Geronimo Stilton

3 in 1

PAPERCUTZ

Geronimo Stilton
GRAPHIC NOVELS AVAILABLE FROM
PAPERCUTZ

#1
"The Discovery
of America"

#2
"The Secret
of the Sphinx"

#3
"The Coliseum
Con"

#4
"Following the
Trail of Marco Polo"

#5
"The Great
Ice Age"

#6
"Who Stole
The Mona Lisa?"

#7
"Dinosaurs
in Action"

#8
"Play It Again,
Mozart!"

#9
"The Weird
Book Machine"

#10
"Geronimo Stilton
Saves the Olympics"

#11
"We'll Always
Have Paris"

#12
"The First Samurai"

#13
"The Fastest Train
in the West"

#14
"The First Mouse
on the Moon"

#15
"All for Stilton,
Stilton for All!"

#16
"Lights, Camera,
Stilton!"

#17
"The Mystery of the
Pirate Ship"

#18
"First to the Last Place
on Earth"

COMING SOON

#19
"Lost in Translation"

**GERONIMO
STILTON REPORTER #1**
"Operation Shufongfong"

**GERONIMO
STILTON REPORTER #2**
"It's My Scoop"

**GERONIMO
STILTON REPORTER #3**
"Stop Acting Around"

**GERONIMO STILTON
3 in 1 #1**

**GERONIMO STILTON
3 in 1 #2**

**GERONIMO STILTON
3 in 1 #3**

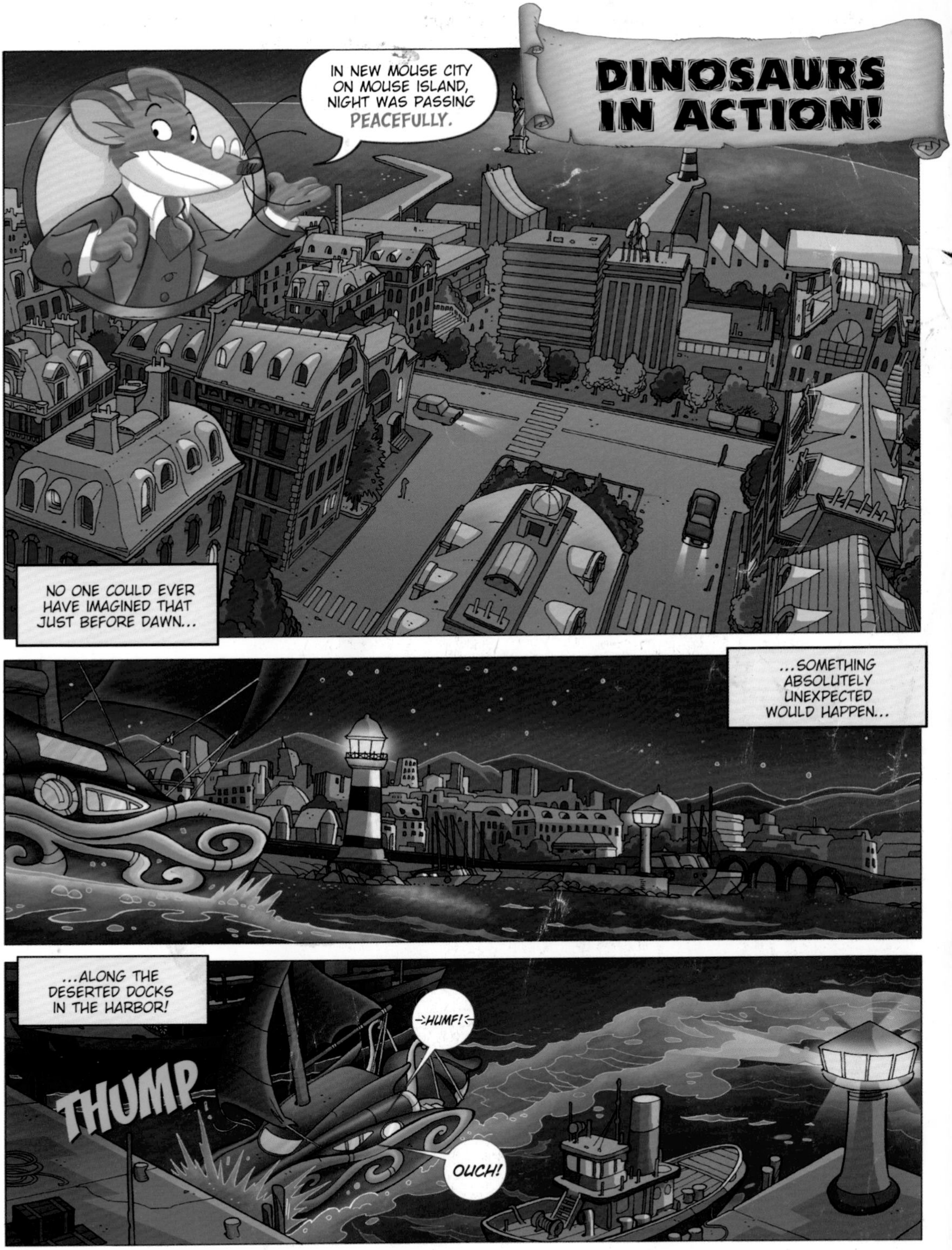
DINOSAURS IN ACTION!
IN NEW MOUSE CITY ON MOUSE ISLAND, NIGHT WAS PASSING PEACEFULLY.
NO ONE COULD EVER HAVE IMAGINED THAT JUST BEFORE DAWN...
...SOMETHING ABSOLUTELY UNEXPECTED WOULD HAPPEN...
...ALONG THE DESERTED DOCKS IN THE HARBOR!
THUMP
HUMF!
OUCH!

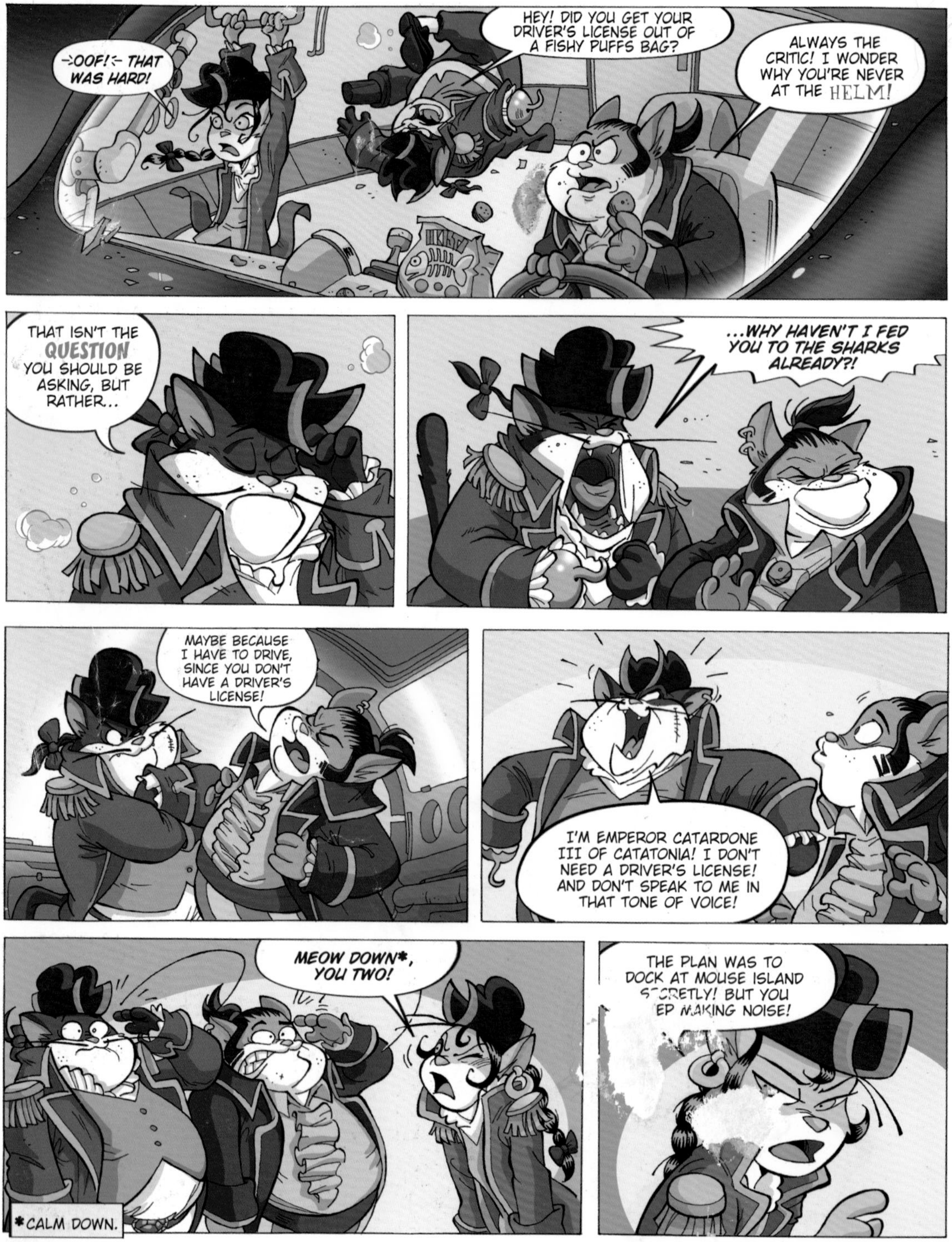

–OOF!– THAT WAS HARD!
HEY! DID YOU GET YOUR DRIVER'S LICENSE OUT OF A FISHY PUFFS BAG?
ALWAYS THE CRITIC! I WONDER WHY YOU'RE NEVER AT THE HELM!
THAT ISN'T THE QUESTION YOU SHOULD BE ASKING, BUT RATHER...
...WHY HAVEN'T I FED YOU TO THE SHARKS ALREADY?!
MAYBE BECAUSE I HAVE TO DRIVE, SINCE YOU DON'T HAVE A DRIVER'S LICENSE!
I'M EMPEROR CATARDONE III OF CATATONIA! I DON'T NEED A DRIVER'S LICENSE! AND DON'T SPEAK TO ME IN THAT TONE OF VOICE!
MEOW DOWN*, YOU TWO!
THE PLAN WAS TO DOCK AT MOUSE ISLAND S CRETLY! BUT YOU EP MAKING NOISE!
*CALM DOWN.

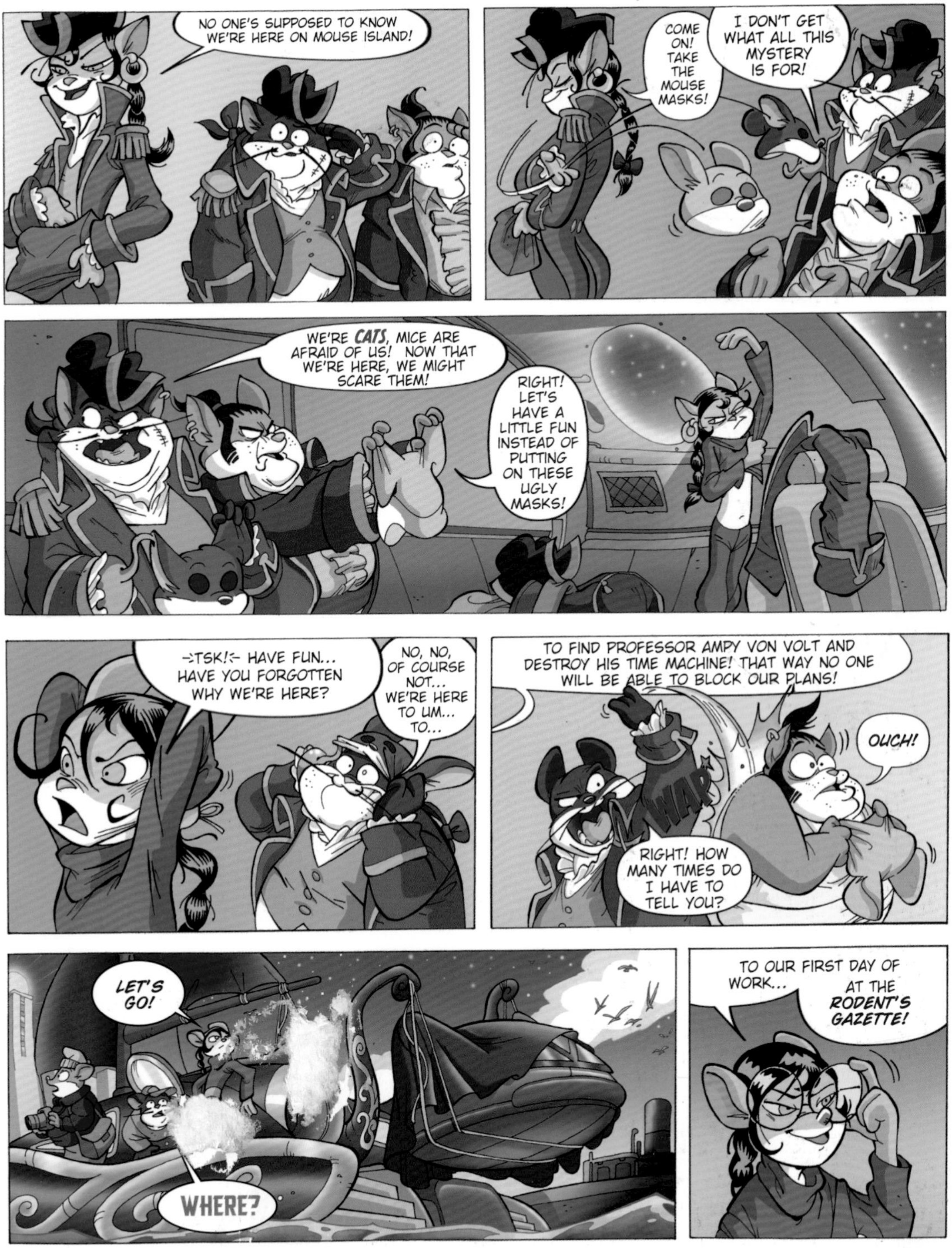

NO ONE'S SUPPOSED TO KNOW WE'RE HERE ON MOUSE ISLAND!
COME ON! TAKE THE MOUSE MASKS!
I DON'T GET WHAT ALL THIS MYSTERY IS FOR!
WE'RE CATS, MICE ARE AFRAID OF US! NOW THAT WE'RE HERE, WE MIGHT SCARE THEM!
RIGHT! LET'S HAVE A LITTLE FUN INSTEAD OF PUTTING ON THESE UGLY MASKS!
-TSK!- HAVE FUN... HAVE YOU FORGOTTEN WHY WE'RE HERE?
NO, NO, OF COURSE NOT... WE'RE HERE TO UM... TO...
TO FIND PROFESSOR AMPY VON VOLT AND DESTROY HIS TIME MACHINE! THAT WAY NO ONE WILL BE ABLE TO BLOCK OUR PLANS!
WAP
OUCH!
RIGHT! HOW MANY TIMES DO I HAVE TO TELL YOU?
LET'S GO!
WHERE?
TO OUR FIRST DAY OF WORK... AT THE RODENT'S GAZETTE!

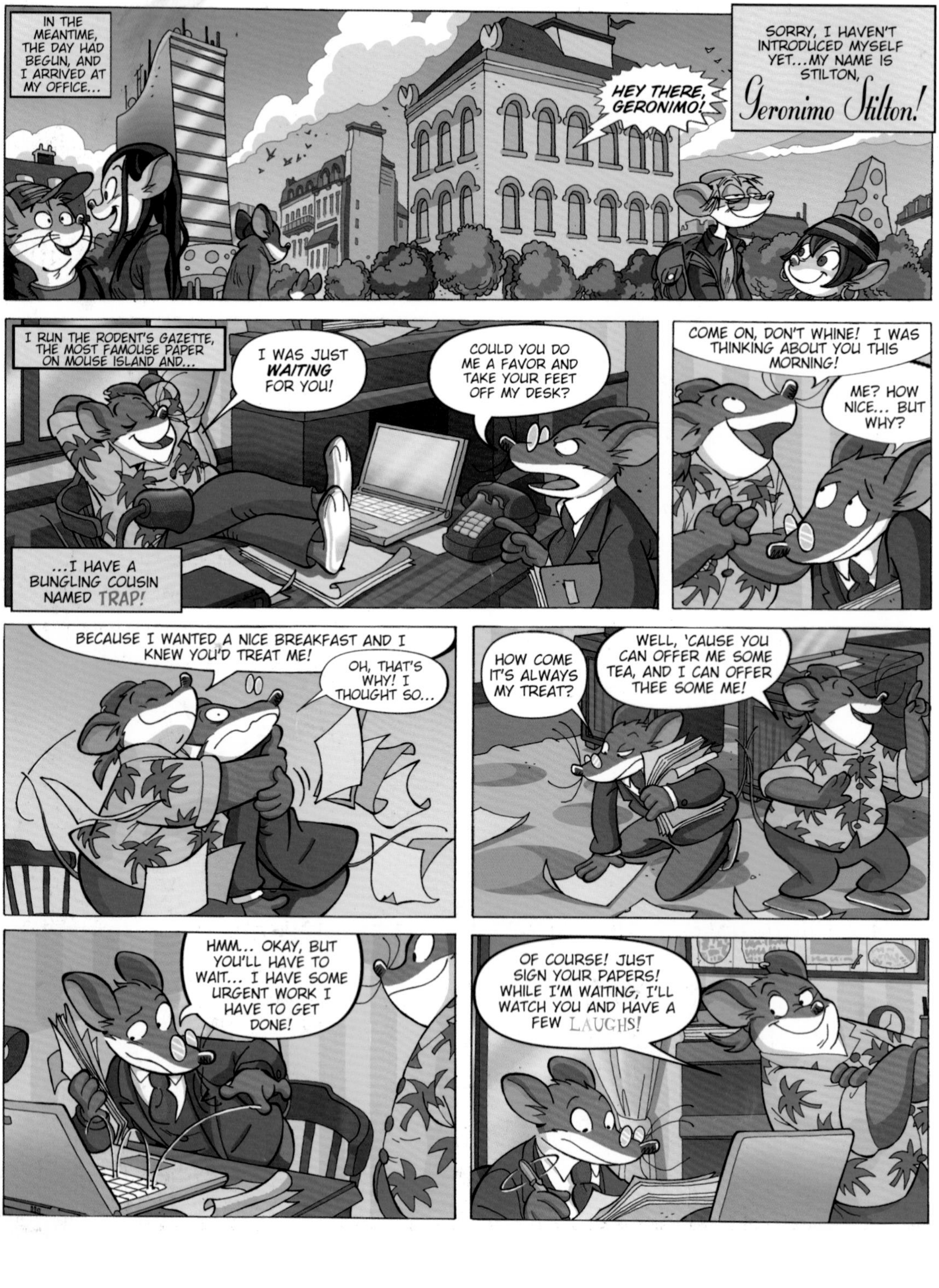
IN THE MEANTIME, THE DAY HAD BEGUN, AND I ARRIVED AT MY OFFICE...
HEY THERE, GERONIMO!
SORRY, I HAVEN'T INTRODUCED MYSELF YET...MY NAME IS STILTON,
Geronimo Stilton!
I RUN THE RODENT'S GAZETTE, THE MOST FAMOUSE PAPER ON MOUSE ISLAND AND...
I WAS JUST WAITING FOR YOU!
COULD YOU DO ME A FAVOR AND TAKE YOUR FEET OFF MY DESK?
...I HAVE A BUNGLING COUSIN NAMED TRAP!
COME ON, DON'T WHINE! I WAS THINKING ABOUT YOU THIS MORNING!
ME? HOW NICE... BUT WHY?
BECAUSE I WANTED A NICE BREAKFAST AND I KNEW YOU'D TREAT ME!
OH, THAT'S WHY! I THOUGHT SO...
HOW COME IT'S ALWAYS MY TREAT?
WELL, 'CAUSE YOU CAN OFFER ME SOME TEA, AND I CAN OFFER THEE SOME ME!
HMM... OKAY, BUT YOU'LL HAVE TO WAIT... I HAVE SOME URGENT WORK I HAVE TO GET DONE!
OF COURSE! JUST SIGN YOUR PAPERS! WHILE I'M WAITING, I'LL WATCH YOU AND HAVE A FEW LAUGHS!

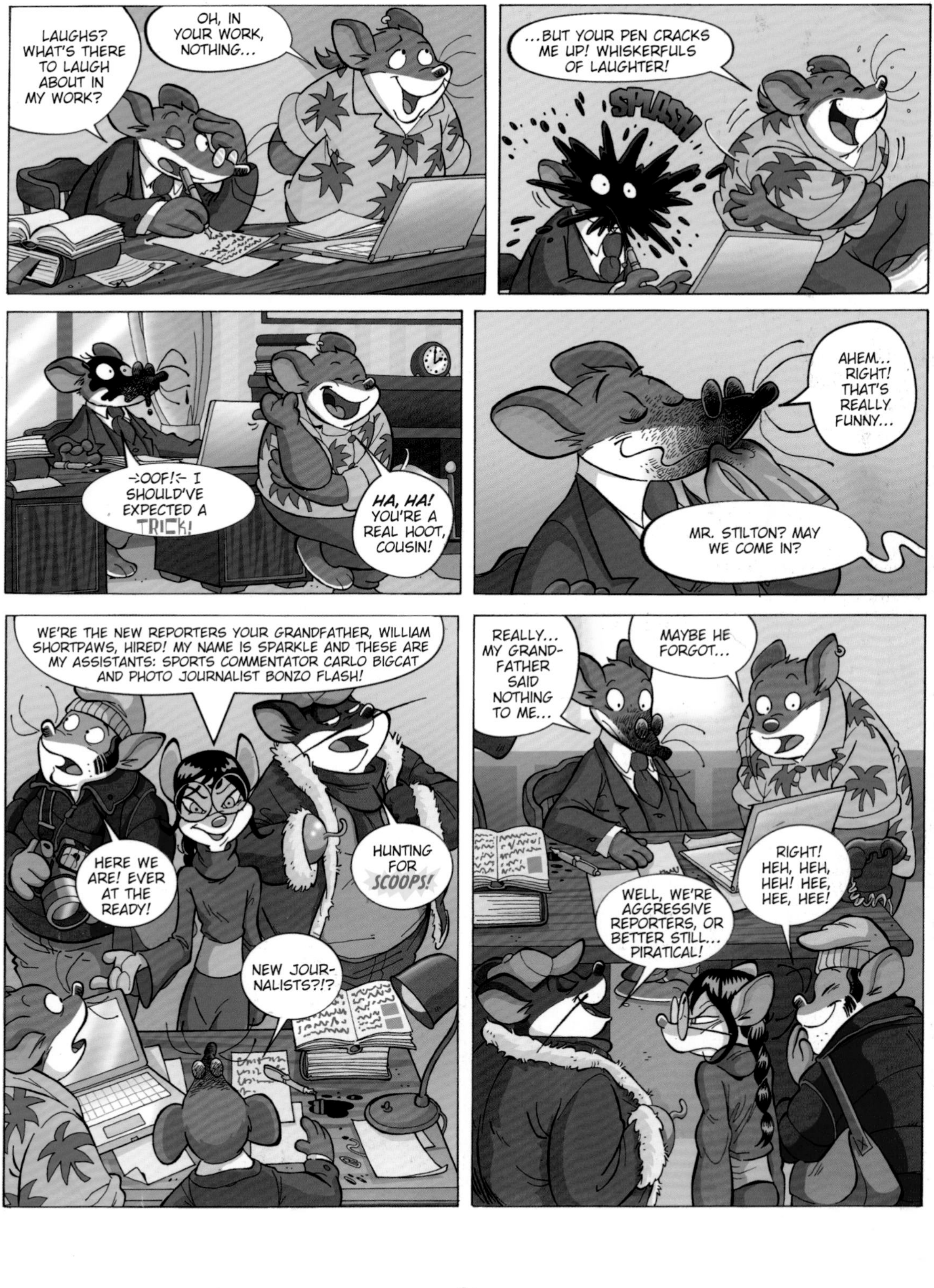
LAUGHS? WHAT'S THERE TO LAUGH ABOUT IN MY WORK?
OH, IN YOUR WORK, NOTHING...
...BUT YOUR PEN CRACKS ME UP! WHISKERFULS OF LAUGHTER!
SPLASH
→OOF!← I SHOULD'VE EXPECTED A TRICK!
HA, HA! YOU'RE A REAL HOOT, COUSIN!
AHEM... RIGHT! THAT'S REALLY FUNNY...
MR. STILTON? MAY WE COME IN?
WE'RE THE NEW REPORTERS YOUR GRANDFATHER, WILLIAM SHORTPAWS, HIRED! MY NAME IS SPARKLE AND THESE ARE MY ASSISTANTS: SPORTS COMMENTATOR CARLO BIGCAT AND PHOTO JOURNALIST BONZO FLASH!
HERE WE ARE! EVER AT THE READY!
HUNTING FOR SCOOPS!
NEW JOURNALISTS?!?
REALLY... MY GRANDFATHER SAID NOTHING TO ME...
MAYBE HE FORGOT...
WELL, WE'RE AGGRESSIVE REPORTERS, OR BETTER STILL... PIRATICAL!
RIGHT! HEH, HEH, HEH! HEE, HEE, HEE!

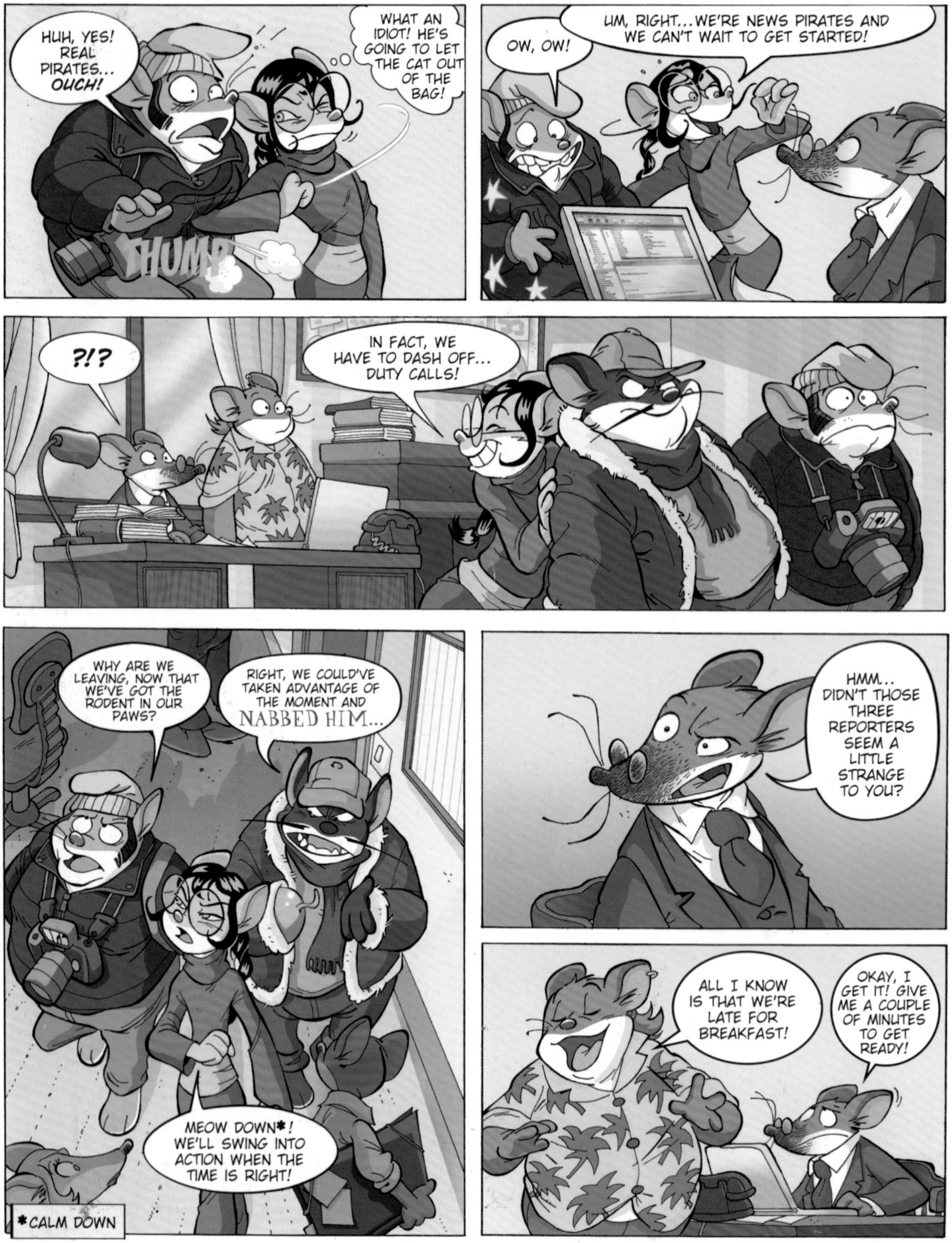
HUH, YES! REAL PIRATES... OUCH!
WHAT AN IDIOT! HE'S GOING TO LET THE CAT OUT OF THE BAG!
THUMP
OW, OW!
UM, RIGHT... WE'RE NEWS PIRATES AND WE CAN'T WAIT TO GET STARTED!
?!?
IN FACT, WE HAVE TO DASH OFF... DUTY CALLS!
WHY ARE WE LEAVING, NOW THAT WE'VE GOT THE RODENT IN OUR PAWS?
RIGHT, WE COULD'VE TAKEN ADVANTAGE OF THE MOMENT AND NABBED HIM...
MEOW DOWN*! WE'LL SWING INTO ACTION WHEN THE TIME IS RIGHT!
*CALM DOWN
HMM... DIDN'T THOSE THREE REPORTERS SEEM A LITTLE STRANGE TO YOU?
ALL I KNOW IS THAT WE'RE LATE FOR BREAKFAST!
OKAY, I GET IT! GIVE ME A COUPLE OF MINUTES TO GET READY!

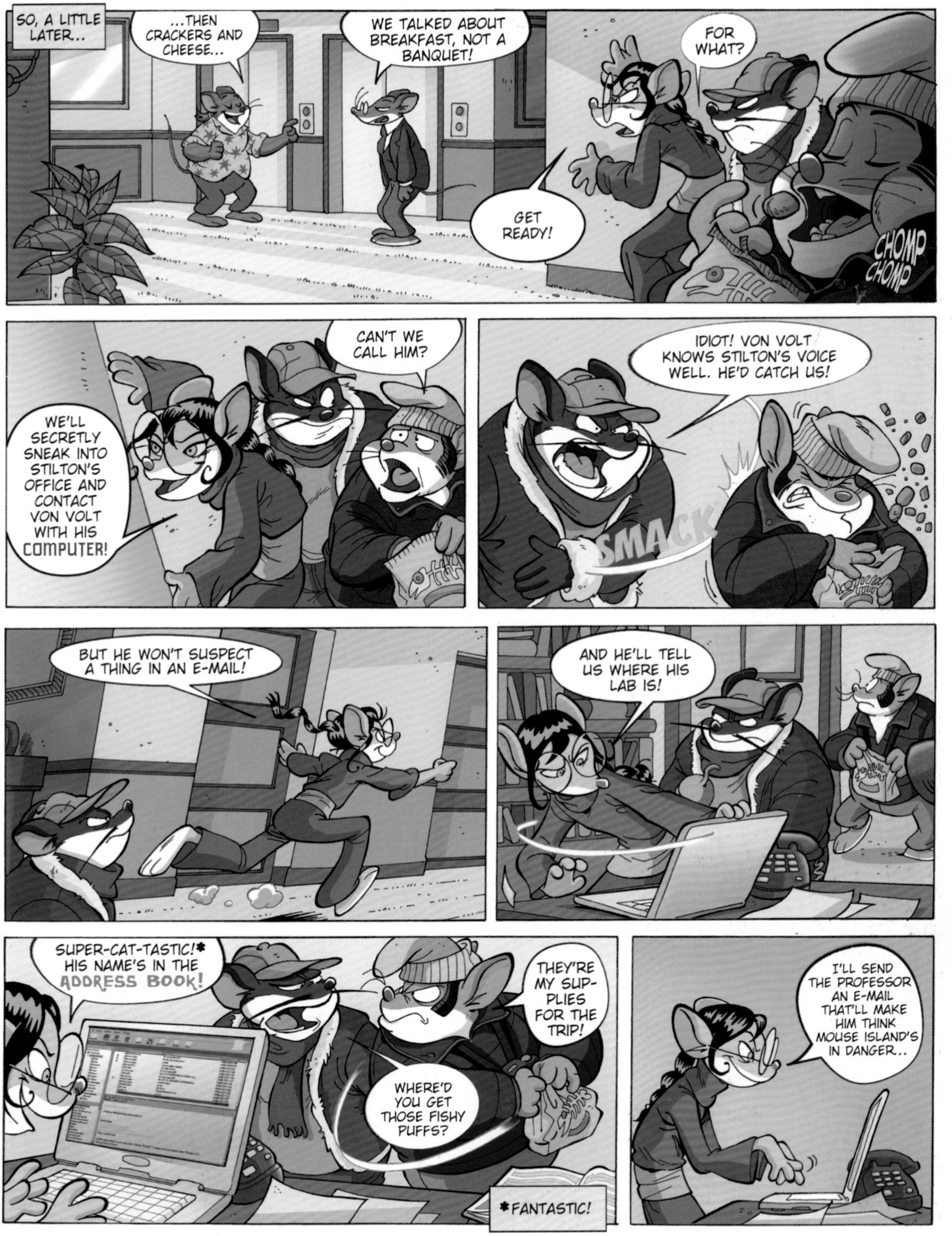
SO, A LITTLE LATER...
...THEN CRACKERS AND CHEESE...
WE TALKED ABOUT BREAKFAST, NOT A BANQUET!
FOR WHAT?
GET READY!
CHOMP CHOMP
CAN'T WE CALL HIM?
WE'LL SECRETLY SNEAK INTO STILTON'S OFFICE AND CONTACT VON VOLT WITH HIS COMPUTER!
IDIOT! VON VOLT KNOWS STILTON'S VOICE WELL. HE'D CATCH US!
SMACK
BUT HE WON'T SUSPECT A THING IN AN E-MAIL!
AND HE'LL TELL US WHERE HIS LAB IS!
SUPER-CAT-TASTIC!* HIS NAME'S IN THE ADDRESS BOOK!
THEY'RE MY SUPPLIES FOR THE TRIP!
WHERE'D YOU GET THOSE FISHY PUFFS?
*FANTASTIC!
I'LL SEND THE PROFESSOR AN E-MAIL THAT'LL MAKE HIM THINK MOUSE ISLAND'S IN DANGER...

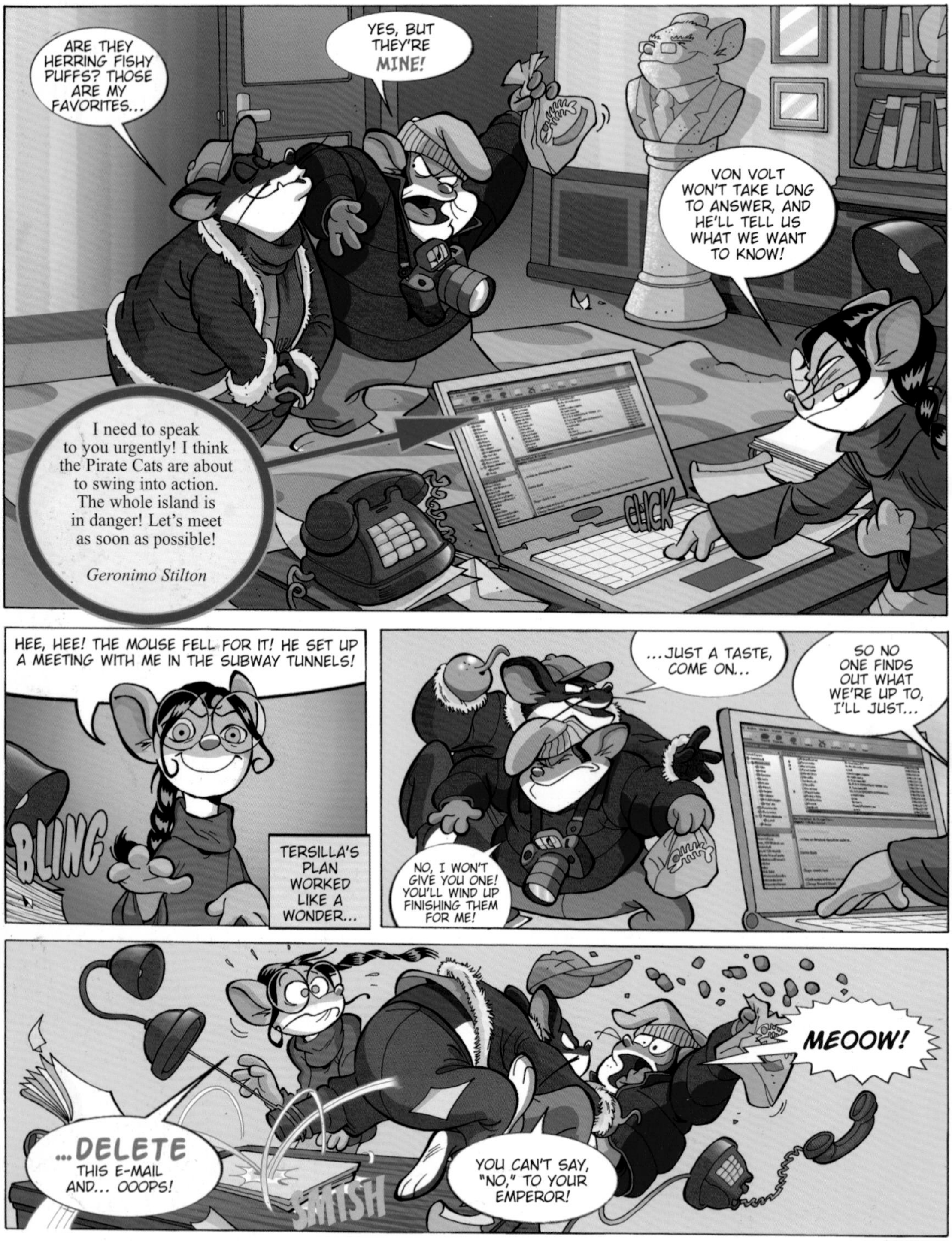

ARE THEY HERRING FISHY PUFFS? THOSE ARE MY FAVORITES...
YES, BUT THEY'RE MINE!
VON VOLT WON'T TAKE LONG TO ANSWER, AND HE'LL TELL US WHAT WE WANT TO KNOW!
I need to speak to you urgently! I think the Pirate Cats are about to swing into action. The whole island is in danger! Let's meet as soon as possible!
Geronimo Stilton
CLICK
HEE, HEE! THE MOUSE FELL FOR IT! HE SET UP A MEETING WITH ME IN THE SUBWAY TUNNELS!
BLING
TERSILLA'S PLAN WORKED LIKE A WONDER...
...JUST A TASTE, COME ON...
NO, I WON'T GIVE YOU ONE! YOU'LL WIND UP FINISHING THEM FOR ME!
SO NO ONE FINDS OUT WHAT WE'RE UP TO, I'LL JUST...
MEOOW!
...DELETE THIS E-MAIL AND... OOOPS!
SMISH
YOU CAN'T SAY, "NO," TO YOUR EMPEROR!

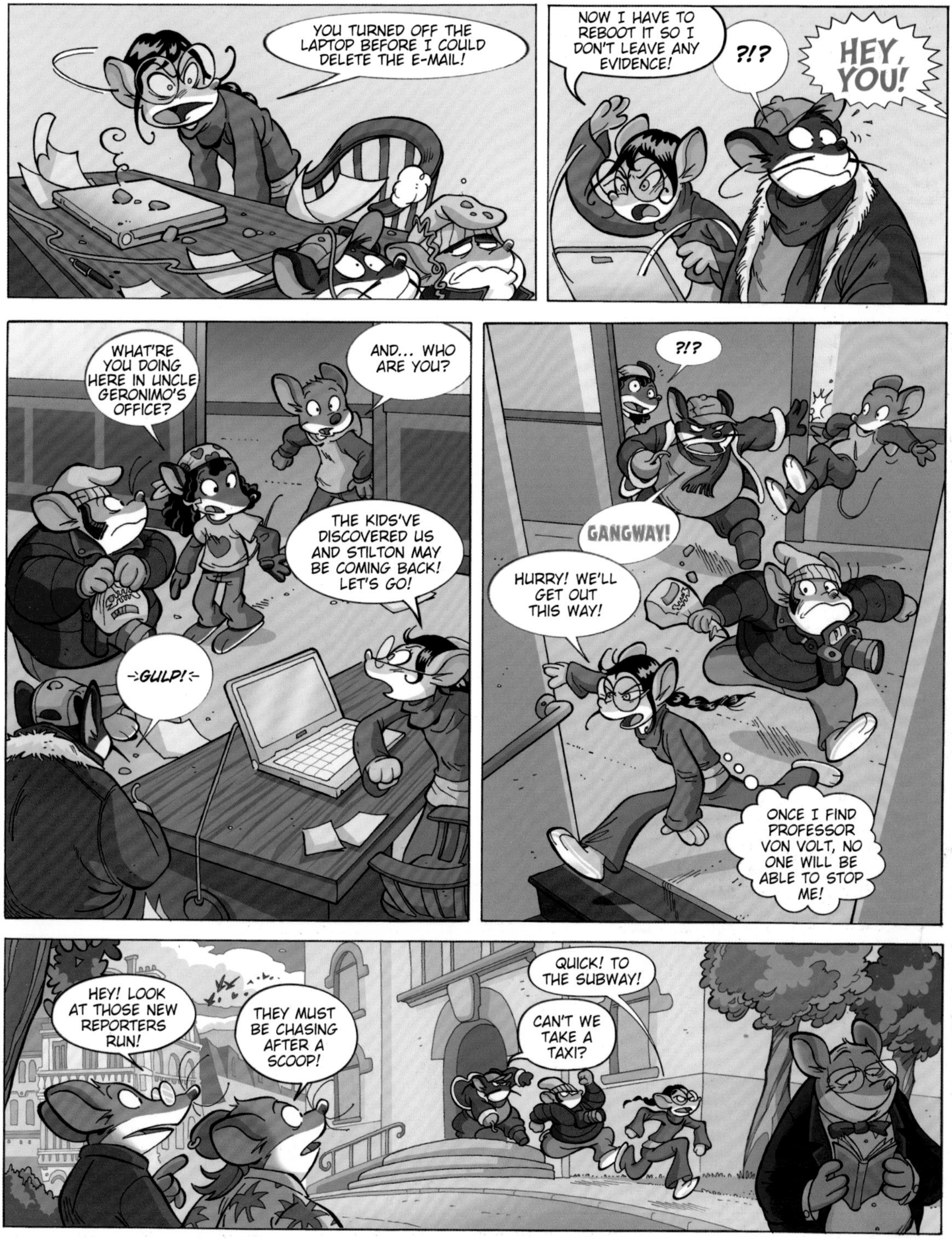
YOU TURNED OFF THE LAPTOP BEFORE I COULD DELETE THE E-MAIL!
NOW I HAVE TO REBOOT IT SO I DON'T LEAVE ANY EVIDENCE!
?!?
HEY, YOU!
WHAT'RE YOU DOING HERE IN UNCLE GERONIMO'S OFFICE?
AND... WHO ARE YOU?
THE KIDS'VE DISCOVERED US AND STILTON MAY BE COMING BACK! LET'S GO!
GULP!
?!?
GANGWAY!
HURRY! WE'LL GET OUT THIS WAY!
ONCE I FIND PROFESSOR VON VOLT, NO ONE WILL BE ABLE TO STOP ME!
HEY! LOOK AT THOSE NEW REPORTERS RUN!
THEY MUST BE CHASING AFTER A SCOOP!
QUICK! TO THE SUBWAY!
CAN'T WE TAKE A TAXI?

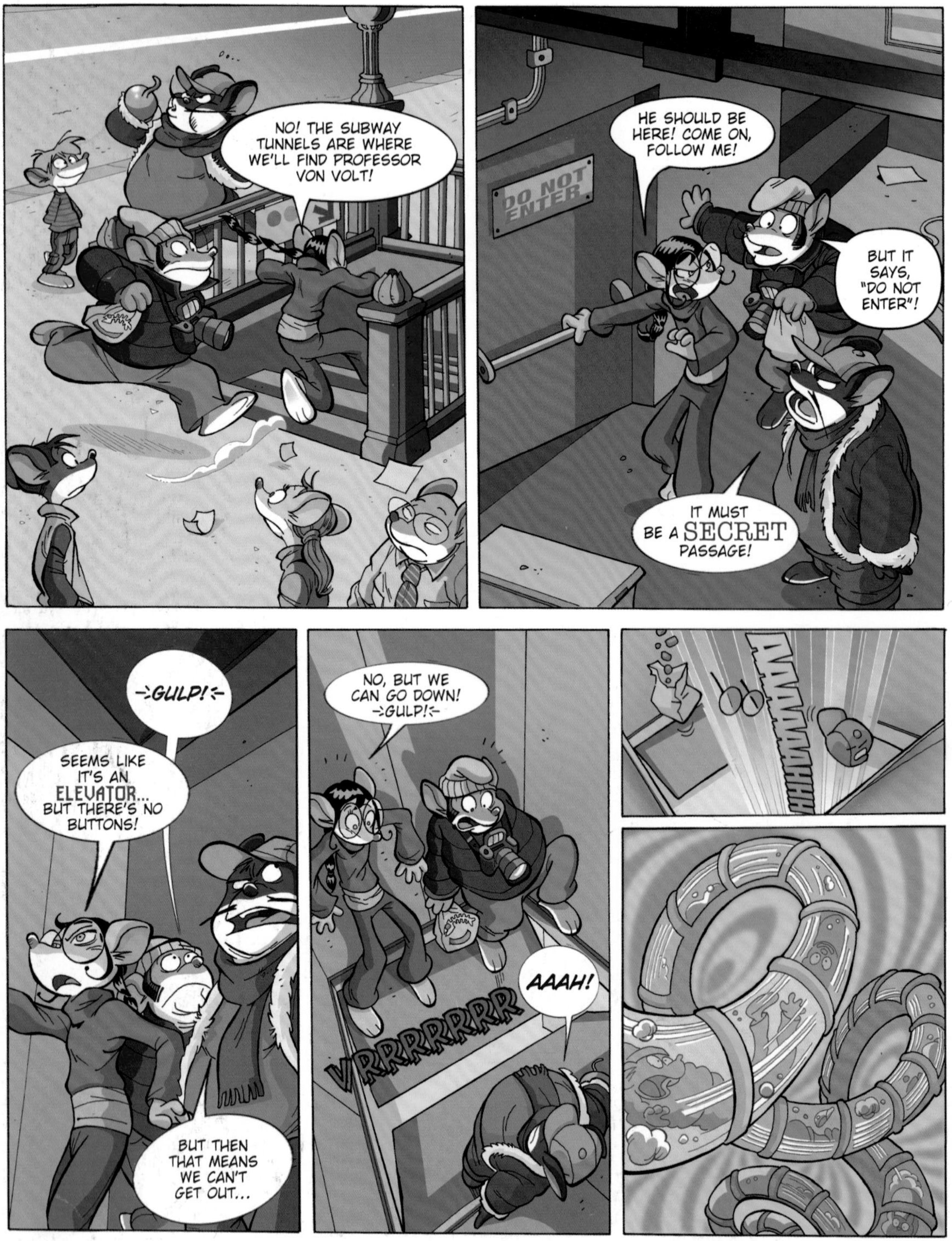
NO! THE SUBWAY TUNNELS ARE WHERE WE'LL FIND PROFESSOR VON VOLT!
HE SHOULD BE HERE! COME ON, FOLLOW ME!
DO NOT ENTER
BUT IT SAYS, "DO NOT ENTER"!
IT MUST BE A SECRET PASSAGE!
-GULP!-
SEEMS LIKE IT'S AN ELEVATOR... BUT THERE'S NO BUTTONS!
BUT THEN THAT MEANS WE CAN'T GET OUT...
NO, BUT WE CAN GO DOWN! -GULP!-
AAAH!

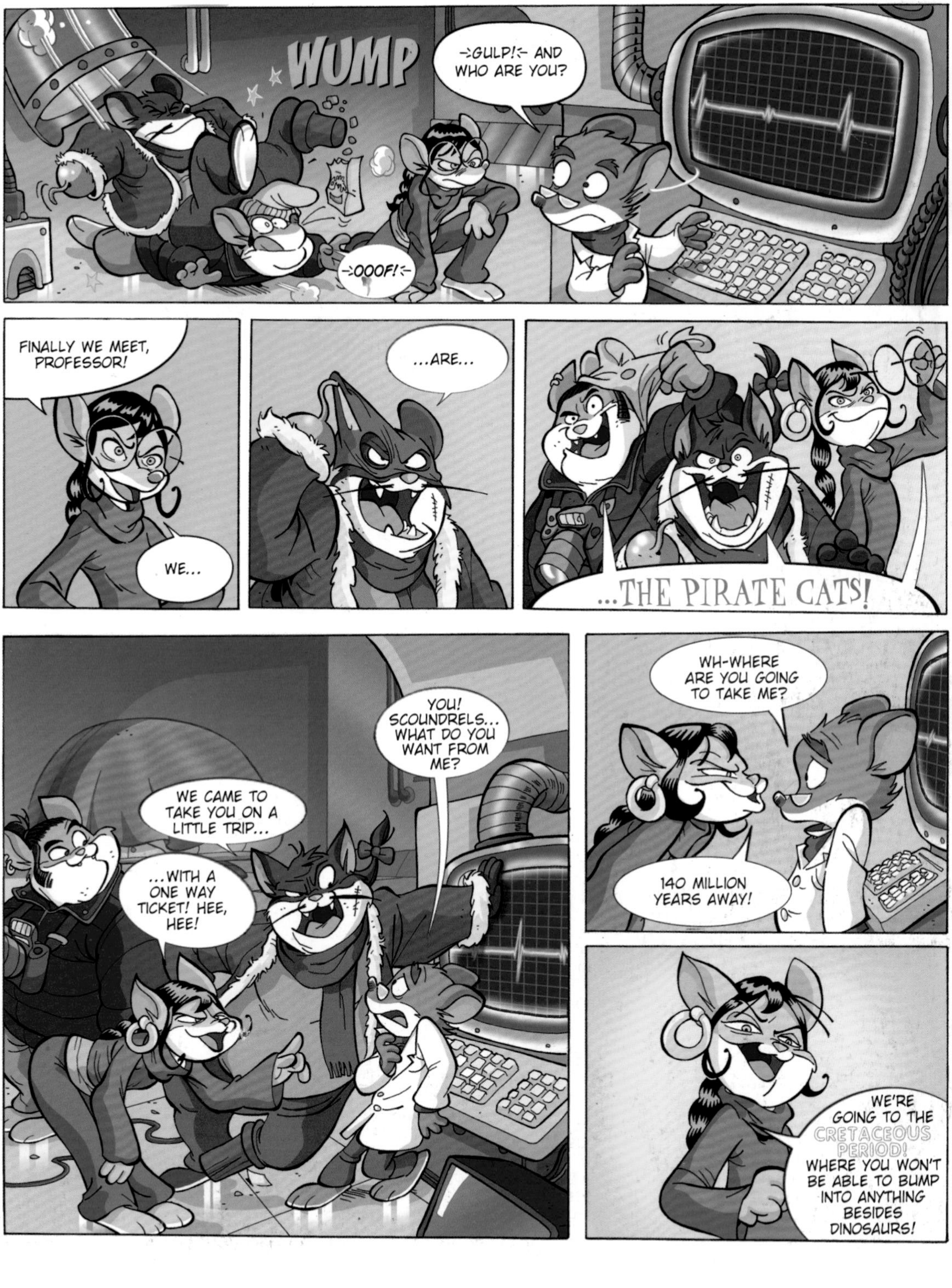
WUMP
-GULP!- AND WHO ARE YOU?
-OOOF!-
FINALLY WE MEET, PROFESSOR!
WE...
...ARE...
...THE PIRATE CATS!
YOU! SCOUNDRELS... WHAT DO YOU WANT FROM ME?
WE CAME TO TAKE YOU ON A LITTLE TRIP...
...WITH A ONE WAY TICKET! HEE, HEE!
WH-WHERE ARE YOU GOING TO TAKE ME?
140 MILLION YEARS AWAY!
WE'RE GOING TO THE CRETACEOUS PERIOD! WHERE YOU WON'T BE ABLE TO BUMP INTO ANYTHING BESIDES DINOSAURS!

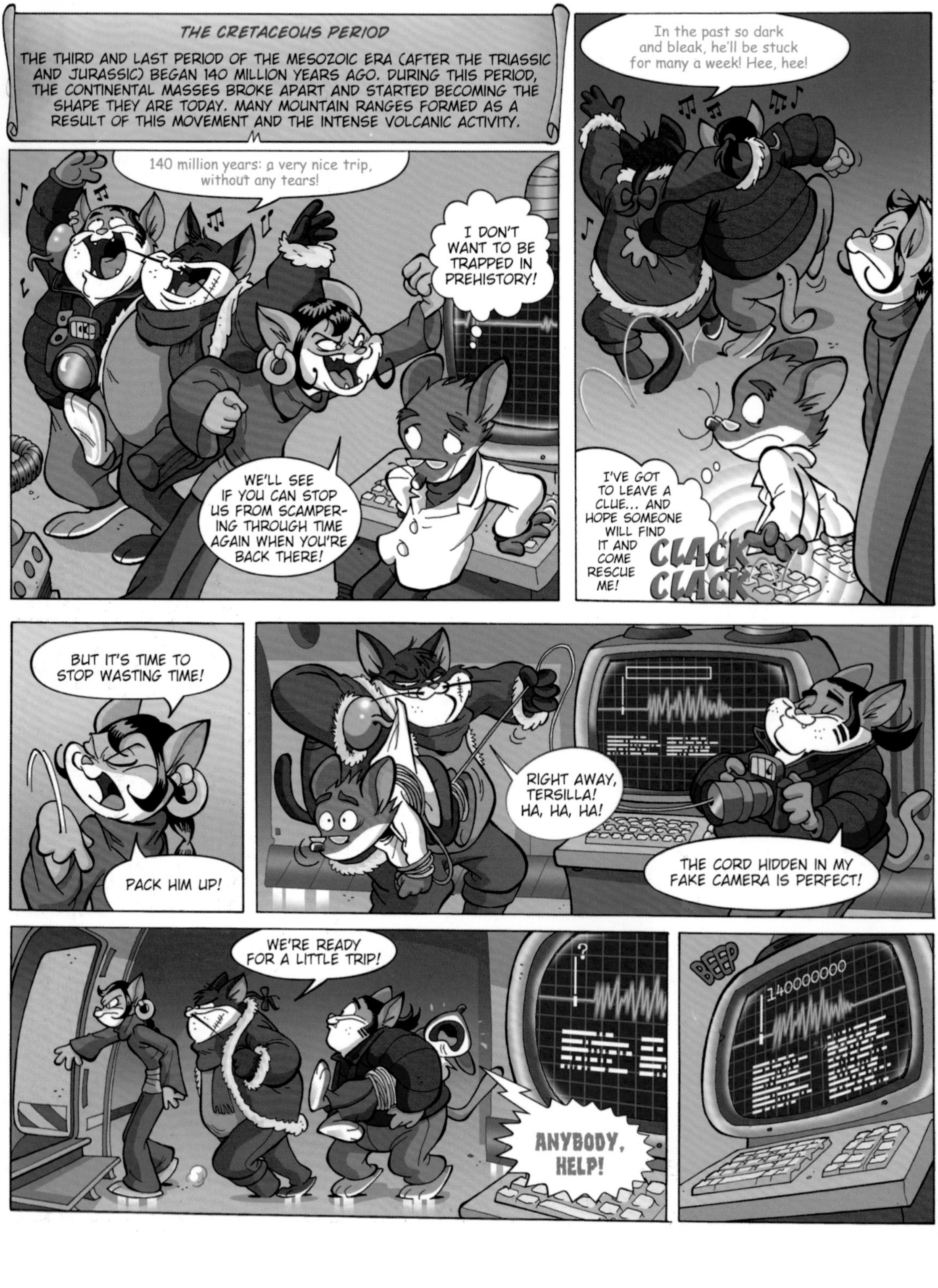
THE CRETACEOUS PERIOD
THE THIRD AND LAST PERIOD OF THE MESOZOIC ERA (AFTER THE TRIASSIC AND JURASSIC) BEGAN 140 MILLION YEARS AGO. DURING THIS PERIOD, THE CONTINENTAL MASSES BROKE APART AND STARTED BECOMING THE SHAPE THEY ARE TODAY. MANY MOUNTAIN RANGES FORMED AS A RESULT OF THIS MOVEMENT AND THE INTENSE VOLCANIC ACTIVITY.
140 million years: a very nice trip, without any tears!
I DON'T WANT TO BE TRAPPED IN PREHISTORY!
WE'LL SEE IF YOU CAN STOP US FROM SCAMPERING THROUGH TIME AGAIN WHEN YOU'RE BACK THERE!
In the past so dark and bleak, he'll be stuck for many a week! Hee, hee!
I'VE GOT TO LEAVE A CLUE... AND HOPE SOMEONE WILL FIND IT AND COME RESCUE ME!
CLACK CLACK
BUT IT'S TIME TO STOP WASTING TIME!
PACK HIM UP!
RIGHT AWAY, TERSILLA! HA, HA, HA!
THE CORD HIDDEN IN MY FAKE CAMERA IS PERFECT!
WE'RE READY FOR A LITTLE TRIP!
ANYBODY, HELP!
BEEP
140000000

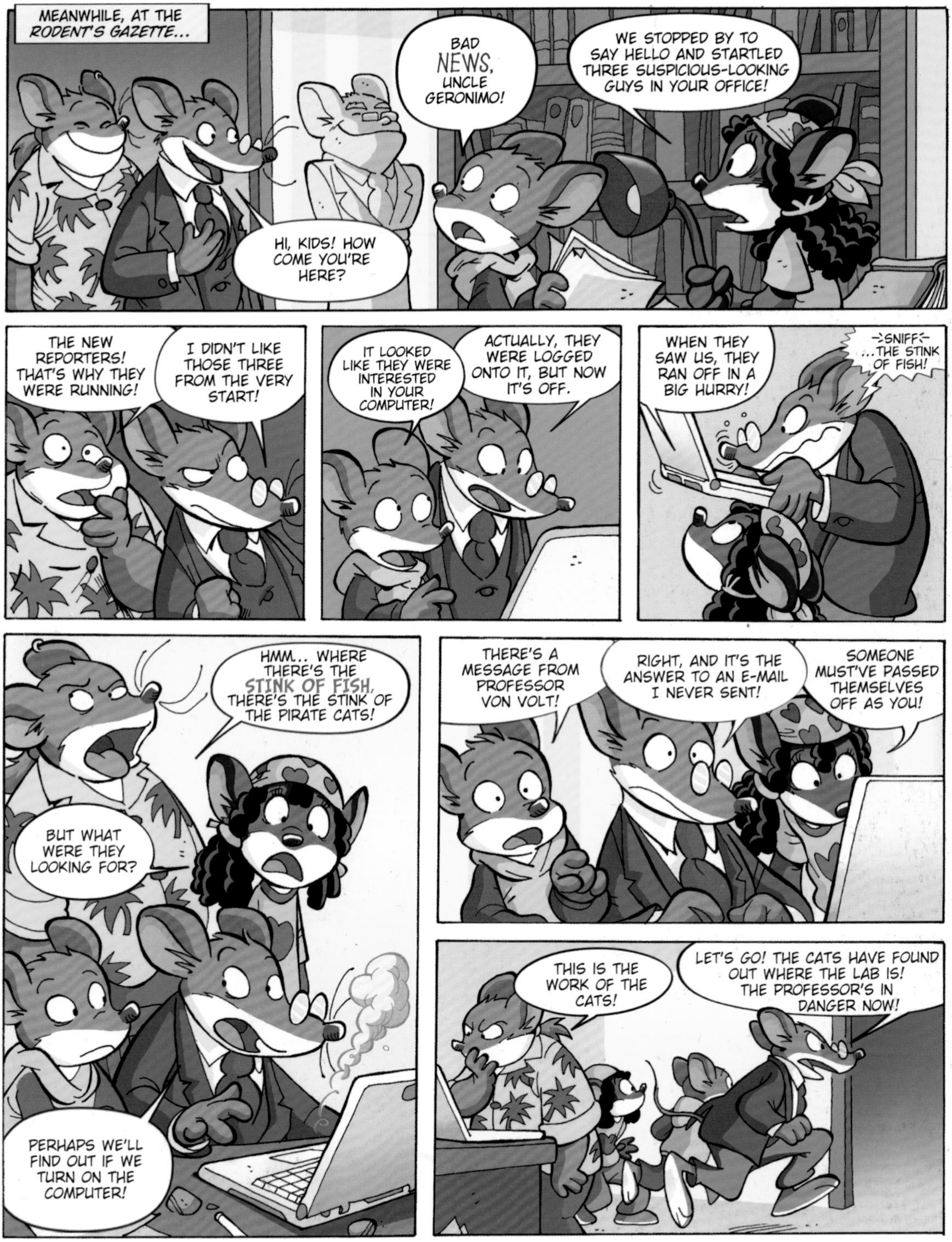
MEANWHILE, AT THE RODENT'S GAZETTE...
HI, KIDS! HOW COME YOU'RE HERE?
BAD NEWS, UNCLE GERONIMO!
WE STOPPED BY TO SAY HELLO AND STARTLED THREE SUSPICIOUS-LOOKING GUYS IN YOUR OFFICE!
THE NEW REPORTERS! THAT'S WHY THEY WERE RUNNING!
I DIDN'T LIKE THOSE THREE FROM THE VERY START!
IT LOOKED LIKE THEY WERE INTERESTED IN YOUR COMPUTER!
ACTUALLY, THEY WERE LOGGED ONTO IT, BUT NOW IT'S OFF.
WHEN THEY SAW US, THEY RAN OFF IN A BIG HURRY!
SNIFF ...THE STINK OF FISH!
HMM... WHERE THERE'S THE STINK OF FISH, THERE'S THE STINK OF THE PIRATE CATS!
BUT WHAT WERE THEY LOOKING FOR?
PERHAPS WE'LL FIND OUT IF WE TURN ON THE COMPUTER!
THERE'S A MESSAGE FROM PROFESSOR VON VOLT!
RIGHT, AND IT'S THE ANSWER TO AN E-MAIL I NEVER SENT!
SOMEONE MUST'VE PASSED THEMSELVES OFF AS YOU!
THIS IS THE WORK OF THE CATS!
LET'S GO! THE CATS HAVE FOUND OUT WHERE THE LAB IS! THE PROFESSOR'S IN DANGER NOW!

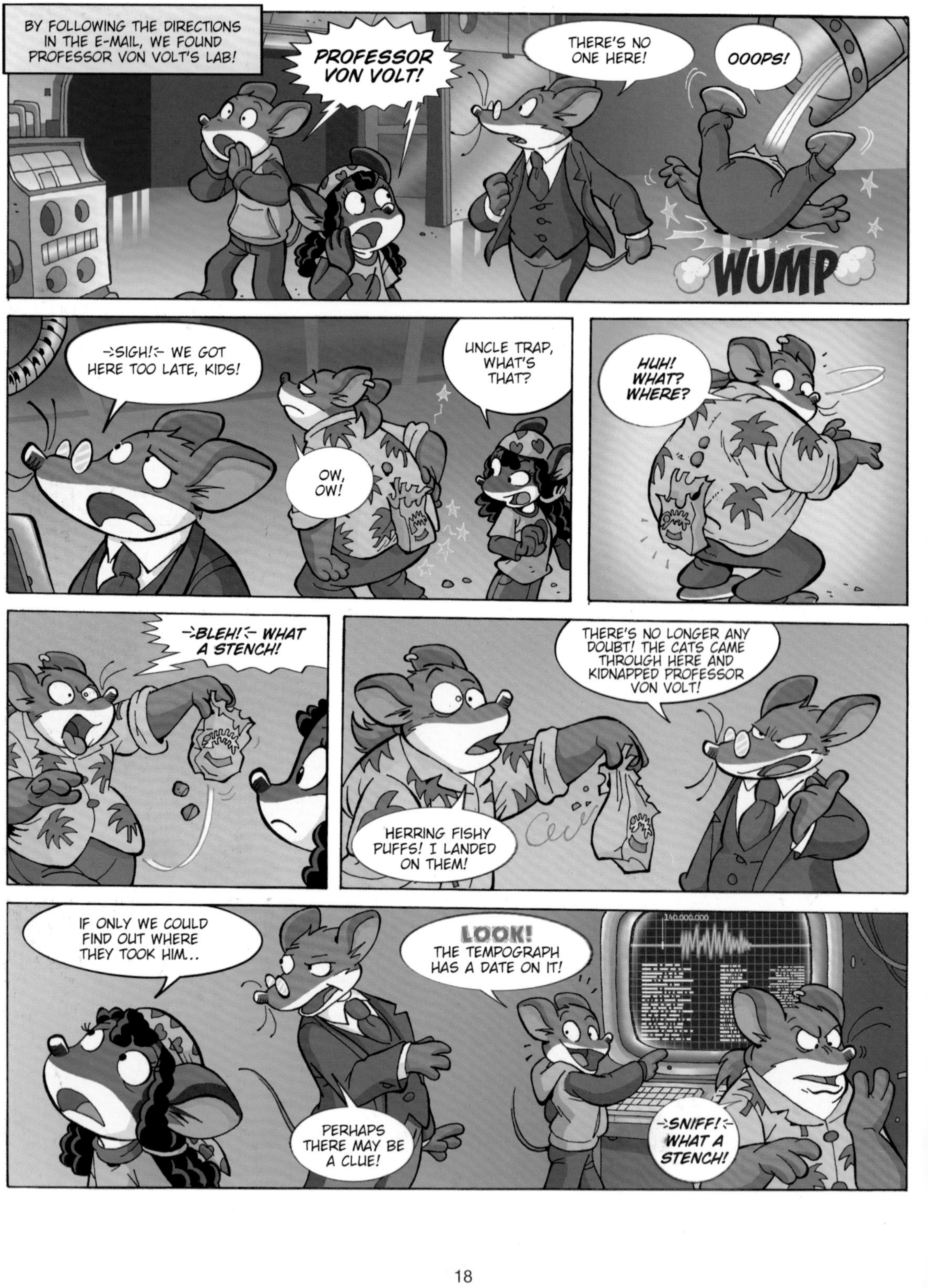

BY FOLLOWING THE DIRECTIONS IN THE E-MAIL, WE FOUND PROFESSOR VON VOLT'S LAB!
PROFESSOR VON VOLT!
THERE'S NO ONE HERE!
OOOPS!
WUMP
-SIGH!- WE GOT HERE TOO LATE, KIDS!
UNCLE TRAP, WHAT'S THAT?
OW, OW!
HUH! WHAT? WHERE?
-BLEH!- WHAT A STENCH!
THERE'S NO LONGER ANY DOUBT! THE CATS CAME THROUGH HERE AND KIDNAPPED PROFESSOR VON VOLT!
HERRING FISHY PUFFS! I LANDED ON THEM!
IF ONLY WE COULD FIND OUT WHERE THEY TOOK HIM...
PERHAPS THERE MAY BE A CLUE!
LOOK! THE TEMPOGRAPH HAS A DATE ON IT!
140.000.000
-SNIFF!- WHAT A STENCH!

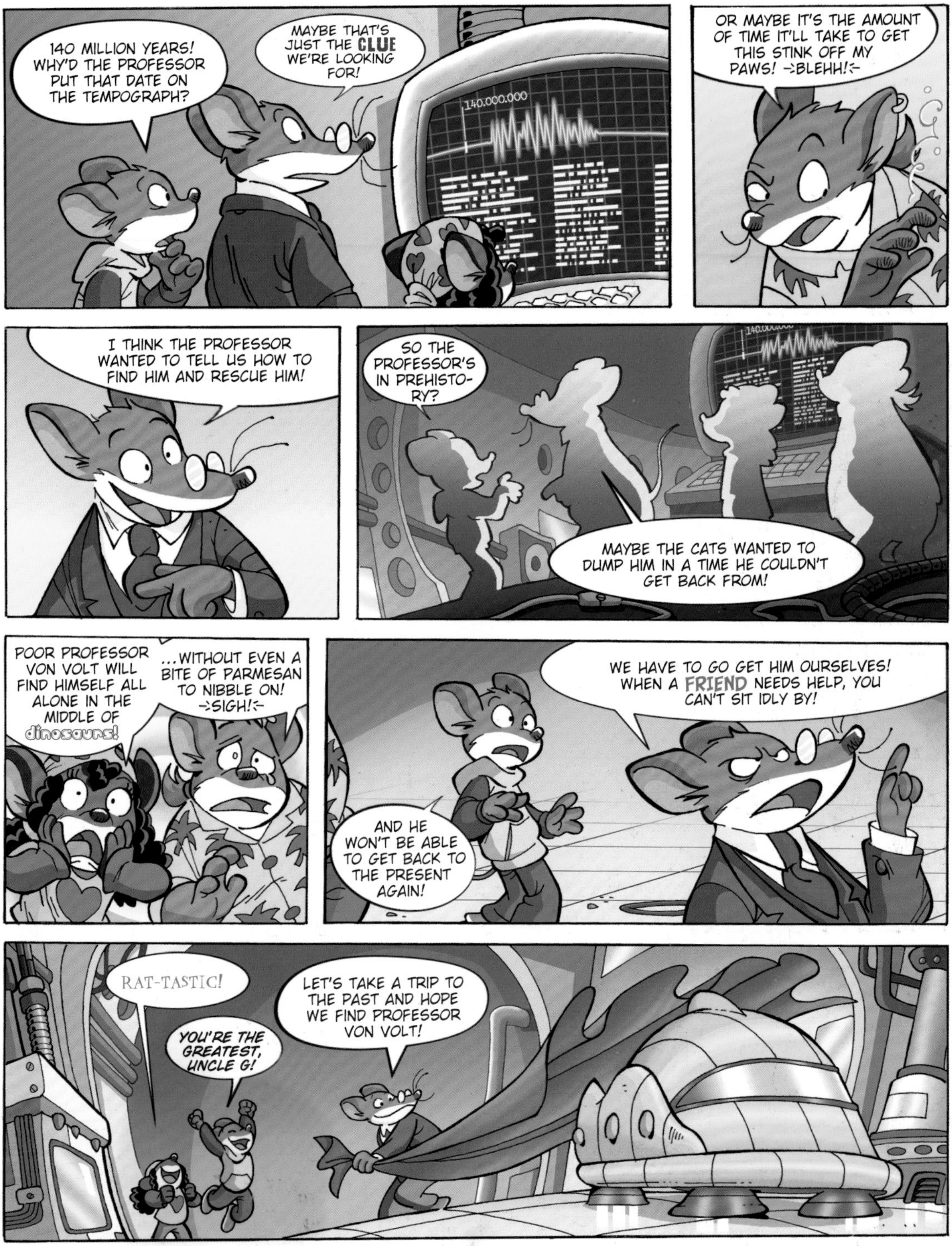
140 MILLION YEARS! WHY'D THE PROFESSOR PUT THAT DATE ON THE TEMPOGRAPH?
MAYBE THAT'S JUST THE CLUE WE'RE LOOKING FOR!
140.000.000
OR MAYBE IT'S THE AMOUNT OF TIME IT'LL TAKE TO GET THIS STINK OFF MY PAWS! ->BLEHH!<-
I THINK THE PROFESSOR WANTED TO TELL US HOW TO FIND HIM AND RESCUE HIM!
SO THE PROFESSOR'S IN PREHISTO-RY?
MAYBE THE CATS WANTED TO DUMP HIM IN A TIME HE COULDN'T GET BACK FROM!
POOR PROFESSOR VON VOLT WILL FIND HIMSELF ALL ALONE IN THE MIDDLE OF dinosaurs!
...WITHOUT EVEN A BITE OF PARMESAN TO NIBBLE ON! ->SIGH!<-
WE HAVE TO GO GET HIM OURSELVES! WHEN A FRIEND NEEDS HELP, YOU CAN'T SIT IDLY BY!
AND HE WON'T BE ABLE TO GET BACK TO THE PRESENT AGAIN!
RAT-TASTIC!
YOU'RE THE GREATEST, UNCLE G!
LET'S TAKE A TRIP TO THE PAST AND HOPE WE FIND PROFESSOR VON VOLT!

YOU'RE RIGHT, WE CAN GO BACK, BUT... WE DON'T KNOW ANYTHING ABOUT **PREHISTORY!**

...AND THIS TIME, THE PROFESSOR ISN'T AROUND TO GIVE US INFORMATION THAT CAN HELP US OUT!

BUT I KNOW WHO CAN GIVE US A HAND!

MY FRIEND AND PALEONTOLOGIST... KAREN VON FOSSILS! SHE'S THE DIRECTOR OF THE NEW MOUSE CITY NATURAL HISTORY MUSEUM AND A DINOSAUR EXPERT!

Karen Von Fossils

"KAREN WAS EXCITED AND CAME RIGHT AWAY!"

I'M SO GLAD I CAN HELP YOU...

...PLUS I'VE ALWAYS WANTED TO VISIT PREHISTORY!

140,000.00

THEN GET YOURSELF READY FOR THE TRIP OF YOUR DREAMS!

PROFESSOR VON VOLT ALREADY SET OUR DESTINATION TIME!

START UP THE SPEEDRAT!

WITH PLEASURE!

THAT'S THE TAKEOFF BUTTON...WILL YOU DO US THE HONOR, DOCTOR VON FOSSILS?

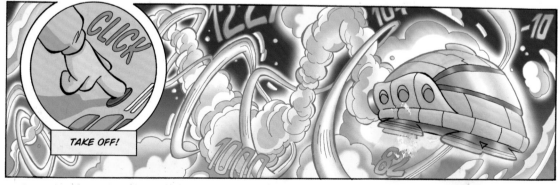

CLICK

TAKE OFF!

20

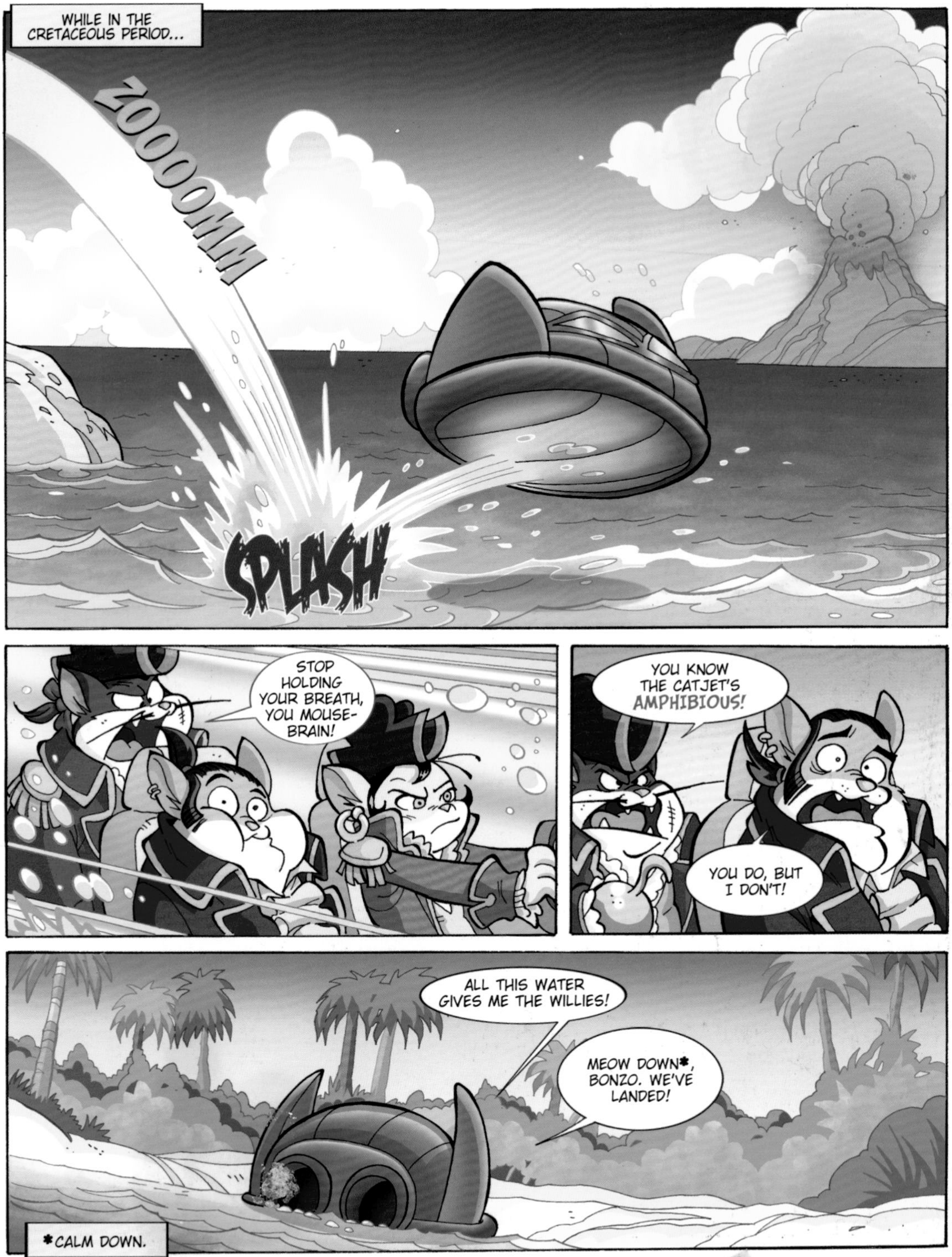

WHILE IN THE CRETACEOUS PERIOD...
ZOOOOMM
SPLASH
STOP HOLDING YOUR BREATH, YOU MOUSE-BRAIN!
YOU KNOW THE CATJET'S AMPHIBIOUS!
YOU DO, BUT I DON'T!
ALL THIS WATER GIVES ME THE WILLIES!
MEOW DOWN*, BONZO. WE'VE LANDED!
*CALM DOWN.

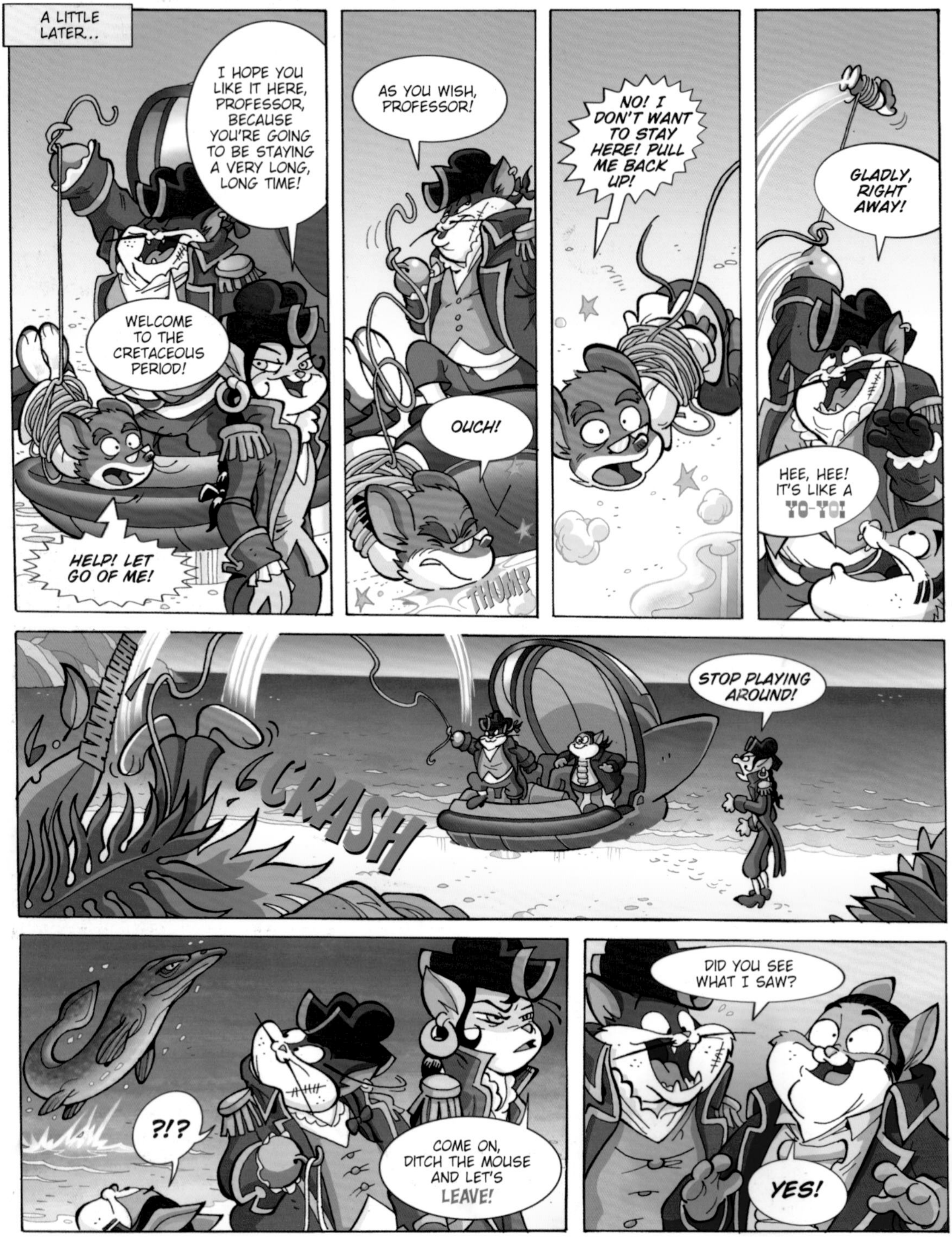
A LITTLE LATER...
I HOPE YOU LIKE IT HERE, PROFESSOR, BECAUSE YOU'RE GOING TO BE STAYING A VERY LONG, LONG TIME!
WELCOME TO THE CRETACEOUS PERIOD!
HELP! LET GO OF ME!
AS YOU WISH, PROFESSOR!
OUCH!
THUMP
NO! I DON'T WANT TO STAY HERE! PULL ME BACK UP!
GLADLY, RIGHT AWAY!
HEE, HEE! IT'S LIKE A YO-YO!
AAAAAHHH
CRASH
STOP PLAYING AROUND!
?!?
COME ON, DITCH THE MOUSE AND LET'S LEAVE!
DID YOU SEE WHAT I SAW?
YES!

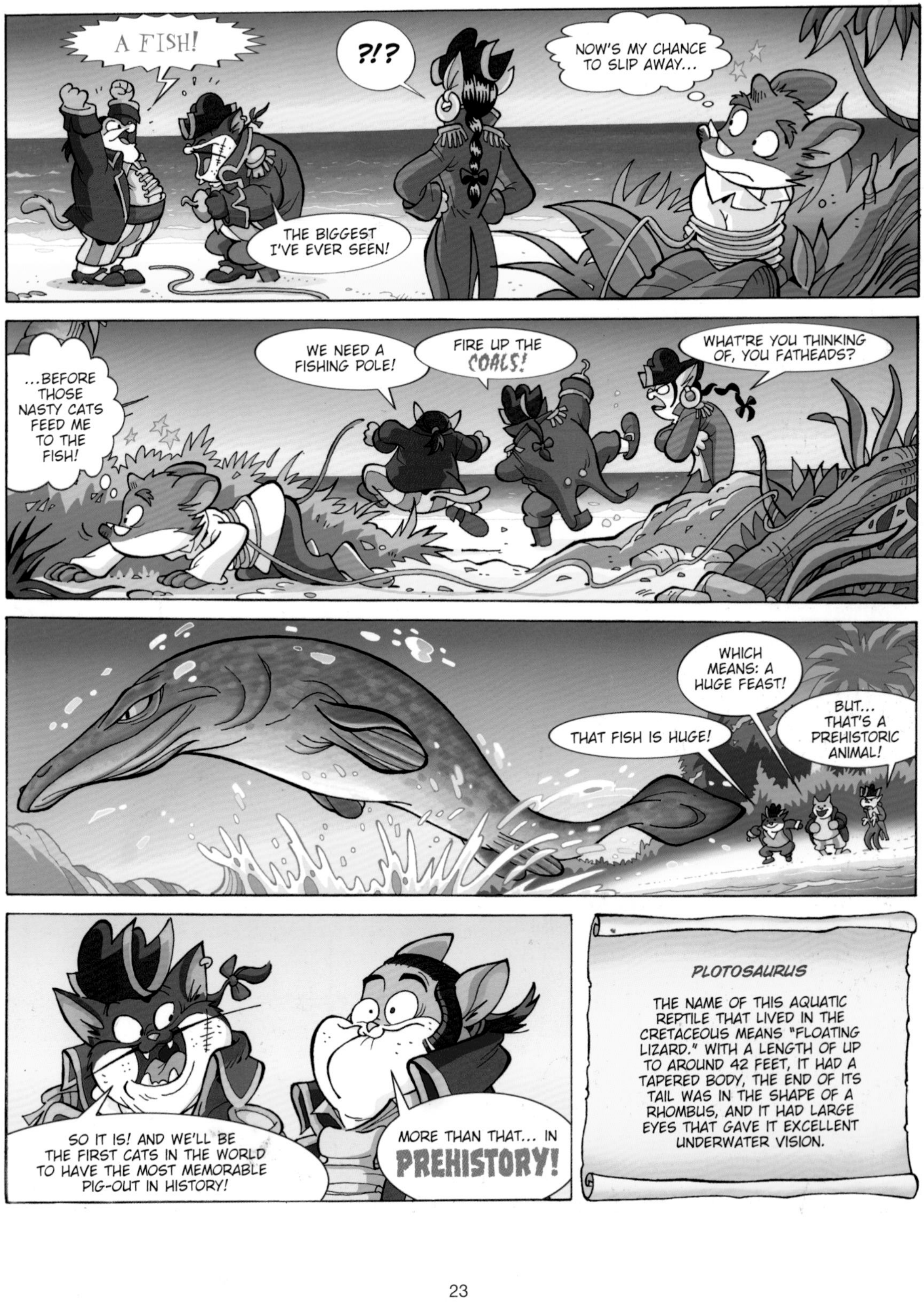
A FISH!
?!?
NOW'S MY CHANCE TO SLIP AWAY...
THE BIGGEST I'VE EVER SEEN!
...BEFORE THOSE NASTY CATS FEED ME TO THE FISH!
WE NEED A FISHING POLE!
FIRE UP THE COALS!
WHAT'RE YOU THINKING OF, YOU FATHEADS?
THAT FISH IS HUGE!
WHICH MEANS: A HUGE FEAST!
BUT... THAT'S A PREHISTORIC ANIMAL!
SO IT IS! AND WE'LL BE THE FIRST CATS IN THE WORLD TO HAVE THE MOST MEMORABLE PIG-OUT IN HISTORY!
MORE THAN THAT... IN PREHISTORY!
PLOTOSAURUS
THE NAME OF THIS AQUATIC REPTILE THAT LIVED IN THE CRETACEOUS MEANS "FLOATING LIZARD." WITH A LENGTH OF UP TO AROUND 42 FEET, IT HAD A TAPERED BODY, THE END OF ITS TAIL WAS IN THE SHAPE OF A RHOMBUS, AND IT HAD LARGE EYES THAT GAVE IT EXCELLENT UNDERWATER VISION.

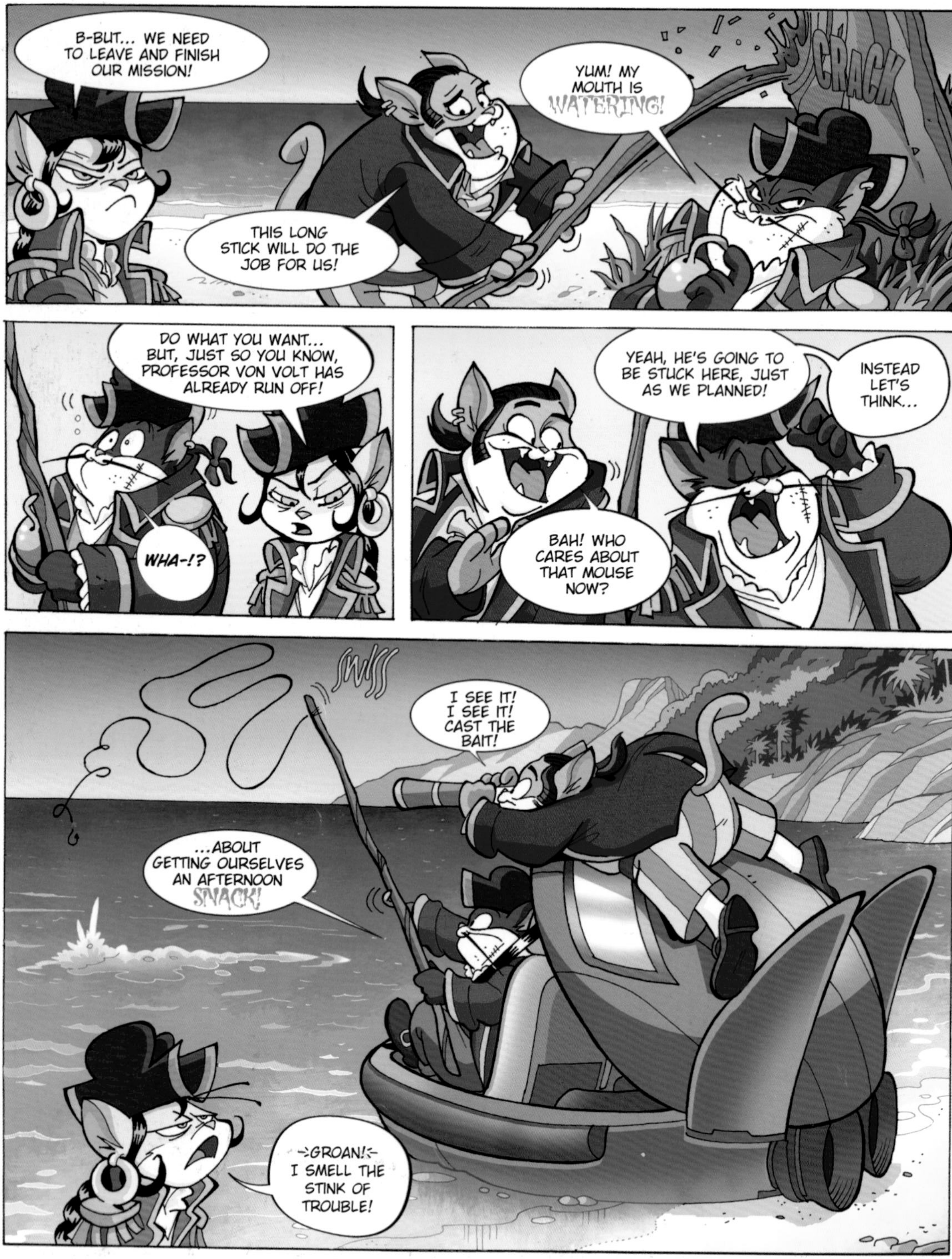

B-BUT... WE NEED TO LEAVE AND FINISH OUR MISSION!
CRACK
YUM! MY MOUTH IS WATERING!
THIS LONG STICK WILL DO THE JOB FOR US!
DO WHAT YOU WANT... BUT, JUST SO YOU KNOW, PROFESSOR VON VOLT HAS ALREADY RUN OFF!
WHA-!?
YEAH, HE'S GOING TO BE STUCK HERE, JUST AS WE PLANNED!
BAH! WHO CARES ABOUT THAT MOUSE NOW?
INSTEAD LET'S THINK...
SWISS
I SEE IT! I SEE IT! CAST THE BAIT!
...ABOUT GETTING OURSELVES AN AFTERNOON SNACK!
-GROAN!- I SMELL THE STINK OF TROUBLE!

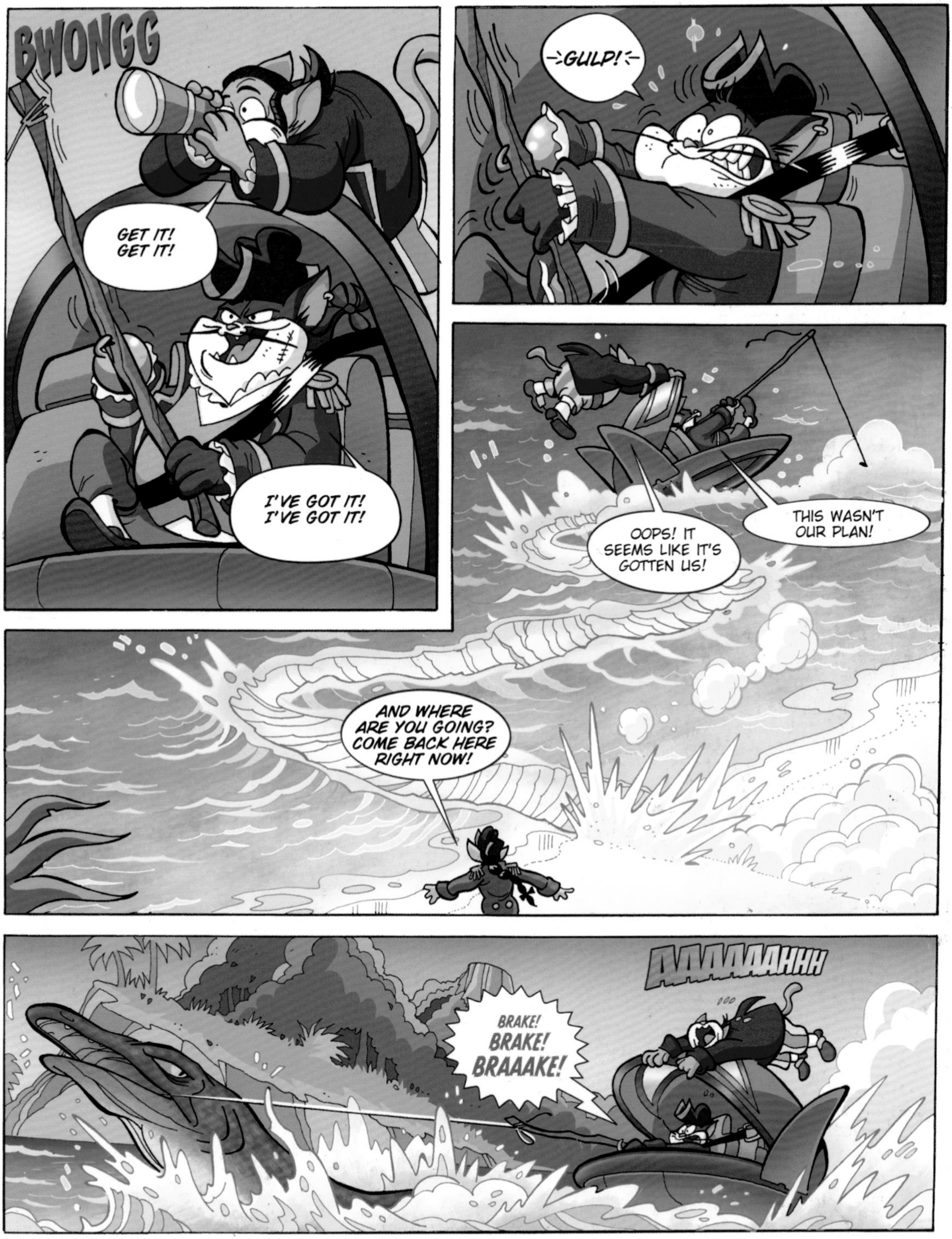
BWONGG
GET IT! GET IT!
I'VE GOT IT! I'VE GOT IT!
-GULP!-
OOPS! IT SEEMS LIKE IT'S GOTTEN US!
THIS WASN'T OUR PLAN!
AND WHERE ARE YOU GOING? COME BACK HERE RIGHT NOW!
AAAAAAHHH
BRAKE! BRAKE! BRAAAKE!

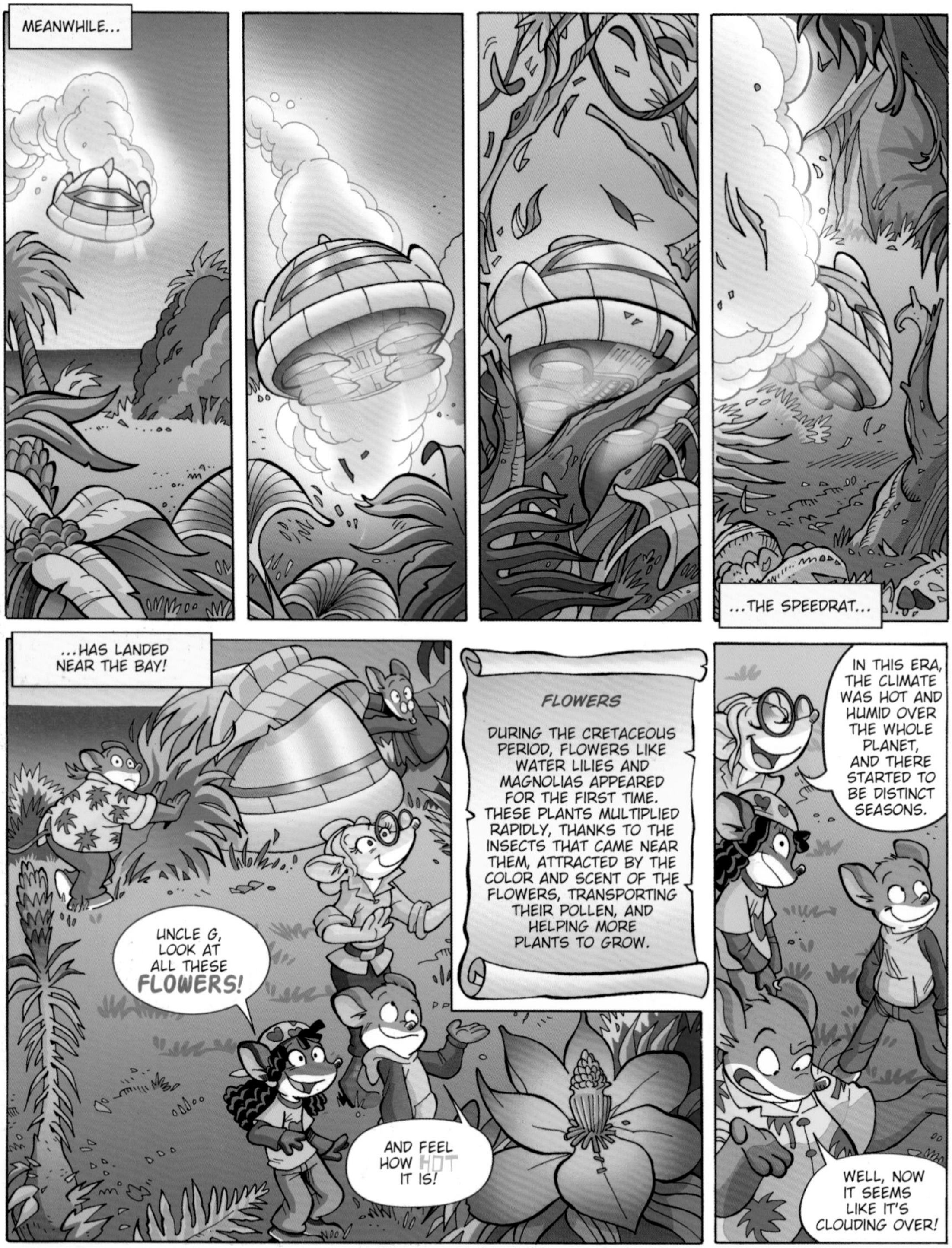
MEANWHILE...
...THE SPEEDRAT...
...HAS LANDED NEAR THE BAY!
FLOWERS
DURING THE CRETACEOUS PERIOD, FLOWERS LIKE WATER LILIES AND MAGNOLIAS APPEARED FOR THE FIRST TIME. THESE PLANTS MULTIPLIED RAPIDLY, THANKS TO THE INSECTS THAT CAME NEAR THEM, ATTRACTED BY THE COLOR AND SCENT OF THE FLOWERS, TRANSPORTING THEIR POLLEN, AND HELPING MORE PLANTS TO GROW.
UNCLE G, LOOK AT ALL THESE FLOWERS!
AND FEEL HOW HOT IT IS!
IN THIS ERA, THE CLIMATE WAS HOT AND HUMID OVER THE WHOLE PLANET, AND THERE STARTED TO BE DISTINCT SEASONS.
WELL, NOW IT SEEMS LIKE IT'S CLOUDING OVER!

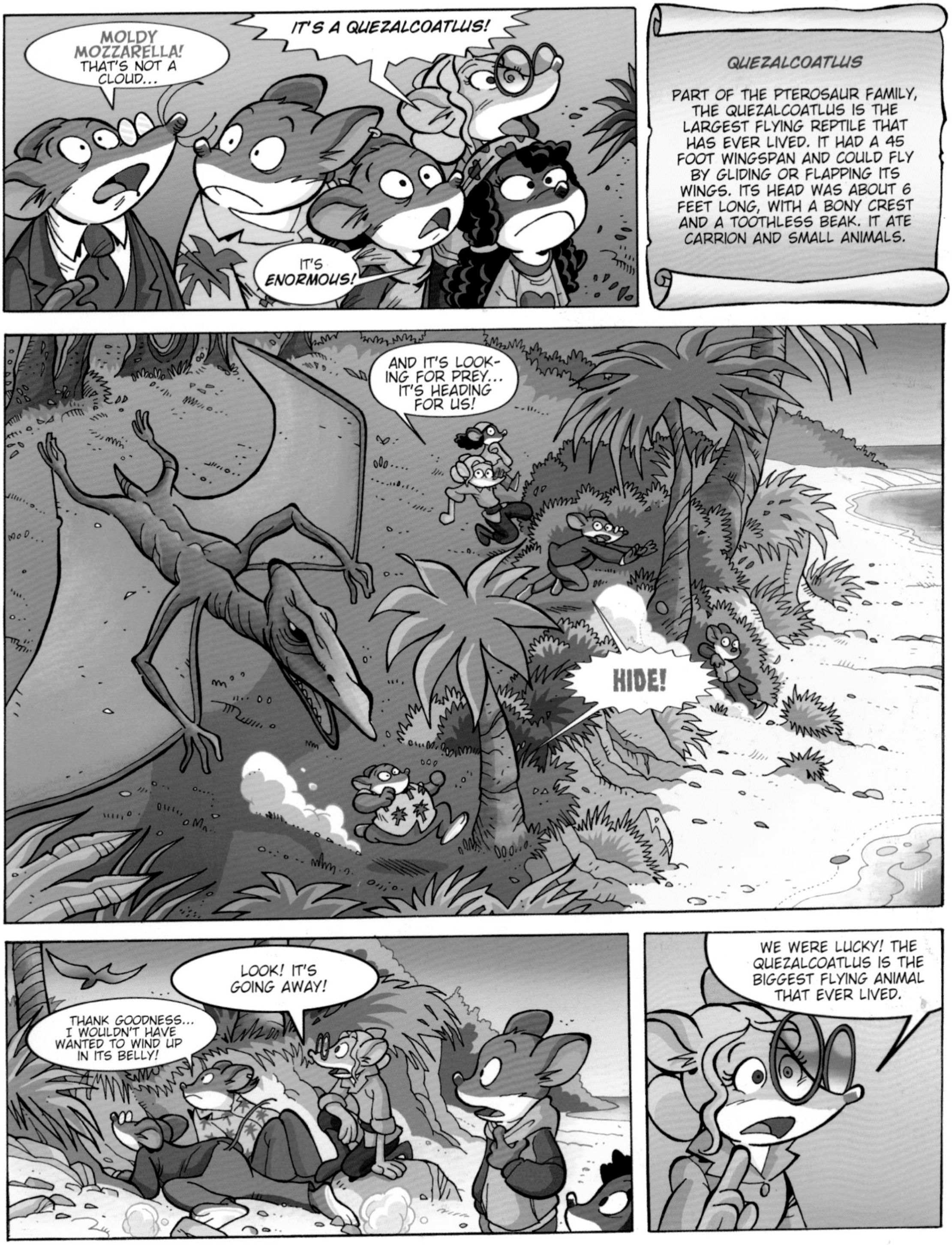
MOLDY MOZZARELLA! THAT'S NOT A CLOUD...
IT'S A QUEZALCOATLUS!
IT'S ENORMOUS!
QUEZALCOATLUS
PART OF THE PTEROSAUR FAMILY, THE QUEZALCOATLUS IS THE LARGEST FLYING REPTILE THAT HAS EVER LIVED. IT HAD A 45 FOOT WINGSPAN AND COULD FLY BY GLIDING OR FLAPPING ITS WINGS. ITS HEAD WAS ABOUT 6 FEET LONG, WITH A BONY CREST AND A TOOTHLESS BEAK. IT ATE CARRION AND SMALL ANIMALS.
AND IT'S LOOKING FOR PREY... IT'S HEADING FOR US!
HIDE!
THANK GOODNESS... I WOULDN'T HAVE WANTED TO WIND UP IN ITS BELLY!
LOOK! IT'S GOING AWAY!
WE WERE LUCKY! THE QUEZALCOATLUS IS THE BIGGEST FLYING ANIMAL THAT EVER LIVED.

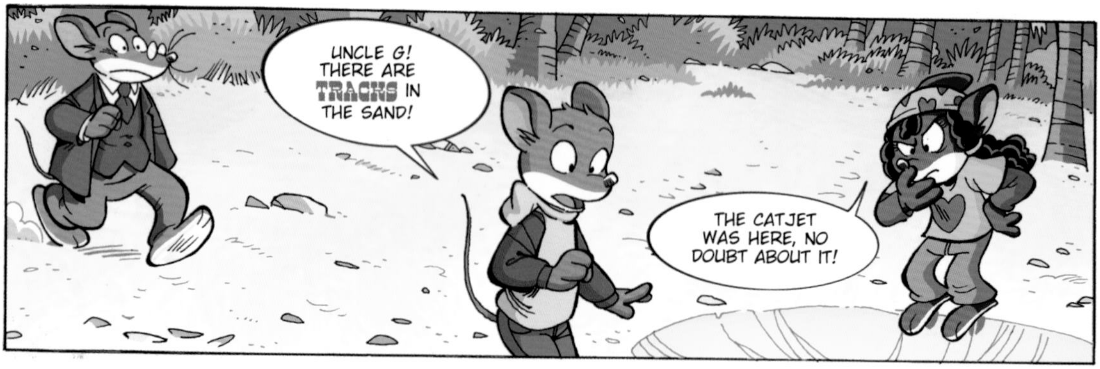
UNCLE G! THERE ARE TRACKS IN THE SAND!
THE CATJET WAS HERE, NO DOUBT ABOUT IT!

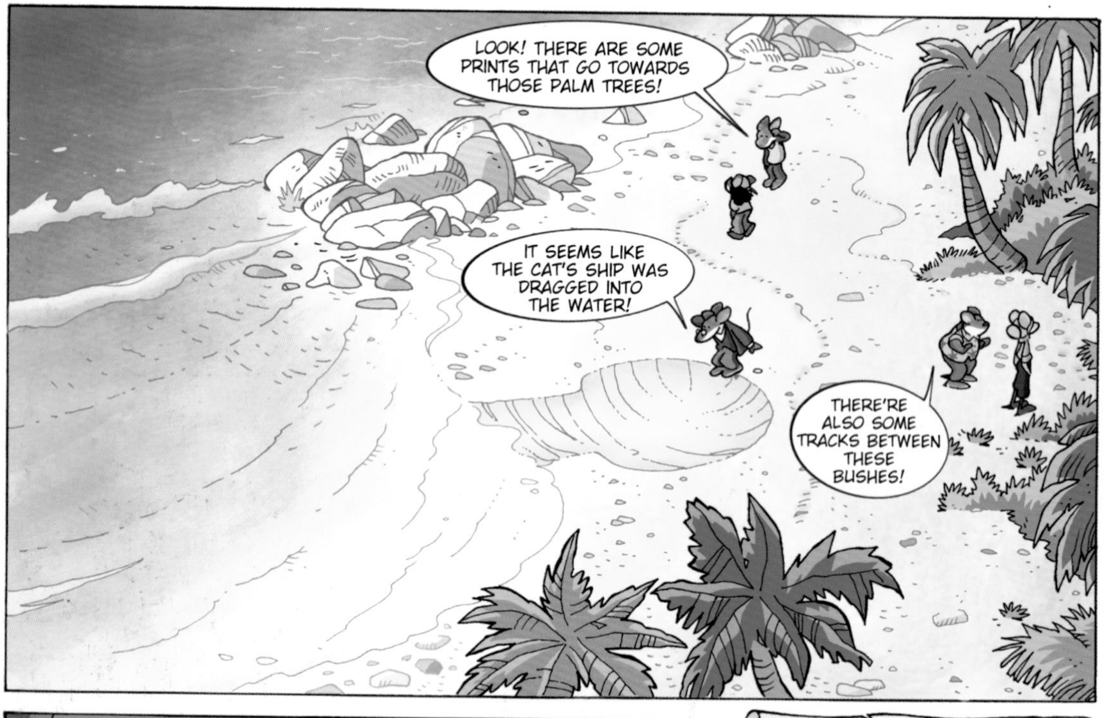
LOOK! THERE ARE SOME PRINTS THAT GO TOWARDS THOSE PALM TREES!
IT SEEMS LIKE THE CAT'S SHIP WAS DRAGGED INTO THE WATER!
THERE'RE ALSO SOME TRACKS BETWEEN THESE BUSHES!

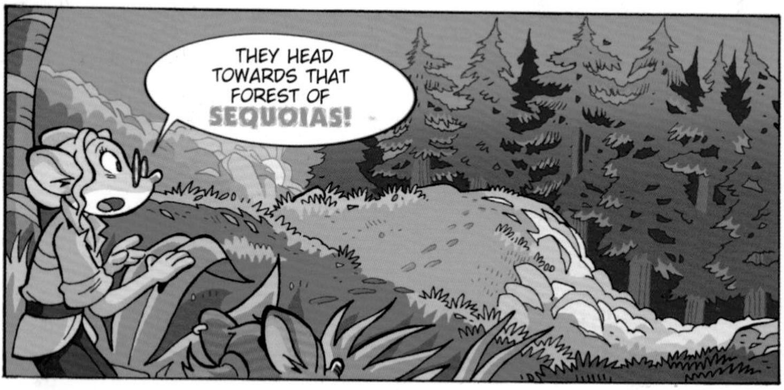
THEY HEAD TOWARDS THAT FOREST OF SEQUOIAS!

PLANTS AND FLOWERS

IN THE CRETACEOUS PERIOD, IN ADDITION TO THE TREE FERNS THAT HAD ALREADY APPEARED IN THE JURASSIC PERIOD, THERE WERE ALSO THE ANCESTORS OF MODERN PALM TREES, AS WELL AS THE FIRST SEQUOIAS. SEQUOIA LEAVES WERE GREATLY PRIZED BY THE LARGE HERBIVOROUS DINOSAURS. SEQUOIA TREES HAVE SURVIVED TO TODAY.

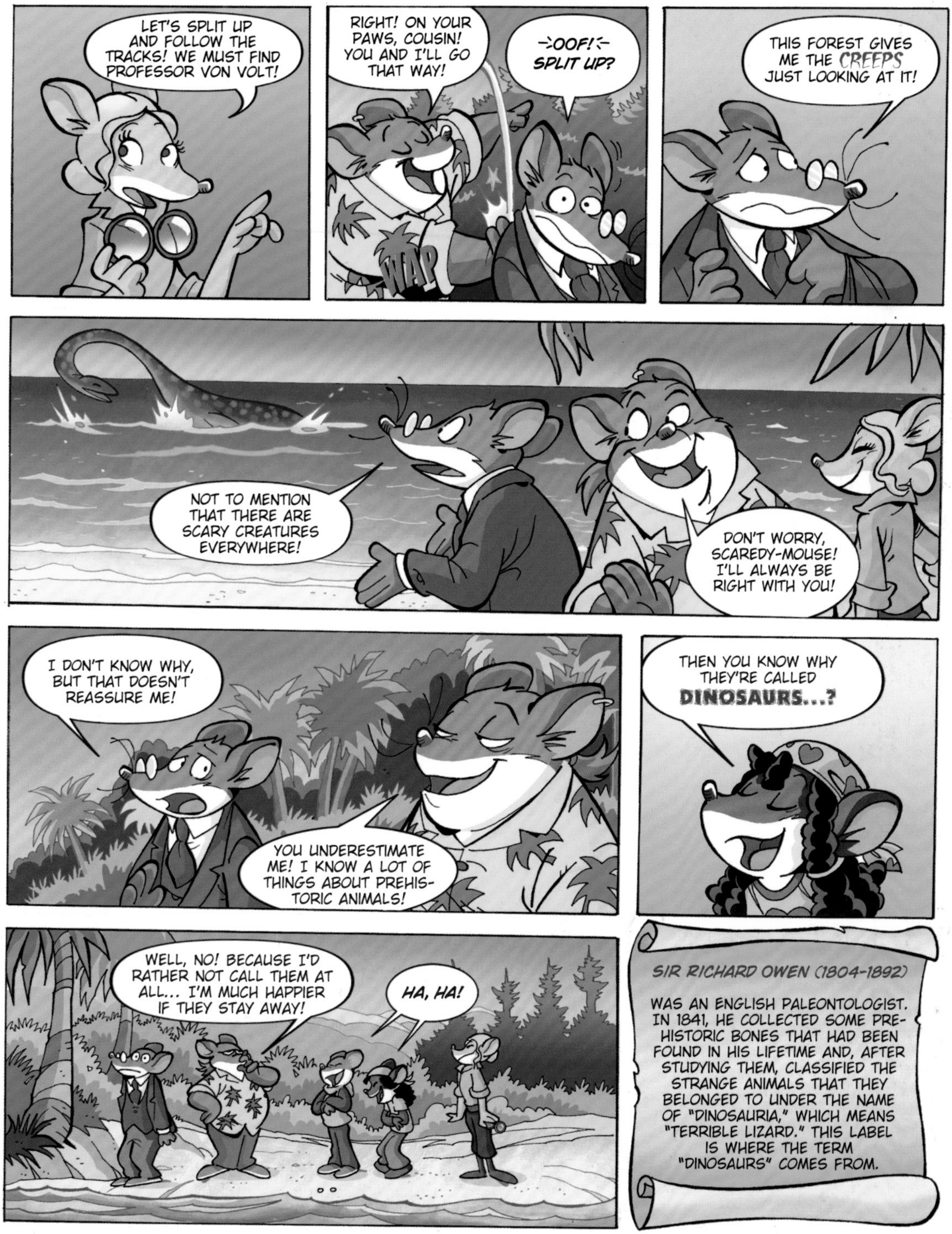
LET'S SPLIT UP AND FOLLOW THE TRACKS! WE MUST FIND PROFESSOR VON VOLT!
RIGHT! ON YOUR PAWS, COUSIN! YOU AND I'LL GO THAT WAY!
OOF! SPLIT UP?
WAP
THIS FOREST GIVES ME THE CREEPS JUST LOOKING AT IT!
NOT TO MENTION THAT THERE ARE SCARY CREATURES EVERYWHERE!
DON'T WORRY, SCAREDY-MOUSE! I'LL ALWAYS BE RIGHT WITH YOU!
I DON'T KNOW WHY, BUT THAT DOESN'T REASSURE ME!
YOU UNDERESTIMATE ME! I KNOW A LOT OF THINGS ABOUT PREHISTORIC ANIMALS!
THEN YOU KNOW WHY THEY'RE CALLED DINOSAURS...?
WELL, NO! BECAUSE I'D RATHER NOT CALL THEM AT ALL... I'M MUCH HAPPIER IF THEY STAY AWAY!
HA, HA!
SIR RICHARD OWEN (1804-1892)
WAS AN ENGLISH PALEONTOLOGIST. IN 1841, HE COLLECTED SOME PREHISTORIC BONES THAT HAD BEEN FOUND IN HIS LIFETIME AND, AFTER STUDYING THEM, CLASSIFIED THE STRANGE ANIMALS THAT THEY BELONGED TO UNDER THE NAME OF "DINOSAURIA," WHICH MEANS "TERRIBLE LIZARD." THIS LABEL IS WHERE THE TERM "DINOSAURS" COMES FROM.

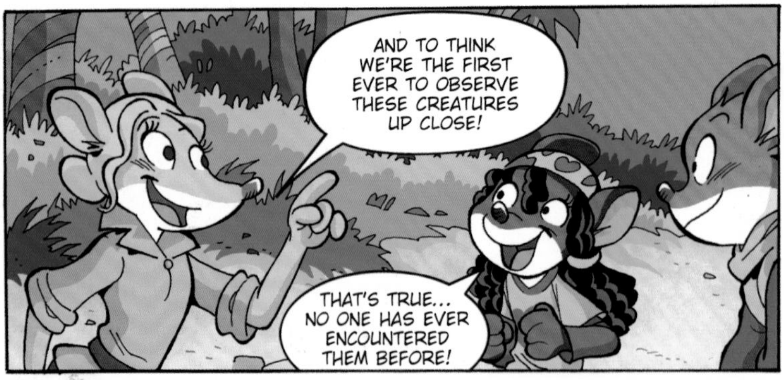
AND TO THINK WE'RE THE FIRST EVER TO OBSERVE THESE CREATURES UP CLOSE!
THAT'S TRUE... NO ONE HAS EVER ENCOUNTERED THEM BEFORE!

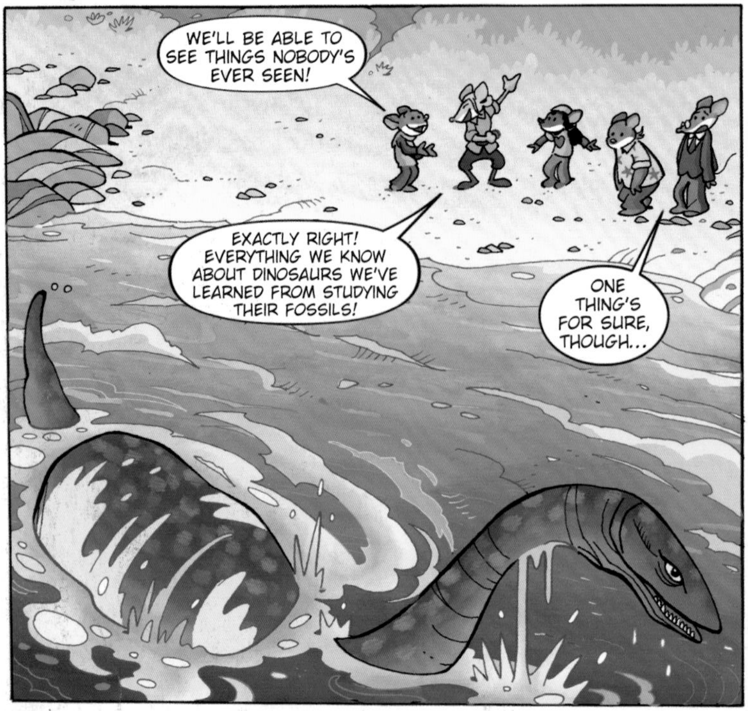
WE'LL BE ABLE TO SEE THINGS NOBODY'S EVER SEEN!
EXACTLY RIGHT! EVERYTHING WE KNOW ABOUT DINOSAURS WE'VE LEARNED FROM STUDYING THEIR FOSSILS!
ONE THING'S FOR SURE, THOUGH...

HOW FOSSILS ARE FORMED

WHAT PALEONTOLOGISTS KNOW ABOUT DINOSAURS COMES FROM STUDYING THE FOSSILS THAT HAVE BEEN UNCOVERED. FOSSILS ARE THE REMAINS OF PLANTS AND ANIMALS THAT HAVE BEEN PRESERVED UNTIL OUR DAY. THIS PROCESS OF PRESERVATION, WHICH IS CALLED "MINERALIZATION," COULD ONLY TAKE PLACE IN CERTAIN SITUATIONS, FOR EXAMPLE, WHEN THE BODY OF A DEAD DINOSAUR WAS NEAR A RIVER OR A LAKE, OR HAD BEEN CARRIED TO THE SEA AND SANK TO THE BOTTOM. IN THAT CASE, THE BOTTOM OF THE SEA WAS COVERED BY DIRT AND OTHER SEDIMENTS THAT SLOWED DOWN THE DECOMPOSITION OF THE BODY. AT THIS POINT, DUE TO VARIOUS CHEMICAL REACTIONS, THE ORGANIC SUBSTANCE IN THE BODY WAS TRANSFORMED INTO MINERAL MATTER. SO FOSSILS ARE THE REMAINS OF ANIMALS OR PLANTS THAT DIDN'T DISAPPEAR BECAUSE THEY WERE TRANSFORMED INTO ROCKS OVER TIME. DUE TO THIS TRANSFORMATION, WE CANNOT REPRODUCE SOME OF THE CHARACTERISTICS OF THESE ANCIENT LIVING BEINGS, SUCH AS, FOR EXAMPLE, THEIR COLOR. IN ADDITION, SCHOLARS HAVEN'T ALWAYS RECONSTRUCTED THE MINERALIZED REMAINS OF DINOSAURS IN THE RIGHT WAY, WHICH HAS SOMETIMES LED TO MISTAKES IN ASSEMBLING THEIR SKELETONS.

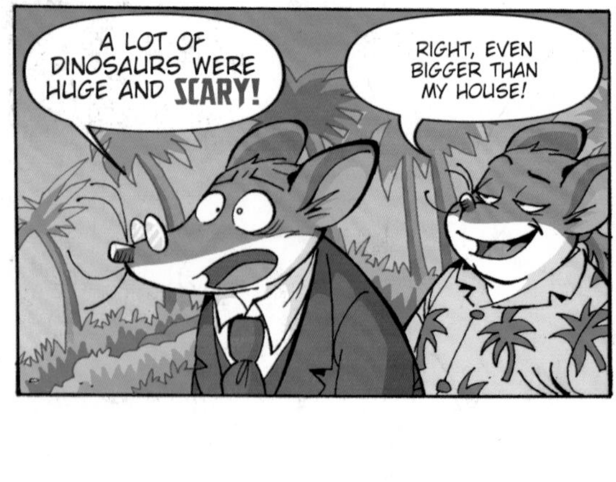
A LOT OF DINOSAURS WERE HUGE AND SCARY!
RIGHT, EVEN BIGGER THAN MY HOUSE!

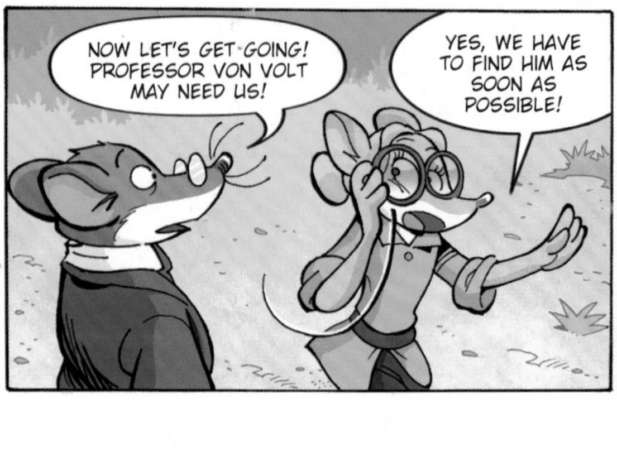
NOW LET'S GET GOING! PROFESSOR VON VOLT MAY NEED US!
YES, WE HAVE TO FIND HIM AS SOON AS POSSIBLE!

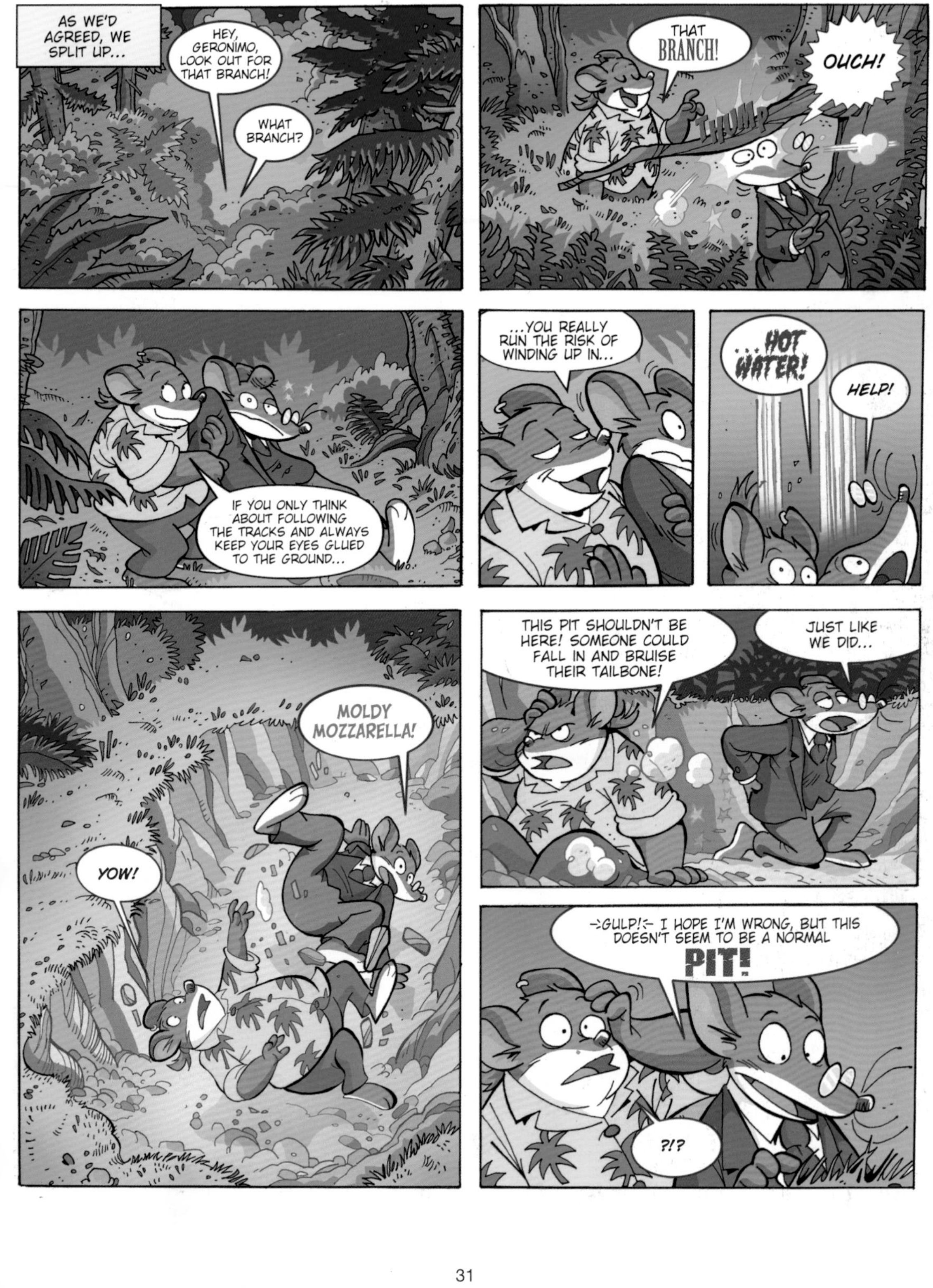
AS WE'D AGREED, WE SPLIT UP...
HEY, GERONIMO, LOOK OUT FOR THAT BRANCH!
WHAT BRANCH?
THAT BRANCH!
THUMP
OUCH!
IF YOU ONLY THINK ABOUT FOLLOWING THE TRACKS AND ALWAYS KEEP YOUR EYES GLUED TO THE GROUND...
...YOU REALLY RUN THE RISK OF WINDING UP IN...
...HOT WATER!
HELP!
MOLDY MOZZARELLA!
YOW!
THIS PIT SHOULDN'T BE HERE! SOMEONE COULD FALL IN AND BRUISE THEIR TAILBONE!
JUST LIKE WE DID...
GULP! I HOPE I'M WRONG, BUT THIS DOESN'T SEEM TO BE A NORMAL PIT!
?!?

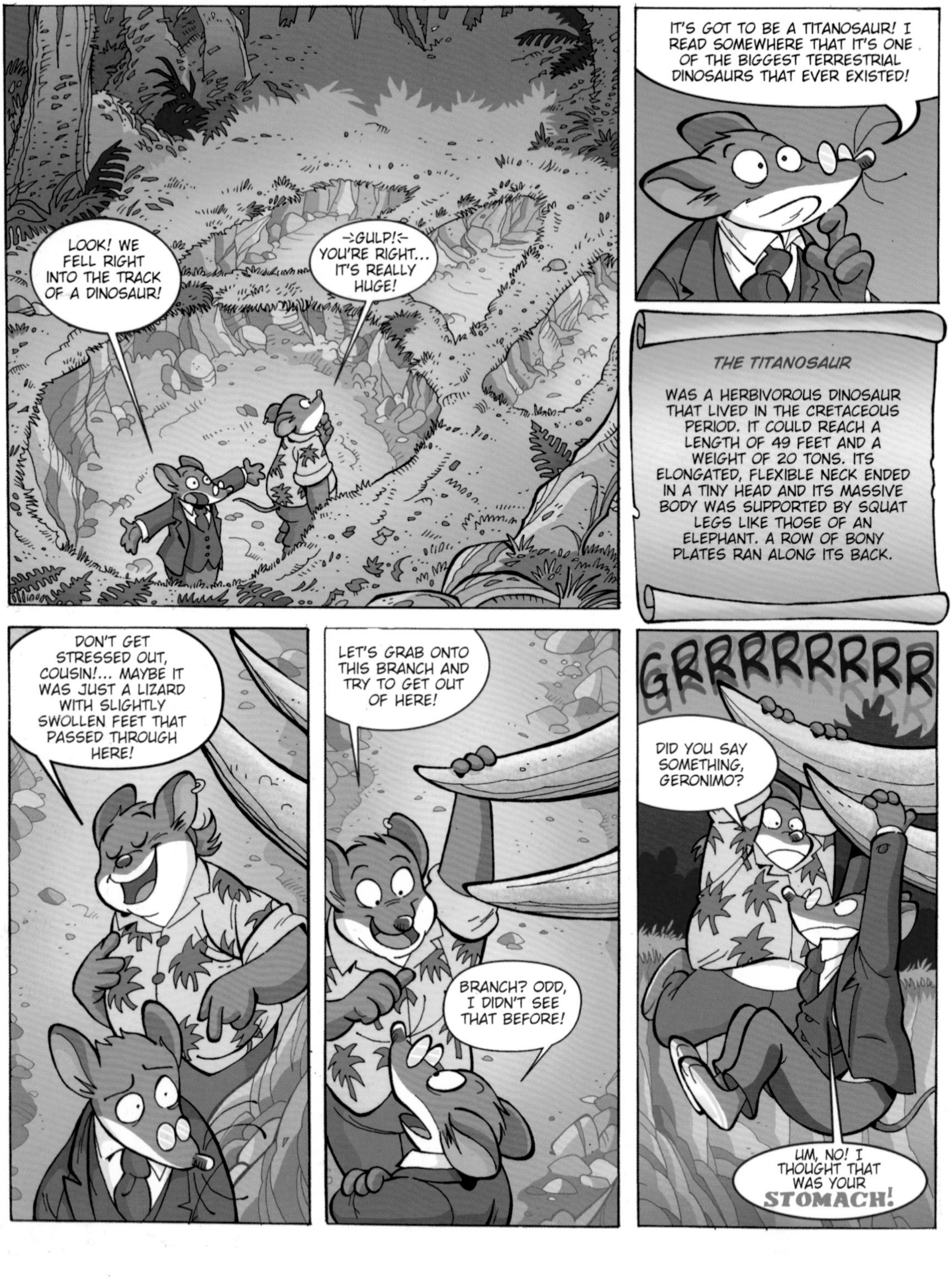
LOOK! WE FELL RIGHT INTO THE TRACK OF A DINOSAUR!
-GULP!- YOU'RE RIGHT... IT'S REALLY HUGE!
IT'S GOT TO BE A TITANOSAUR! I READ SOMEWHERE THAT IT'S ONE OF THE BIGGEST TERRESTRIAL DINOSAURS THAT EVER EXISTED!
THE TITANOSAUR
WAS A HERBIVOROUS DINOSAUR THAT LIVED IN THE CRETACEOUS PERIOD. IT COULD REACH A LENGTH OF 49 FEET AND A WEIGHT OF 20 TONS. ITS ELONGATED, FLEXIBLE NECK ENDED IN A TINY HEAD AND ITS MASSIVE BODY WAS SUPPORTED BY SQUAT LEGS LIKE THOSE OF AN ELEPHANT. A ROW OF BONY PLATES RAN ALONG ITS BACK.
DON'T GET STRESSED OUT, COUSIN!... MAYBE IT WAS JUST A LIZARD WITH SLIGHTLY SWOLLEN FEET THAT PASSED THROUGH HERE!
LET'S GRAB ONTO THIS BRANCH AND TRY TO GET OUT OF HERE!
BRANCH? ODD, I DIDN'T SEE THAT BEFORE!
GRRRRRRRR
DID YOU SAY SOMETHING, GERONIMO?
UM, NO! I THOUGHT THAT WAS YOUR STOMACH!

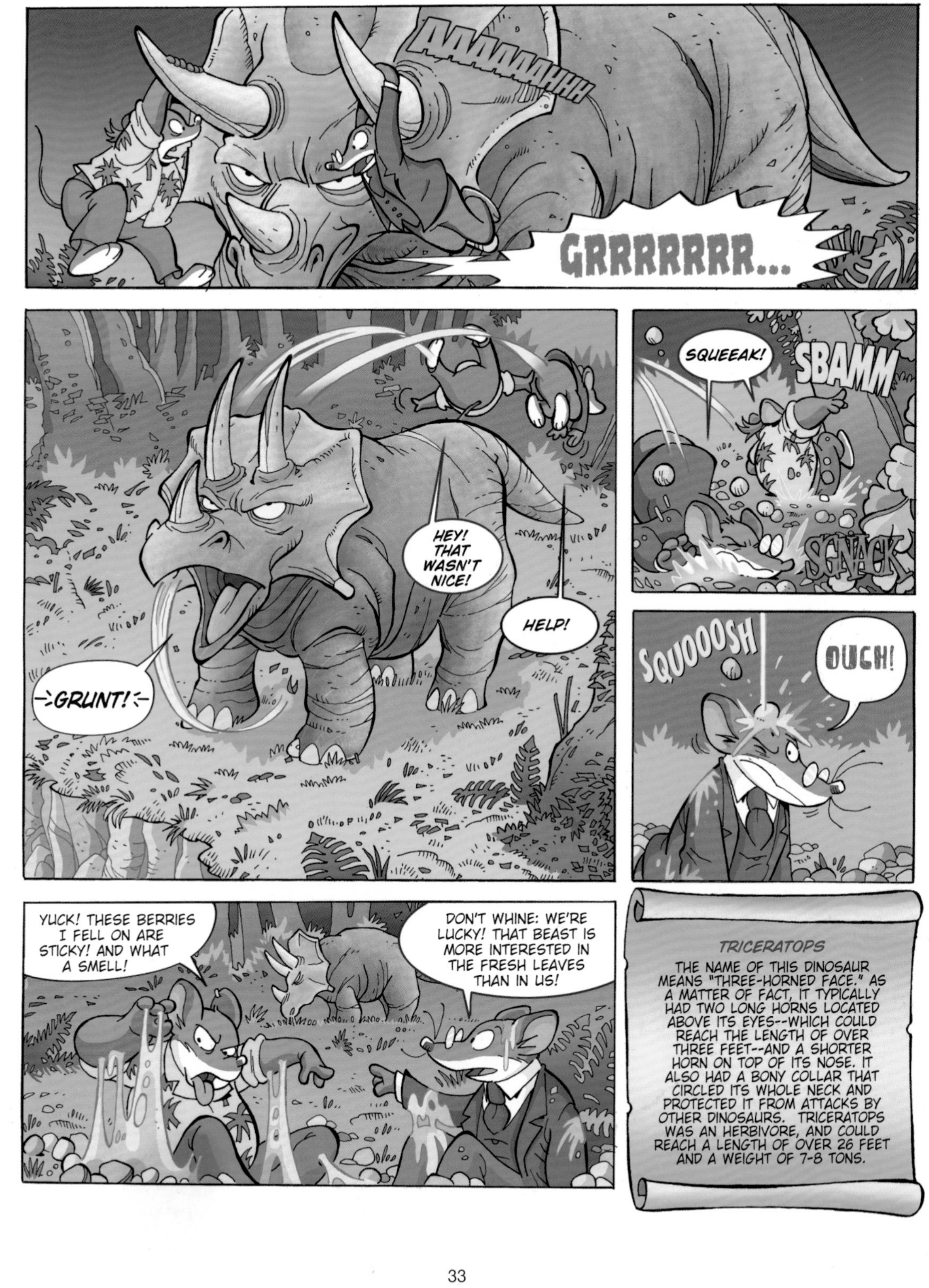

AAAAAAAHHHH
GRRRRRRR...
HEY! THAT WASN'T NICE!
HELP!
GRUNT!
SQUEEAK!
SBAMM
SCNACK
SQUOOOSH
OUCH!
YUCK! THESE BERRIES I FELL ON ARE STICKY! AND WHAT A SMELL!
DON'T WHINE: WE'RE LUCKY! THAT BEAST IS MORE INTERESTED IN THE FRESH LEAVES THAN IN US!
TRICERATOPS
THE NAME OF THIS DINOSAUR MEANS "THREE-HORNED FACE." AS A MATTER OF FACT, IT TYPICALLY HAD TWO LONG HORNS LOCATED ABOVE ITS EYES--WHICH COULD REACH THE LENGTH OF OVER THREE FEET--AND A SHORTER HORN ON TOP OF ITS NOSE. IT ALSO HAD A BONY COLLAR THAT CIRCLED ITS WHOLE NECK AND PROTECTED IT FROM ATTACKS BY OTHER DINOSAURS. TRICERATOPS WAS AN HERBIVORE, AND COULD REACH A LENGTH OF OVER 26 FEET AND A WEIGHT OF 7-8 TONS.

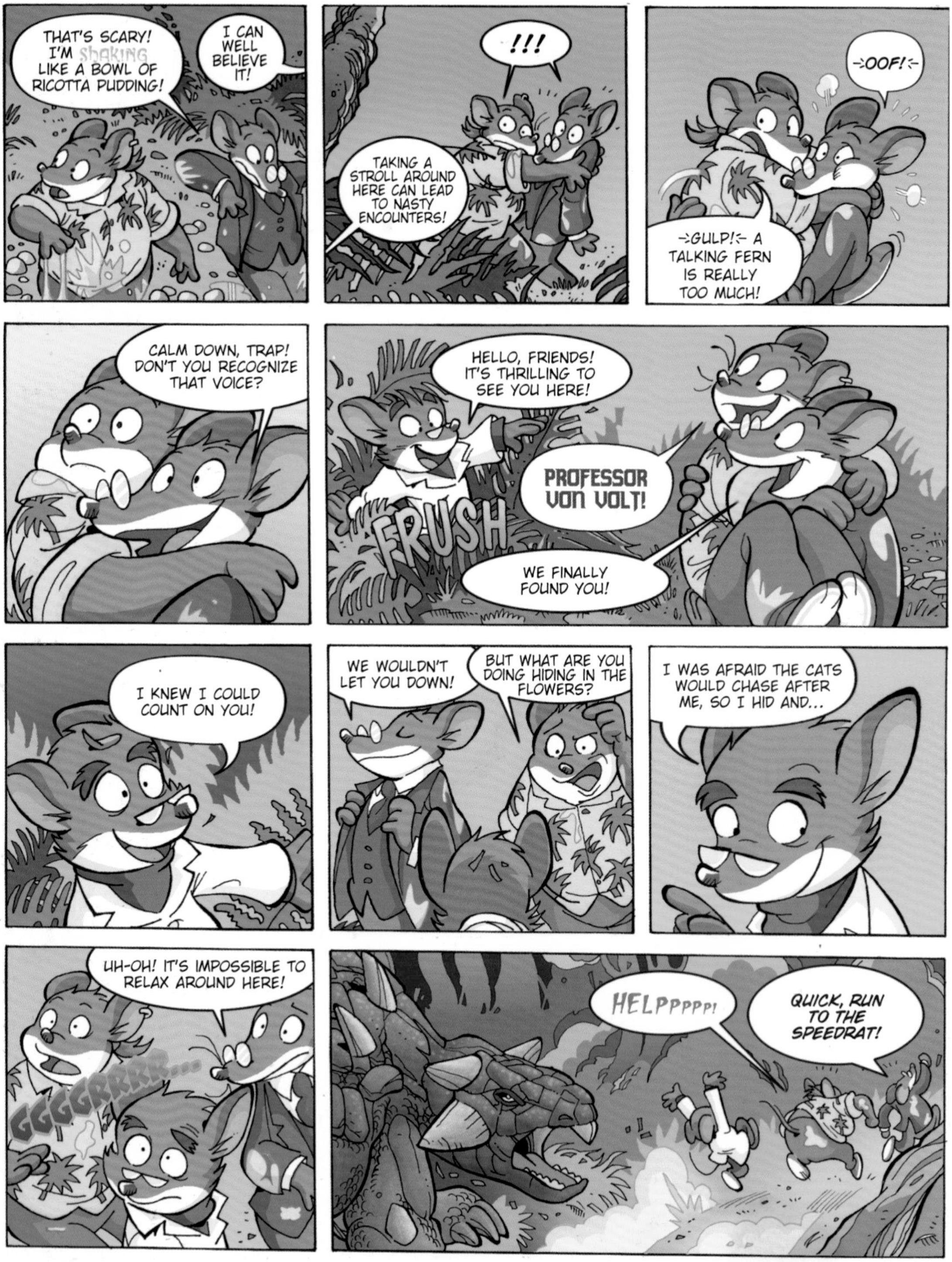
THAT'S SCARY! I'M SHAKING LIKE A BOWL OF RICOTTA PUDDING!
I CAN WELL BELIEVE IT!
!!!
TAKING A STROLL AROUND HERE CAN LEAD TO NASTY ENCOUNTERS!
-OOF!-
-GULP!- A TALKING FERN IS REALLY TOO MUCH!
CALM DOWN, TRAP! DON'T YOU RECOGNIZE THAT VOICE?
HELLO, FRIENDS! IT'S THRILLING TO SEE YOU HERE!
FRUSH
PROFESSOR VON VOLT!
WE FINALLY FOUND YOU!
I KNEW I COULD COUNT ON YOU!
WE WOULDN'T LET YOU DOWN!
BUT WHAT ARE YOU DOING HIDING IN THE FLOWERS?
I WAS AFRAID THE CATS WOULD CHASE AFTER ME, SO I HID AND...
UH-OH! IT'S IMPOSSIBLE TO RELAX AROUND HERE!
GGGGRRRR...
HELPPPPP!
QUICK, RUN TO THE SPEEDRAT!

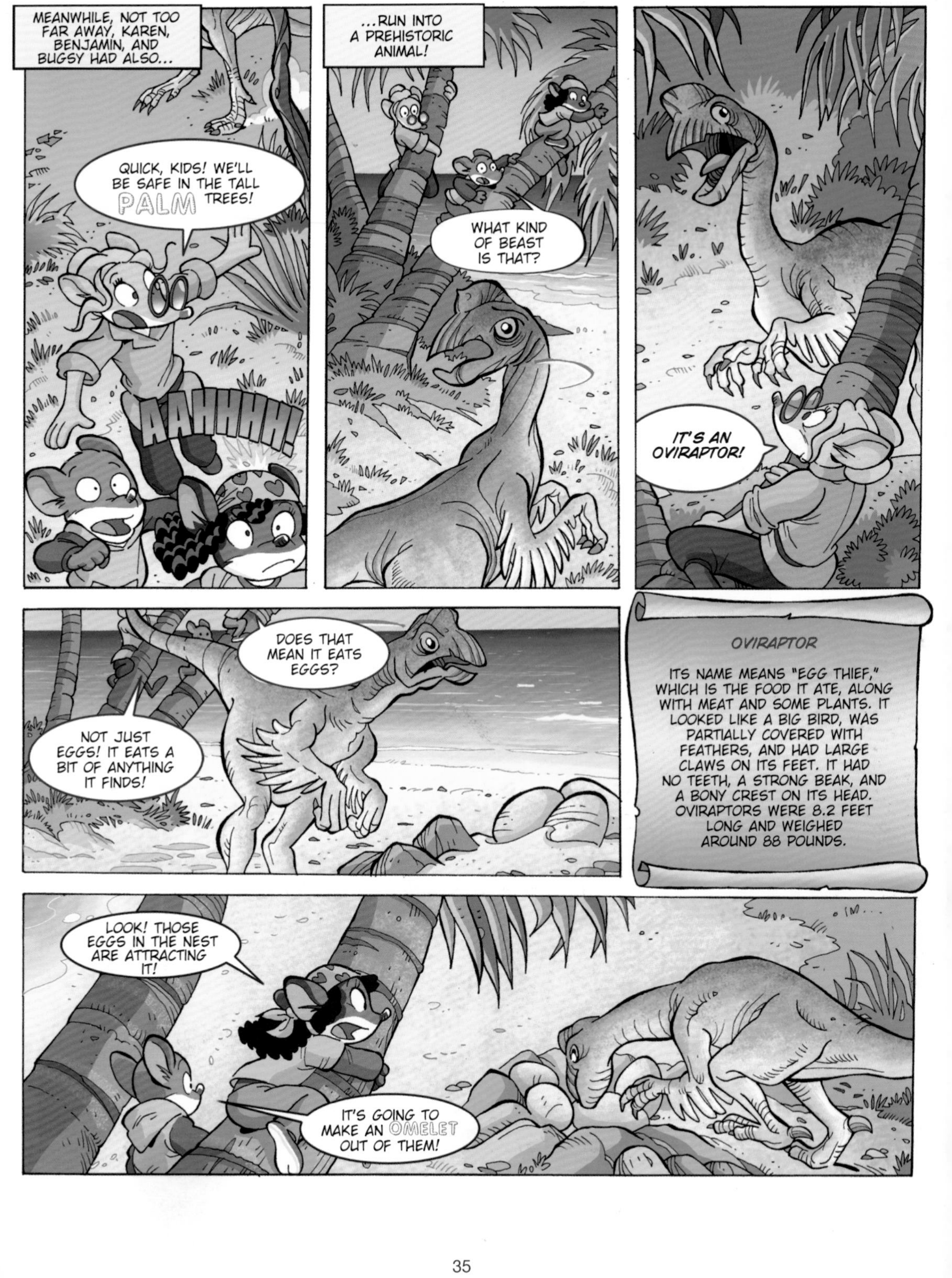
MEANWHILE, NOT TOO FAR AWAY, KAREN, BENJAMIN, AND BUGSY HAD ALSO...
QUICK, KIDS! WE'LL BE SAFE IN THE TALL PALM TREES!
AAHHHH!
...RUN INTO A PREHISTORIC ANIMAL!
WHAT KIND OF BEAST IS THAT?
IT'S AN OVIRAPTOR!
DOES THAT MEAN IT EATS EGGS?
NOT JUST EGGS! IT EATS A BIT OF ANYTHING IT FINDS!
OVIRAPTOR
ITS NAME MEANS "EGG THIEF," WHICH IS THE FOOD IT ATE, ALONG WITH MEAT AND SOME PLANTS. IT LOOKED LIKE A BIG BIRD, WAS PARTIALLY COVERED WITH FEATHERS, AND HAD LARGE CLAWS ON ITS FEET. IT HAD NO TEETH, A STRONG BEAK, AND A BONY CREST ON ITS HEAD. OVIRAPTORS WERE 8.2 FEET LONG AND WEIGHED AROUND 88 POUNDS.
LOOK! THOSE EGGS IN THE NEST ARE ATTRACTING IT!
IT'S GOING TO MAKE AN OMELET OUT OF THEM!

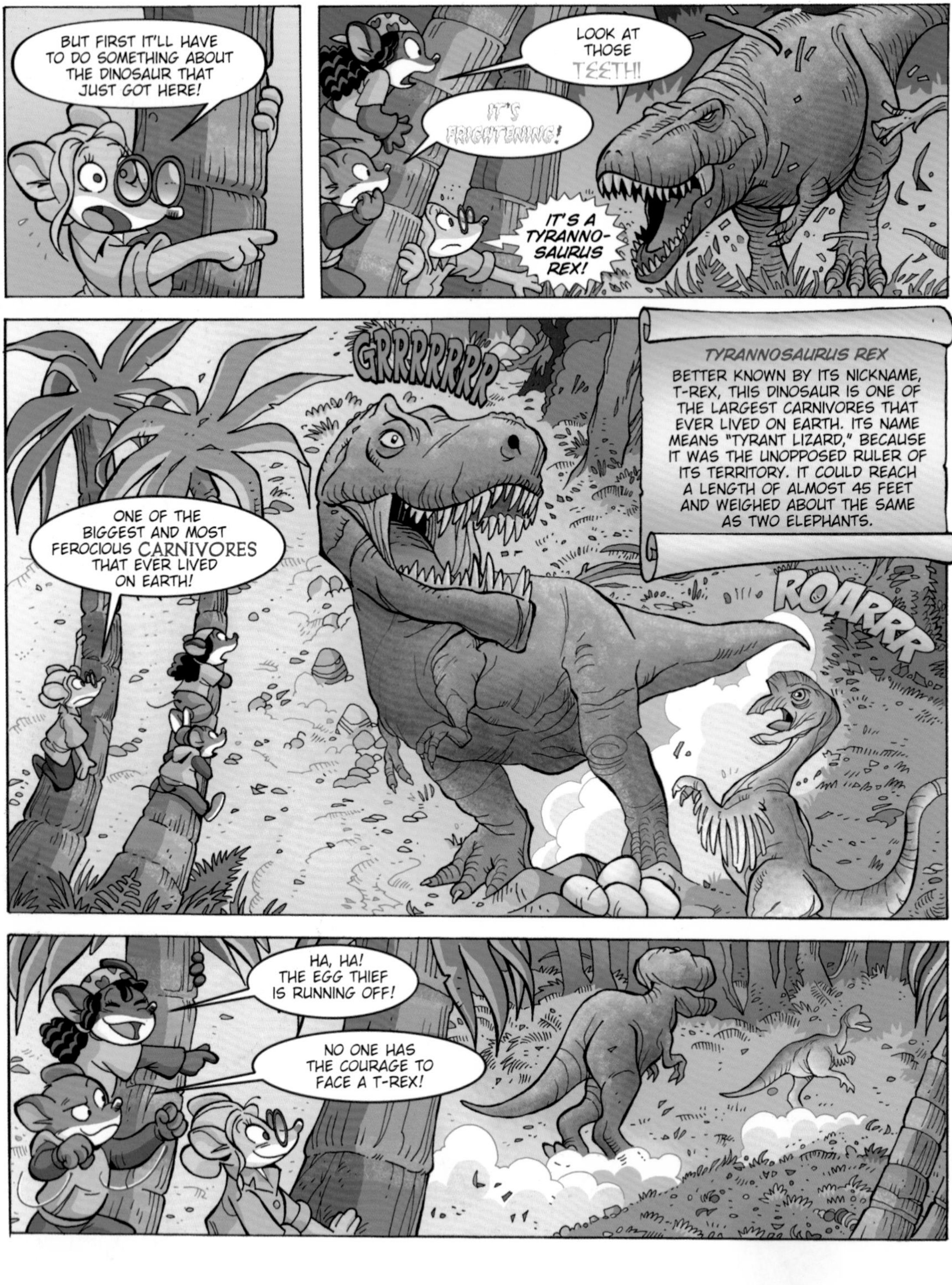
BUT FIRST IT'LL HAVE TO DO SOMETHING ABOUT THE DINOSAUR THAT JUST GOT HERE!
LOOK AT THOSE TEETH!
IT'S FRIGHTENING!
IT'S A TYRANNO-SAURUS REX!
GRRRRRRR
TYRANNOSAURUS REX
BETTER KNOWN BY ITS NICKNAME, T-REX, THIS DINOSAUR IS ONE OF THE LARGEST CARNIVORES THAT EVER LIVED ON EARTH. ITS NAME MEANS "TYRANT LIZARD," BECAUSE IT WAS THE UNOPPOSED RULER OF ITS TERRITORY. IT COULD REACH A LENGTH OF ALMOST 45 FEET AND WEIGHED ABOUT THE SAME AS TWO ELEPHANTS.
ONE OF THE BIGGEST AND MOST FEROCIOUS CARNIVORES THAT EVER LIVED ON EARTH!
ROARRRR
HA, HA! THE EGG THIEF IS RUNNING OFF!
NO ONE HAS THE COURAGE TO FACE A T-REX!

LET'S GET AWAY FROM HERE BEFORE THE TYRANNOSAURUS SEES US!

HEY! THERE'S SOMETHING OUT THERE IN THE MIDDLE OF THE SEA!

YOU'RE RIGHT! ANOTHER *CHASE*!

?!?

IT'S THE CATS! BUT THEY'RE NOT ALONE!

INCREDIBLE! THEY'RE BEING DRAGGED BY A PLOTOSAURUS AND CHASED BY AN ELASMOSAURUS...

ELASMOSAURUS

THE NAME OF THIS AQUATIC REPTILE, WHICH MEANS "RIBBON LIZARD," COMES FROM ITS NECK, WHICH COULD EXCEED 22 FEET IN LENGTH. BECAUSE OF ITS FLIPPERS, IT WAS ABLE TO MOVE WITH GREAT AGILITY AND CATCH FISH AND CRUSTACEANS, AND IT COULD ALSO EMERGE FROM THE WATER SUDDENLY TO CATCH FLYING REPTILES THAT GOT NEAR THE SURFACE.

THEY'RE HEADED RIGHT FOR THE *CORAL REEF*!

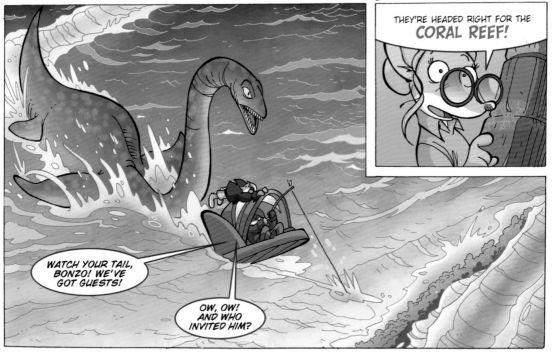

WATCH YOUR TAIL, BONZO! WE'VE GOT GUESTS!

OW, OW! AND WHO INVITED HIM?

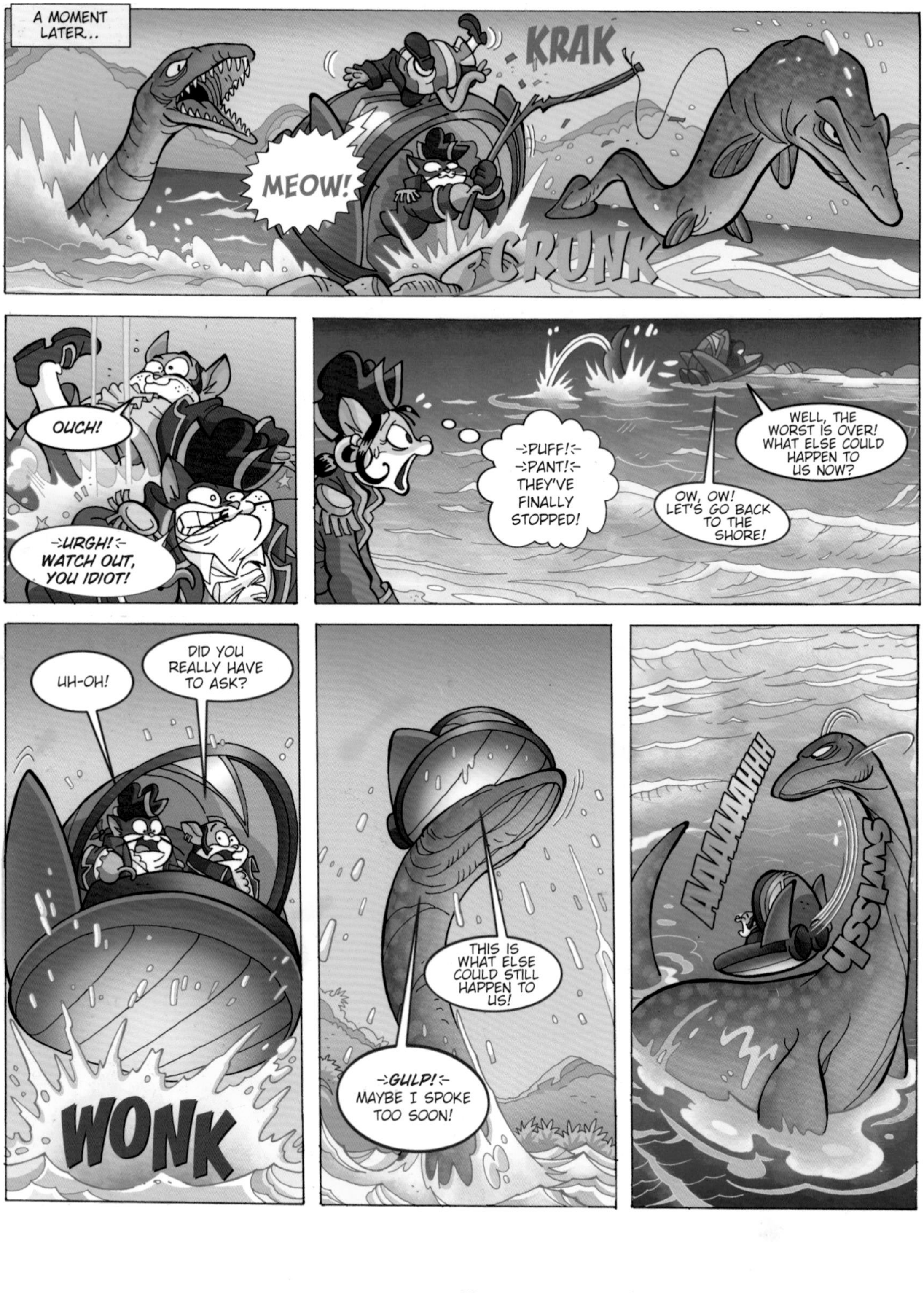

A MOMENT LATER...
KRAK
MEOW!
CRUNK
OUCH!
-URGH!- WATCH OUT, YOU IDIOT!
-PUFF!- -PANT!- THEY'VE FINALLY STOPPED!
OW, OW! LET'S GO BACK TO THE SHORE!
WELL, THE WORST IS OVER! WHAT ELSE COULD HAPPEN TO US NOW?
UH-OH!
DID YOU REALLY HAVE TO ASK?
WONK
THIS IS WHAT ELSE COULD STILL HAPPEN TO US!
-GULP!- MAYBE I SPOKE TOO SOON!
AAAAAAHHH
SWISSSH

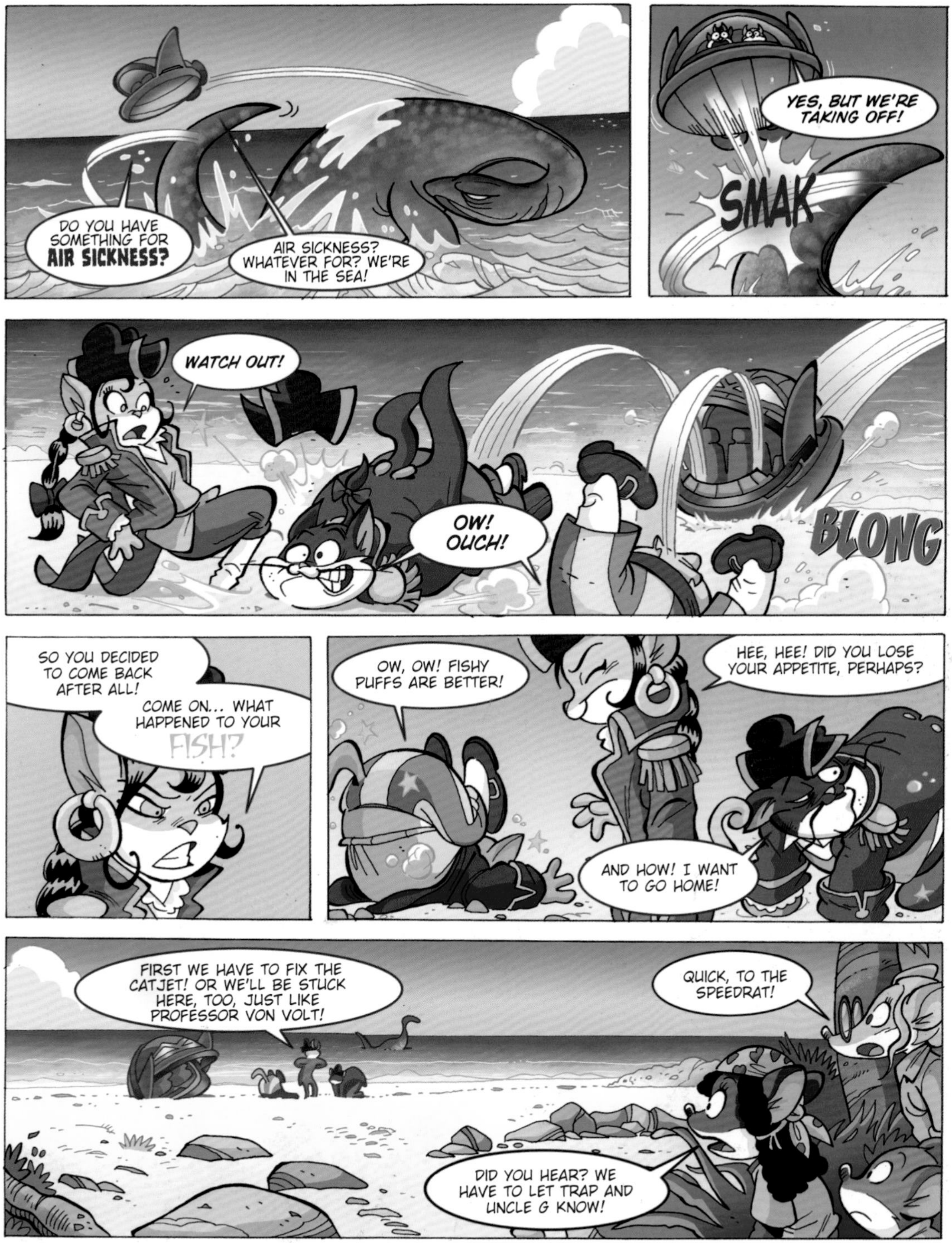
DO YOU HAVE SOMETHING FOR AIR SICKNESS?
AIR SICKNESS? WHATEVER FOR? WE'RE IN THE SEA!
YES, BUT WE'RE TAKING OFF!
SMAK
WATCH OUT!
OW! OUCH!
BLONG
SO YOU DECIDED TO COME BACK AFTER ALL!
COME ON... WHAT HAPPENED TO YOUR FISH?
OW, OW! FISHY PUFFS ARE BETTER!
HEE, HEE! DID YOU LOSE YOUR APPETITE, PERHAPS?
AND HOW! I WANT TO GO HOME!
FIRST WE HAVE TO FIX THE CATJET! OR WE'LL BE STUCK HERE, TOO, JUST LIKE PROFESSOR VON VOLT!
QUICK, TO THE SPEEDRAT!
DID YOU HEAR? WE HAVE TO LET TRAP AND UNCLE G KNOW!

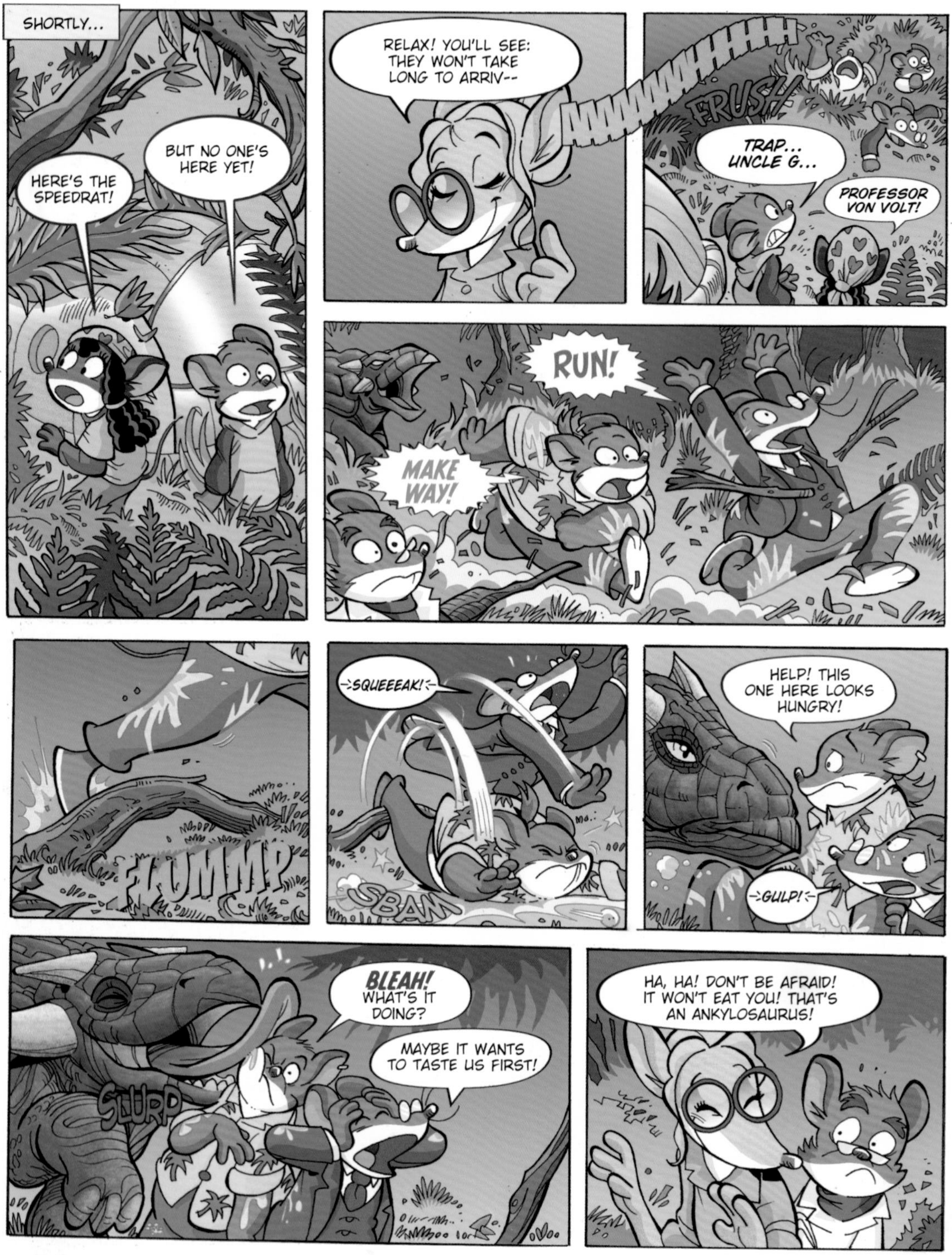
SHORTLY...
HERE'S THE SPEEDRAT!
BUT NO ONE'S HERE YET!
RELAX! YOU'LL SEE: THEY WON'T TAKE LONG TO ARRIV--
AAAAAAAHHHHHH
FRUSH
TRAP... UNCLE G...
PROFESSOR VON VOLT!
RUN!
MAKE WAY!
FLUMMP
SQUEEEAK!
SBAM
HELP! THIS ONE HERE LOOKS HUNGRY!
GULP!
SLURP
BLEAH! WHAT'S IT DOING?
MAYBE IT WANTS TO TASTE US FIRST!
HA, HA! DON'T BE AFRAID! IT WON'T EAT YOU! THAT'S AN ANKYLOSAURUS!

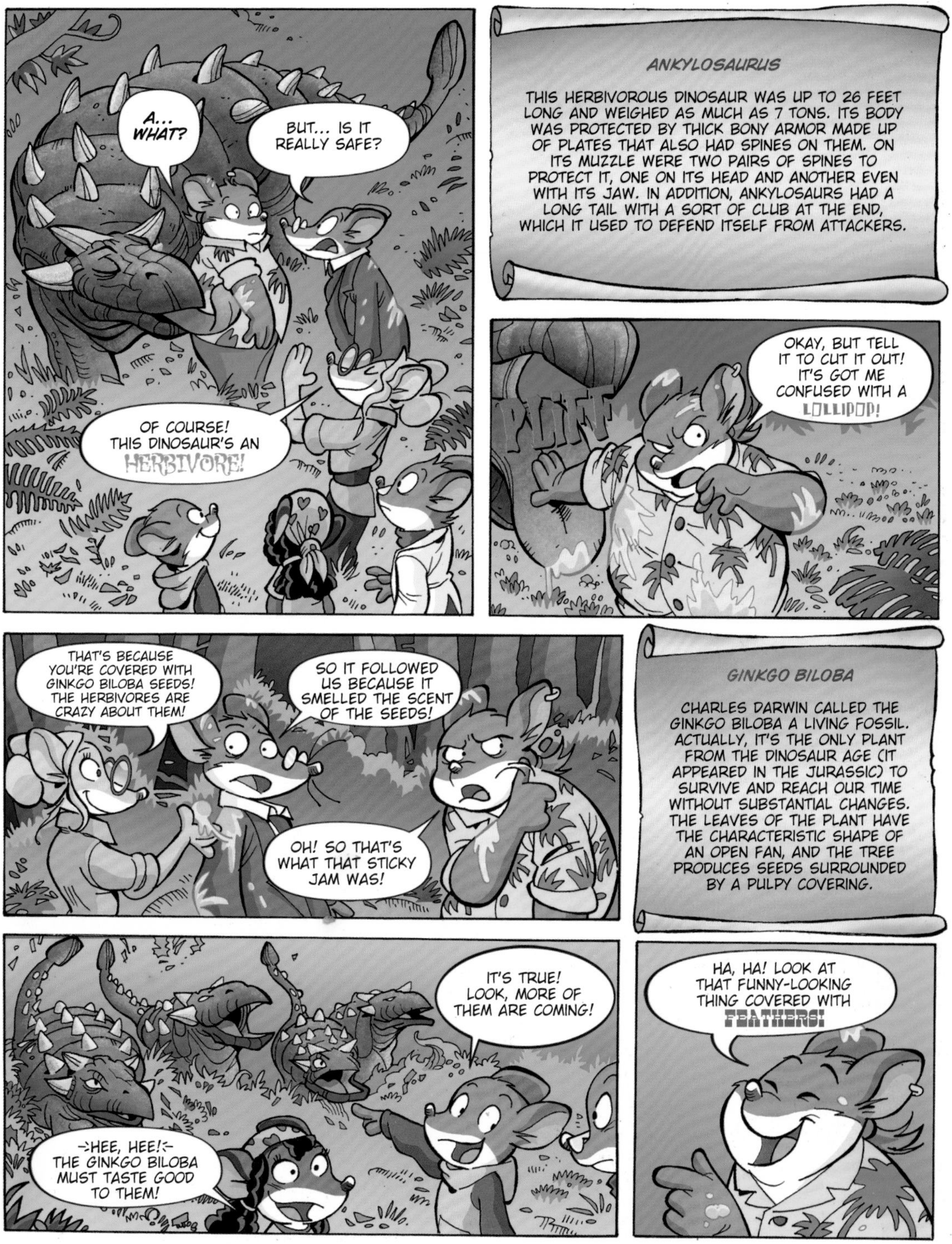
A... WHAT?
BUT... IS IT REALLY SAFE?
OF COURSE! THIS DINOSAUR'S AN HERBIVORE!
ANKYLOSAURUS
THIS HERBIVOROUS DINOSAUR WAS UP TO 26 FEET LONG AND WEIGHED AS MUCH AS 7 TONS. ITS BODY WAS PROTECTED BY THICK BONY ARMOR MADE UP OF PLATES THAT ALSO HAD SPINES ON THEM. ON ITS MUZZLE WERE TWO PAIRS OF SPINES TO PROTECT IT, ONE ON ITS HEAD AND ANOTHER EVEN WITH ITS JAW. IN ADDITION, ANKYLOSAURS HAD A LONG TAIL WITH A SORT OF CLUB AT THE END, WHICH IT USED TO DEFEND ITSELF FROM ATTACKERS.
OKAY, BUT TELL IT TO CUT IT OUT! IT'S GOT ME CONFUSED WITH A LOLLIPOP!
THAT'S BECAUSE YOU'RE COVERED WITH GINKGO BILOBA SEEDS! THE HERBIVORES ARE CRAZY ABOUT THEM!
SO IT FOLLOWED US BECAUSE IT SMELLED THE SCENT OF THE SEEDS!
OH! SO THAT'S WHAT THAT STICKY JAM WAS!
GINKGO BILOBA
CHARLES DARWIN CALLED THE GINKGO BILOBA A LIVING FOSSIL. ACTUALLY, IT'S THE ONLY PLANT FROM THE DINOSAUR AGE (IT APPEARED IN THE JURASSIC) TO SURVIVE AND REACH OUR TIME WITHOUT SUBSTANTIAL CHANGES. THE LEAVES OF THE PLANT HAVE THE CHARACTERISTIC SHAPE OF AN OPEN FAN, AND THE TREE PRODUCES SEEDS SURROUNDED BY A PULPY COVERING.
IT'S TRUE! LOOK, MORE OF THEM ARE COMING!
HEE, HEE! THE GINKGO BILOBA MUST TASTE GOOD TO THEM!
HA, HA! LOOK AT THAT FUNNY-LOOKING THING COVERED WITH FEATHERS!

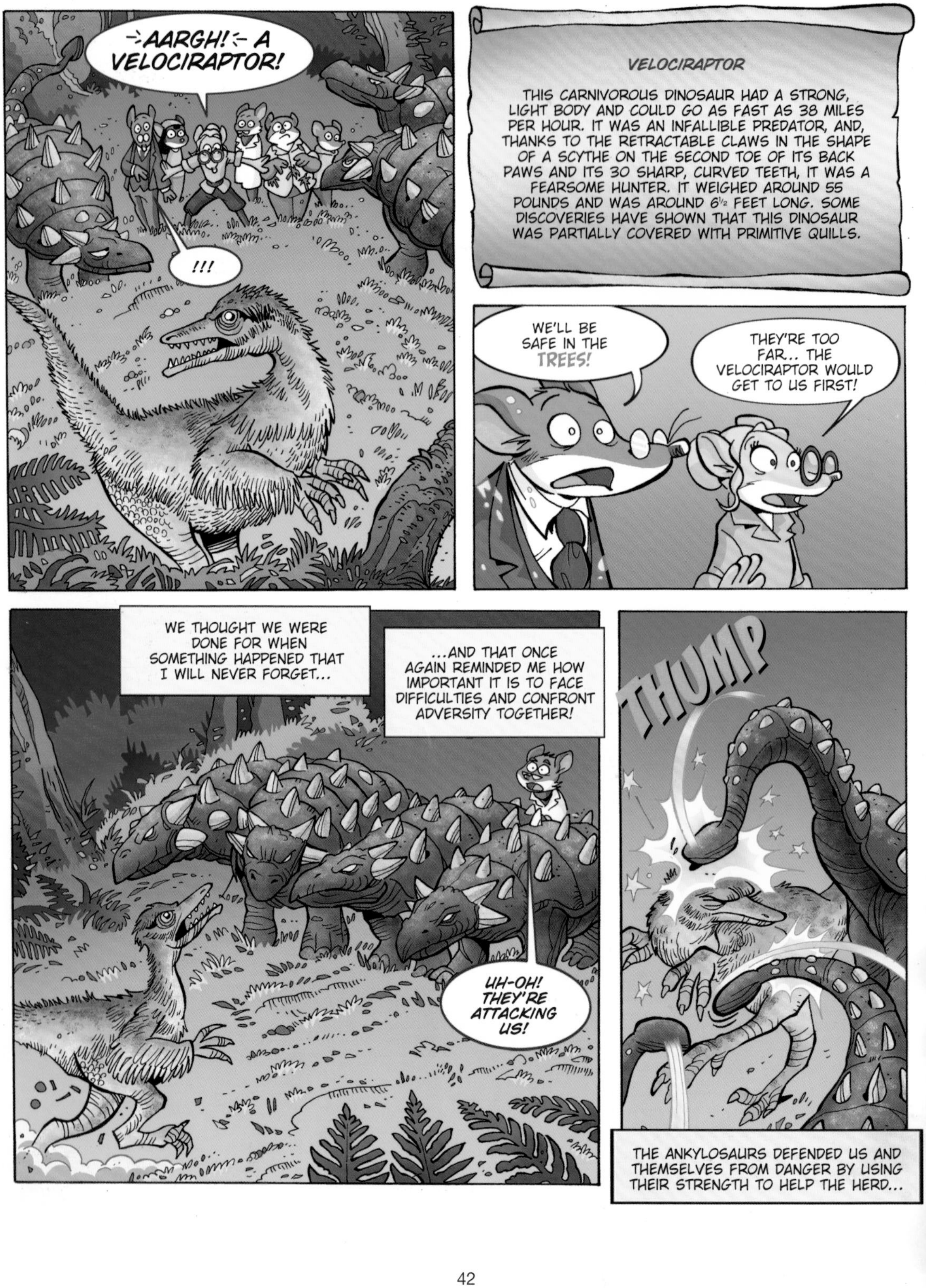

AARGH! A VELOCIRAPTOR!
!!!
VELOCIRAPTOR
THIS CARNIVOROUS DINOSAUR HAD A STRONG, LIGHT BODY AND COULD GO AS FAST AS 38 MILES PER HOUR. IT WAS AN INFALLIBLE PREDATOR, AND, THANKS TO THE RETRACTABLE CLAWS IN THE SHAPE OF A SCYTHE ON THE SECOND TOE OF ITS BACK PAWS AND ITS 30 SHARP, CURVED TEETH, IT WAS A FEARSOME HUNTER. IT WEIGHED AROUND 55 POUNDS AND WAS AROUND 6½ FEET LONG. SOME DISCOVERIES HAVE SHOWN THAT THIS DINOSAUR WAS PARTIALLY COVERED WITH PRIMITIVE QUILLS.
WE'LL BE SAFE IN THE TREES!
THEY'RE TOO FAR... THE VELOCIRAPTOR WOULD GET TO US FIRST!
WE THOUGHT WE WERE DONE FOR WHEN SOMETHING HAPPENED THAT I WILL NEVER FORGET...
...AND THAT ONCE AGAIN REMINDED ME HOW IMPORTANT IT IS TO FACE DIFFICULTIES AND CONFRONT ADVERSITY TOGETHER!
UH-OH! THEY'RE ATTACKING US!
THUMP
THE ANKYLOSAURS DEFENDED US AND THEMSELVES FROM DANGER BY USING THEIR STRENGTH TO HELP THE HERD...

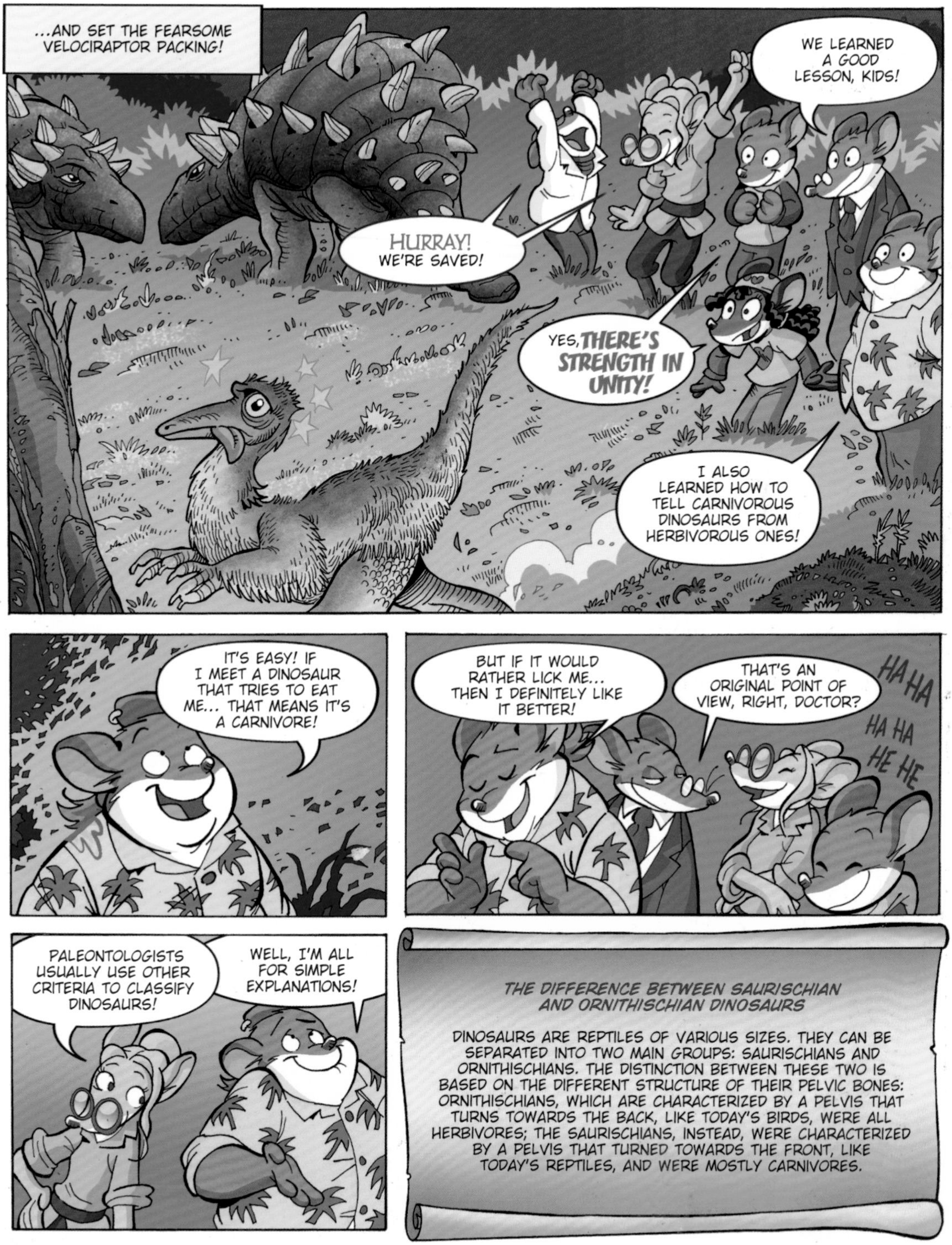
...AND SET THE FEARSOME VELOCIRAPTOR PACKING!
WE LEARNED A GOOD LESSON, KIDS!
HURRAY! WE'RE SAVED!
YES, THERE'S STRENGTH IN UNITY!
I ALSO LEARNED HOW TO TELL CARNIVOROUS DINOSAURS FROM HERBIVOROUS ONES!
IT'S EASY! IF I MEET A DINOSAUR THAT TRIES TO EAT ME... THAT MEANS IT'S A CARNIVORE!
BUT IF IT WOULD RATHER LICK ME... THEN I DEFINITELY LIKE IT BETTER!
THAT'S AN ORIGINAL POINT OF VIEW, RIGHT, DOCTOR?
HA HA
HA HA
HE HE
PALEONTOLOGISTS USUALLY USE OTHER CRITERIA TO CLASSIFY DINOSAURS!
WELL, I'M ALL FOR SIMPLE EXPLANATIONS!
THE DIFFERENCE BETWEEN SAURISCHIAN AND ORNITHISCHIAN DINOSAURS
DINOSAURS ARE REPTILES OF VARIOUS SIZES. THEY CAN BE SEPARATED INTO TWO MAIN GROUPS: SAURISCHIANS AND ORNITHISCHIANS. THE DISTINCTION BETWEEN THESE TWO IS BASED ON THE DIFFERENT STRUCTURE OF THEIR PELVIC BONES: ORNITHISCHIANS, WHICH ARE CHARACTERIZED BY A PELVIS THAT TURNS TOWARDS THE BACK, LIKE TODAY'S BIRDS, WERE ALL HERBIVORES; THE SAURISCHIANS, INSTEAD, WERE CHARACTERIZED BY A PELVIS THAT TURNED TOWARDS THE FRONT, LIKE TODAY'S REPTILES, AND WERE MOSTLY CARNIVORES.

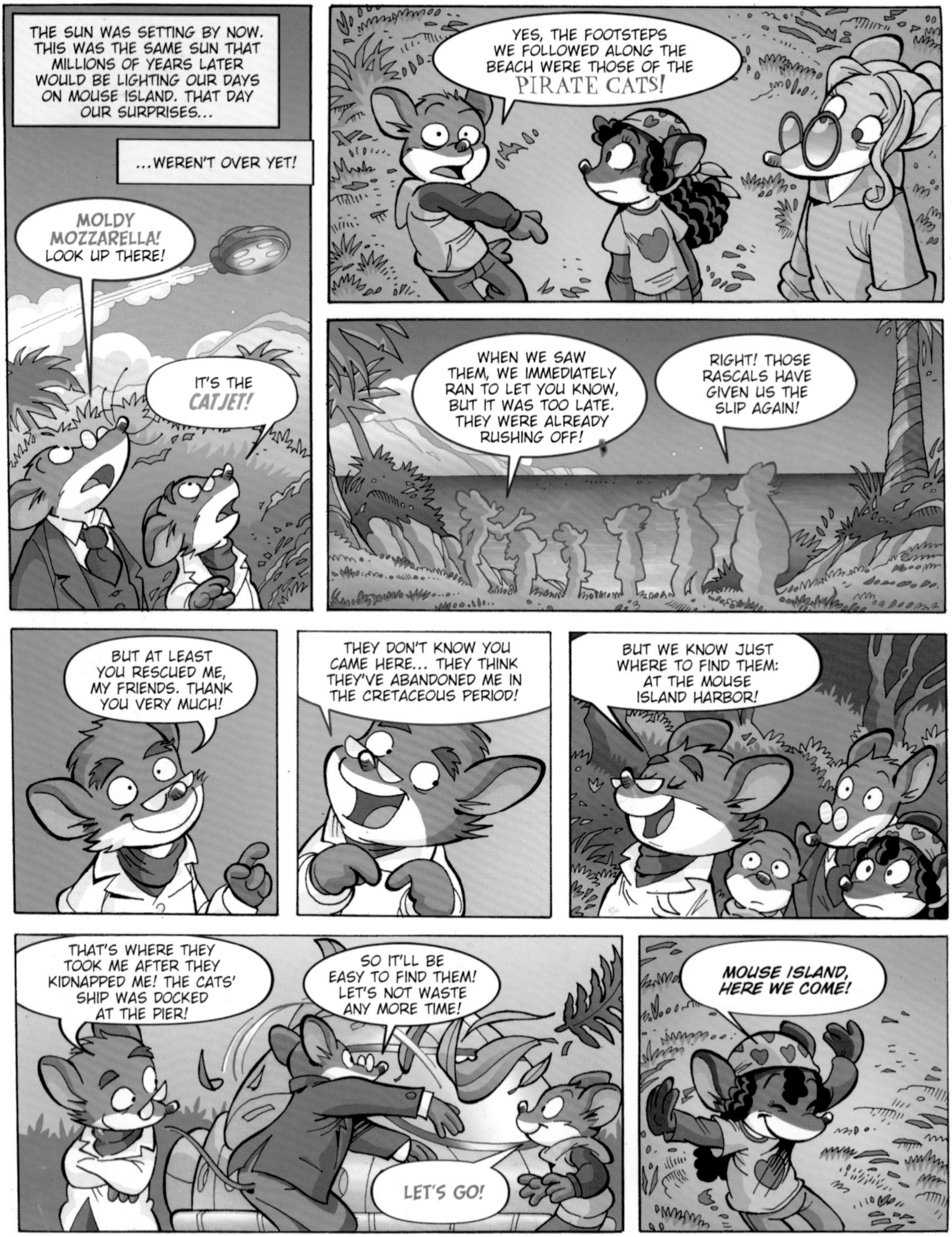
THE SUN WAS SETTING BY NOW. THIS WAS THE SAME SUN THAT MILLIONS OF YEARS LATER WOULD BE LIGHTING OUR DAYS ON MOUSE ISLAND. THAT DAY OUR SURPRISES...
...WEREN'T OVER YET!
MOLDY MOZZARELLA! LOOK UP THERE!
IT'S THE CATJET!
YES, THE FOOTSTEPS WE FOLLOWED ALONG THE BEACH WERE THOSE OF THE PIRATE CATS!
WHEN WE SAW THEM, WE IMMEDIATELY RAN TO LET YOU KNOW, BUT IT WAS TOO LATE. THEY WERE ALREADY RUSHING OFF!
RIGHT! THOSE RASCALS HAVE GIVEN US THE SLIP AGAIN!
BUT AT LEAST YOU RESCUED ME, MY FRIENDS. THANK YOU VERY MUCH!
THEY DON'T KNOW YOU CAME HERE... THEY THINK THEY'VE ABANDONED ME IN THE CRETACEOUS PERIOD!
BUT WE KNOW JUST WHERE TO FIND THEM: AT THE MOUSE ISLAND HARBOR!
THAT'S WHERE THEY TOOK ME AFTER THEY KIDNAPPED ME! THE CATS' SHIP WAS DOCKED AT THE PIER!
SO IT'LL BE EASY TO FIND THEM! LET'S NOT WASTE ANY MORE TIME!
LET'S GO!
MOUSE ISLAND, HERE WE COME!

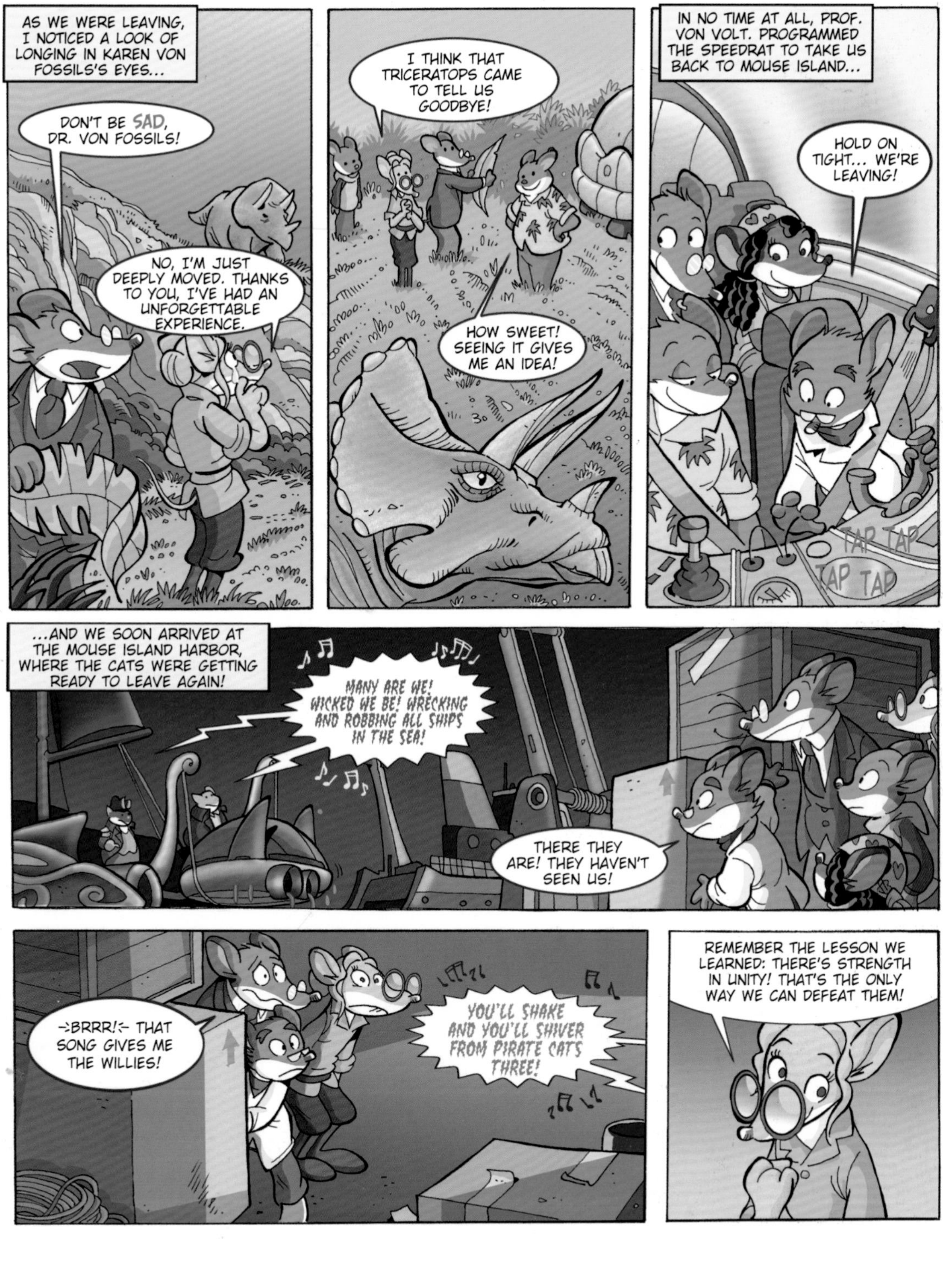

AS WE WERE LEAVING, I NOTICED A LOOK OF LONGING IN KAREN VON FOSSILS'S EYES...
DON'T BE SAD, DR. VON FOSSILS!
NO, I'M JUST DEEPLY MOVED. THANKS TO YOU, I'VE HAD AN UNFORGETTABLE EXPERIENCE.
I THINK THAT TRICERATOPS CAME TO TELL US GOODBYE!
HOW SWEET! SEEING IT GIVES ME AN IDEA!
IN NO TIME AT ALL, PROF. VON VOLT. PROGRAMMED THE SPEEDRAT TO TAKE US BACK TO MOUSE ISLAND...
HOLD ON TIGHT... WE'RE LEAVING!
TAP TAP
TAP TAP
...AND WE SOON ARRIVED AT THE MOUSE ISLAND HARBOR, WHERE THE CATS WERE GETTING READY TO LEAVE AGAIN!
MANY ARE WE! WICKED WE BE! WRECKING AND ROBBING ALL SHIPS IN THE SEA!
THERE THEY ARE! THEY HAVEN'T SEEN US!
BRRR! THAT SONG GIVES ME THE WILLIES!
YOU'LL SHAKE AND YOU'LL SHIVER FROM PIRATE CATS THREE!
REMEMBER THE LESSON WE LEARNED: THERE'S STRENGTH IN UNITY! THAT'S THE ONLY WAY WE CAN DEFEAT THEM!

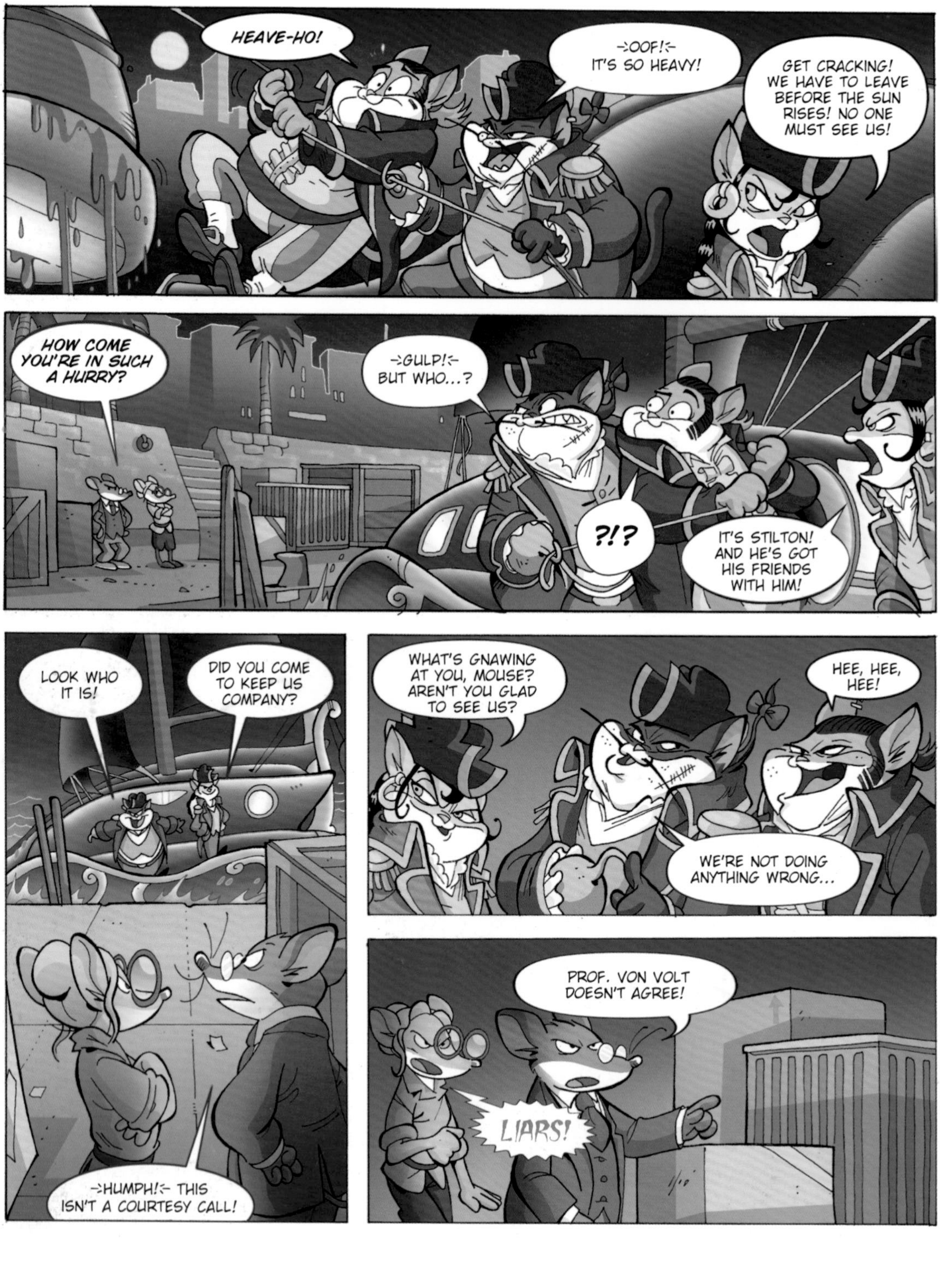
HEAVE-HO!
-OOF!- IT'S SO HEAVY!
GET CRACKING! WE HAVE TO LEAVE BEFORE THE SUN RISES! NO ONE MUST SEE US!
HOW COME YOU'RE IN SUCH A HURRY?
-GULP!- BUT WHO...?
?!?
IT'S STILTON! AND HE'S GOT HIS FRIENDS WITH HIM!
LOOK WHO IT IS!
DID YOU COME TO KEEP US COMPANY?
-HUMPH!- THIS ISN'T A COURTESY CALL!
WHAT'S GNAWING AT YOU, MOUSE? AREN'T YOU GLAD TO SEE US?
HEE, HEE, HEE!
WE'RE NOT DOING ANYTHING WRONG...
PROF. VON VOLT DOESN'T AGREE!
LIARS!

:-TSK!:- YOUR NOSY PARKER FRIEND! WE'VE GOT HIM OUT OF THE WAY NOW! HE'S SOMEWHERE WHERE HE'LL HAVE LOTS OF FUN!

AND NOW YOU'LL MEET THE SAME END!

RIGHT! DON'T LET US INTIMIDATE YOU TWO RODENTS!

YOU COUNTED WRONG... IT'S NOT JUST THESE TWO!

BUT... HOW IS THIS POSSIBLE?!?

:-GULP!:-

PROFESSOR VON VOLT!

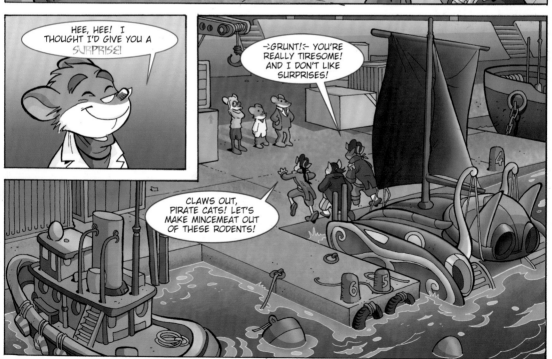

HEE, HEE! I THOUGHT I'D GIVE YOU A SURPRISE!

:-GRUNT!:- YOU'RE REALLY TIRESOME! AND I DON'T LIKE SURPRISES!

CLAWS OUT, PIRATE CATS! LET'S MAKE MINCEMEAT OUT OF THESE RODENTS!

47

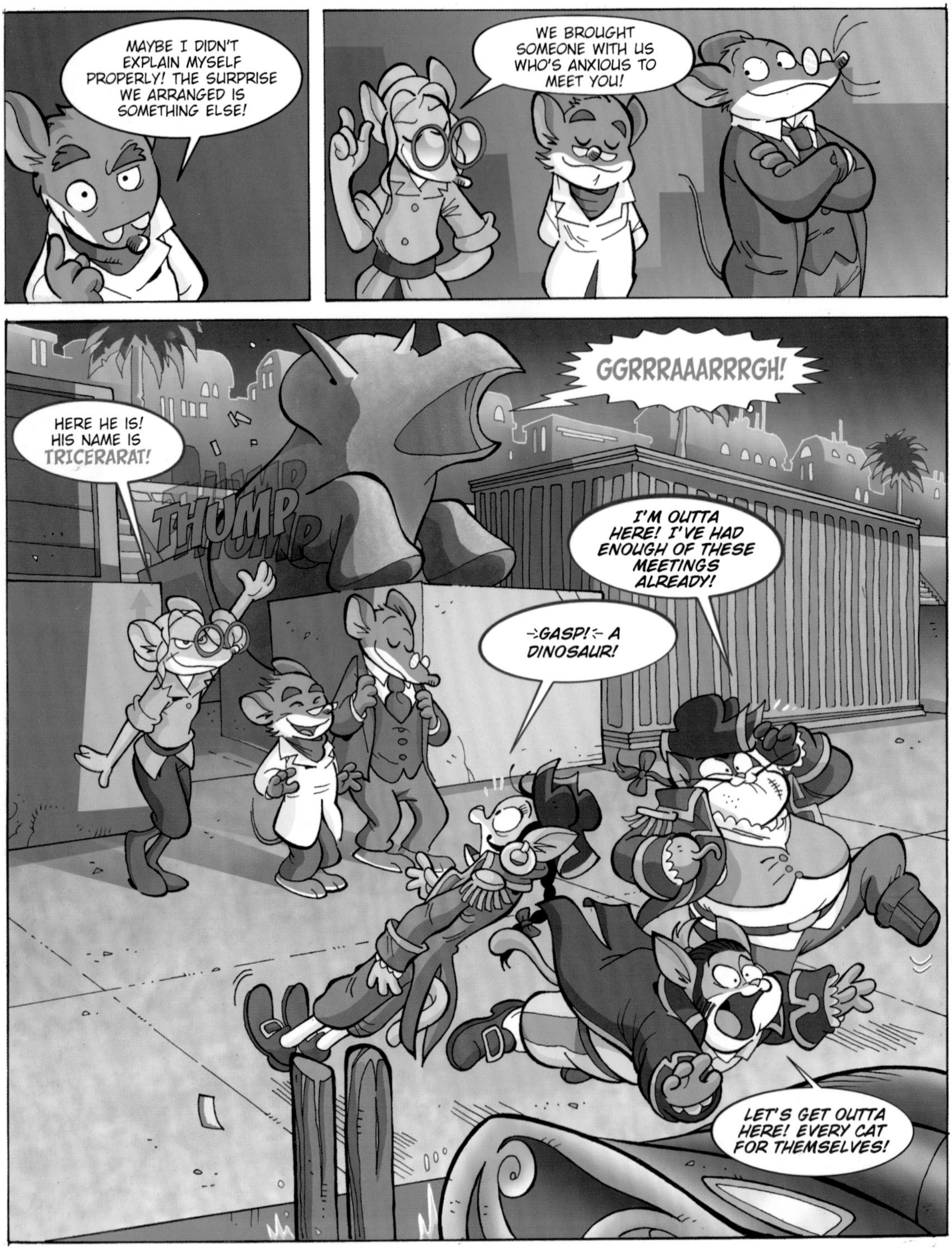
MAYBE I DIDN'T EXPLAIN MYSELF PROPERLY! THE SURPRISE WE ARRANGED IS SOMETHING ELSE!
WE BROUGHT SOMEONE WITH US WHO'S ANXIOUS TO MEET YOU!
GGRRRAAARRRGH!
HERE HE IS! HIS NAME IS TRICERARAT!
THUMP
THUMP
I'M OUTTA HERE! I'VE HAD ENOUGH OF THESE MEETINGS ALREADY!
-GASP!- A DINOSAUR!
LET'S GET OUTTA HERE! EVERY CAT FOR THEMSELVES!

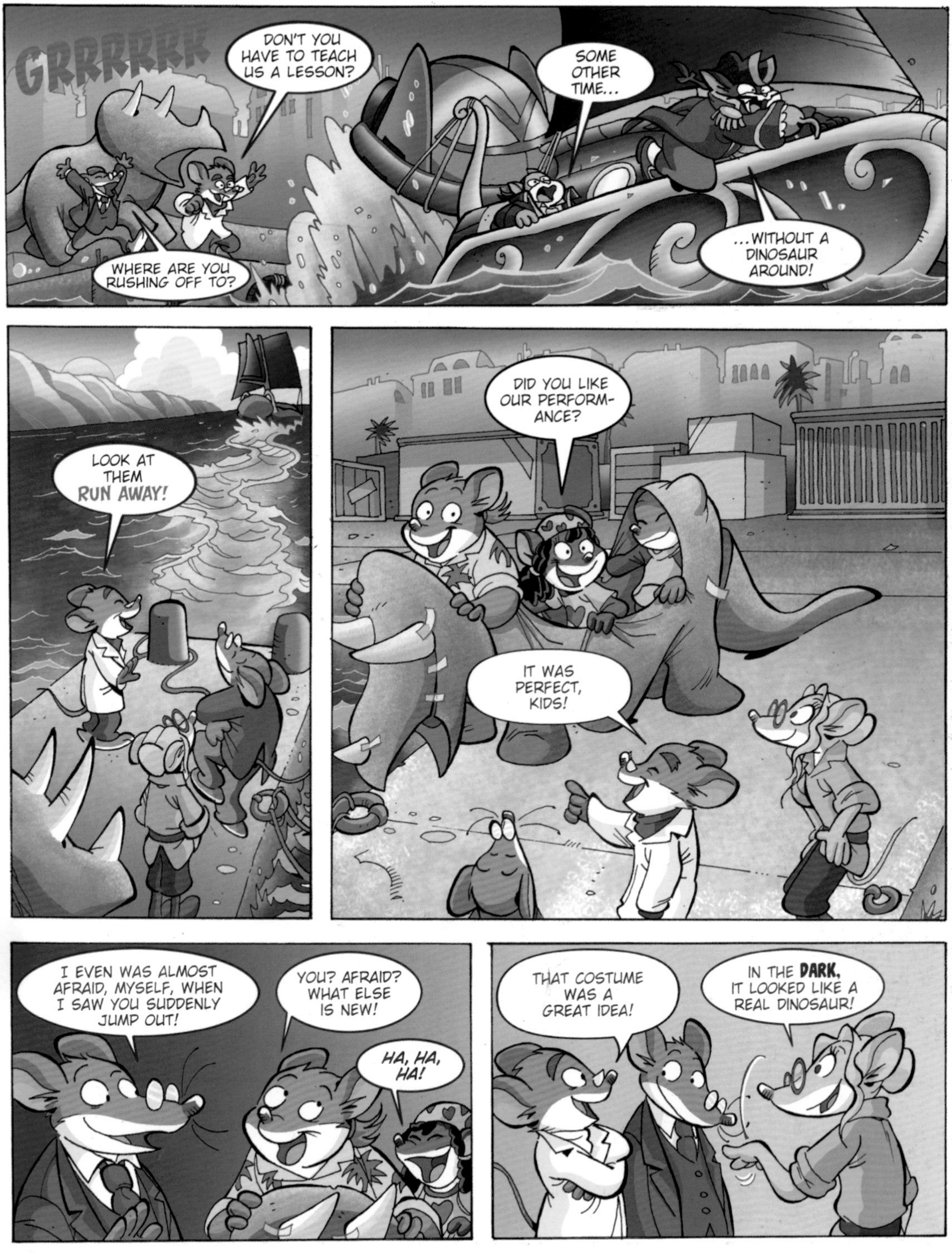
GRRRRRK
DON'T YOU HAVE TO TEACH US A LESSON?
WHERE ARE YOU RUSHING OFF TO?
SOME OTHER TIME...
...WITHOUT A DINOSAUR AROUND!
LOOK AT THEM RUN AWAY!
DID YOU LIKE OUR PERFORM-ANCE?
IT WAS PERFECT, KIDS!
I EVEN WAS ALMOST AFRAID, MYSELF, WHEN I SAW YOU SUDDENLY JUMP OUT!
YOU? AFRAID? WHAT ELSE IS NEW!
HA, HA, HA!
THAT COSTUME WAS A GREAT IDEA!
IN THE DARK, IT LOOKED LIKE A REAL DINOSAUR!

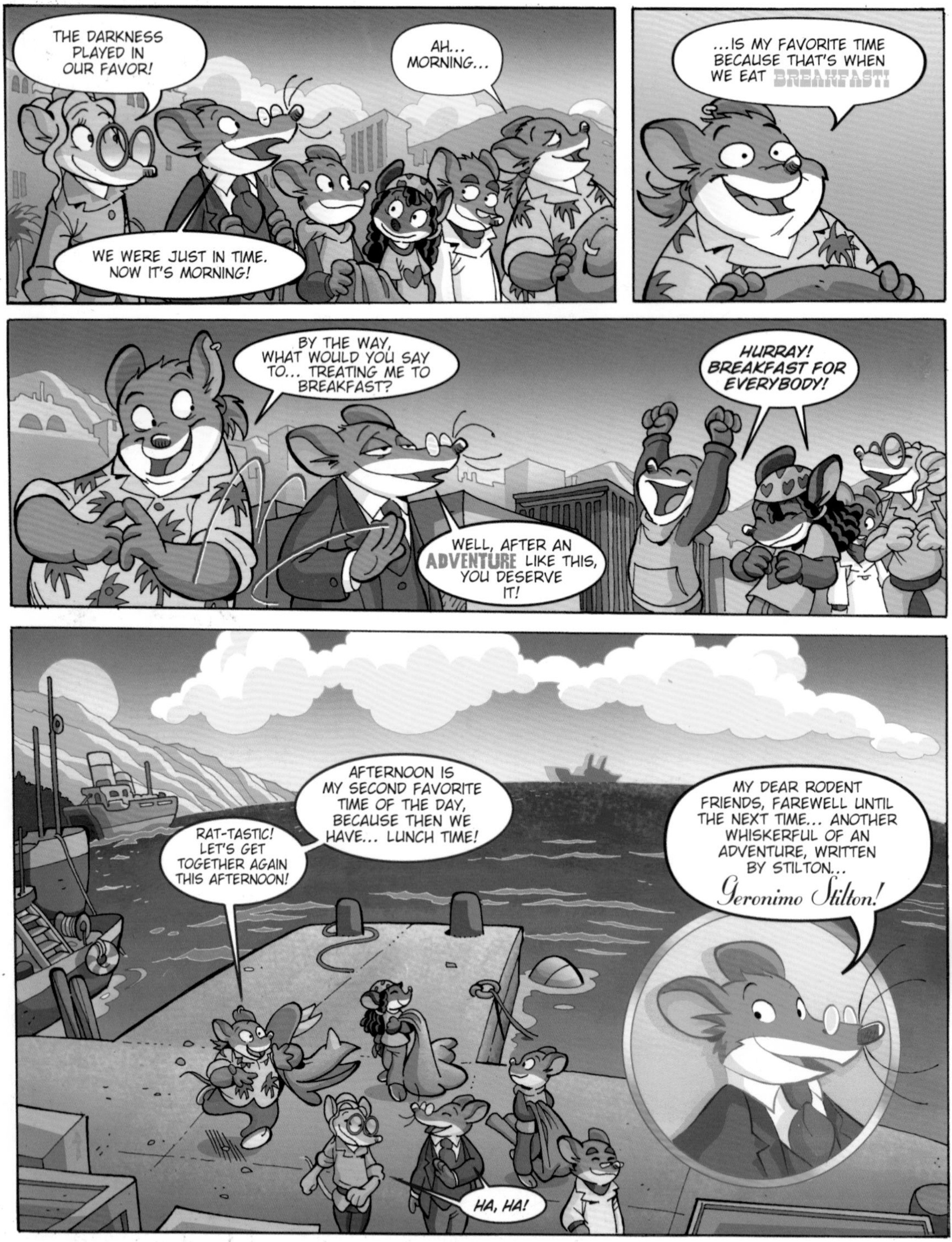
THE DARKNESS PLAYED IN OUR FAVOR!
AH... MORNING...
WE WERE JUST IN TIME. NOW IT'S MORNING!
...IS MY FAVORITE TIME BECAUSE THAT'S WHEN WE EAT BREAKFAST!
BY THE WAY, WHAT WOULD YOU SAY TO... TREATING ME TO BREAKFAST?
WELL, AFTER AN ADVENTURE LIKE THIS, YOU DESERVE IT!
HURRAY! BREAKFAST FOR EVERYBODY!
AFTERNOON IS MY SECOND FAVORITE TIME OF THE DAY, BECAUSE THEN WE HAVE... LUNCH TIME!
RAT-TASTIC! LET'S GET TOGETHER AGAIN THIS AFTERNOON!
MY DEAR RODENT FRIENDS, FAREWELL UNTIL THE NEXT TIME... ANOTHER WHISKERFUL OF AN ADVENTURE, WRITTEN BY STILTON... Geronimo Stilton!
HA, HA!

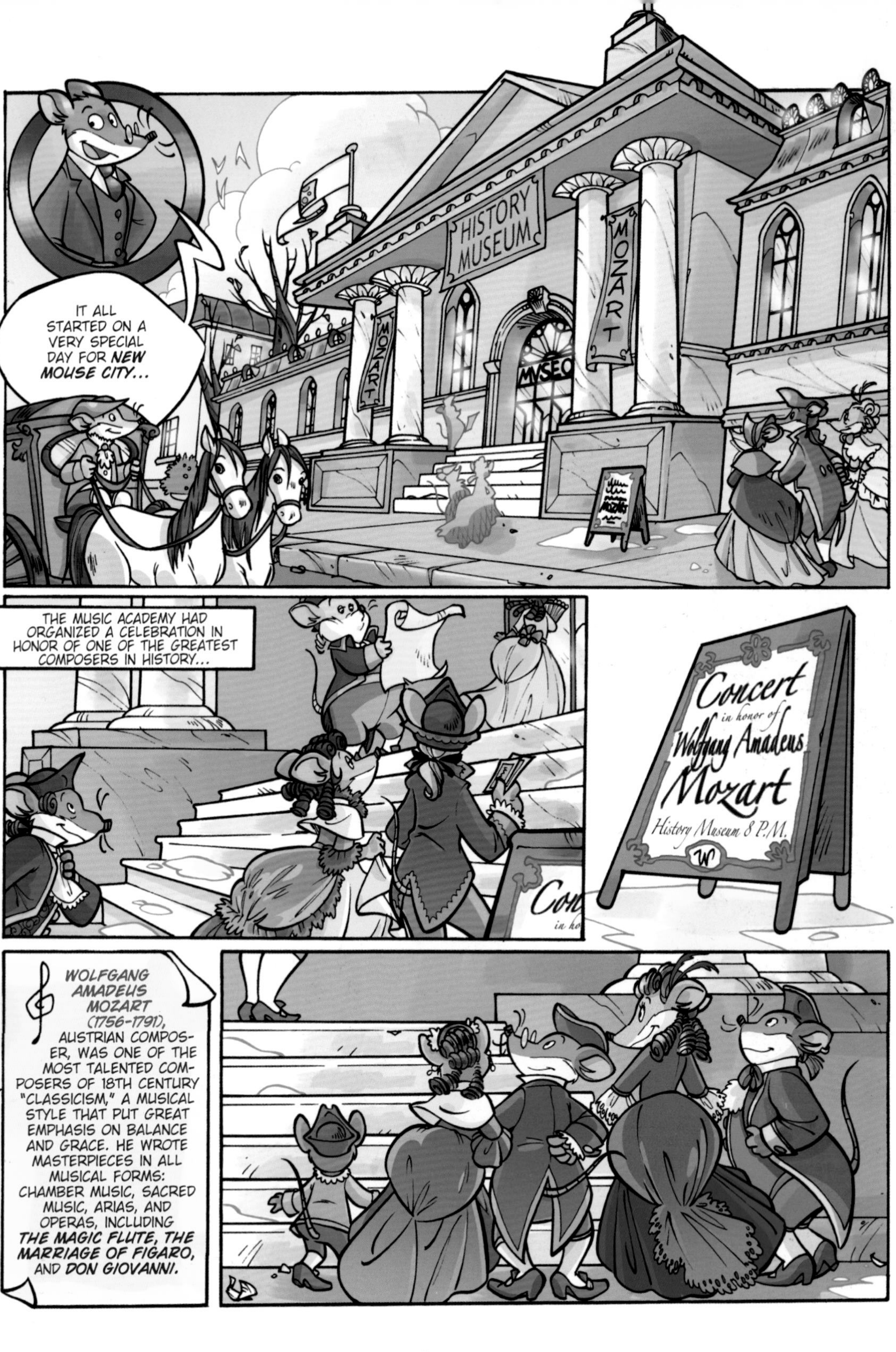

IT ALL STARTED ON A VERY SPECIAL DAY FOR **NEW MOUSE CITY**...
HISTORY MUSEUM
MOZART
MUSEO
THE MUSIC ACADEMY HAD ORGANIZED A CELEBRATION IN HONOR OF ONE OF THE GREATEST COMPOSERS IN HISTORY...
Concert in honor of Wolfgang Amadeus Mozart History Museum 8 P.M.
WOLFGANG AMADEUS MOZART (1756-1791), AUSTRIAN COMPOSER, WAS ONE OF THE MOST TALENTED COMPOSERS OF 18TH CENTURY "CLASSICISM," A MUSICAL STYLE THAT PUT GREAT EMPHASIS ON BALANCE AND GRACE. HE WROTE MASTERPIECES IN ALL MUSICAL FORMS: CHAMBER MUSIC, SACRED MUSIC, ARIAS, AND OPERAS, INCLUDING ***THE MAGIC FLUTE, THE MARRIAGE OF FIGARO,*** AND ***DON GIOVANNI.***

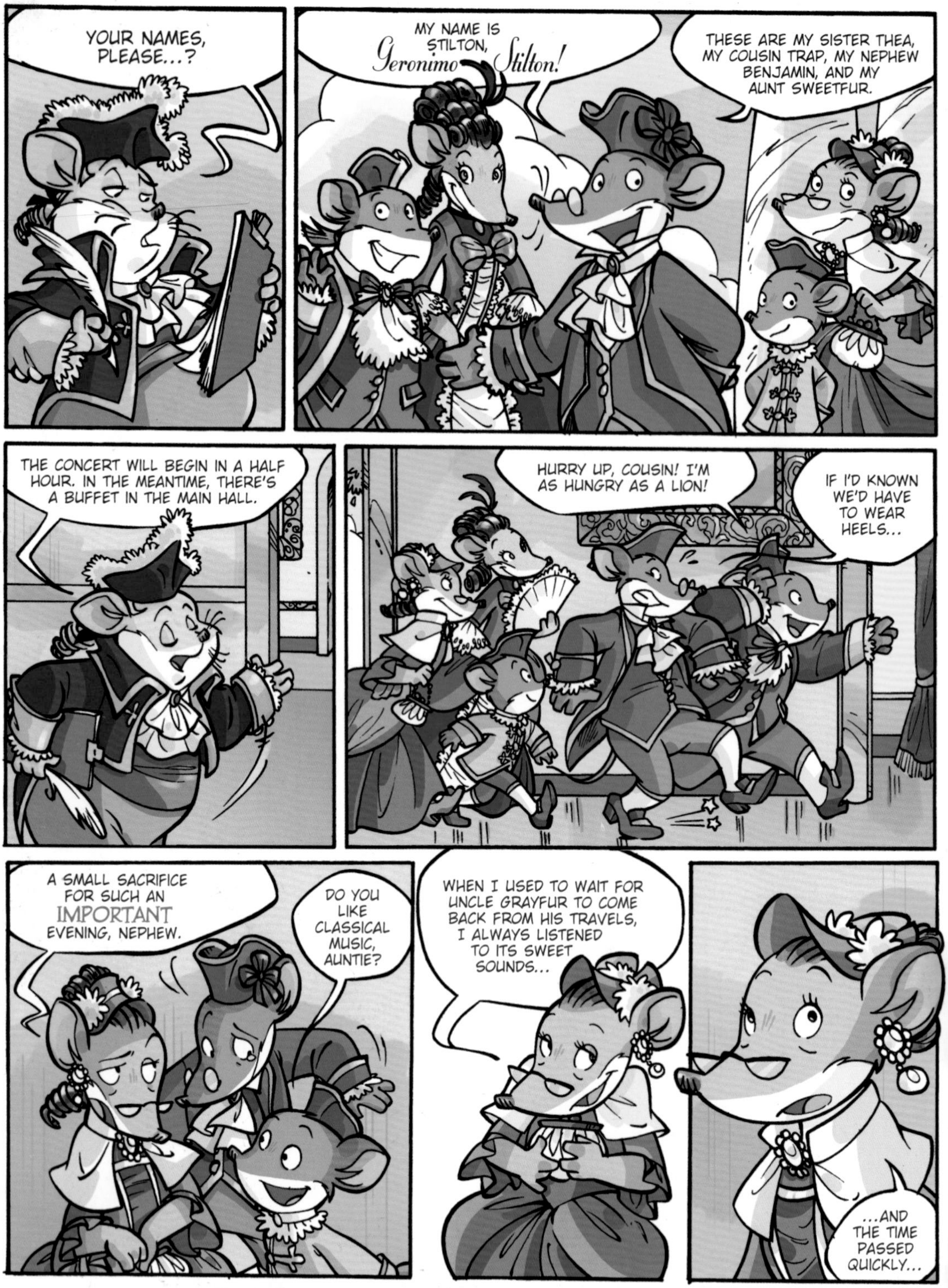

YOUR NAMES, PLEASE...?
MY NAME IS STILTON, Geronimo Stilton!
THESE ARE MY SISTER THEA, MY COUSIN TRAP, MY NEPHEW BENJAMIN, AND MY AUNT SWEETFUR.
THE CONCERT WILL BEGIN IN A HALF HOUR. IN THE MEANTIME, THERE'S A BUFFET IN THE MAIN HALL.
HURRY UP, COUSIN! I'M AS HUNGRY AS A LION!
IF I'D KNOWN WE'D HAVE TO WEAR HEELS...
A SMALL SACRIFICE FOR SUCH AN IMPORTANT EVENING, NEPHEW.
DO YOU LIKE CLASSICAL MUSIC, AUNTIE?
WHEN I USED TO WAIT FOR UNCLE GRAYFUR TO COME BACK FROM HIS TRAVELS, I ALWAYS LISTENED TO ITS SWEET SOUNDS...
...AND THE TIME PASSED QUICKLY...

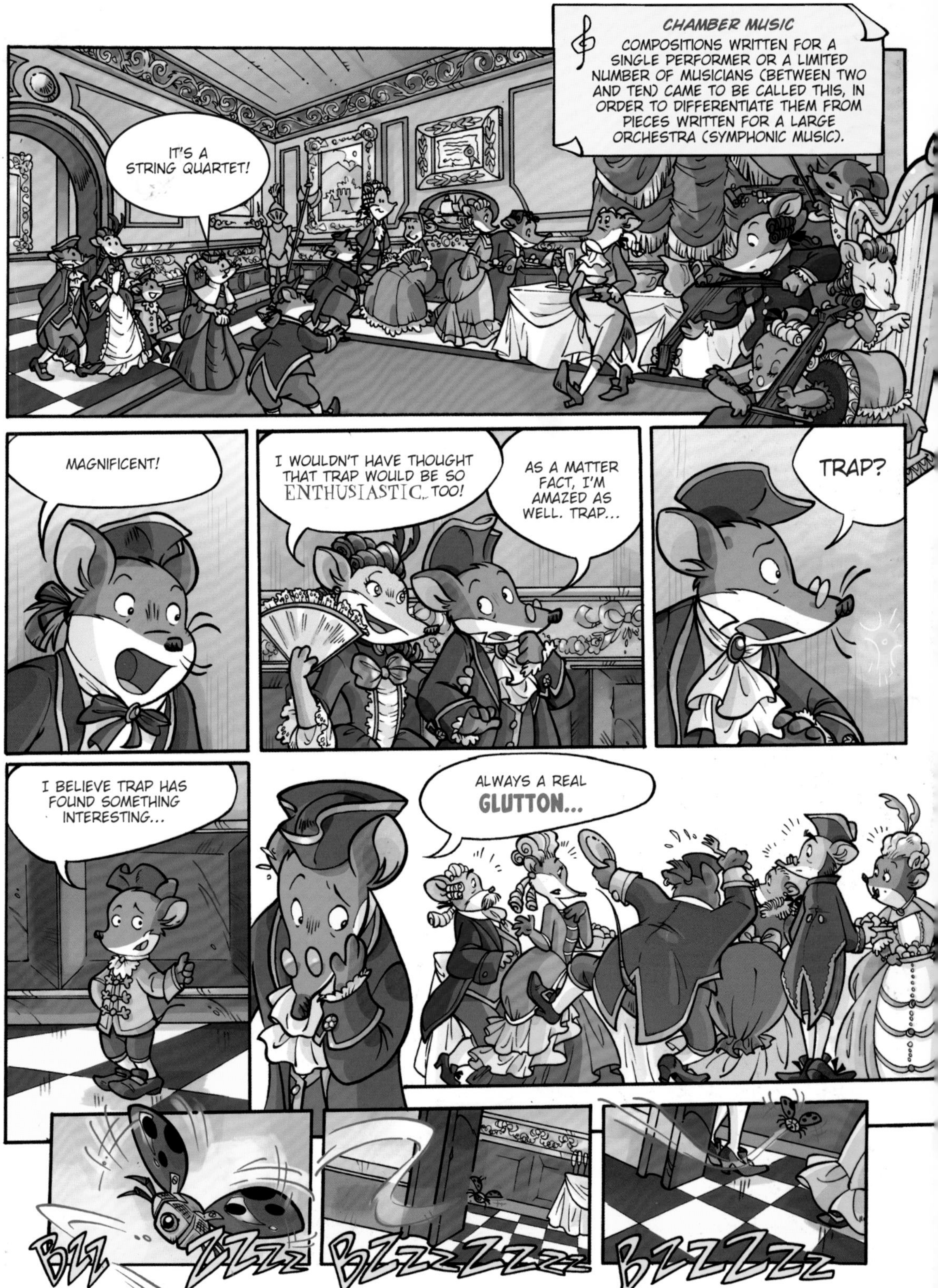
CHAMBER MUSIC
COMPOSITIONS WRITTEN FOR A SINGLE PERFORMER OR A LIMITED NUMBER OF MUSICIANS (BETWEEN TWO AND TEN) CAME TO BE CALLED THIS, IN ORDER TO DIFFERENTIATE THEM FROM PIECES WRITTEN FOR A LARGE ORCHESTRA (SYMPHONIC MUSIC).
IT'S A STRING QUARTET!
MAGNIFICENT!
I WOULDN'T HAVE THOUGHT THAT TRAP WOULD BE SO ENTHUSIASTIC... TOO!
AS A MATTER FACT, I'M AMAZED AS WELL. TRAP...
TRAP?
I BELIEVE TRAP HAS FOUND SOMETHING INTERESTING...
ALWAYS A REAL GLUTTON...
BZZ
ZZZzz
BZZzzzZZzzz
BZZZZZZzz

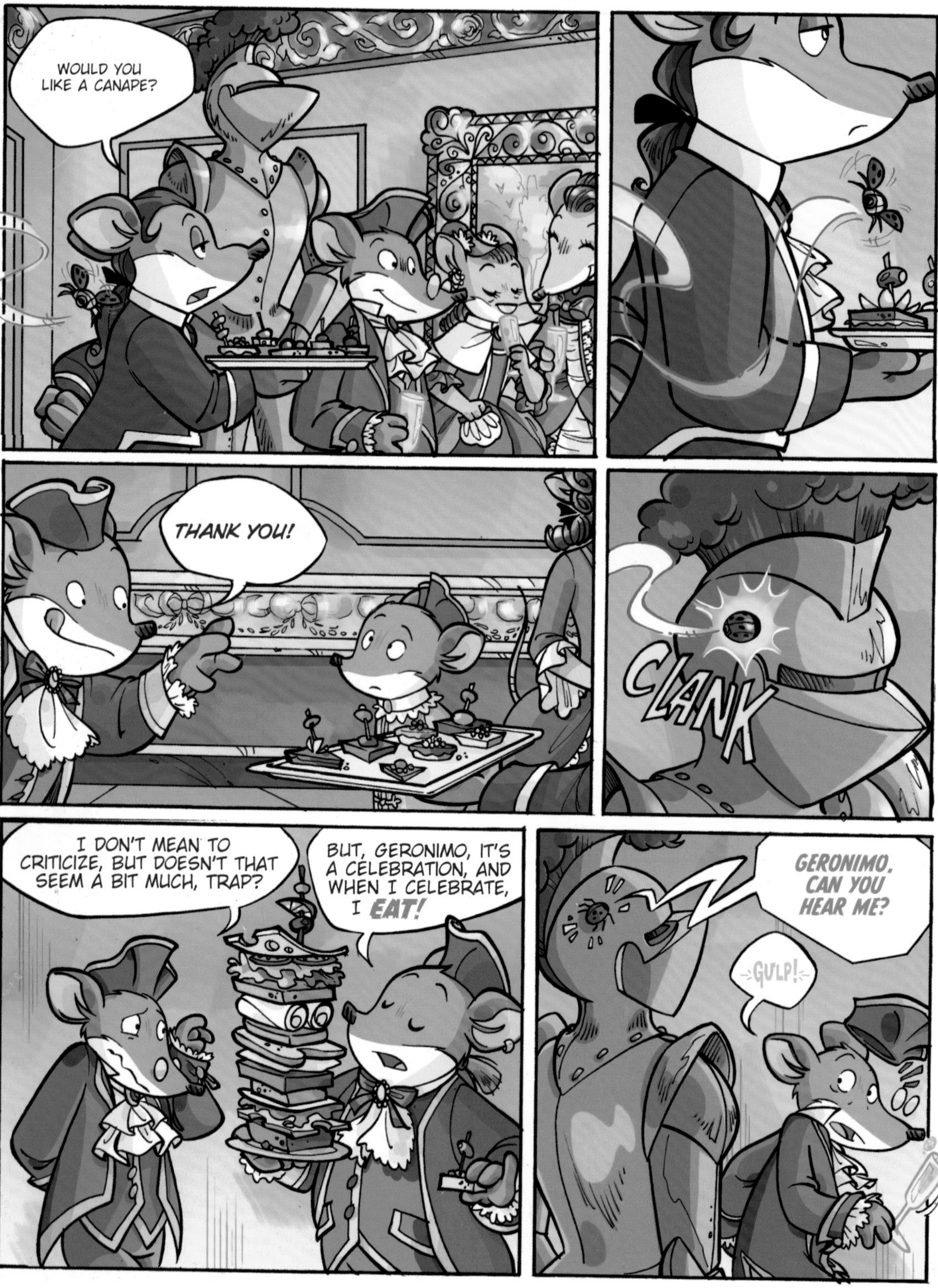
WOULD YOU LIKE A CANAPE?
THANK YOU!
CLANK
I DON'T MEAN TO CRITICIZE, BUT DOESN'T THAT SEEM A BIT MUCH, TRAP?
BUT, GERONIMO, IT'S A CELEBRATION, AND WHEN I CELEBRATE, I EAT!
GERONIMO. CAN YOU HEAR ME?
GULP!

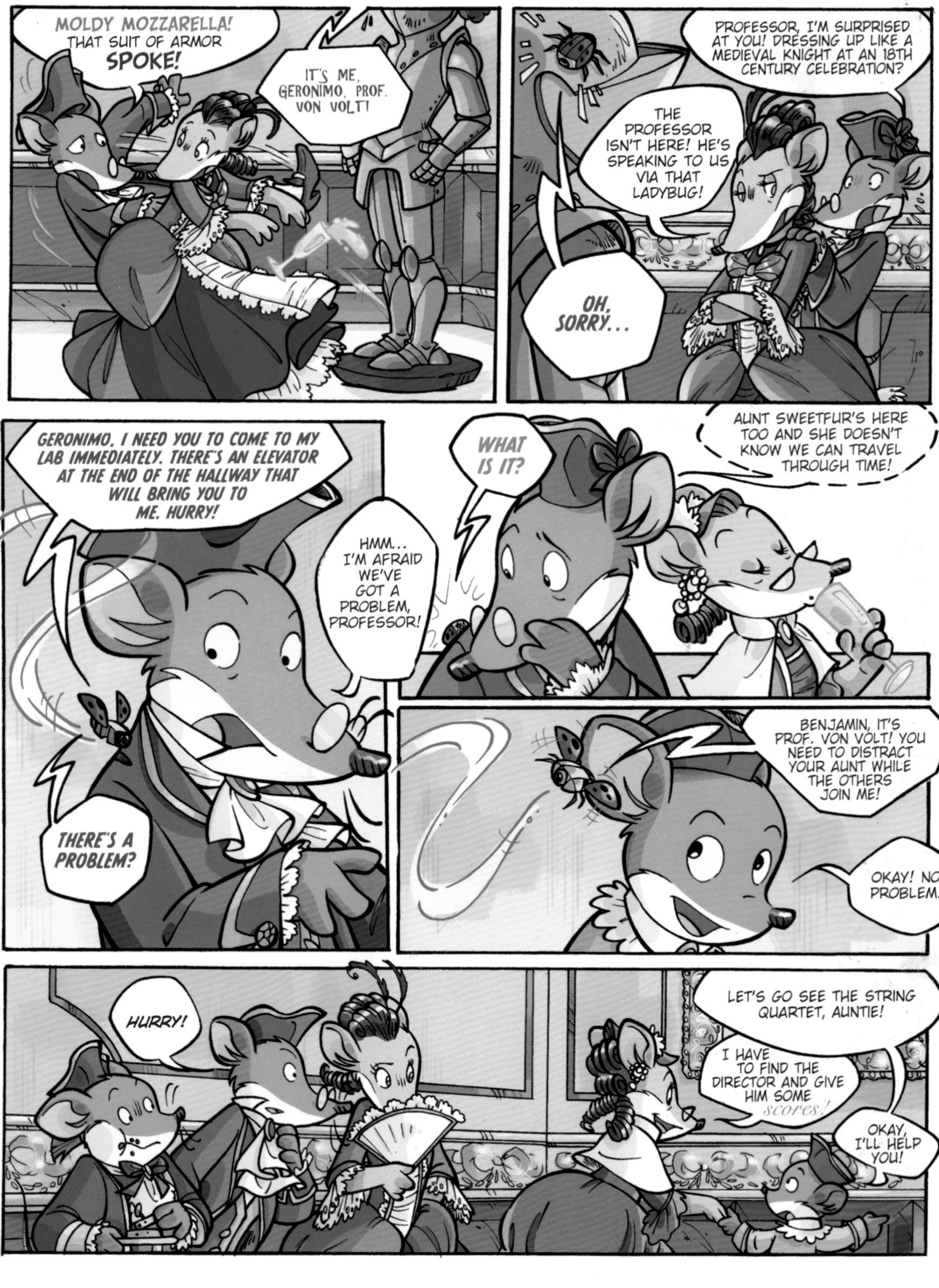
MOLDY MOZZARELLA! THAT SUIT OF ARMOR SPOKE!
IT'S ME, GERONIMO, PROF. VON VOLT!
PROFESSOR, I'M SURPRISED AT YOU! DRESSING UP LIKE A MEDIEVAL KNIGHT AT AN 18TH CENTURY CELEBRATION?
THE PROFESSOR ISN'T HERE! HE'S SPEAKING TO US VIA THAT LADYBUG!
OH, SORRY...
GERONIMO, I NEED YOU TO COME TO MY LAB IMMEDIATELY. THERE'S AN ELEVATOR AT THE END OF THE HALLWAY THAT WILL BRING YOU TO ME. HURRY!
THERE'S A PROBLEM?
HMM... I'M AFRAID WE'VE GOT A PROBLEM, PROFESSOR!
WHAT IS IT?
AUNT SWEETFUR'S HERE TOO AND SHE DOESN'T KNOW WE CAN TRAVEL THROUGH TIME!
BENJAMIN, IT'S PROF. VON VOLT! YOU NEED TO DISTRACT YOUR AUNT WHILE THE OTHERS JOIN ME!
OKAY! NO PROBLEM.
HURRY!
LET'S GO SEE THE STRING QUARTET, AUNTIE!
I HAVE TO FIND THE DIRECTOR AND GIVE HIM SOME scores!
OKAY, I'LL HELP YOU!

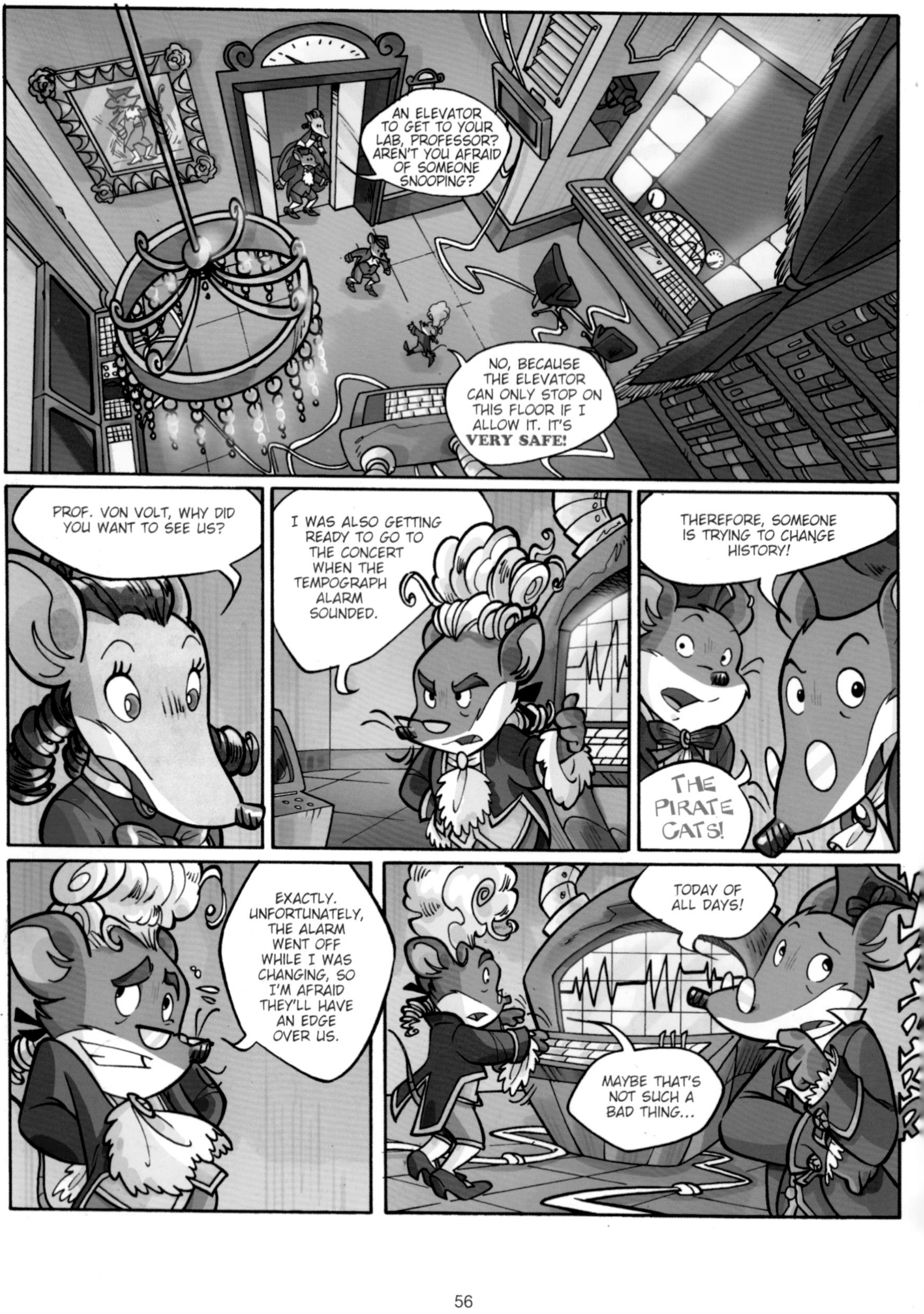

AN ELEVATOR TO GET TO YOUR LAB, PROFESSOR? AREN'T YOU AFRAID OF SOMEONE SNOOPING?
NO, BECAUSE THE ELEVATOR CAN ONLY STOP ON THIS FLOOR IF I ALLOW IT. IT'S VERY SAFE!
PROF. VON VOLT, WHY DID YOU WANT TO SEE US?
I WAS ALSO GETTING READY TO GO TO THE CONCERT WHEN THE TEMPOGRAPH ALARM SOUNDED.
THEREFORE, SOMEONE IS TRYING TO CHANGE HISTORY!
THE PIRATE CATS!
EXACTLY. UNFORTUNATELY, THE ALARM WENT OFF WHILE I WAS CHANGING, SO I'M AFRAID THEY'LL HAVE AN EDGE OVER US.
TODAY OF ALL DAYS!
MAYBE THAT'S NOT SUCH A BAD THING...

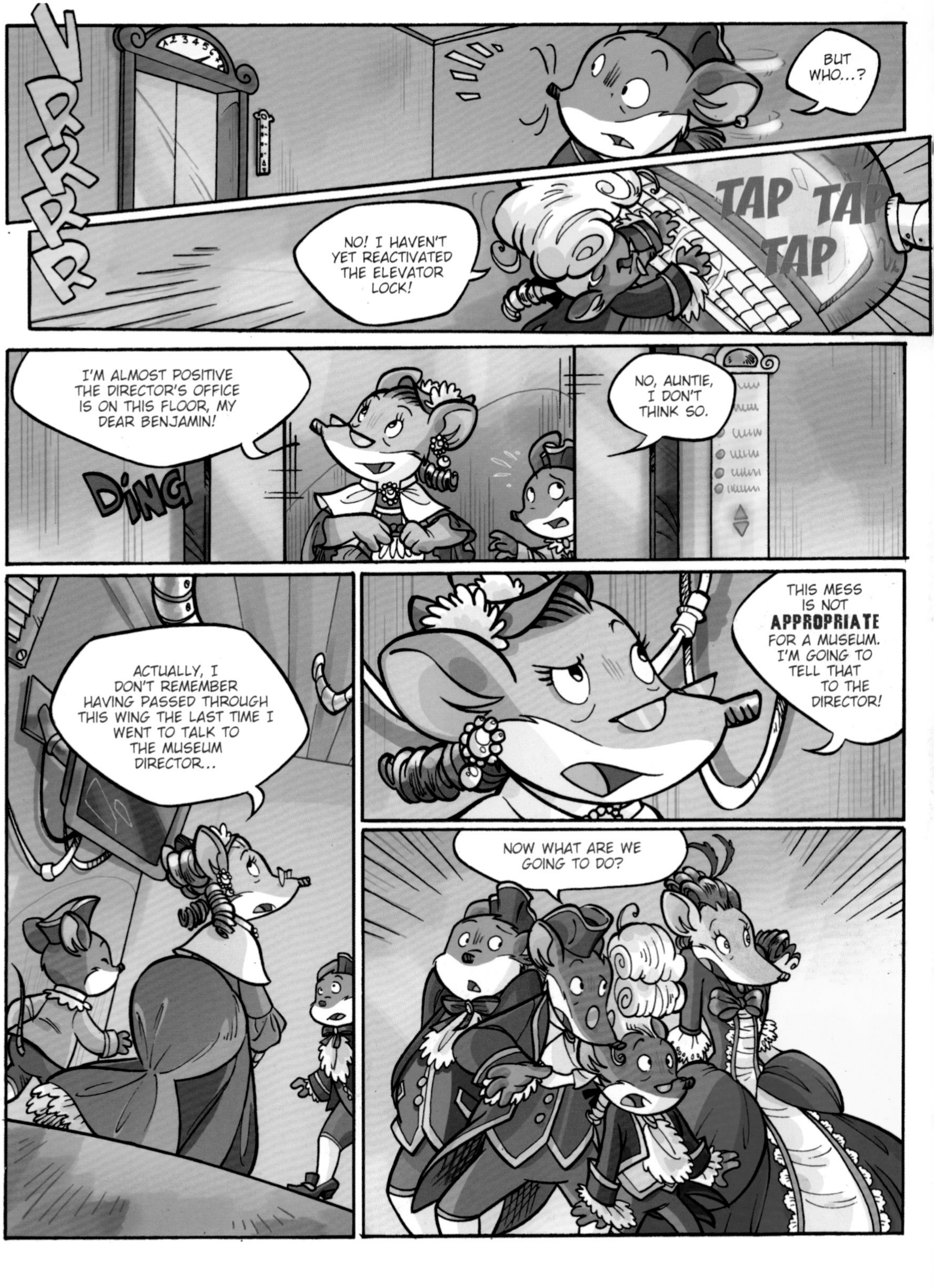
VRRRR
BUT WHO...?
TAP TAP TAP
NO! I HAVEN'T YET REACTIVATED THE ELEVATOR LOCK!
I'M ALMOST POSITIVE THE DIRECTOR'S OFFICE IS ON THIS FLOOR, MY DEAR BENJAMIN!
DING
NO, AUNTIE, I DON'T THINK SO.
ACTUALLY, I DON'T REMEMBER HAVING PASSED THROUGH THIS WING THE LAST TIME I WENT TO TALK TO THE MUSEUM DIRECTOR...
THIS MESS IS NOT APPROPRIATE FOR A MUSEUM. I'M GOING TO TELL THAT TO THE DIRECTOR!
NOW WHAT ARE WE GOING TO DO?

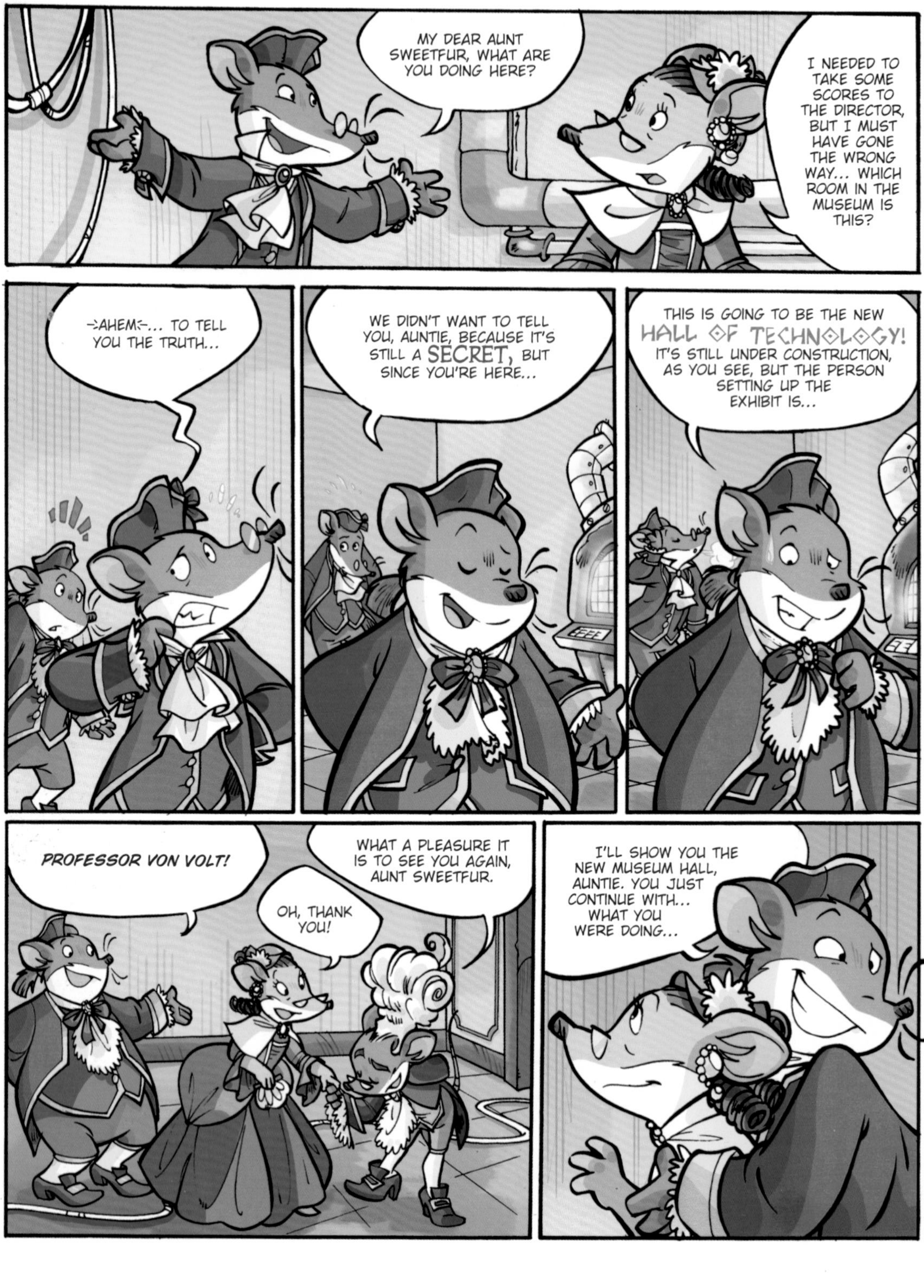
MY DEAR AUNT SWEETFUR, WHAT ARE YOU DOING HERE?
I NEEDED TO TAKE SOME SCORES TO THE DIRECTOR, BUT I MUST HAVE GONE THE WRONG WAY... WHICH ROOM IN THE MUSEUM IS THIS?
-AHEM-... TO TELL YOU THE TRUTH...
WE DIDN'T WANT TO TELL YOU, AUNTIE, BECAUSE IT'S STILL A SECRET, BUT SINCE YOU'RE HERE...
THIS IS GOING TO BE THE NEW HALL OF TECHNOLOGY! IT'S STILL UNDER CONSTRUCTION, AS YOU SEE, BUT THE PERSON SETTING UP THE EXHIBIT IS...
PROFESSOR VON VOLT!
WHAT A PLEASURE IT IS TO SEE YOU AGAIN, AUNT SWEETFUR.
OH, THANK YOU!
I'LL SHOW YOU THE NEW MUSEUM HALL, AUNTIE. YOU JUST CONTINUE WITH... WHAT YOU WERE DOING...

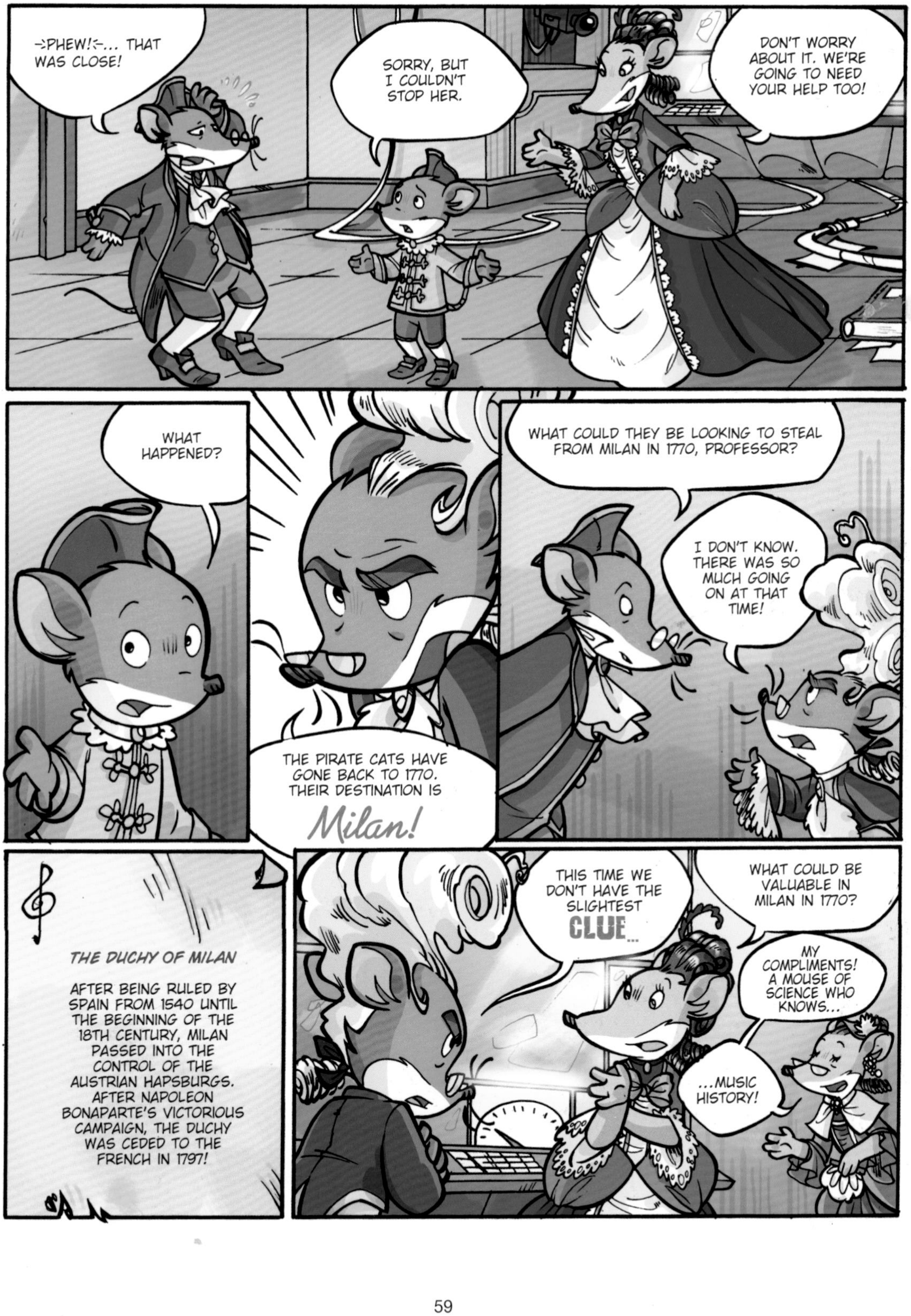

-PHEW!-... THAT WAS CLOSE!
SORRY, BUT I COULDN'T STOP HER.
DON'T WORRY ABOUT IT. WE'RE GOING TO NEED YOUR HELP TOO!
WHAT HAPPENED?
THE PIRATE CATS HAVE GONE BACK TO 1770. THEIR DESTINATION IS
Milan!
WHAT COULD THEY BE LOOKING TO STEAL FROM MILAN IN 1770, PROFESSOR?
I DON'T KNOW. THERE WAS SO MUCH GOING ON AT THAT TIME!
THE DUCHY OF MILAN
AFTER BEING RULED BY SPAIN FROM 1540 UNTIL THE BEGINNING OF THE 18TH CENTURY, MILAN PASSED INTO THE CONTROL OF THE AUSTRIAN HAPSBURGS. AFTER NAPOLEON BONAPARTE'S VICTORIOUS CAMPAIGN, THE DUCHY WAS CEDED TO THE FRENCH IN 1797!
THIS TIME WE DON'T HAVE THE SLIGHTEST CLUE...
WHAT COULD BE VALUABLE IN MILAN IN 1770?
MY COMPLIMENTS! A MOUSE OF SCIENCE WHO KNOWS...
...MUSIC HISTORY!

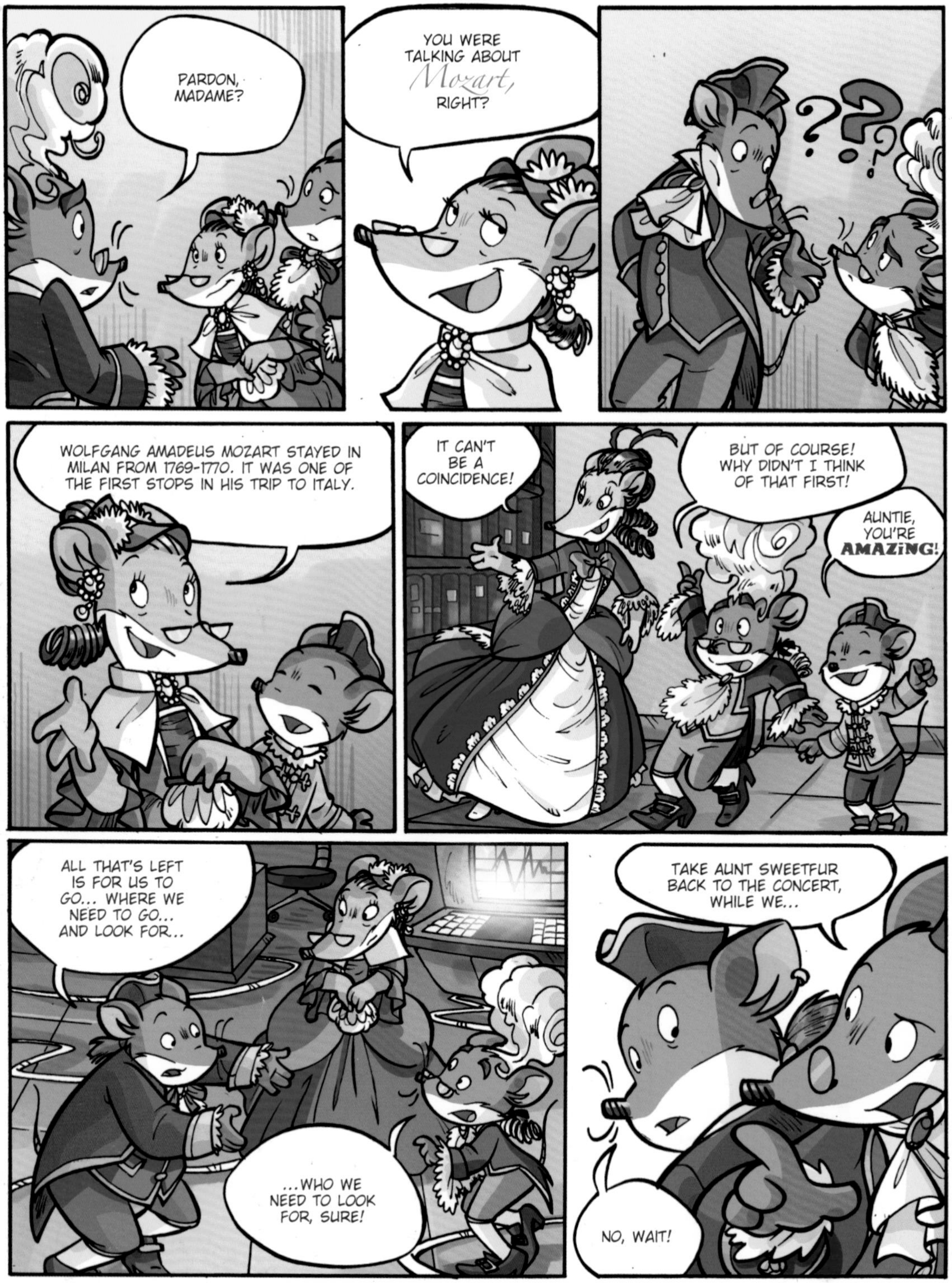
PARDON, MADAME?
YOU WERE TALKING ABOUT Mozart, RIGHT?
?? ?
WOLFGANG AMADEUS MOZART STAYED IN MILAN FROM 1769-1770. IT WAS ONE OF THE FIRST STOPS IN HIS TRIP TO ITALY.
IT CAN'T BE A COINCIDENCE!
BUT OF COURSE! WHY DIDN'T I THINK OF THAT FIRST!
AUNTIE, YOU'RE AMAZING!
ALL THAT'S LEFT IS FOR US TO GO... WHERE WE NEED TO GO... AND LOOK FOR...
...WHO WE NEED TO LOOK FOR, SURE!
TAKE AUNT SWEETFUR BACK TO THE CONCERT, WHILE WE...
NO, WAIT!

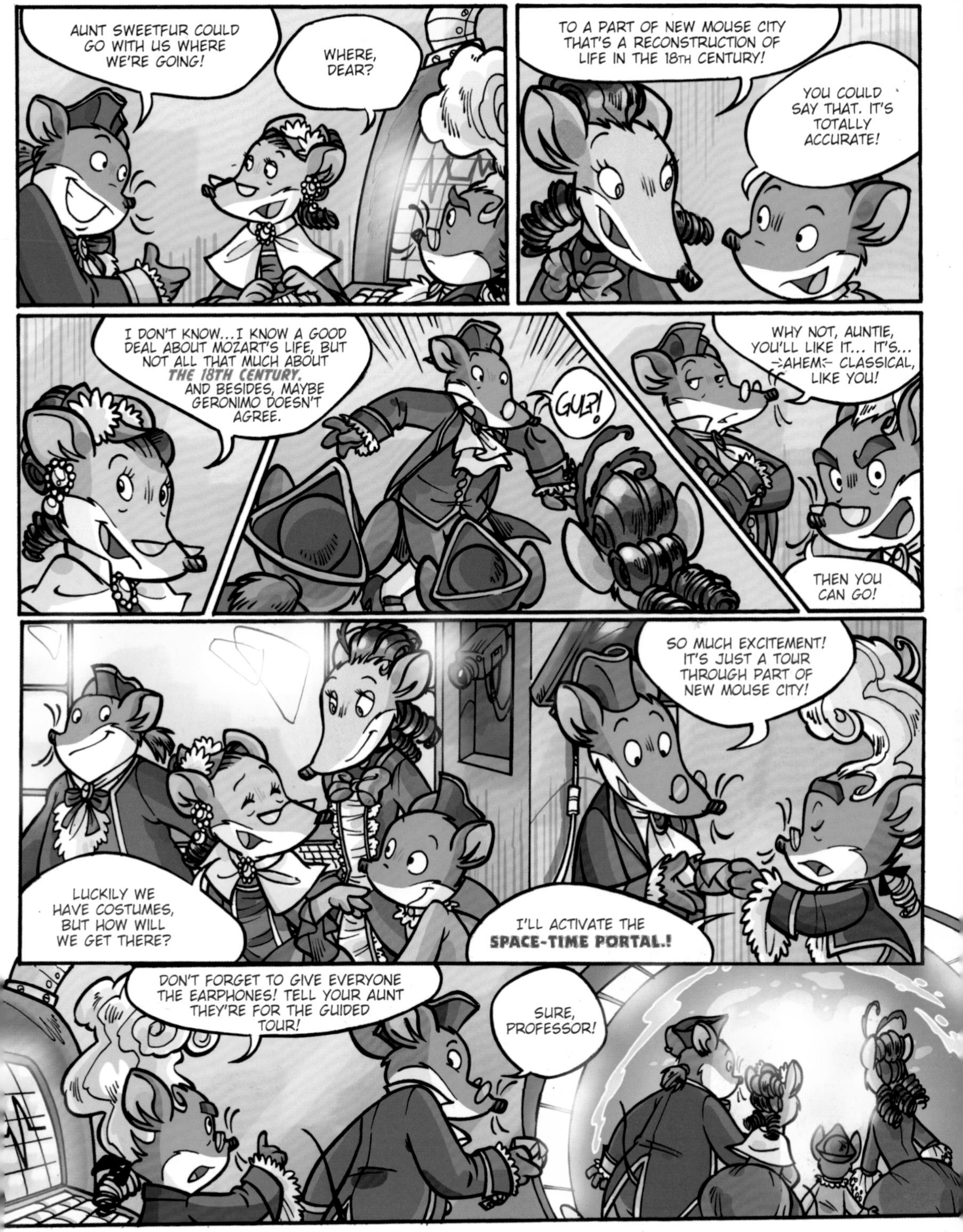
AUNT SWEETFUR COULD GO WITH US WHERE WE'RE GOING!
WHERE, DEAR?
TO A PART OF NEW MOUSE CITY THAT'S A RECONSTRUCTION OF LIFE IN THE 18TH CENTURY!
YOU COULD SAY THAT. IT'S TOTALLY ACCURATE!
I DON'T KNOW...I KNOW A GOOD DEAL ABOUT MOZART'S LIFE, BUT NOT ALL THAT MUCH ABOUT THE 18TH CENTURY. AND BESIDES, MAYBE GERONIMO DOESN'T AGREE.
GULP!
WHY NOT, AUNTIE, YOU'LL LIKE IT... IT'S... AHEM CLASSICAL, LIKE YOU!
THEN YOU CAN GO!
LUCKILY WE HAVE COSTUMES, BUT HOW WILL WE GET THERE?
SO MUCH EXCITEMENT! IT'S JUST A TOUR THROUGH PART OF NEW MOUSE CITY!
I'LL ACTIVATE THE SPACE-TIME PORTAL.!
DON'T FORGET TO GIVE EVERYONE THE EARPHONES! TELL YOUR AUNT THEY'RE FOR THE GUIDED TOUR!
SURE, PROFESSOR!

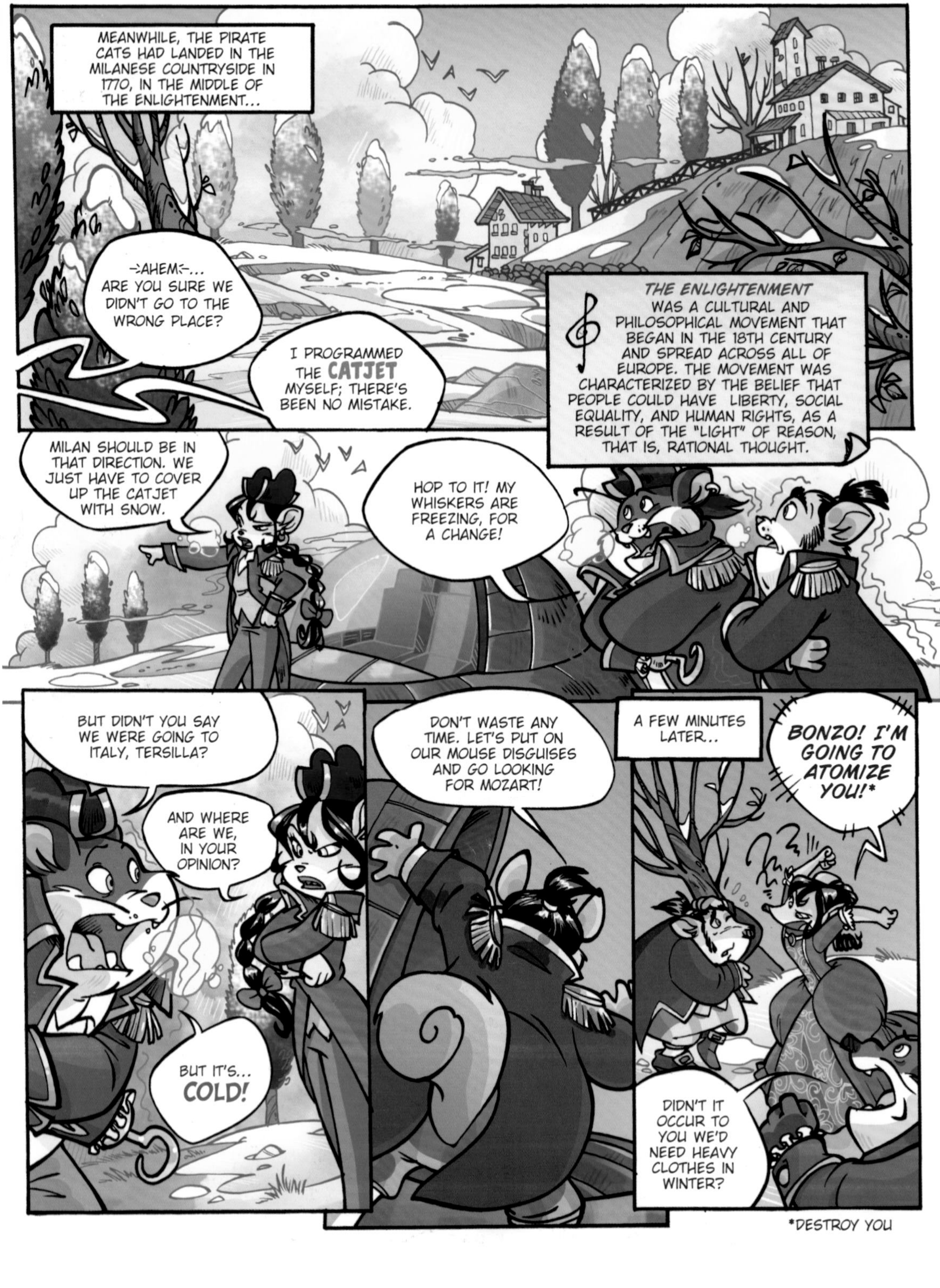
MEANWHILE, THE PIRATE CATS HAD LANDED IN THE MILANESE COUNTRYSIDE IN 1770, IN THE MIDDLE OF THE ENLIGHTENMENT...
-AHEM-... ARE YOU SURE WE DIDN'T GO TO THE WRONG PLACE?
I PROGRAMMED THE CATJET MYSELF; THERE'S BEEN NO MISTAKE.
THE ENLIGHTENMENT WAS A CULTURAL AND PHILOSOPHICAL MOVEMENT THAT BEGAN IN THE 18TH CENTURY AND SPREAD ACROSS ALL OF EUROPE. THE MOVEMENT WAS CHARACTERIZED BY THE BELIEF THAT PEOPLE COULD HAVE LIBERTY, SOCIAL EQUALITY, AND HUMAN RIGHTS, AS A RESULT OF THE "LIGHT" OF REASON, THAT IS, RATIONAL THOUGHT.
MILAN SHOULD BE IN THAT DIRECTION. WE JUST HAVE TO COVER UP THE CATJET WITH SNOW.
HOP TO IT! MY WHISKERS ARE FREEZING, FOR A CHANGE!
BUT DIDN'T YOU SAY WE WERE GOING TO ITALY, TERSILLA?
AND WHERE ARE WE, IN YOUR OPINION?
BUT IT'S... COLD!
DON'T WASTE ANY TIME. LET'S PUT ON OUR MOUSE DISGUISES AND GO LOOKING FOR MOZART!
A FEW MINUTES LATER...
BONZO! I'M GOING TO ATOMIZE YOU!*
DIDN'T IT OCCUR TO YOU WE'D NEED HEAVY CLOTHES IN WINTER?

*DESTROY YOU

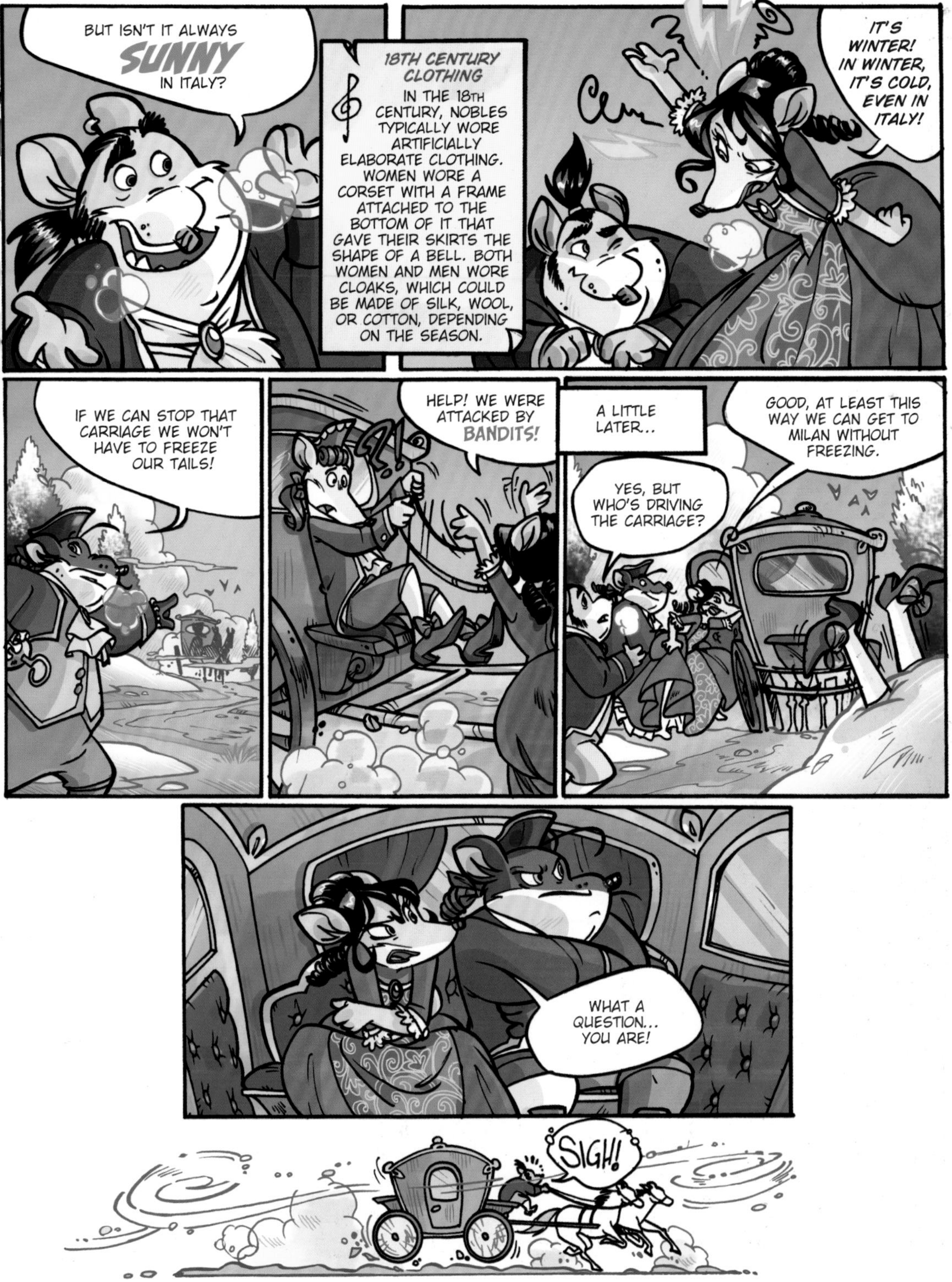
BUT ISN'T IT ALWAYS SUNNY IN ITALY?
18TH CENTURY CLOTHING
IN THE 18TH CENTURY, NOBLES TYPICALLY WORE ARTIFICIALLY ELABORATE CLOTHING. WOMEN WORE A CORSET WITH A FRAME ATTACHED TO THE BOTTOM OF IT THAT GAVE THEIR SKIRTS THE SHAPE OF A BELL. BOTH WOMEN AND MEN WORE CLOAKS, WHICH COULD BE MADE OF SILK, WOOL, OR COTTON, DEPENDING ON THE SEASON.
IT'S WINTER! IN WINTER, IT'S COLD, EVEN IN ITALY!
IF WE CAN STOP THAT CARRIAGE WE WON'T HAVE TO FREEZE OUR TAILS!
HELP! WE WERE ATTACKED BY BANDITS!
A LITTLE LATER...
GOOD, AT LEAST THIS WAY WE CAN GET TO MILAN WITHOUT FREEZING.
YES, BUT WHO'S DRIVING THE CARRIAGE?
WHAT A QUESTION... YOU ARE!
SIGH!

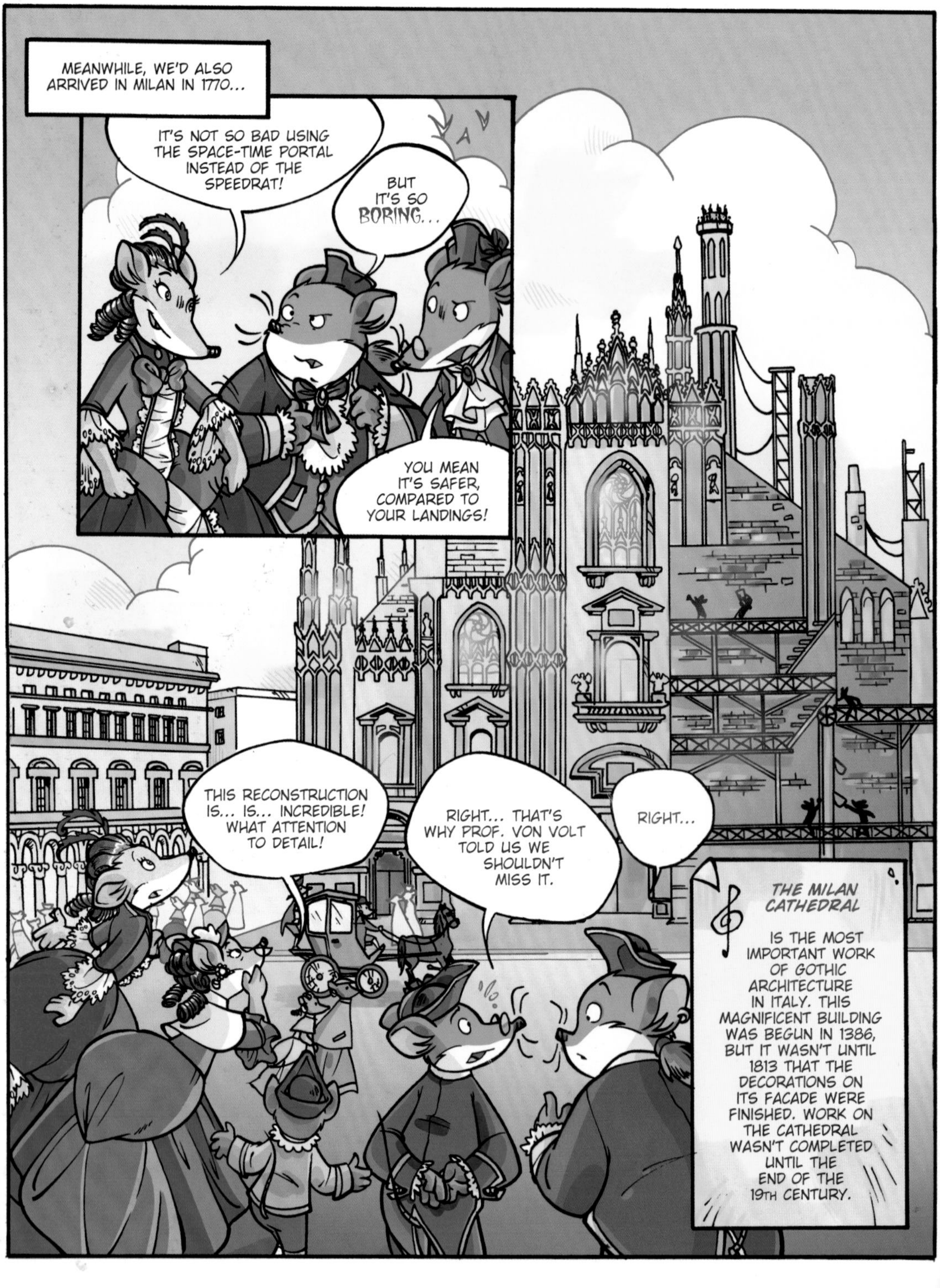

MEANWHILE, WE'D ALSO ARRIVED IN MILAN IN 1770...
IT'S NOT SO BAD USING THE SPACE-TIME PORTAL INSTEAD OF THE SPEEDRAT!
BUT IT'S SO BORING...
YOU MEAN IT'S SAFER, COMPARED TO YOUR LANDINGS!
THIS RECONSTRUCTION IS... IS... INCREDIBLE! WHAT ATTENTION TO DETAIL!
RIGHT... THAT'S WHY PROF. VON VOLT TOLD US WE SHOULDN'T MISS IT.
RIGHT...
THE MILAN CATHEDRAL
IS THE MOST IMPORTANT WORK OF GOTHIC ARCHITECTURE IN ITALY. THIS MAGNIFICENT BUILDING WAS BEGUN IN 1386, BUT IT WASN'T UNTIL 1813 THAT THE DECORATIONS ON ITS FACADE WERE FINISHED. WORK ON THE CATHEDRAL WASN'T COMPLETED UNTIL THE END OF THE 19TH CENTURY.

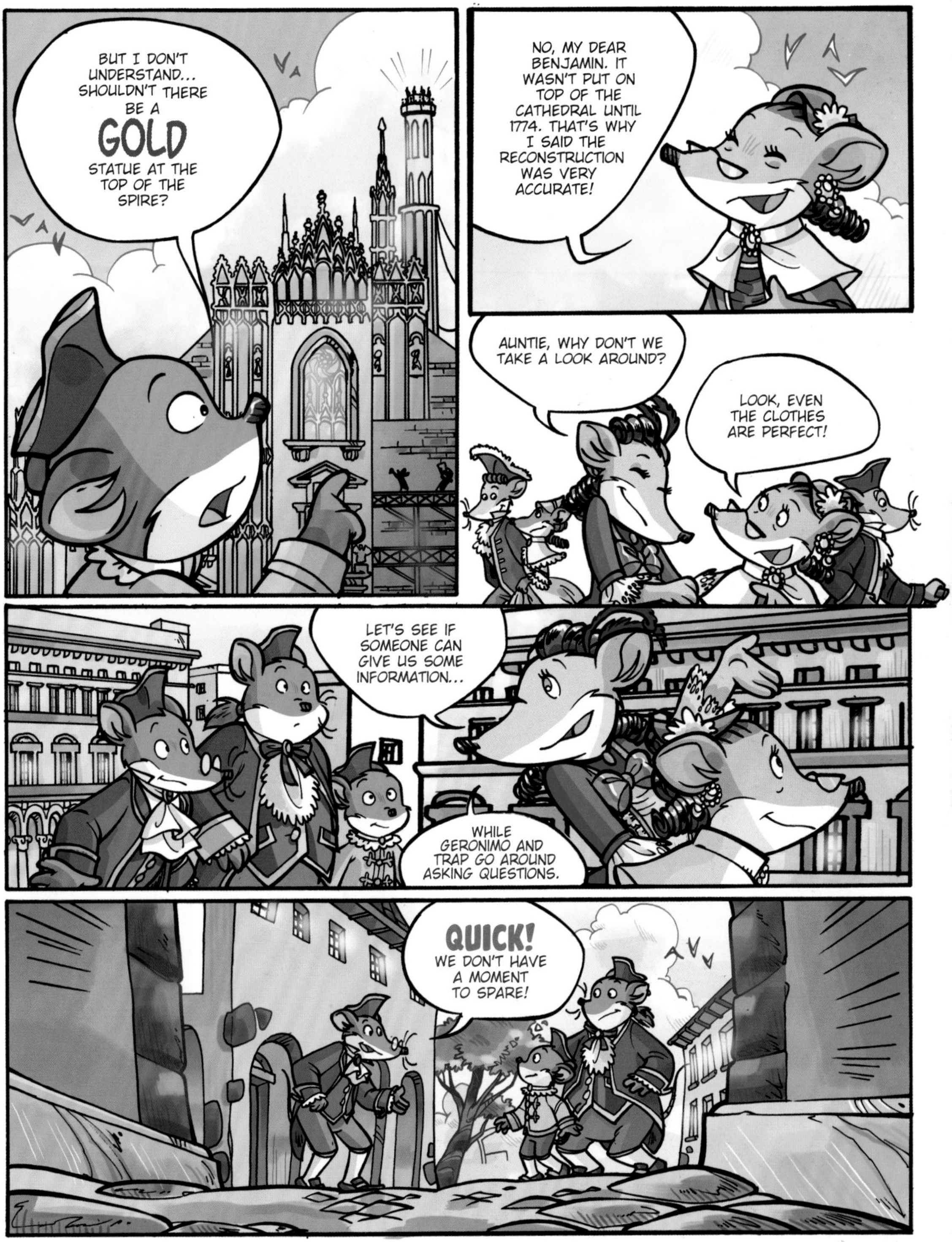
BUT I DON'T UNDERSTAND... SHOULDN'T THERE BE A GOLD STATUE AT THE TOP OF THE SPIRE?
NO, MY DEAR BENJAMIN. IT WASN'T PUT ON TOP OF THE CATHEDRAL UNTIL 1774. THAT'S WHY I SAID THE RECONSTRUCTION WAS VERY ACCURATE!
AUNTIE, WHY DON'T WE TAKE A LOOK AROUND?
LOOK, EVEN THE CLOTHES ARE PERFECT!
LET'S SEE IF SOMEONE CAN GIVE US SOME INFORMATION...
WHILE GERONIMO AND TRAP GO AROUND ASKING QUESTIONS.
QUICK! WE DON'T HAVE A MOMENT TO SPARE!

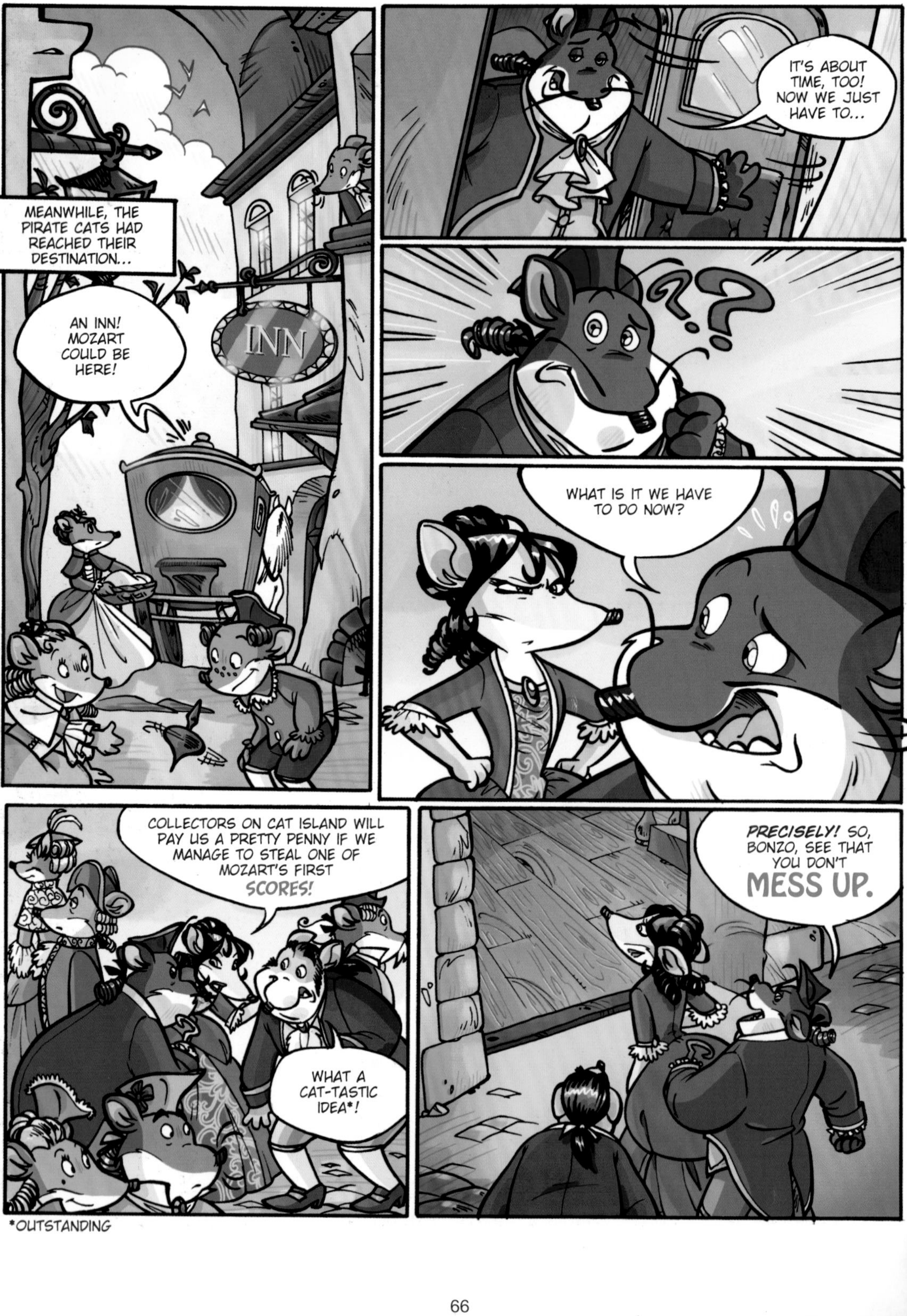
MEANWHILE, THE PIRATE CATS HAD REACHED THEIR DESTINATION...
AN INN! MOZART COULD BE HERE!
INN
IT'S ABOUT TIME, TOO! NOW WE JUST HAVE TO...
??
WHAT IS IT WE HAVE TO DO NOW?
COLLECTORS ON CAT ISLAND WILL PAY US A PRETTY PENNY IF WE MANAGE TO STEAL ONE OF MOZART'S FIRST SCORES!
WHAT A CAT-TASTIC IDEA*!
PRECISELY! SO, BONZO, SEE THAT YOU DON'T MESS UP.

*OUTSTANDING

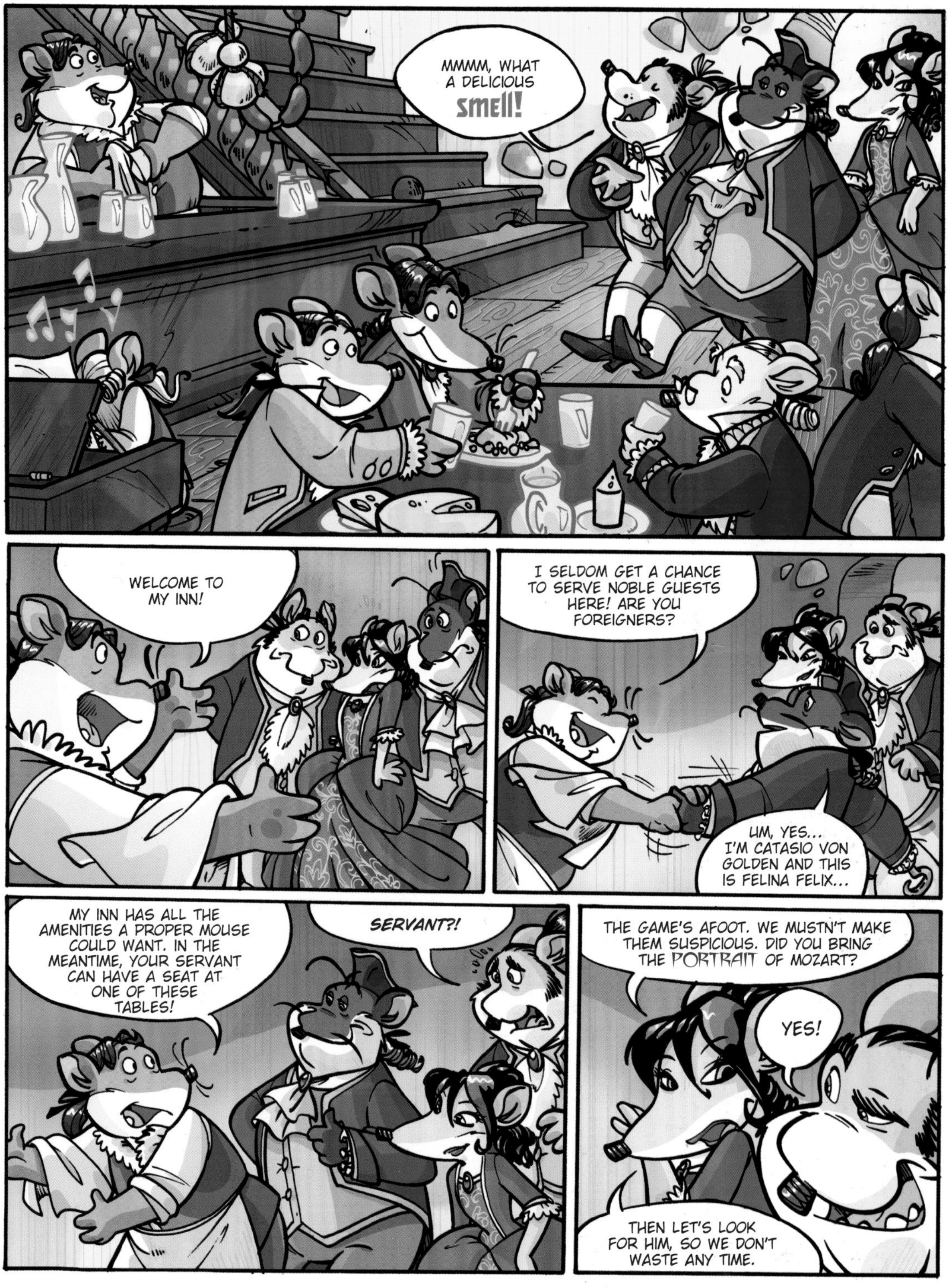
MMMM, WHAT A DELICIOUS SMELL!
WELCOME TO MY INN!
I SELDOM GET A CHANCE TO SERVE NOBLE GUESTS HERE! ARE YOU FOREIGNERS?
UM, YES... I'M CATASIO VON GOLDEN AND THIS IS FELINA FELIX...
MY INN HAS ALL THE AMENITIES A PROPER MOUSE COULD WANT. IN THE MEANTIME, YOUR SERVANT CAN HAVE A SEAT AT ONE OF THESE TABLES!
SERVANT?!
THE GAME'S AFOOT. WE MUSTN'T MAKE THEM SUSPICIOUS. DID YOU BRING THE PORTRAIT OF MOZART?
YES!
THEN LET'S LOOK FOR HIM, SO WE DON'T WASTE ANY TIME.

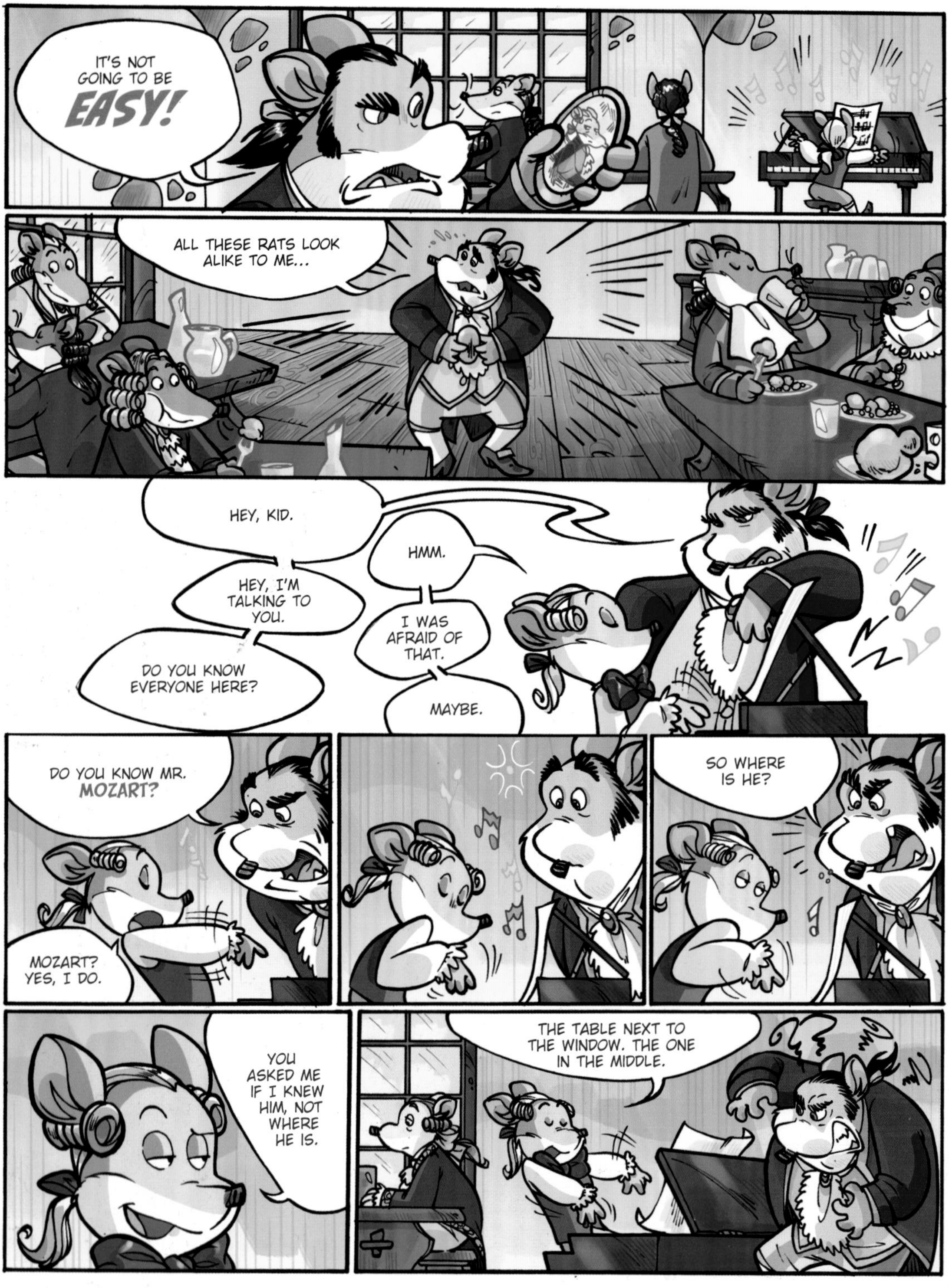
IT'S NOT GOING TO BE EASY!
ALL THESE RATS LOOK ALIKE TO ME...
HEY, KID.
HEY, I'M TALKING TO YOU.
DO YOU KNOW EVERYONE HERE?
HMM.
I WAS AFRAID OF THAT.
MAYBE.
DO YOU KNOW MR. MOZART?
MOZART? YES, I DO.
SO WHERE IS HE?
YOU ASKED ME IF I KNEW HIM, NOT WHERE HE IS.
THE TABLE NEXT TO THE WINDOW. THE ONE IN THE MIDDLE.

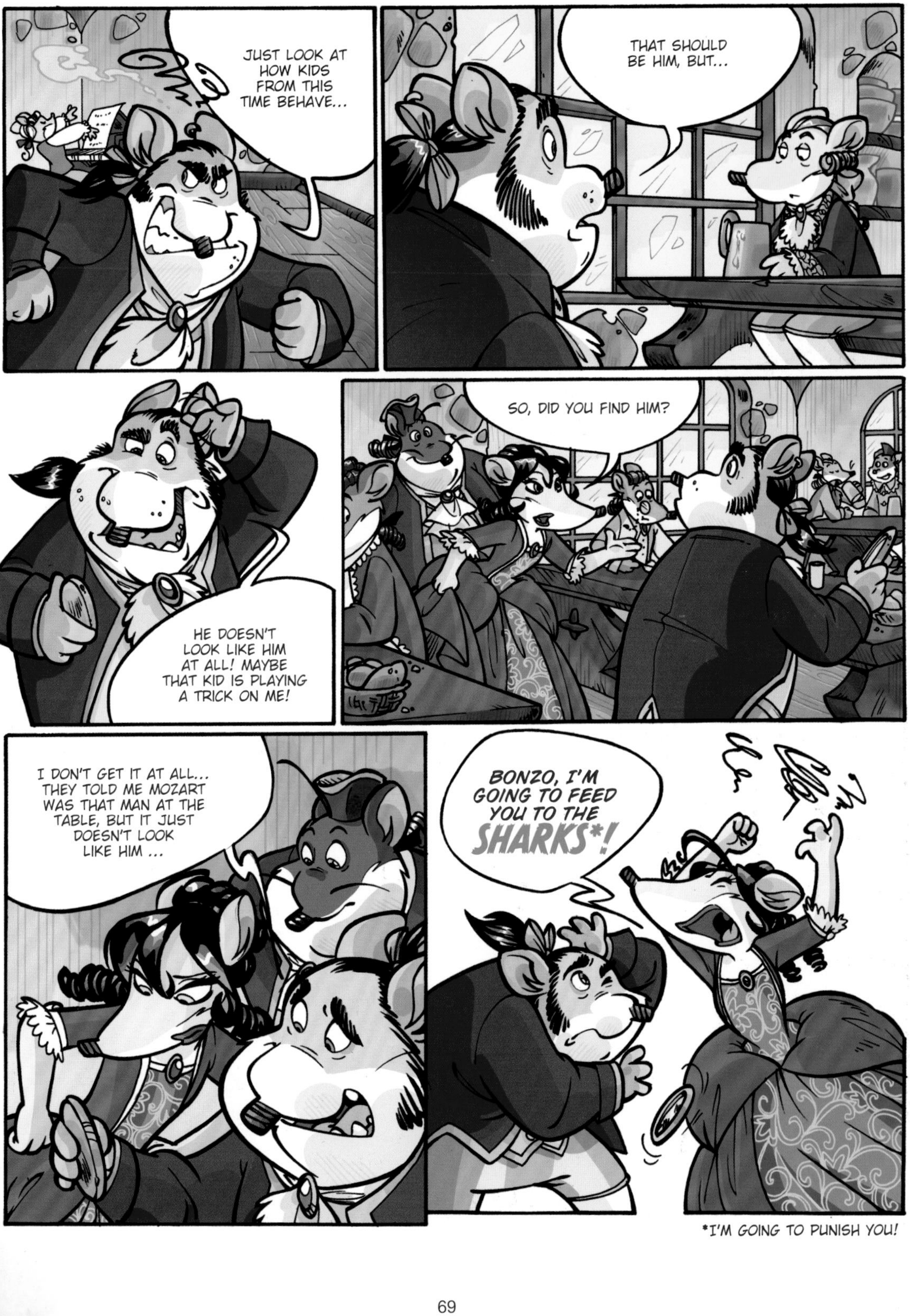
JUST LOOK AT HOW KIDS FROM THIS TIME BEHAVE...
THAT SHOULD BE HIM, BUT...
HE DOESN'T LOOK LIKE HIM AT ALL! MAYBE THAT KID IS PLAYING A TRICK ON ME!
SO, DID YOU FIND HIM?
I DON'T GET IT AT ALL... THEY TOLD ME MOZART WAS THAT MAN AT THE TABLE, BUT IT JUST DOESN'T LOOK LIKE HIM ...
BONZO, I'M GOING TO FEED YOU TO THE SHARKS*!

*I'M GOING TO PUNISH YOU!

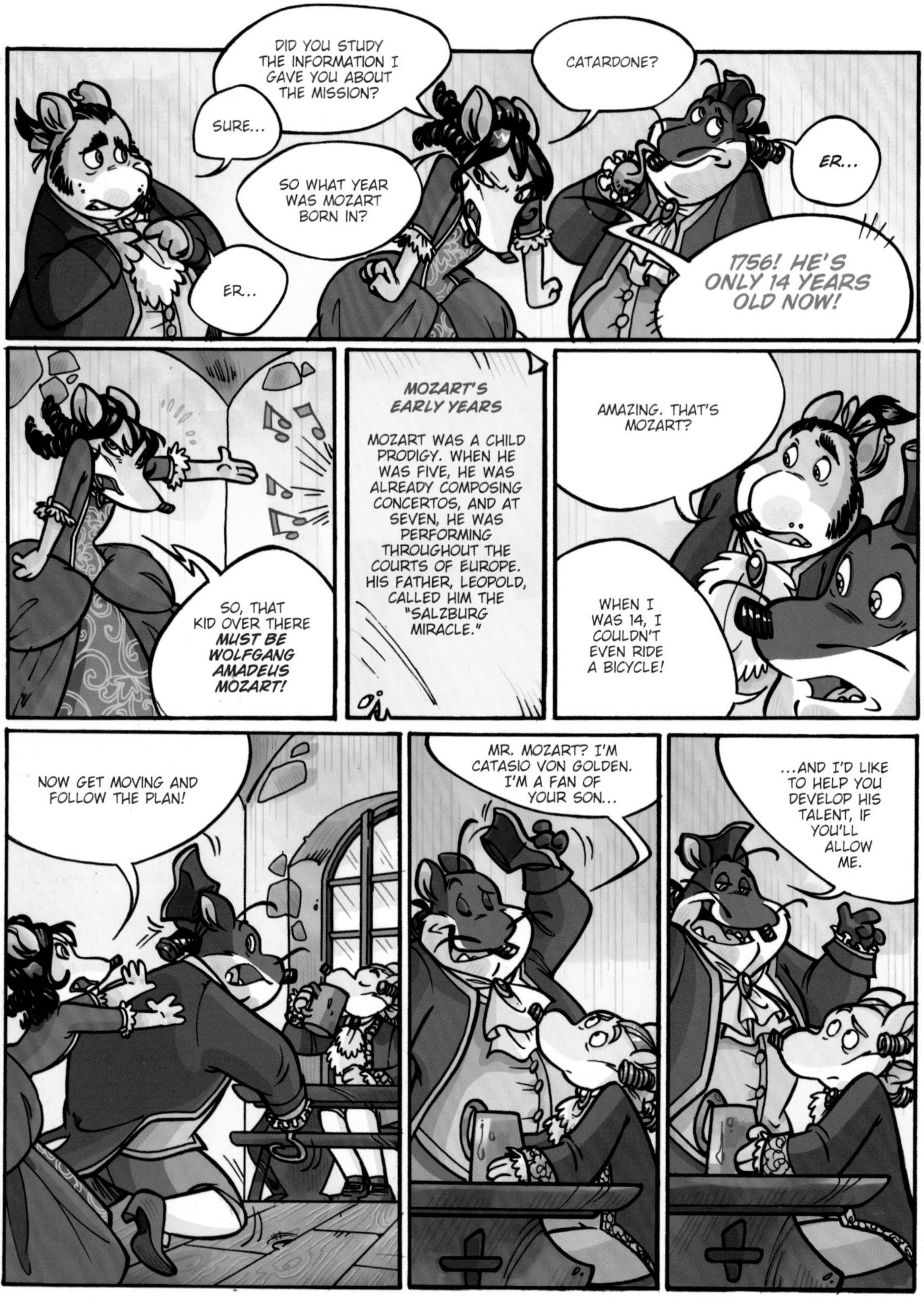
DID YOU STUDY THE INFORMATION I GAVE YOU ABOUT THE MISSION?
SURE...
CATARDONE?
ER...
SO WHAT YEAR WAS MOZART BORN IN?
ER...
1756! HE'S ONLY 14 YEARS OLD NOW!
SO, THAT KID OVER THERE MUST BE WOLFGANG AMADEUS MOZART!
MOZART'S EARLY YEARS
MOZART WAS A CHILD PRODIGY. WHEN HE WAS FIVE, HE WAS ALREADY COMPOSING CONCERTOS, AND AT SEVEN, HE WAS PERFORMING THROUGHOUT THE COURTS OF EUROPE. HIS FATHER, LEOPOLD, CALLED HIM THE "SALZBURG MIRACLE."
AMAZING. THAT'S MOZART?
WHEN I WAS 14, I COULDN'T EVEN RIDE A BICYCLE!
NOW GET MOVING AND FOLLOW THE PLAN!
MR. MOZART? I'M CATASIO VON GOLDEN. I'M A FAN OF YOUR SON...
...AND I'D LIKE TO HELP YOU DEVELOP HIS TALENT, IF YOU'LL ALLOW ME.

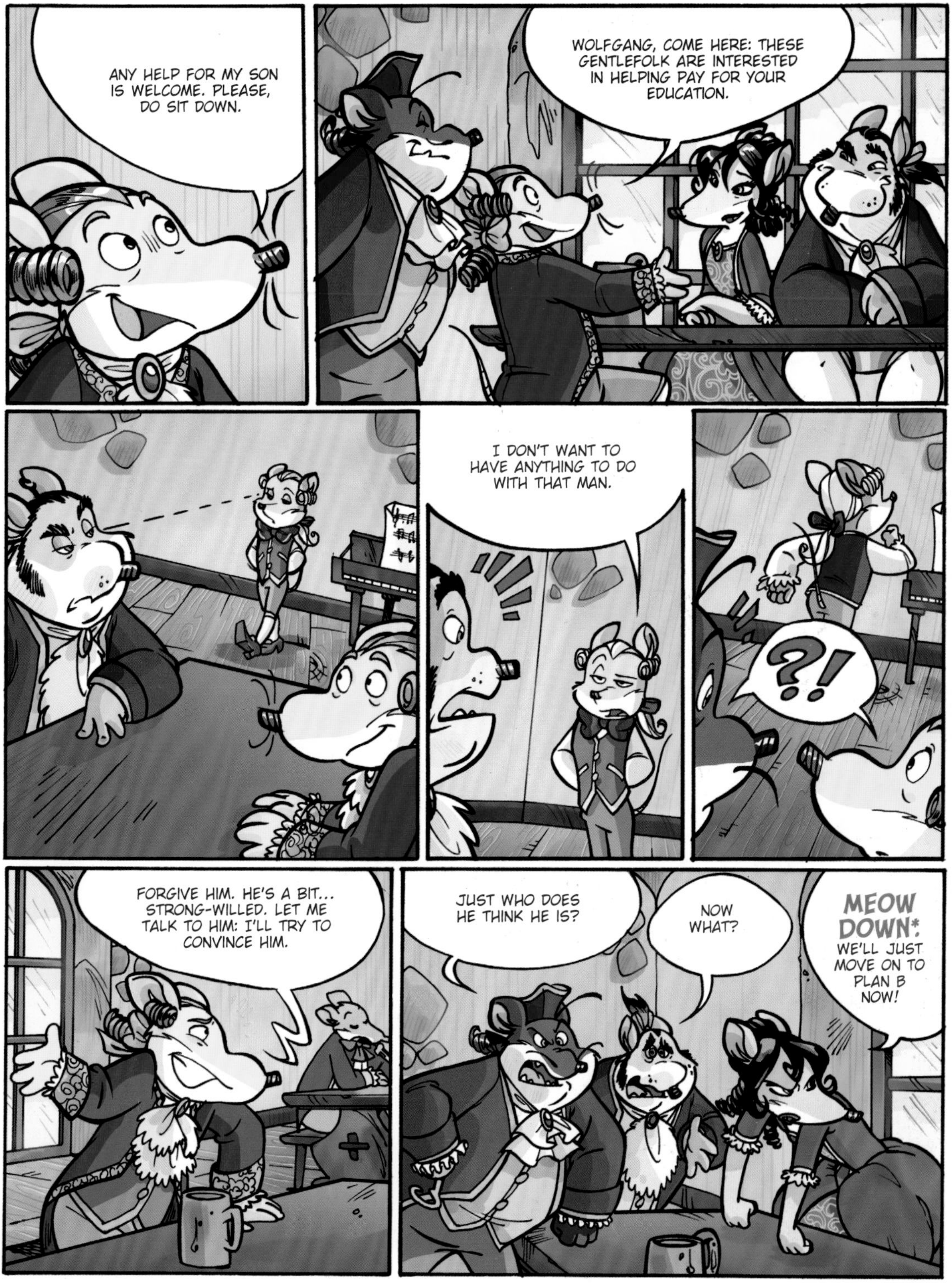
ANY HELP FOR MY SON IS WELCOME. PLEASE, DO SIT DOWN.
WOLFGANG, COME HERE: THESE GENTLEFOLK ARE INTERESTED IN HELPING PAY FOR YOUR EDUCATION.
I DON'T WANT TO HAVE ANYTHING TO DO WITH THAT MAN.
?!
FORGIVE HIM. HE'S A BIT... STRONG-WILLED. LET ME TALK TO HIM: I'LL TRY TO CONVINCE HIM.
JUST WHO DOES HE THINK HE IS?
NOW WHAT?
MEOW DOWN*: WE'LL JUST MOVE ON TO PLAN B NOW!

*CALM DOWN

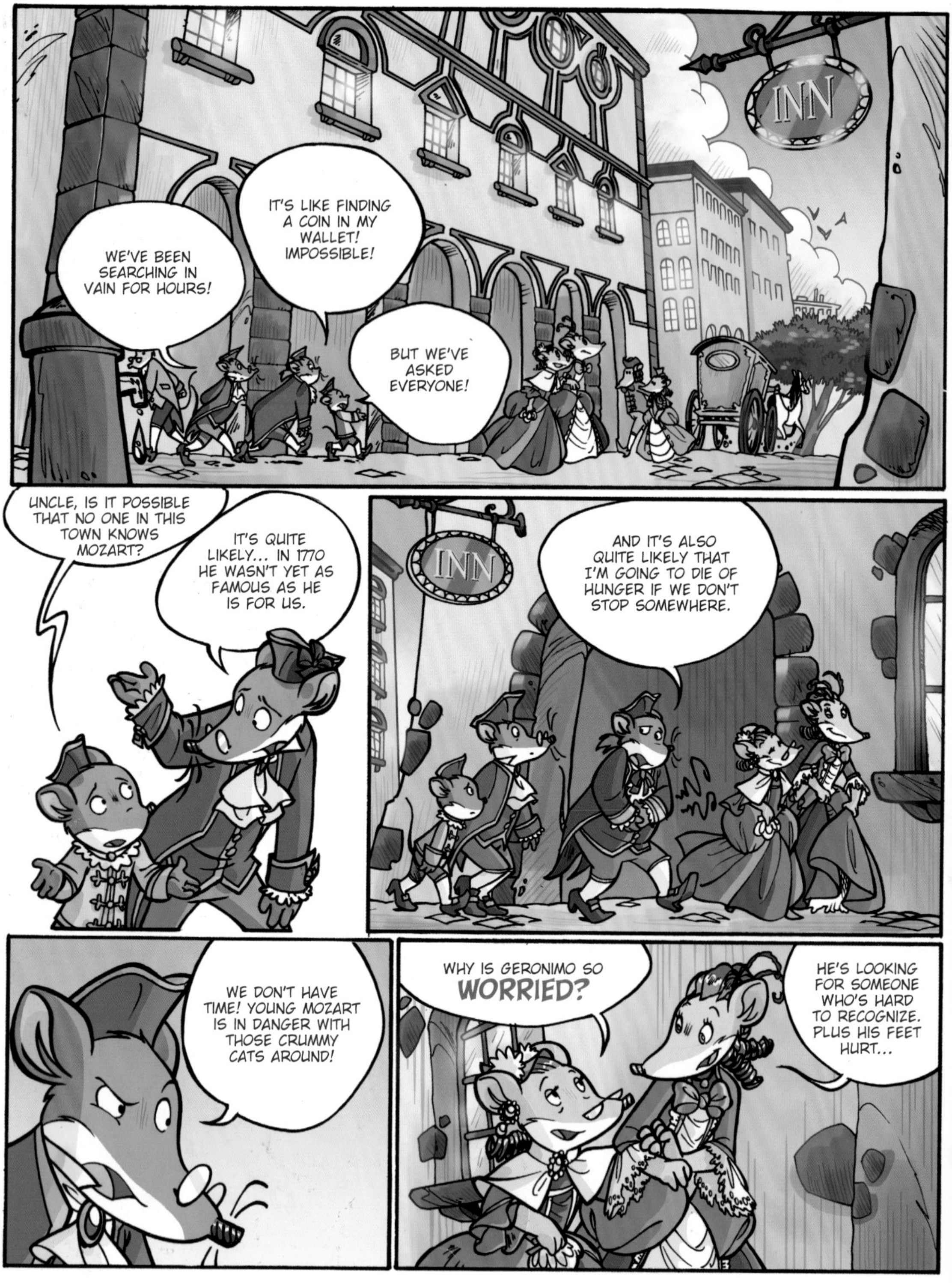
WE'VE BEEN SEARCHING IN VAIN FOR HOURS!
IT'S LIKE FINDING A COIN IN MY WALLET! IMPOSSIBLE!
BUT WE'VE ASKED EVERYONE!
INN
UNCLE, IS IT POSSIBLE THAT NO ONE IN THIS TOWN KNOWS MOZART?
IT'S QUITE LIKELY... IN 1770 HE WASN'T YET AS FAMOUS AS HE IS FOR US.
INN
AND IT'S ALSO QUITE LIKELY THAT I'M GOING TO DIE OF HUNGER IF WE DON'T STOP SOMEWHERE.
WE DON'T HAVE TIME! YOUNG MOZART IS IN DANGER WITH THOSE CRUMMY CATS AROUND!
WHY IS GERONIMO SO **WORRIED?**
HE'S LOOKING FOR SOMEONE WHO'S HARD TO RECOGNIZE. PLUS HIS FEET HURT...

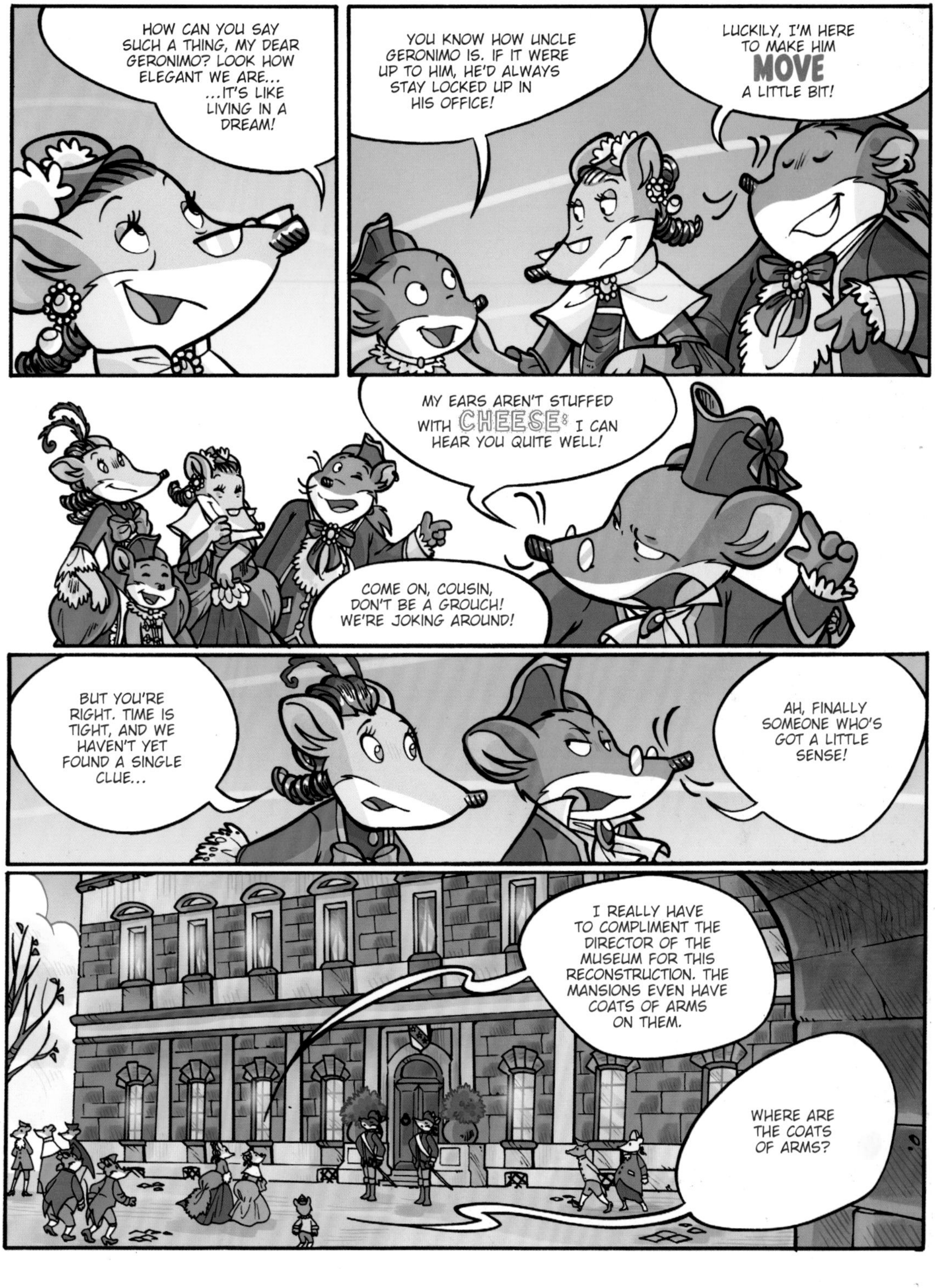
HOW CAN YOU SAY SUCH A THING, MY DEAR GERONIMO? LOOK HOW ELEGANT WE ARE... ...IT'S LIKE LIVING IN A DREAM!
YOU KNOW HOW UNCLE GERONIMO IS. IF IT WERE UP TO HIM, HE'D ALWAYS STAY LOCKED UP IN HIS OFFICE!
LUCKILY, I'M HERE TO MAKE HIM MOVE A LITTLE BIT!
MY EARS AREN'T STUFFED WITH CHEESE: I CAN HEAR YOU QUITE WELL!
COME ON, COUSIN, DON'T BE A GROUCH! WE'RE JOKING AROUND!
BUT YOU'RE RIGHT. TIME IS TIGHT, AND WE HAVEN'T YET FOUND A SINGLE CLUE...
AH, FINALLY SOMEONE WHO'S GOT A LITTLE SENSE!
I REALLY HAVE TO COMPLIMENT THE DIRECTOR OF THE MUSEUM FOR THIS RECONSTRUCTION. THE MANSIONS EVEN HAVE COATS OF ARMS ON THEM.
WHERE ARE THE COATS OF ARMS?

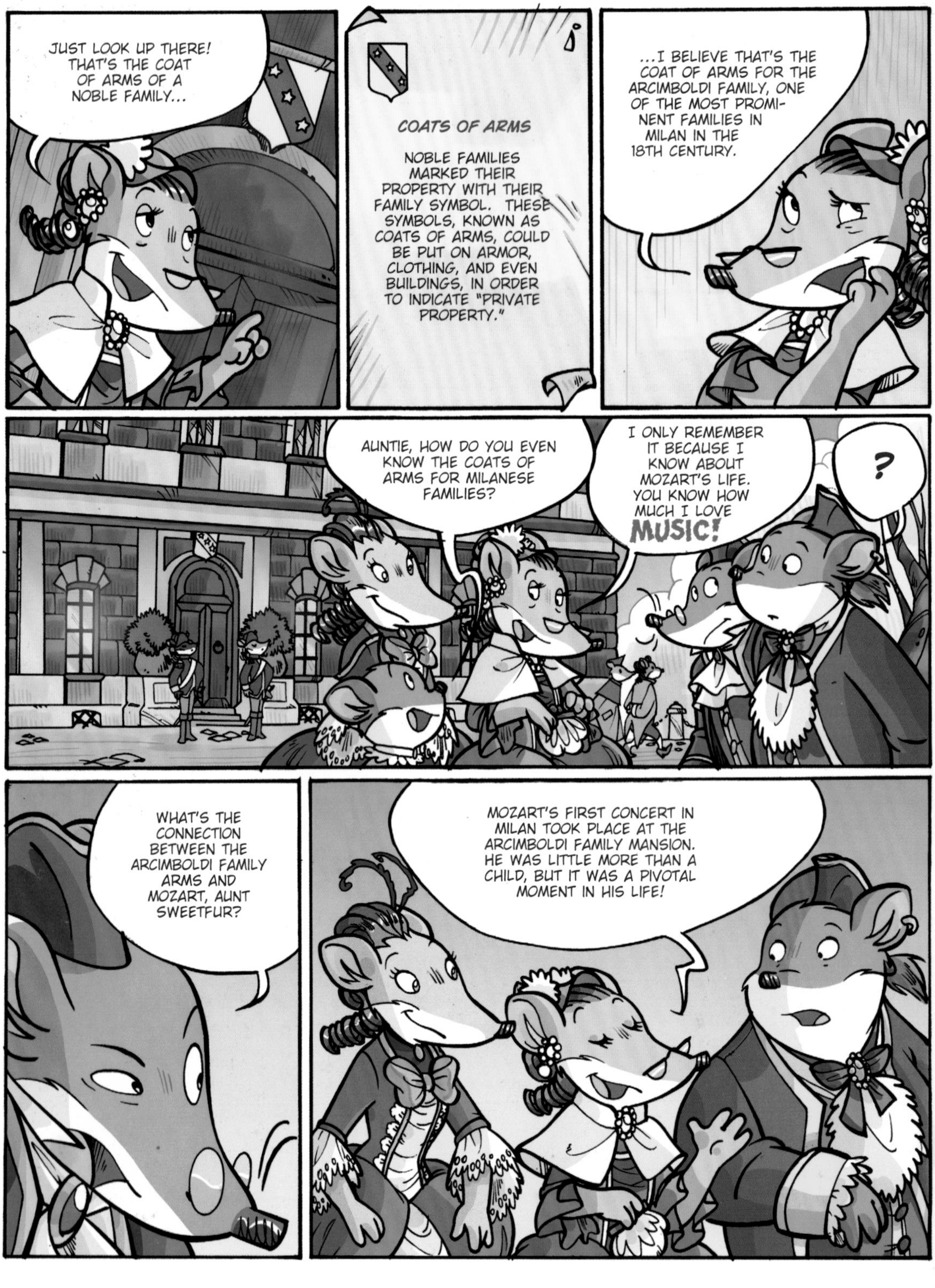

JUST LOOK UP THERE! THAT'S THE COAT OF ARMS OF A NOBLE FAMILY...
COATS OF ARMS
NOBLE FAMILIES MARKED THEIR PROPERTY WITH THEIR FAMILY SYMBOL. THESE SYMBOLS, KNOWN AS COATS OF ARMS, COULD BE PUT ON ARMOR, CLOTHING, AND EVEN BUILDINGS, IN ORDER TO INDICATE "PRIVATE PROPERTY."
...I BELIEVE THAT'S THE COAT OF ARMS FOR THE ARCIMBOLDI FAMILY, ONE OF THE MOST PROMINENT FAMILIES IN MILAN IN THE 18TH CENTURY.
AUNTIE, HOW DO YOU EVEN KNOW THE COATS OF ARMS FOR MILANESE FAMILIES?
I ONLY REMEMBER IT BECAUSE I KNOW ABOUT MOZART'S LIFE. YOU KNOW HOW MUCH I LOVE MUSIC!
?
WHAT'S THE CONNECTION BETWEEN THE ARCIMBOLDI FAMILY ARMS AND MOZART, AUNT SWEETFUR?
MOZART'S FIRST CONCERT IN MILAN TOOK PLACE AT THE ARCIMBOLDI FAMILY MANSION. HE WAS LITTLE MORE THAN A CHILD, BUT IT WAS A PIVOTAL MOMENT IN HIS LIFE!

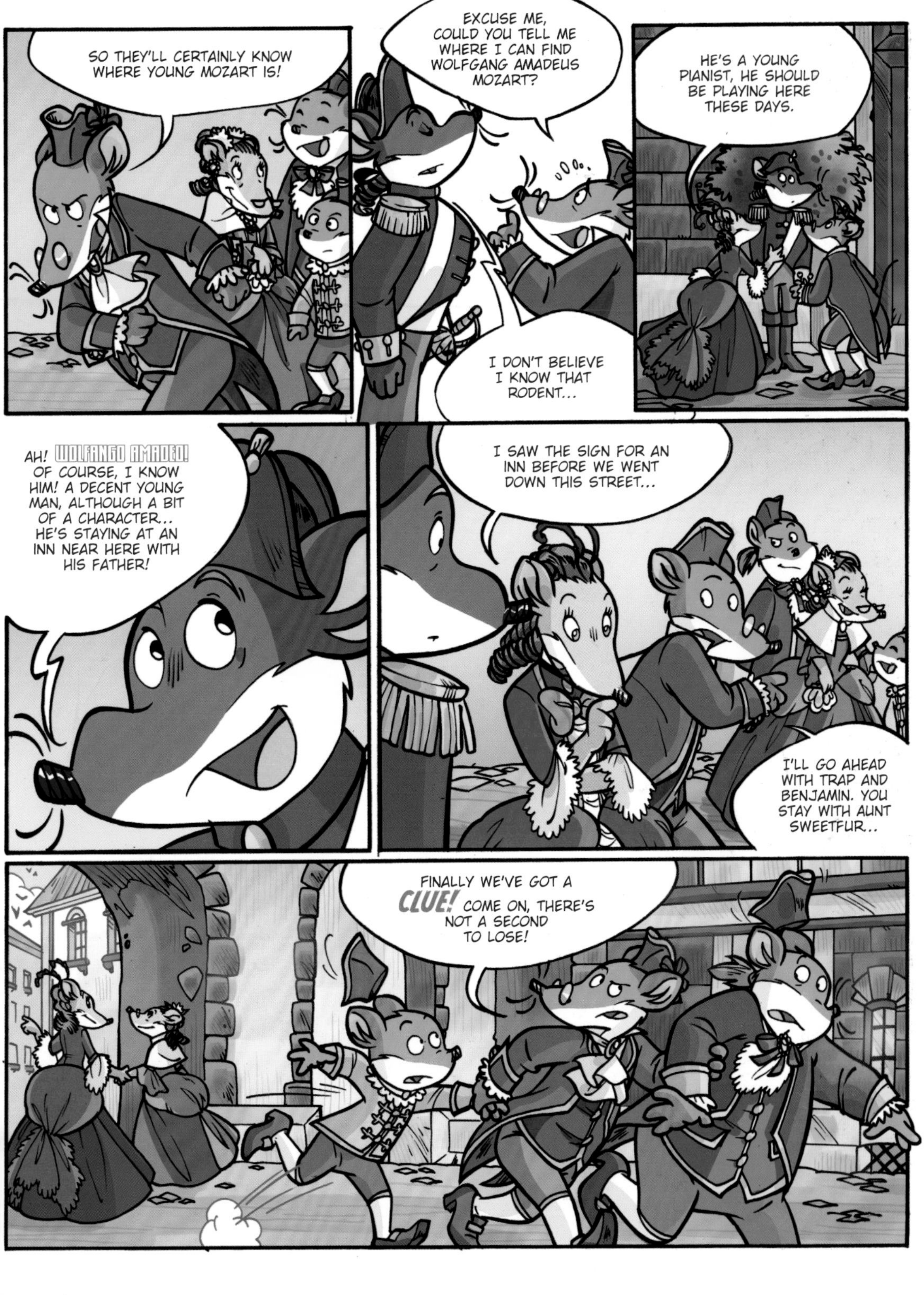
SO THEY'LL CERTAINLY KNOW WHERE YOUNG MOZART IS!
EXCUSE ME, COULD YOU TELL ME WHERE I CAN FIND WOLFGANG AMADEUS MOZART?
I DON'T BELIEVE I KNOW THAT RODENT...
HE'S A YOUNG PIANIST, HE SHOULD BE PLAYING HERE THESE DAYS.
AH! WOLFANGO AMADEO! OF COURSE, I KNOW HIM! A DECENT YOUNG MAN, ALTHOUGH A BIT OF A CHARACTER... HE'S STAYING AT AN INN NEAR HERE WITH HIS FATHER!
I SAW THE SIGN FOR AN INN BEFORE WE WENT DOWN THIS STREET...
I'LL GO AHEAD WITH TRAP AND BENJAMIN. YOU STAY WITH AUNT SWEETFUR...
FINALLY WE'VE GOT A CLUE! COME ON, THERE'S NOT A SECOND TO LOSE!

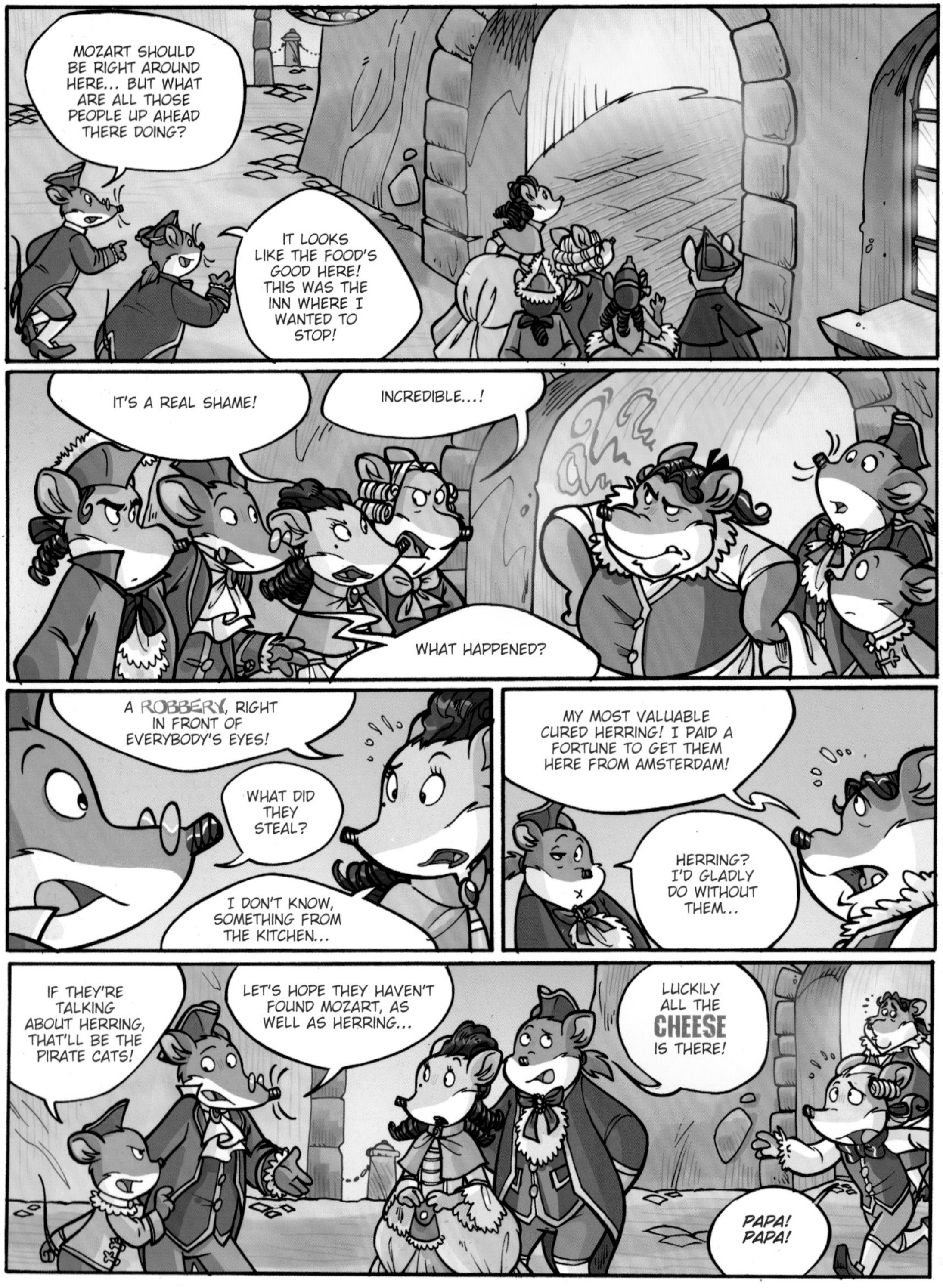
MOZART SHOULD BE RIGHT AROUND HERE... BUT WHAT ARE ALL THOSE PEOPLE UP AHEAD THERE DOING?
IT LOOKS LIKE THE FOOD'S GOOD HERE! THIS WAS THE INN WHERE I WANTED TO STOP!
IT'S A REAL SHAME!
INCREDIBLE...!
WHAT HAPPENED?
A ROBBERY, RIGHT IN FRONT OF EVERYBODY'S EYES!
WHAT DID THEY STEAL?
I DON'T KNOW, SOMETHING FROM THE KITCHEN...
MY MOST VALUABLE CURED HERRING! I PAID A FORTUNE TO GET THEM HERE FROM AMSTERDAM!
HERRING? I'D GLADLY DO WITHOUT THEM...
IF THEY'RE TALKING ABOUT HERRING, THAT'LL BE THE PIRATE CATS!
LET'S HOPE THEY HAVEN'T FOUND MOZART, AS WELL AS HERRING...
LUCKILY ALL THE CHEESE IS THERE!
PAPA! PAPA!

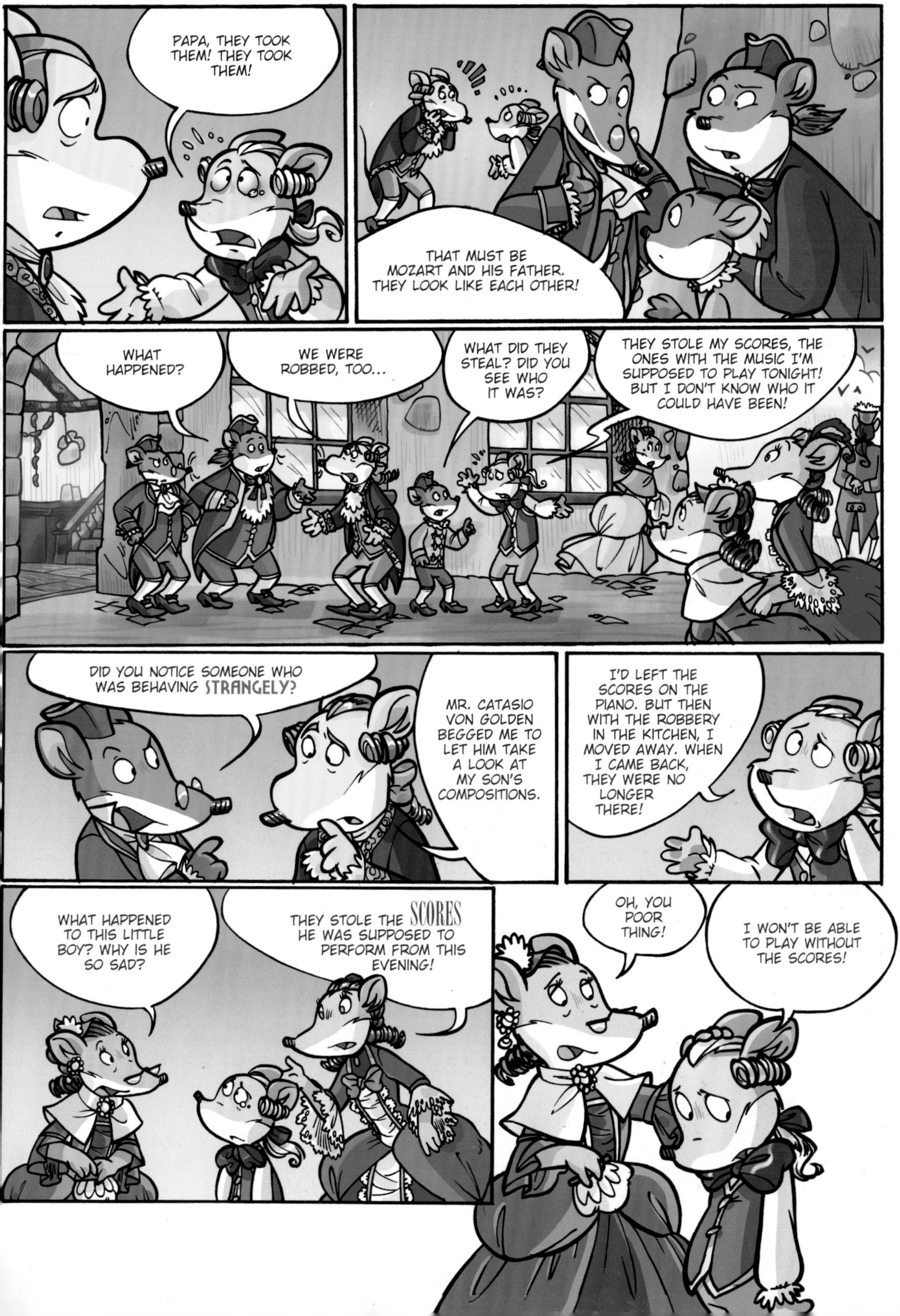
PAPA, THEY TOOK THEM! THEY TOOK THEM!
THAT MUST BE MOZART AND HIS FATHER. THEY LOOK LIKE EACH OTHER!
WHAT HAPPENED?
WE WERE ROBBED, TOO...
WHAT DID THEY STEAL? DID YOU SEE WHO IT WAS?
THEY STOLE MY SCORES, THE ONES WITH THE MUSIC I'M SUPPOSED TO PLAY TONIGHT! BUT I DON'T KNOW WHO IT COULD HAVE BEEN!
DID YOU NOTICE SOMEONE WHO WAS BEHAVING STRANGELY?
MR. CATASIO VON GOLDEN BEGGED ME TO LET HIM TAKE A LOOK AT MY SON'S COMPOSITIONS.
I'D LEFT THE SCORES ON THE PIANO. BUT THEN WITH THE ROBBERY IN THE KITCHEN, I MOVED AWAY. WHEN I CAME BACK, THEY WERE NO LONGER THERE!
WHAT HAPPENED TO THIS LITTLE BOY? WHY IS HE SO SAD?
THEY STOLE THE SCORES HE WAS SUPPOSED TO PERFORM FROM THIS EVENING!
OH, YOU POOR THING!
I WON'T BE ABLE TO PLAY WITHOUT THE SCORES!

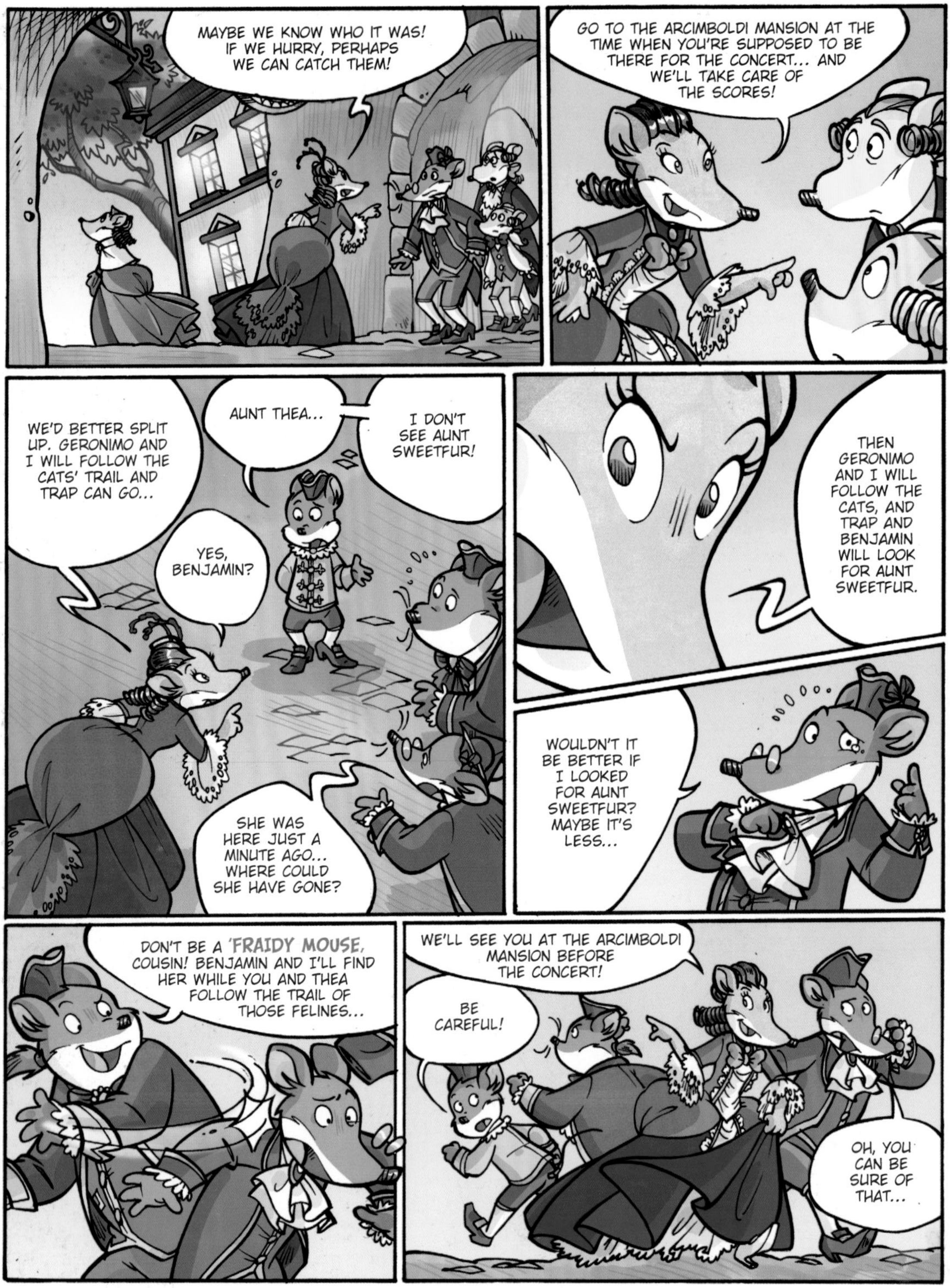

MAYBE WE KNOW WHO IT WAS! IF WE HURRY, PERHAPS WE CAN CATCH THEM!
GO TO THE ARCIMBOLDI MANSION AT THE TIME WHEN YOU'RE SUPPOSED TO BE THERE FOR THE CONCERT... AND WE'LL TAKE CARE OF THE SCORES!
WE'D BETTER SPLIT UP. GERONIMO AND I WILL FOLLOW THE CATS' TRAIL AND TRAP CAN GO...
AUNT THEA...
I DON'T SEE AUNT SWEETFUR!
YES, BENJAMIN?
SHE WAS HERE JUST A MINUTE AGO... WHERE COULD SHE HAVE GONE?
THEN GERONIMO AND I WILL FOLLOW THE CATS, AND TRAP AND BENJAMIN WILL LOOK FOR AUNT SWEETFUR.
WOULDN'T IT BE BETTER IF I LOOKED FOR AUNT SWEETFUR? MAYBE IT'S LESS...
DON'T BE A 'FRAIDY MOUSE, COUSIN! BENJAMIN AND I'LL FIND HER WHILE YOU AND THEA FOLLOW THE TRAIL OF THOSE FELINES...
WE'LL SEE YOU AT THE ARCIMBOLDI MANSION BEFORE THE CONCERT!
BE CAREFUL!
OH, YOU CAN BE SURE OF THAT...

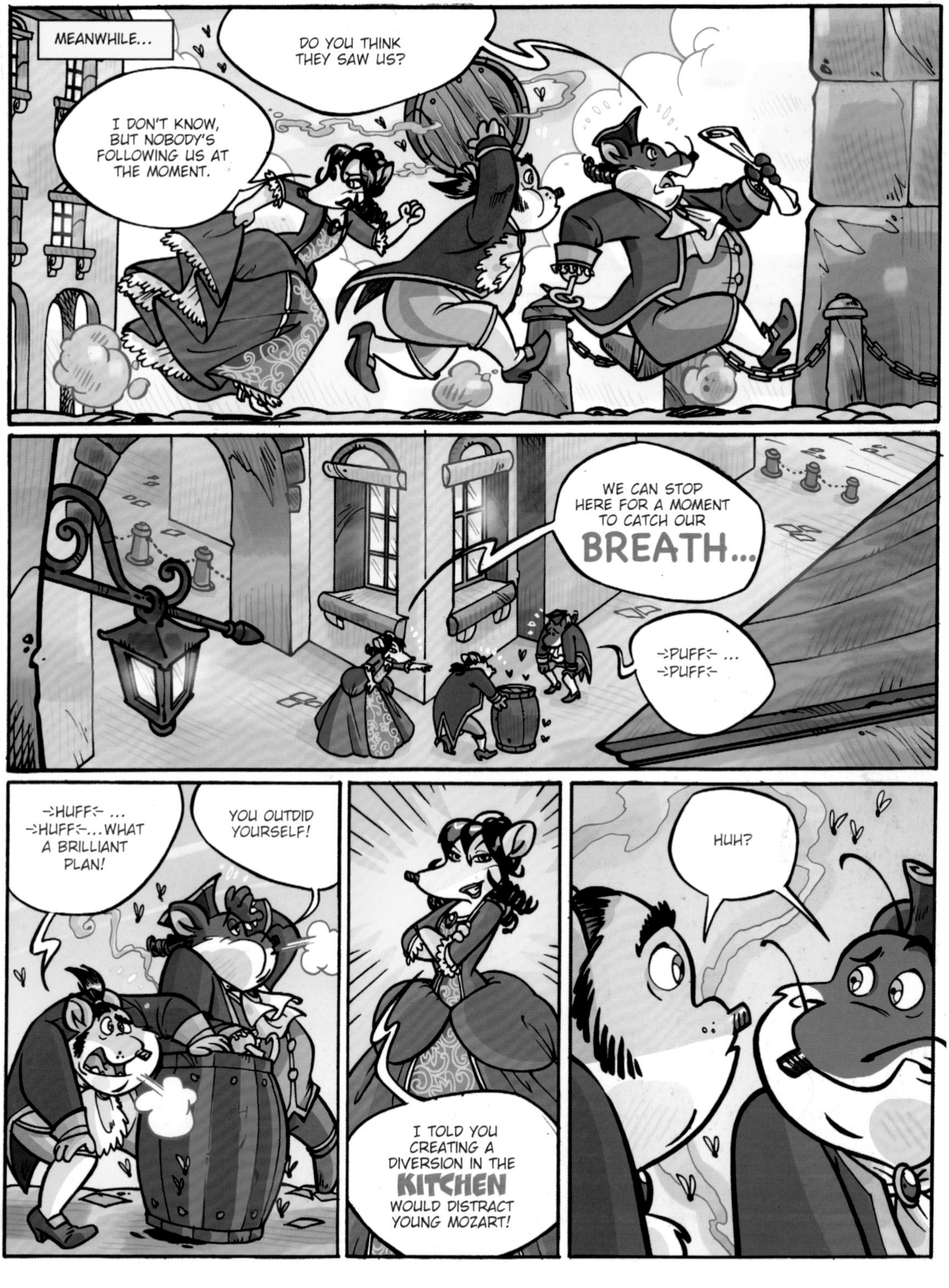
MEANWHILE...
DO YOU THINK THEY SAW US?
I DON'T KNOW, BUT NOBODY'S FOLLOWING US AT THE MOMENT.
WE CAN STOP HERE FOR A MOMENT TO CATCH OUR BREATH...
-PUFF- ... -PUFF-
-HUFF- ... -HUFF-...WHAT A BRILLIANT PLAN!
YOU OUTDID YOURSELF!
I TOLD YOU CREATING A DIVERSION IN THE KITCHEN WOULD DISTRACT YOUNG MOZART!
HUH?

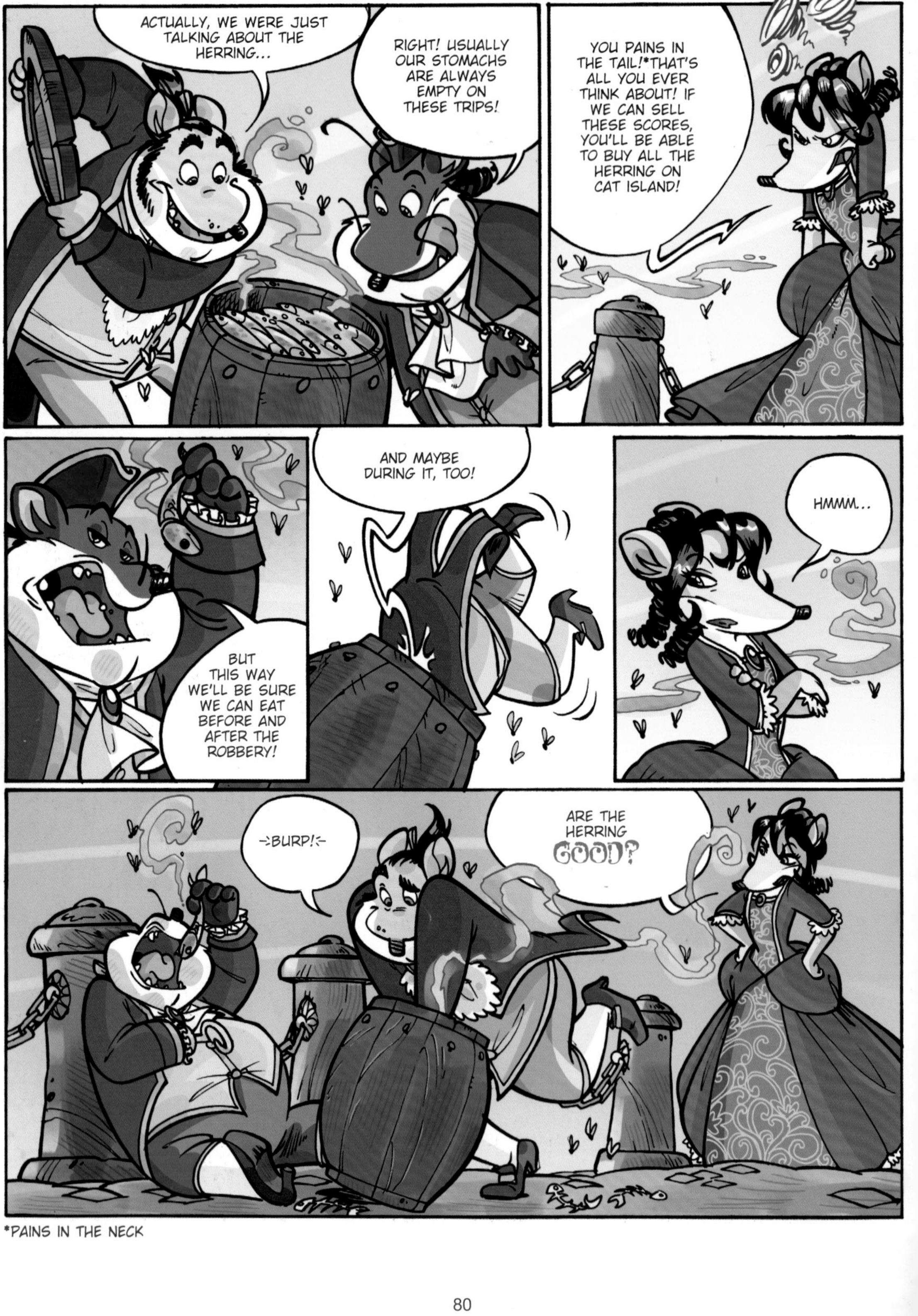
ACTUALLY, WE WERE JUST TALKING ABOUT THE HERRING...
RIGHT! USUALLY OUR STOMACHS ARE ALWAYS EMPTY ON THESE TRIPS!
YOU PAINS IN THE TAIL!*THAT'S ALL YOU EVER THINK ABOUT! IF WE CAN SELL THESE SCORES, YOU'LL BE ABLE TO BUY ALL THE HERRING ON CAT ISLAND!
BUT THIS WAY WE'LL BE SURE WE CAN EAT BEFORE AND AFTER THE ROBBERY!
AND MAYBE DURING IT, TOO!
HMMM...
-BURP!-
ARE THE HERRING GOOD?

*PAINS IN THE NECK

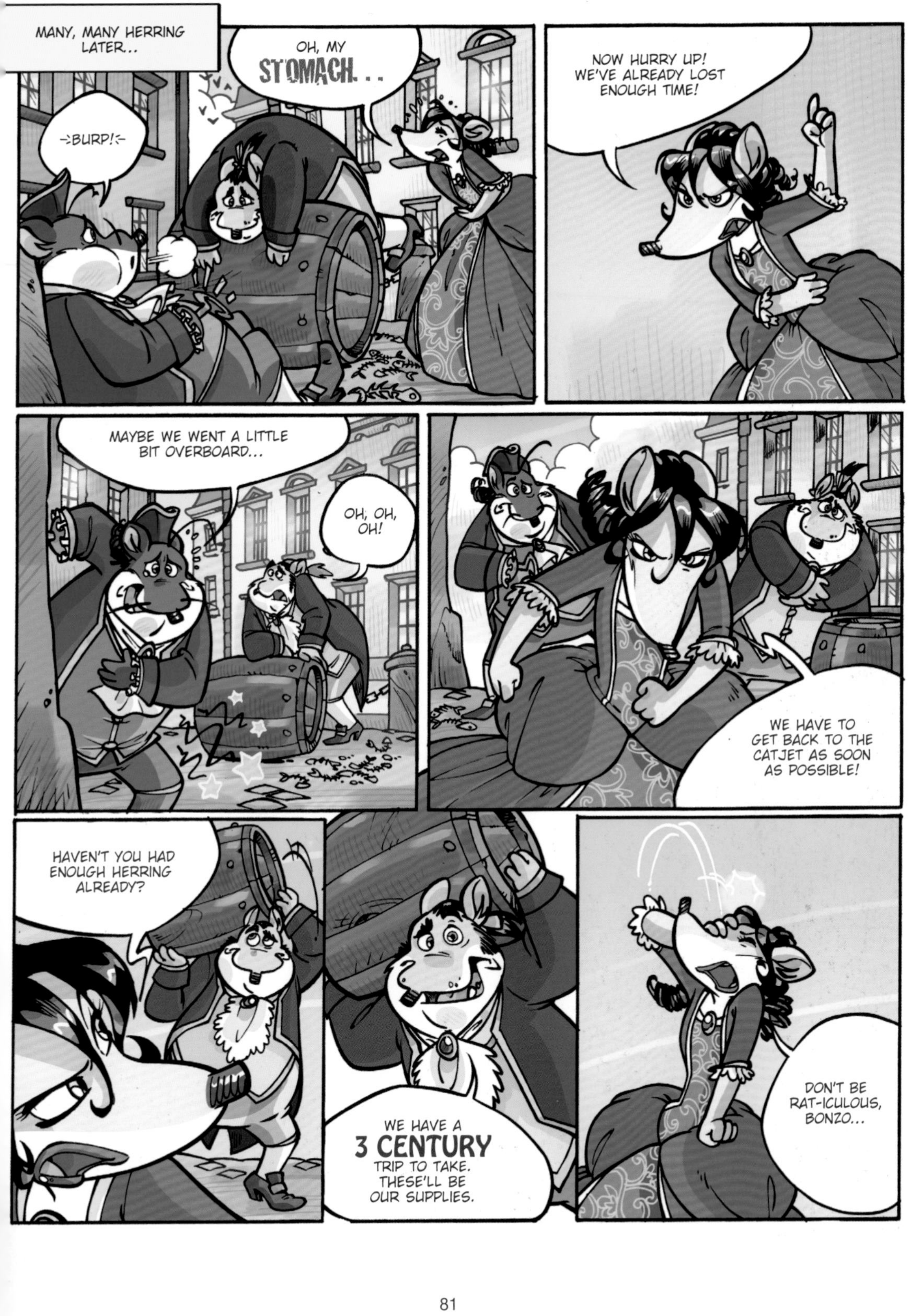
MANY, MANY HERRING LATER...
OH, MY STOMACH...
-BURP!-
NOW HURRY UP! WE'VE ALREADY LOST ENOUGH TIME!
MAYBE WE WENT A LITTLE BIT OVERBOARD...
OH, OH, OH!
WE HAVE TO GET BACK TO THE CATJET AS SOON AS POSSIBLE!
HAVEN'T YOU HAD ENOUGH HERRING ALREADY?
WE HAVE A 3 CENTURY TRIP TO TAKE. THESE'LL BE OUR SUPPLIES.
DON'T BE RAT-ICULOUS, BONZO...

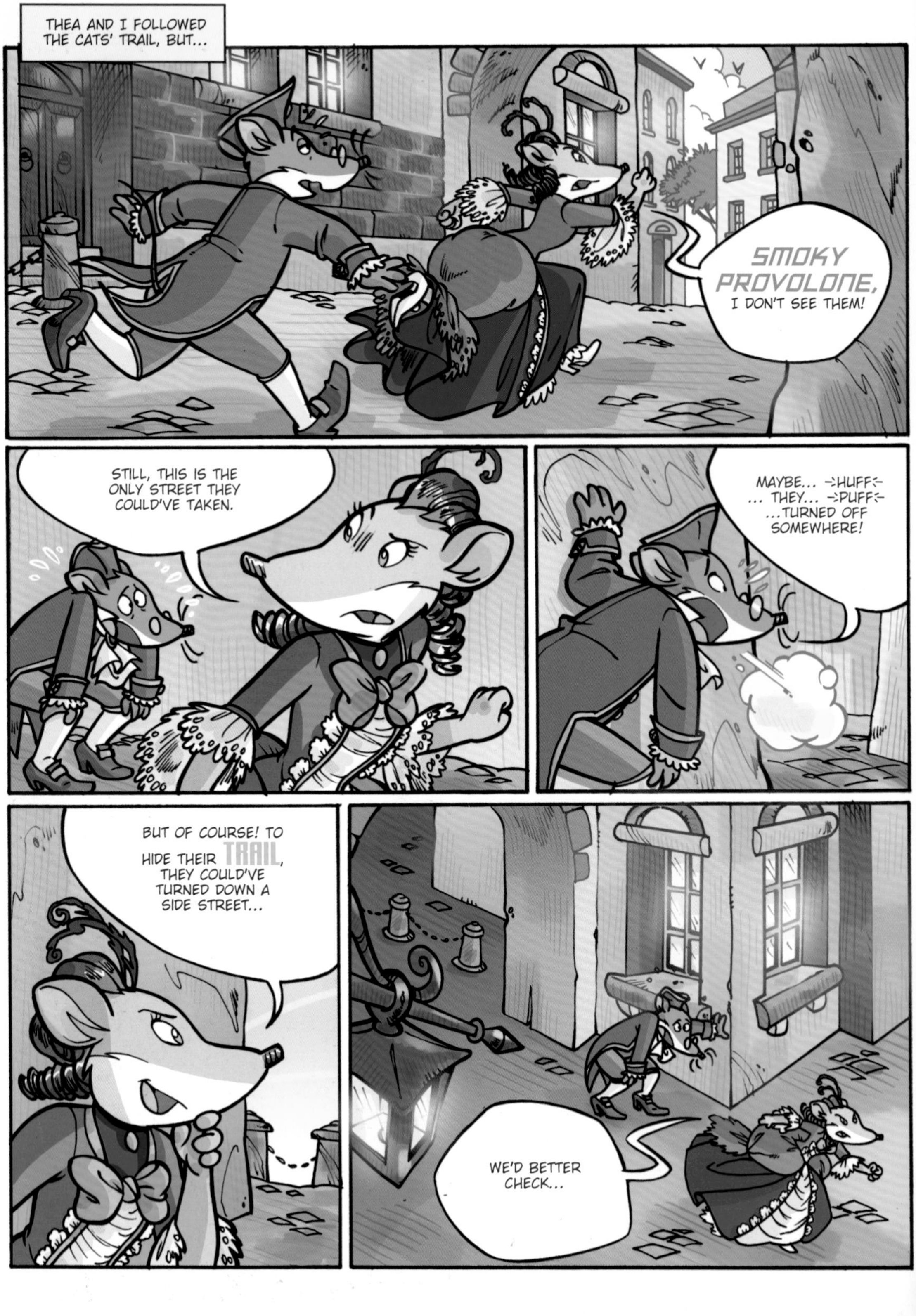
THEA AND I FOLLOWED THE CATS' TRAIL, BUT...
SMOKY PROVOLONE, I DON'T SEE THEM!
STILL, THIS IS THE ONLY STREET THEY COULD'VE TAKEN.
MAYBE... -HUFF- ... THEY... -PUFF- ...TURNED OFF SOMEWHERE!
BUT OF COURSE! TO HIDE THEIR TRAIL, THEY COULD'VE TURNED DOWN A SIDE STREET...
WE'D BETTER CHECK...

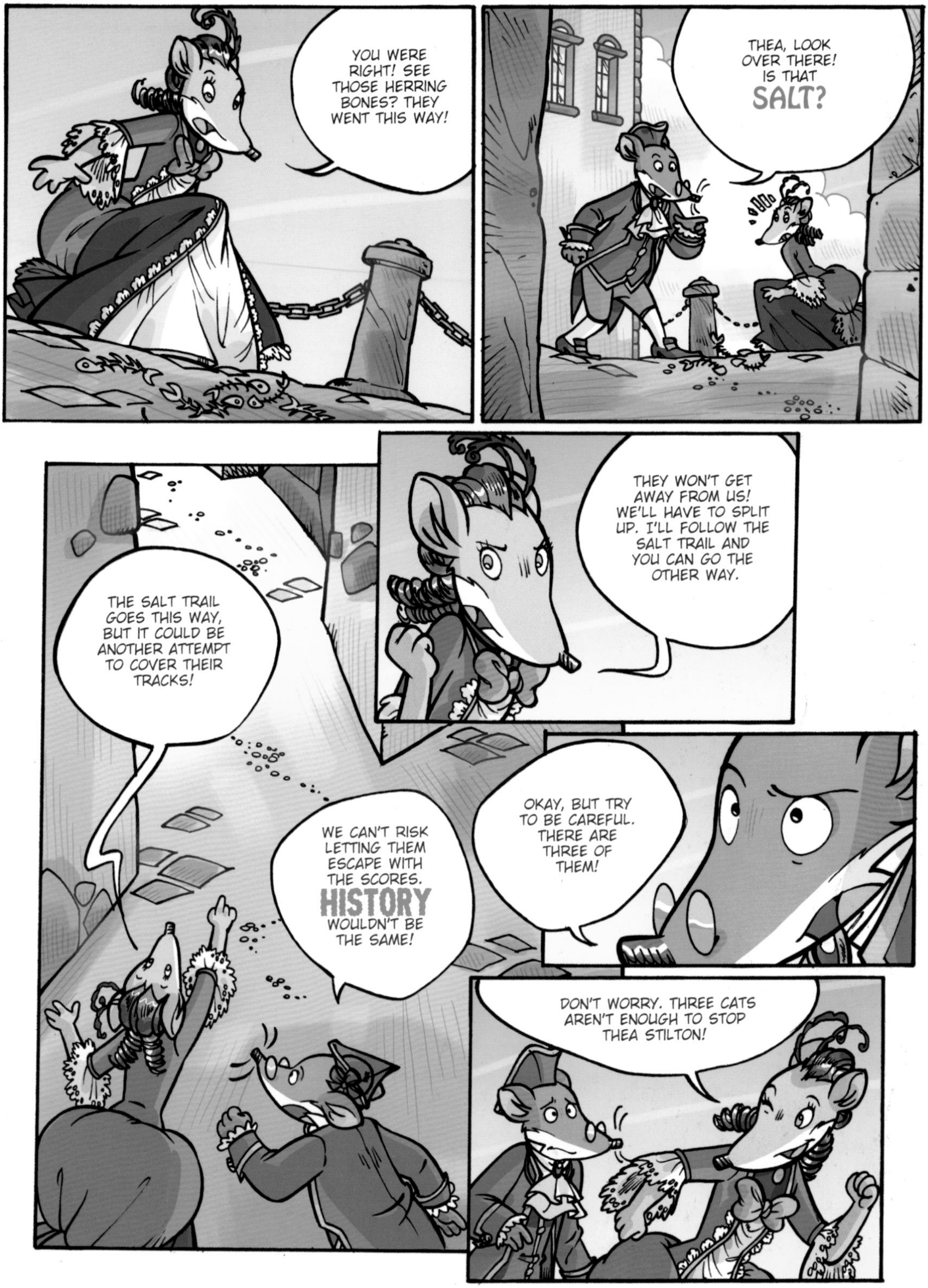
YOU WERE RIGHT! SEE THOSE HERRING BONES? THEY WENT THIS WAY!
THEA, LOOK OVER THERE! IS THAT SALT?
THEY WON'T GET AWAY FROM US! WE'LL HAVE TO SPLIT UP. I'LL FOLLOW THE SALT TRAIL AND YOU CAN GO THE OTHER WAY.
THE SALT TRAIL GOES THIS WAY, BUT IT COULD BE ANOTHER ATTEMPT TO COVER THEIR TRACKS!
WE CAN'T RISK LETTING THEM ESCAPE WITH THE SCORES. HISTORY WOULDN'T BE THE SAME!
OKAY, BUT TRY TO BE CAREFUL. THERE ARE THREE OF THEM!
DON'T WORRY. THREE CATS AREN'T ENOUGH TO STOP THEA STILTON!

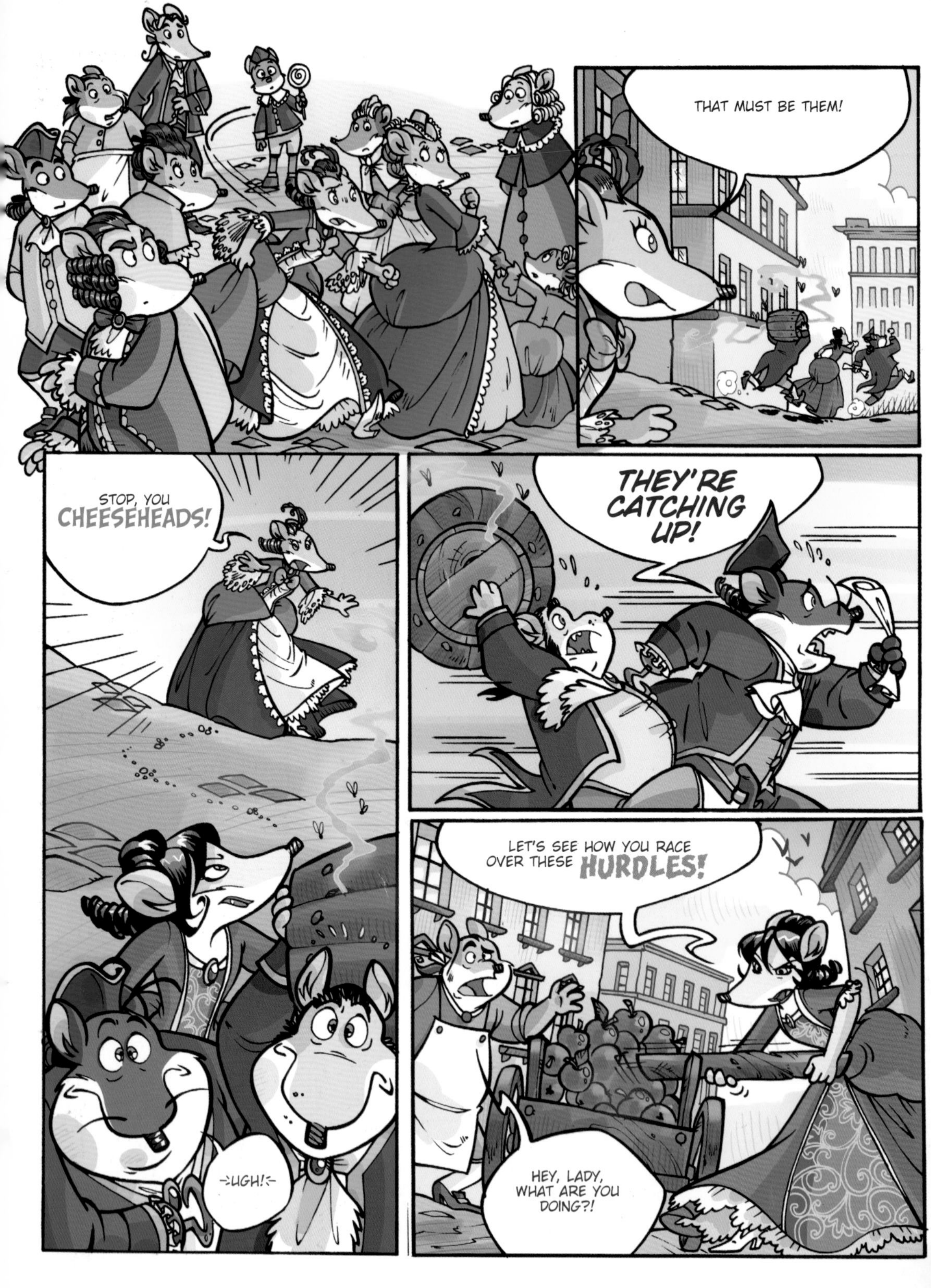
THAT MUST BE THEM!
STOP, YOU CHEESEHEADS!
THEY'RE CATCHING UP!
LET'S SEE HOW YOU RACE OVER THESE HURDLES!
HEY, LADY, WHAT ARE YOU DOING?!
UGH!

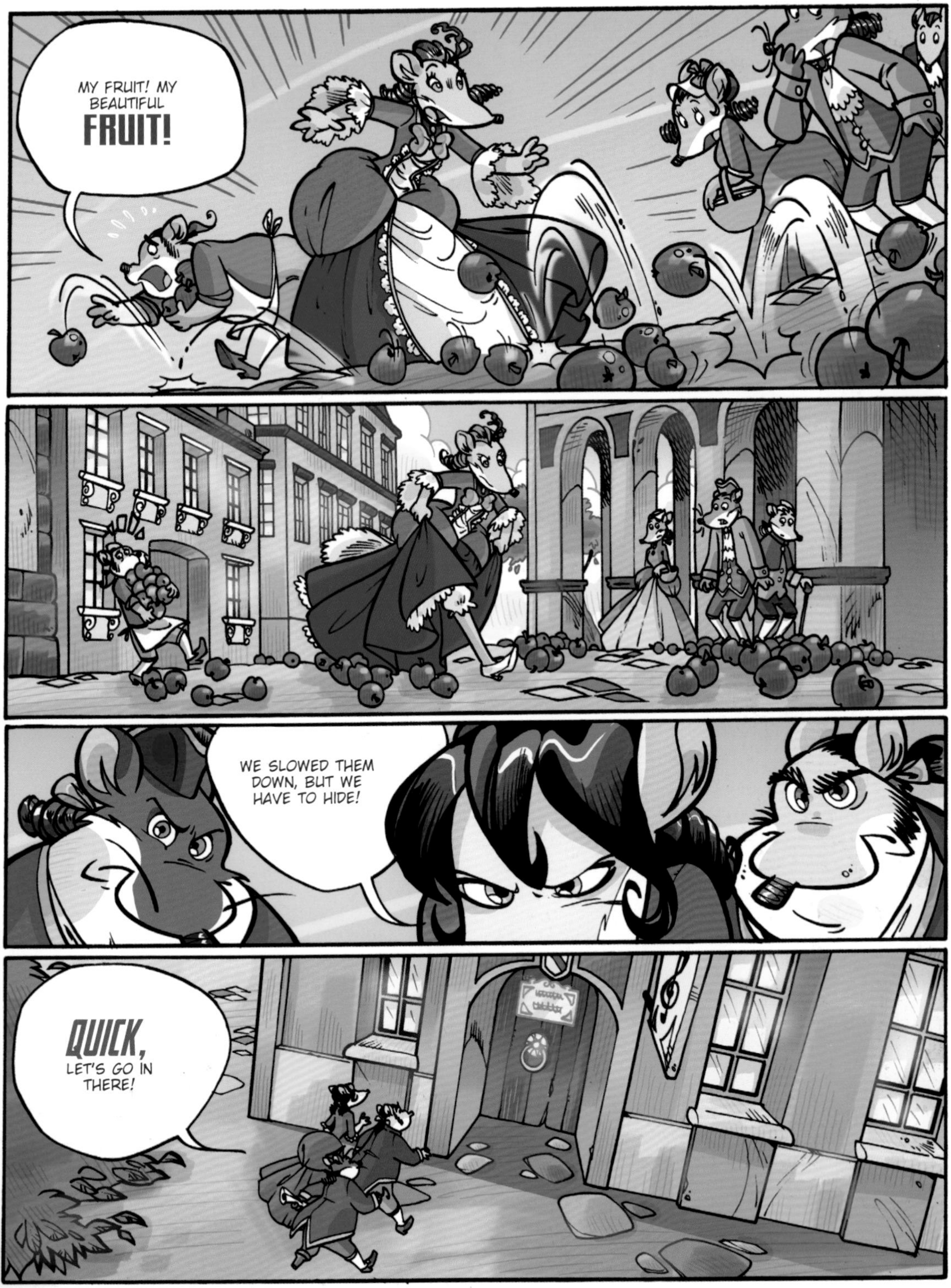
MY FRUIT! MY BEAUTIFUL FRUIT!
WE SLOWED THEM DOWN, BUT WE HAVE TO HIDE!
QUICK, LET'S GO IN THERE!

DING
WHERE ARE WE? WHAT IS THIS PLACE?
IT SEEMS LIKE A MUSICAL INSTRUMENT SHOP... THE BEST PLACE FOR HIDING SCORES!
ARE YOU SURE YOU WANT TO LEAVE THEM HERE?
ONLY WE KNOW THEY'RE IN HERE. AND IN THE MIDST OF THIS MESS, EVEN IF SOMEONE WERE LOOKING FOR THE SCORES, THEY'D NEVER BE ABLE TO FIND ANYTHING!
LET'S COME BACK WHEN THE COAST IS CLEAR!

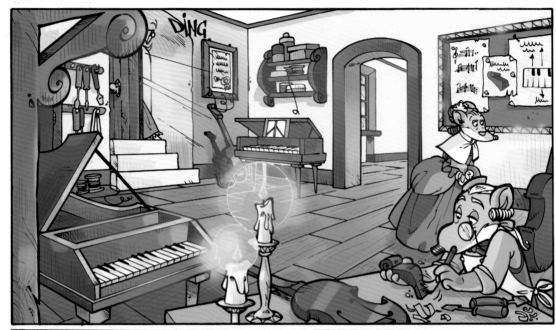

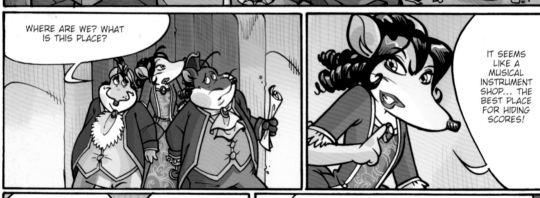

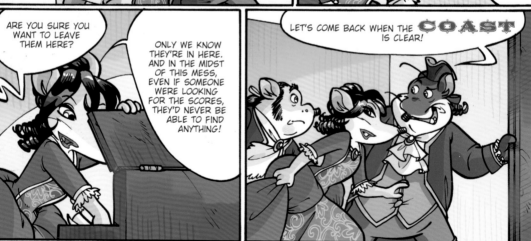

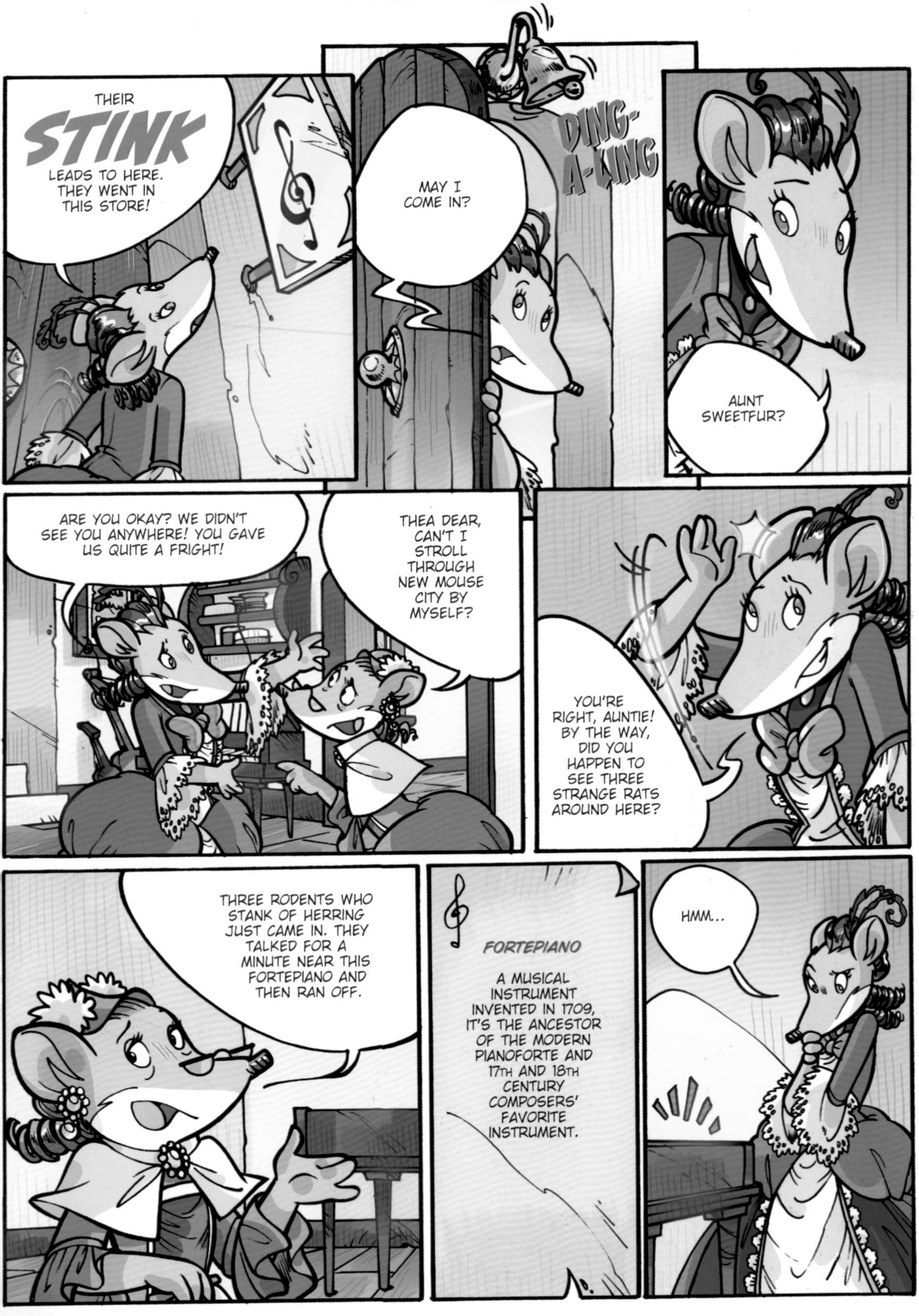
THEIR STINK LEADS TO HERE. THEY WENT IN THIS STORE!
MAY I COME IN?
DING-A-LING
AUNT SWEETFUR?
ARE YOU OKAY? WE DIDN'T SEE YOU ANYWHERE! YOU GAVE US QUITE A FRIGHT!
THEA DEAR, CAN'T I STROLL THROUGH NEW MOUSE CITY BY MYSELF?
YOU'RE RIGHT, AUNTIE! BY THE WAY, DID YOU HAPPEN TO SEE THREE STRANGE RATS AROUND HERE?
THREE RODENTS WHO STANK OF HERRING JUST CAME IN. THEY TALKED FOR A MINUTE NEAR THIS FORTEPIANO AND THEN RAN OFF.
FORTEPIANO
A MUSICAL INSTRUMENT INVENTED IN 1709, IT'S THE ANCESTOR OF THE MODERN PIANOFORTE AND 17TH AND 18TH CENTURY COMPOSERS' FAVORITE INSTRUMENT.
HMM...

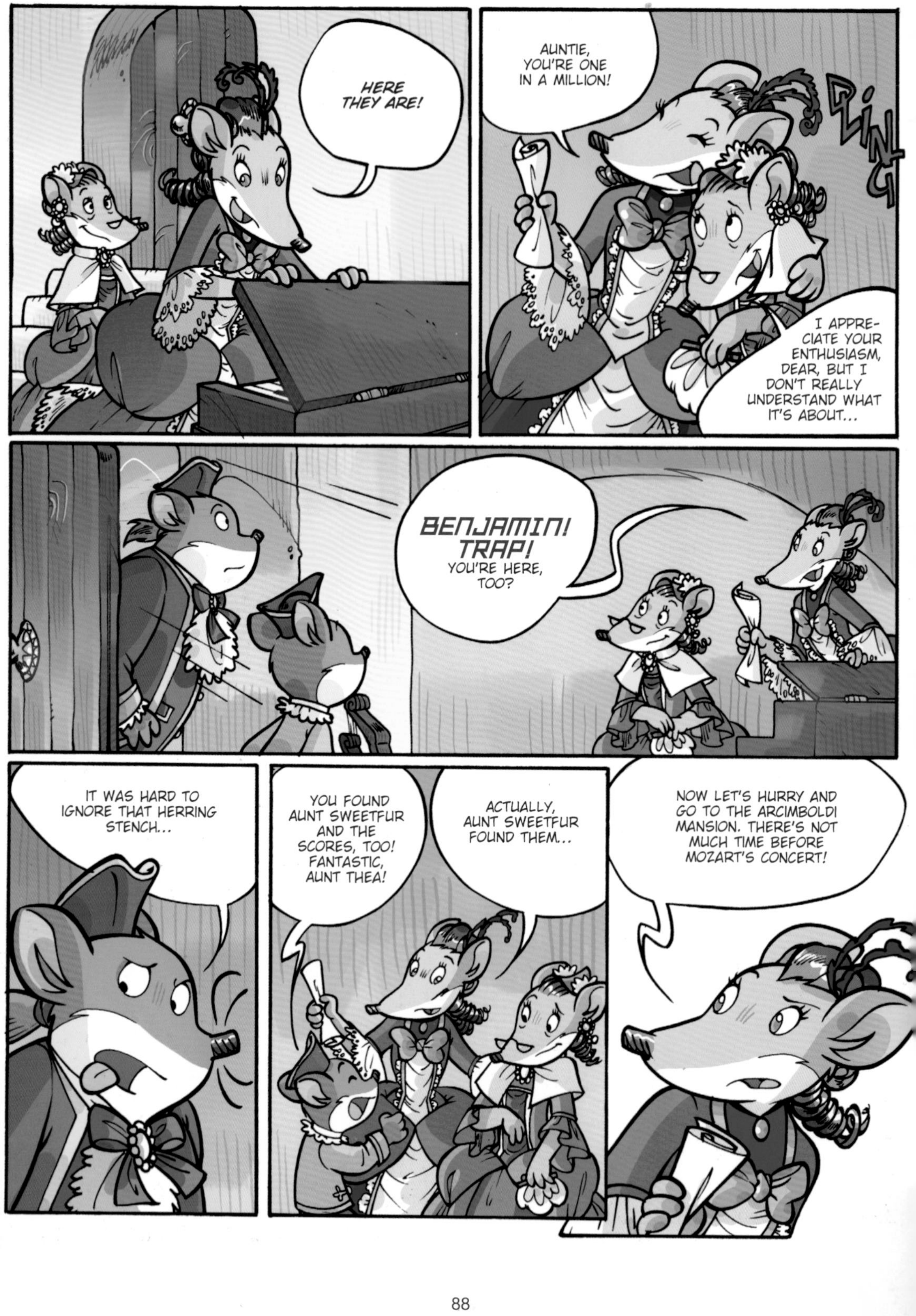
HERE THEY ARE!
AUNTIE, YOU'RE ONE IN A MILLION!
DLING
I APPRECIATE YOUR ENTHUSIASM, DEAR, BUT I DON'T REALLY UNDERSTAND WHAT IT'S ABOUT...
BENJAMIN! TRAP! YOU'RE HERE, TOO?
IT WAS HARD TO IGNORE THAT HERRING STENCH...
YOU FOUND AUNT SWEETFUR AND THE SCORES, TOO! FANTASTIC, AUNT THEA!
ACTUALLY, AUNT SWEETFUR FOUND THEM...
NOW LET'S HURRY AND GO TO THE ARCIMBOLDI MANSION. THERE'S NOT MUCH TIME BEFORE MOZART'S CONCERT!

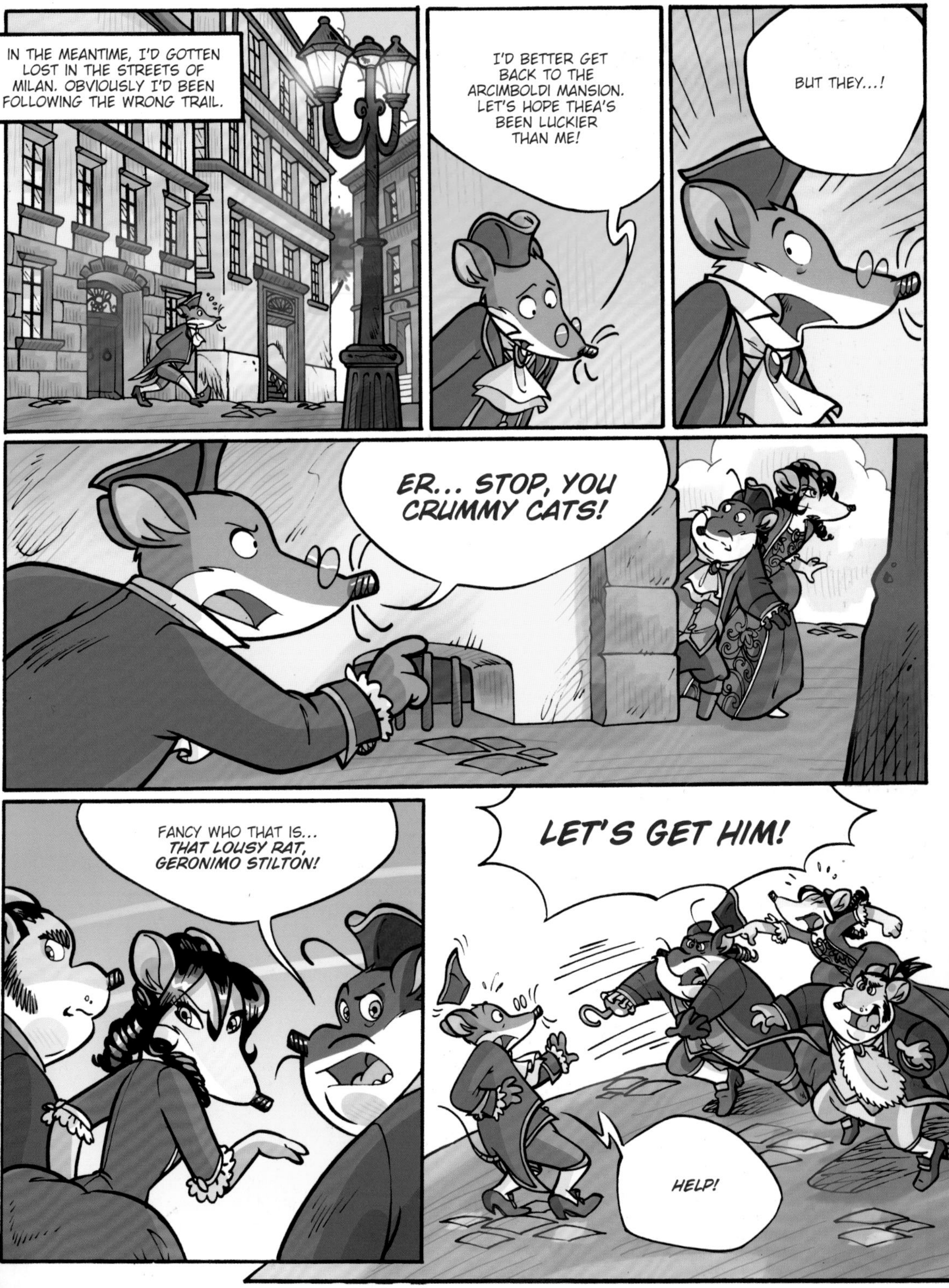
IN THE MEANTIME, I'D GOTTEN LOST IN THE STREETS OF MILAN. OBVIOUSLY I'D BEEN FOLLOWING THE WRONG TRAIL.
I'D BETTER GET BACK TO THE ARCIMBOLDI MANSION. LET'S HOPE THEA'S BEEN LUCKIER THAN ME!
BUT THEY...!
ER... STOP, YOU CRUMMY CATS!
FANCY WHO THAT IS... THAT LOUSY RAT, GERONIMO STILTON!
LET'S GET HIM!
HELP!

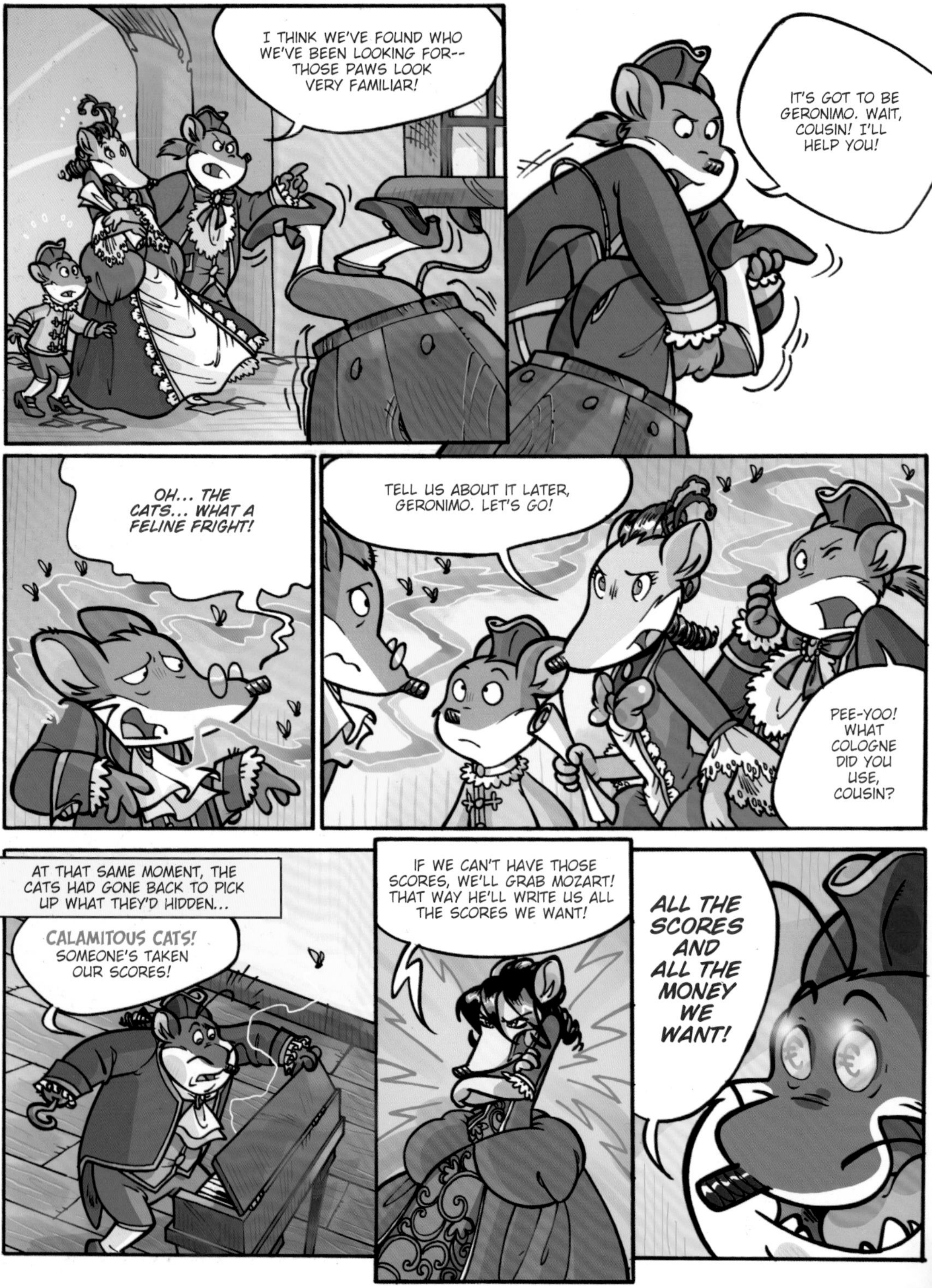
I THINK WE'VE FOUND WHO WE'VE BEEN LOOKING FOR-- THOSE PAWS LOOK VERY FAMILIAR!
IT'S GOT TO BE GERONIMO. WAIT, COUSIN! I'LL HELP YOU!
OH... THE CATS... WHAT A FELINE FRIGHT!
TELL US ABOUT IT LATER, GERONIMO. LET'S GO!
PEE-YOO! WHAT COLOGNE DID YOU USE, COUSIN?
AT THAT SAME MOMENT, THE CATS HAD GONE BACK TO PICK UP WHAT THEY'D HIDDEN...
CALAMITOUS CATS! SOMEONE'S TAKEN OUR SCORES!
IF WE CAN'T HAVE THOSE SCORES, WE'LL GRAB MOZART! THAT WAY HE'LL WRITE US ALL THE SCORES WE WANT!
ALL THE SCORES AND ALL THE MONEY WE WANT!

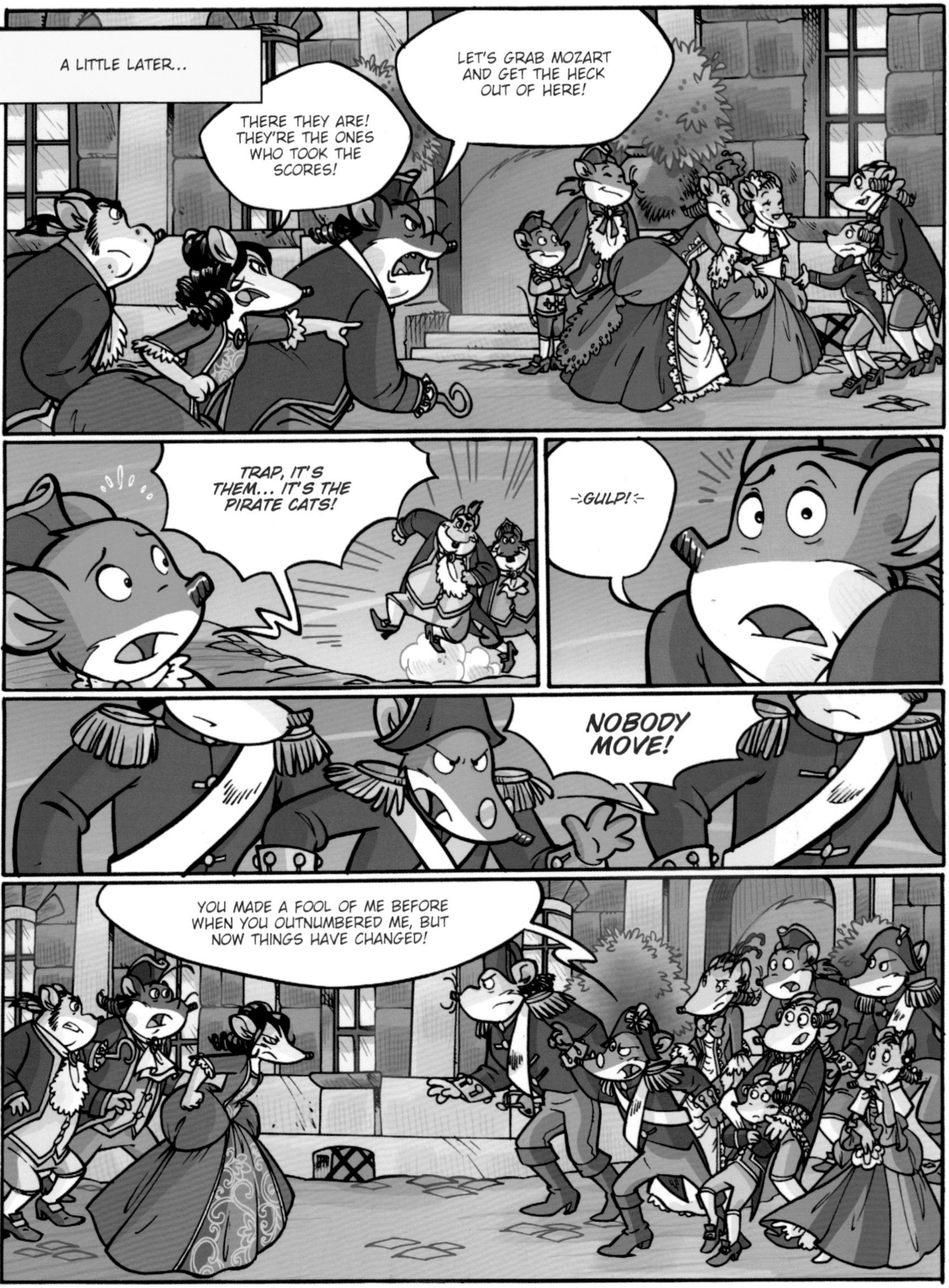
A LITTLE LATER...
THERE THEY ARE! THEY'RE THE ONES WHO TOOK THE SCORES!
LET'S GRAB MOZART AND GET THE HECK OUT OF HERE!
TRAP, IT'S THEM... IT'S THE PIRATE CATS!
GULP!
NOBODY MOVE!
YOU MADE A FOOL OF ME BEFORE WHEN YOU OUTNUMBERED ME, BUT NOW THINGS HAVE CHANGED!

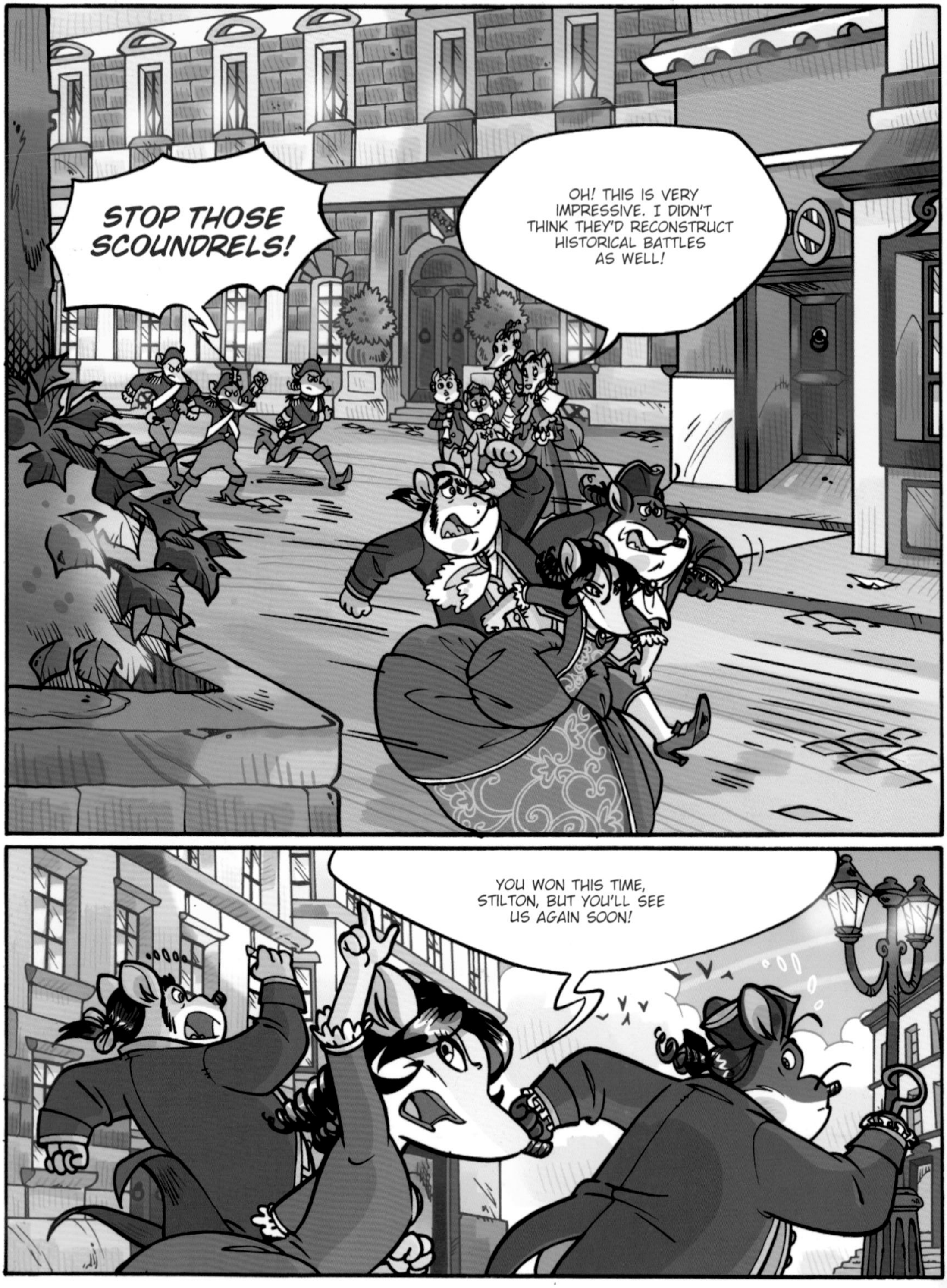
STOP THOSE SCOUNDRELS!
OH! THIS IS VERY IMPRESSIVE. I DIDN'T THINK THEY'D RECONSTRUCT HISTORICAL BATTLES AS WELL!
YOU WON THIS TIME, STILTON, BUT YOU'LL SEE US AGAIN SOON!

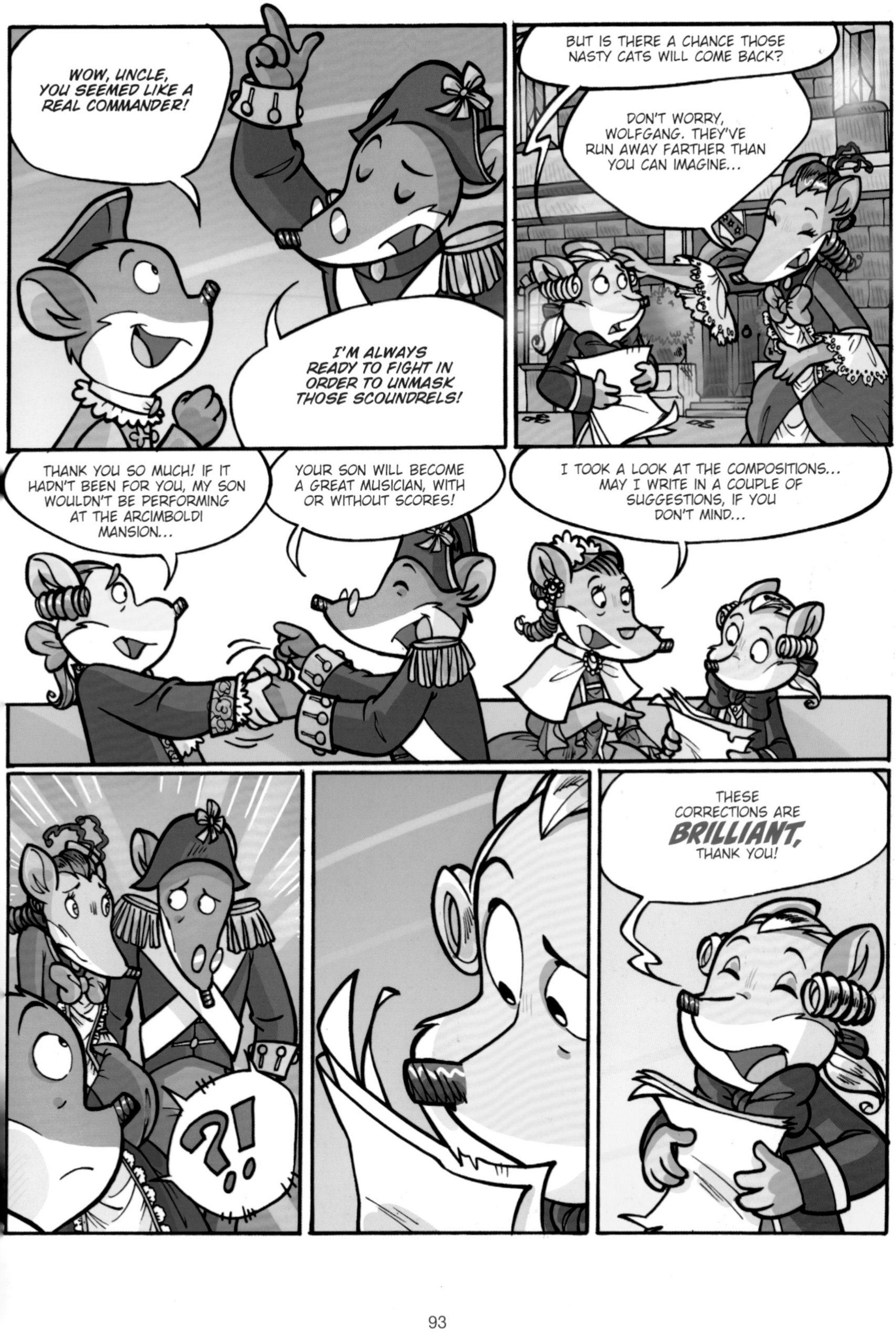

WOW, UNCLE, YOU SEEMED LIKE A REAL COMMANDER!
I'M ALWAYS READY TO FIGHT IN ORDER TO UNMASK THOSE SCOUNDRELS!
BUT IS THERE A CHANCE THOSE NASTY CATS WILL COME BACK?
DON'T WORRY, WOLFGANG. THEY'VE RUN AWAY FARTHER THAN YOU CAN IMAGINE...
THANK YOU SO MUCH! IF IT HADN'T BEEN FOR YOU, MY SON WOULDN'T BE PERFORMING AT THE ARCIMBOLDI MANSION...
YOUR SON WILL BECOME A GREAT MUSICIAN, WITH OR WITHOUT SCORES!
I TOOK A LOOK AT THE COMPOSITIONS... MAY I WRITE IN A COUPLE OF SUGGESTIONS, IF YOU DON'T MIND...
?!
THESE CORRECTIONS ARE BRILLIANT, THANK YOU!

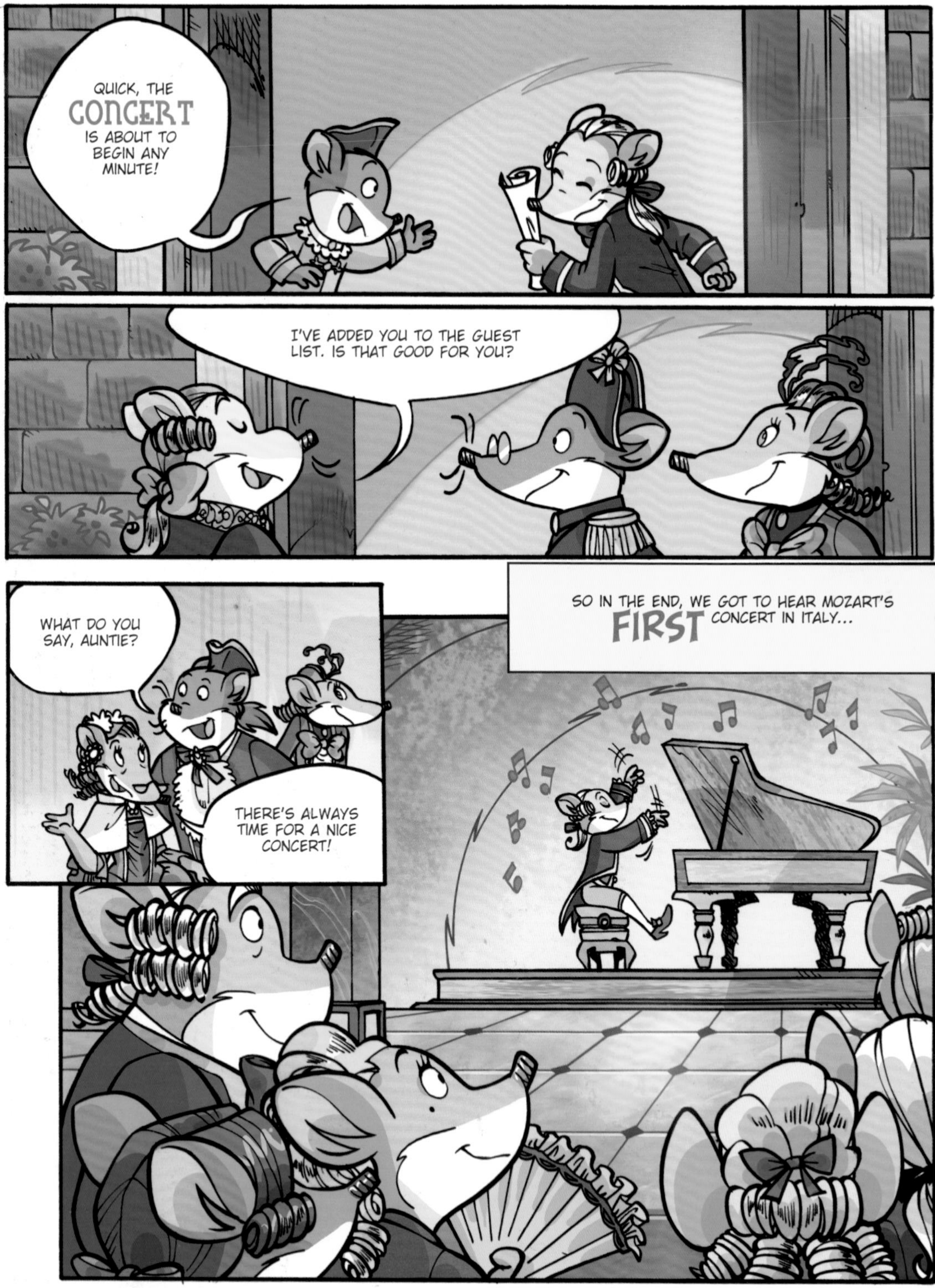
QUICK, THE CONCERT IS ABOUT TO BEGIN ANY MINUTE!
I'VE ADDED YOU TO THE GUEST LIST. IS THAT GOOD FOR YOU?
WHAT DO YOU SAY, AUNTIE?
THERE'S ALWAYS TIME FOR A NICE CONCERT!
SO IN THE END, WE GOT TO HEAR MOZART'S FIRST CONCERT IN ITALY...

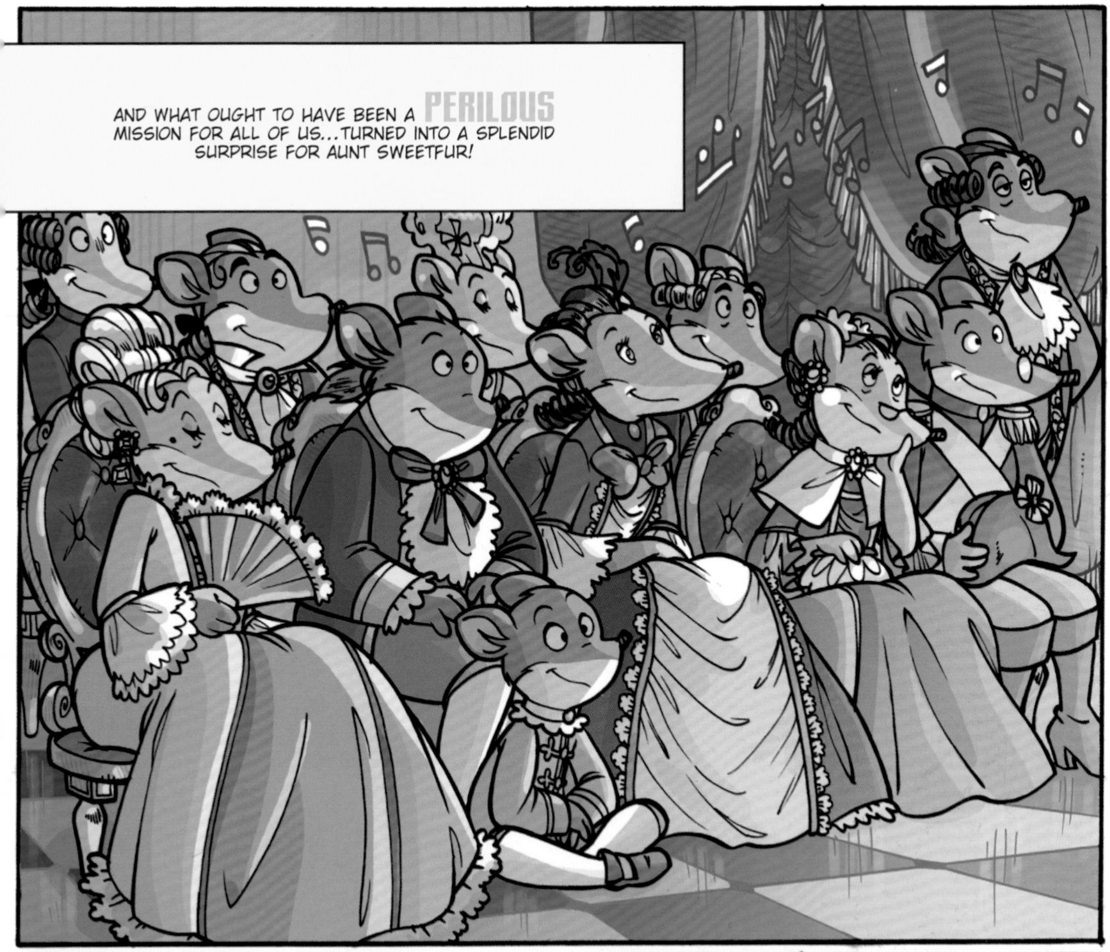
AND WHAT OUGHT TO HAVE BEEN A PERILOUS MISSION FOR ALL OF US...TURNED INTO A SPLENDID SURPRISE FOR AUNT SWEETFUR!

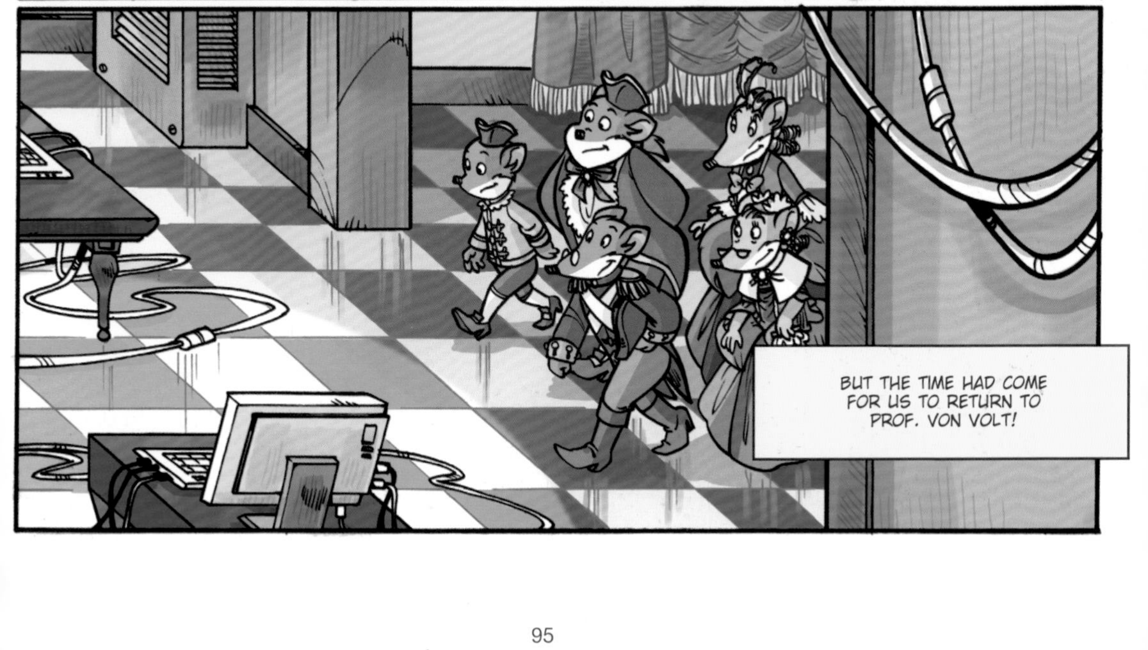
BUT THE TIME HAD COME FOR US TO RETURN TO PROF. VON VOLT!

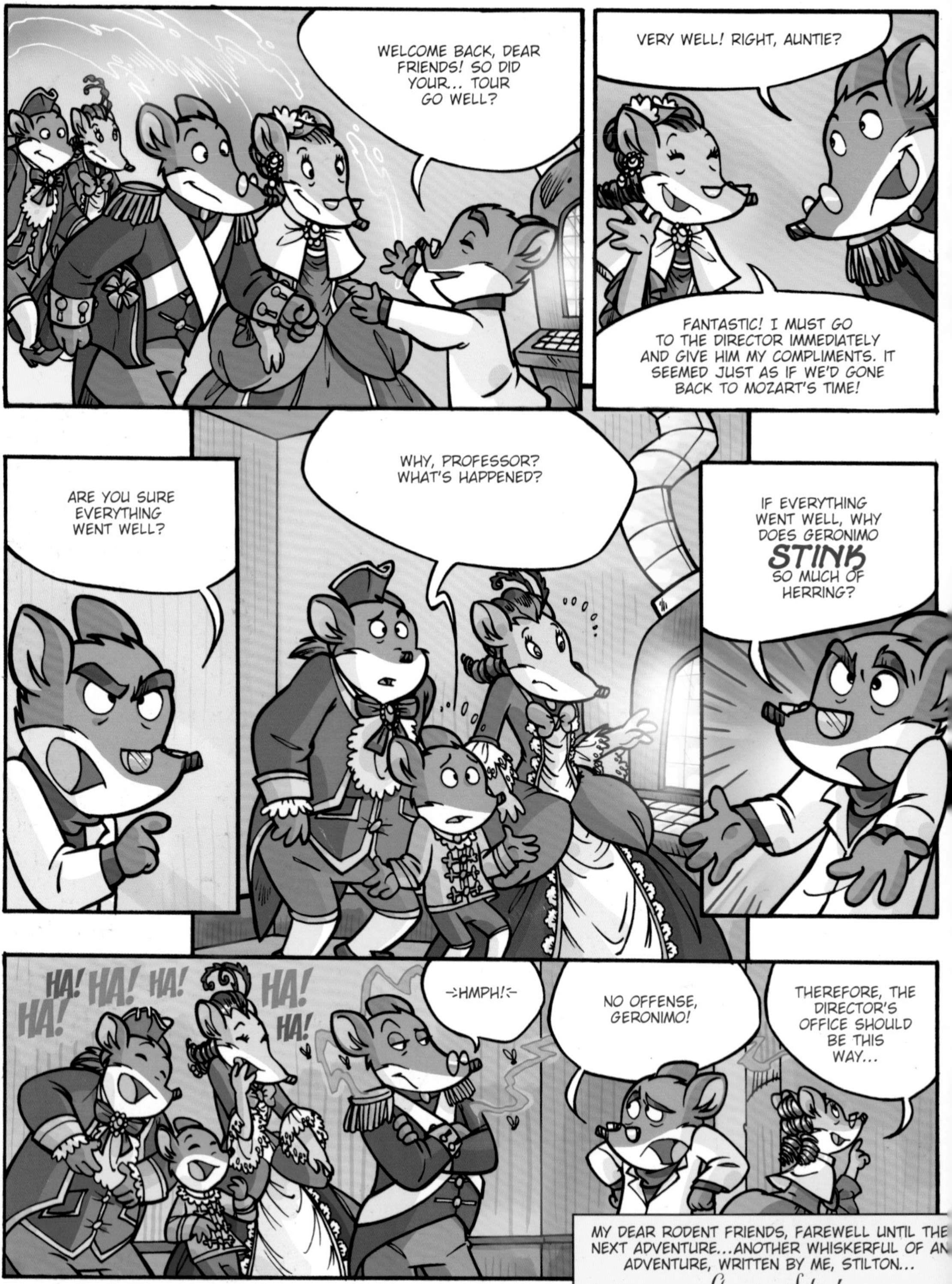
WELCOME BACK, DEAR FRIENDS! SO DID YOUR... TOUR GO WELL?
VERY WELL! RIGHT, AUNTIE?
FANTASTIC! I MUST GO TO THE DIRECTOR IMMEDIATELY AND GIVE HIM MY COMPLIMENTS. IT SEEMED JUST AS IF WE'D GONE BACK TO MOZART'S TIME!
ARE YOU SURE EVERYTHING WENT WELL?
WHY, PROFESSOR? WHAT'S HAPPENED?
IF EVERYTHING WENT WELL, WHY DOES GERONIMO STINK SO MUCH OF HERRING?
HA! HA! HA! HA! HA! HA!
HMPH!
NO OFFENSE, GERONIMO!
THEREFORE, THE DIRECTOR'S OFFICE SHOULD BE THIS WAY...
MY DEAR RODENT FRIENDS, FAREWELL UNTIL THE NEXT ADVENTURE...ANOTHER WHISKERFUL OF AN ADVENTURE, WRITTEN BY ME, STILTON...
Geronimo Stilton!

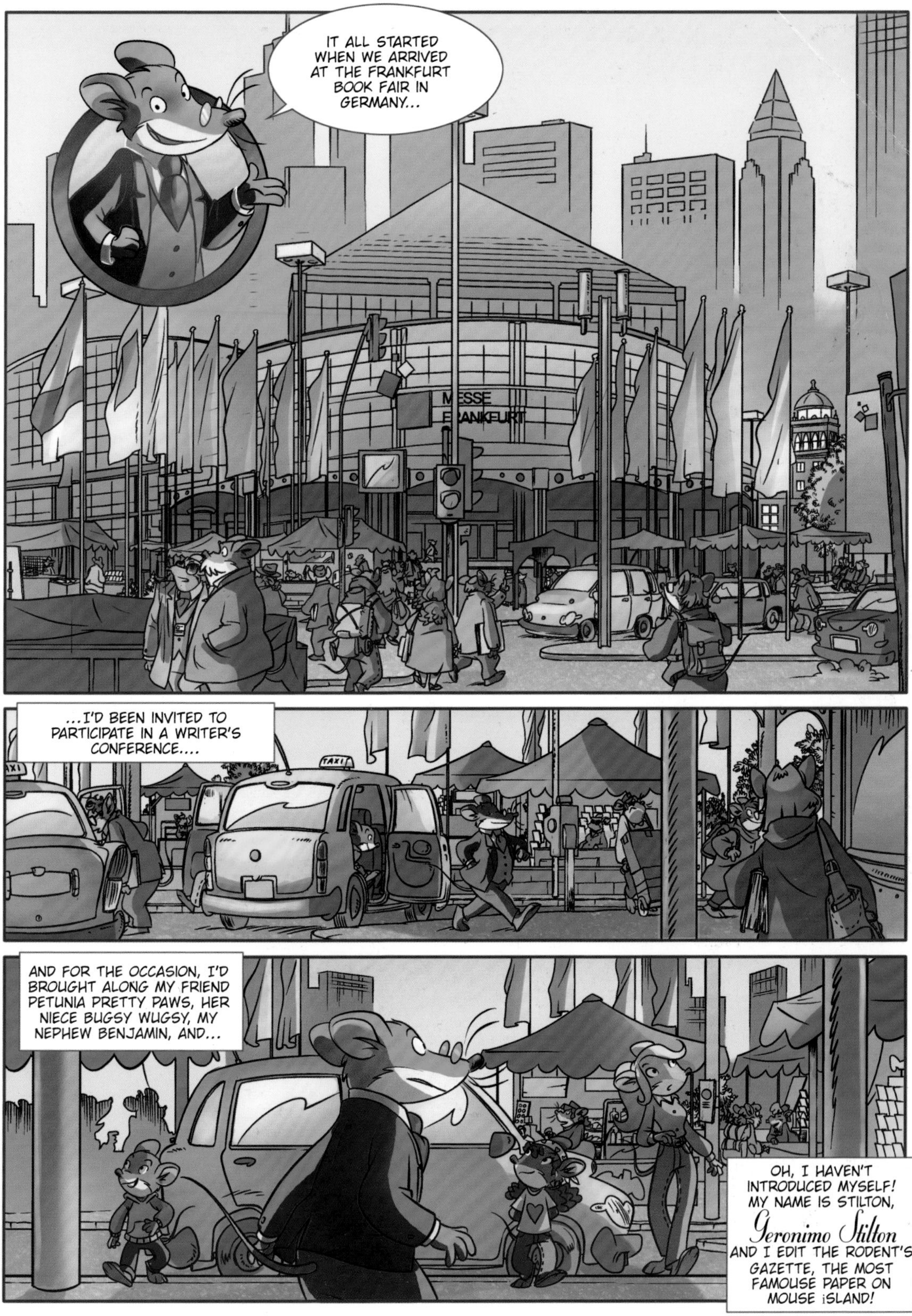

IT ALL STARTED WHEN WE ARRIVED AT THE FRANKFURT BOOK FAIR IN GERMANY...
MESSE FRANKFURT
...I'D BEEN INVITED TO PARTICIPATE IN A WRITER'S CONFERENCE....
TAXI
AND FOR THE OCCASION, I'D BROUGHT ALONG MY FRIEND PETUNIA PRETTY PAWS, HER NIECE BUGSY WUGSY, MY NEPHEW BENJAMIN, AND...
OH, I HAVEN'T INTRODUCED MYSELF! MY NAME IS STILTON, Geronimo Stilton AND I EDIT THE RODENT'S GAZETTE, THE MOST FAMOUSE PAPER ON MOUSE iSLAND!

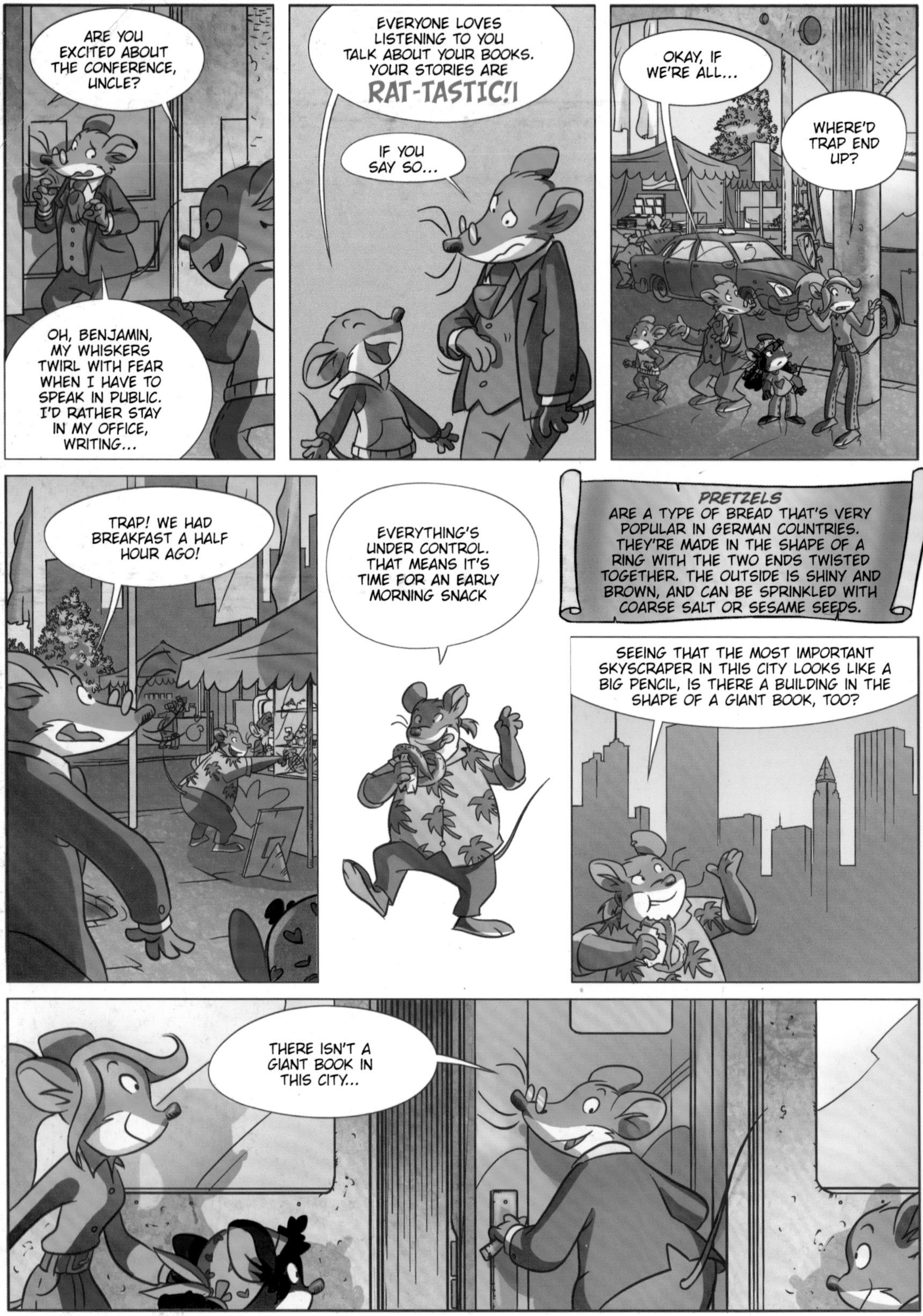
ARE YOU EXCITED ABOUT THE CONFERENCE, UNCLE?
OH, BENJAMIN, MY WHISKERS TWIRL WITH FEAR WHEN I HAVE TO SPEAK IN PUBLIC. I'D RATHER STAY IN MY OFFICE, WRITING...
EVERYONE LOVES LISTENING TO YOU TALK ABOUT YOUR BOOKS. YOUR STORIES ARE RAT-TASTIC!
IF YOU SAY SO...
OKAY, IF WE'RE ALL...
WHERE'D TRAP END UP?
TRAP! WE HAD BREAKFAST A HALF HOUR AGO!
EVERYTHING'S UNDER CONTROL. THAT MEANS IT'S TIME FOR AN EARLY MORNING SNACK
PRETZELS ARE A TYPE OF BREAD THAT'S VERY POPULAR IN GERMAN COUNTRIES. THEY'RE MADE IN THE SHAPE OF A RING WITH THE TWO ENDS TWISTED TOGETHER. THE OUTSIDE IS SHINY AND BROWN, AND CAN BE SPRINKLED WITH COARSE SALT OR SESAME SEEDS.
SEEING THAT THE MOST IMPORTANT SKYSCRAPER IN THIS CITY LOOKS LIKE A BIG PENCIL, IS THERE A BUILDING IN THE SHAPE OF A GIANT BOOK, TOO?
THERE ISN'T A GIANT BOOK IN THIS CITY...

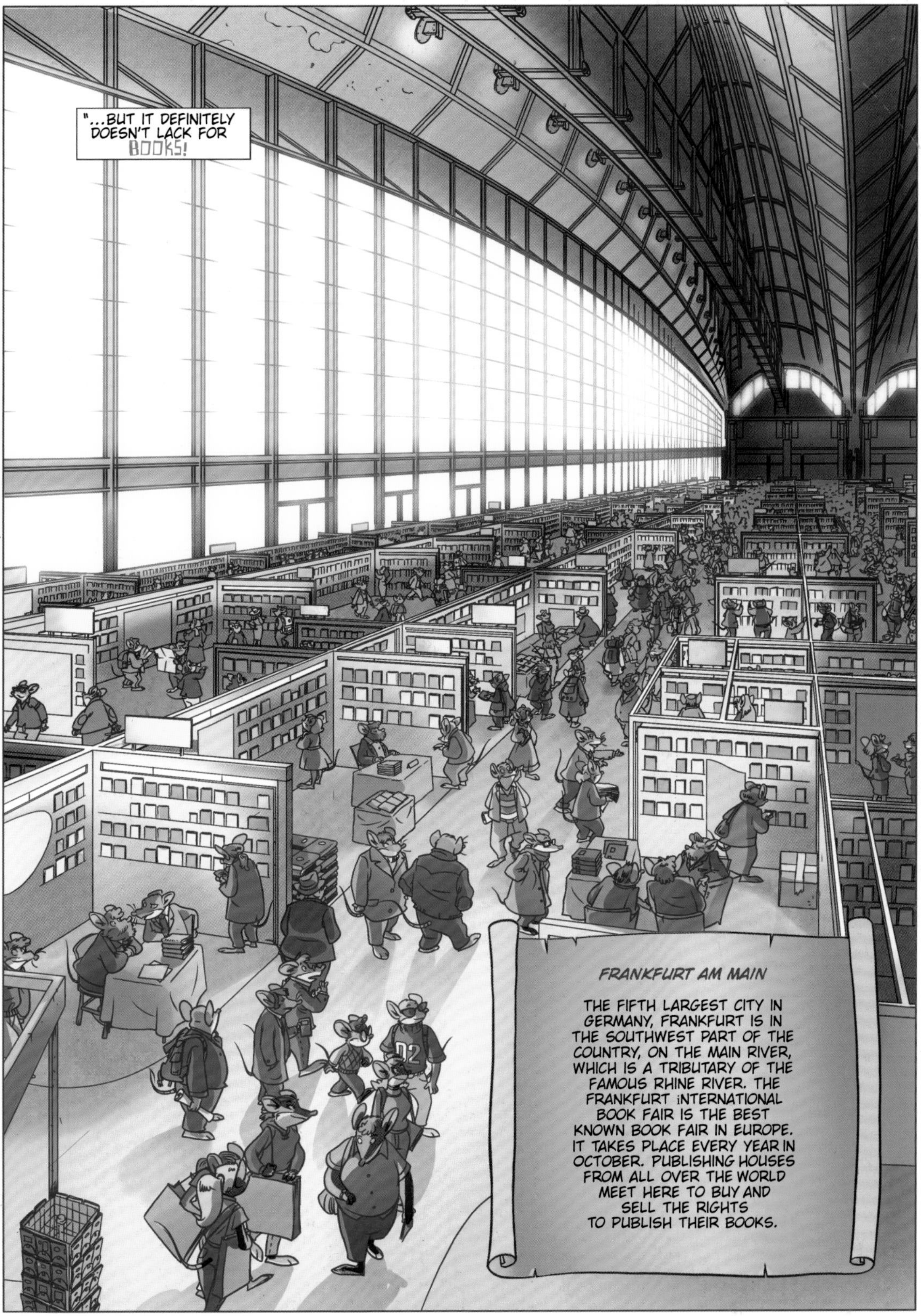
"...BUT IT DEFINITELY DOESN'T LACK FOR BOOKS!
FRANKFURT AM MAIN
THE FIFTH LARGEST CITY IN GERMANY, FRANKFURT IS IN THE SOUTHWEST PART OF THE COUNTRY, ON THE MAIN RIVER, WHICH IS A TRIBUTARY OF THE FAMOUS RHINE RIVER. THE FRANKFURT INTERNATIONAL BOOK FAIR IS THE BEST KNOWN BOOK FAIR IN EUROPE. IT TAKES PLACE EVERY YEAR IN OCTOBER. PUBLISHING HOUSES FROM ALL OVER THE WORLD MEET HERE TO BUY AND SELL THE RIGHTS TO PUBLISH THEIR BOOKS.

WHAT I DIDN'T KNOW WAS THAT PROF. VON VOLT WAS ALSO IN FRANKFURT.

JOURNEY TO MARS

WE CAN'T YET SAY FOR CERTAIN WHEN WE'LL BE ABLE TO REACH THE **RED PLANET**, BUT ACCORDING TO MY ANALYSIS, THE CONDITIONS FOR THE ABOVE MENTIONED JOURNEY WILL ARRIVE IN A RELATIVELY SHORT TIME SPAN.

I HOPE HE WON'T TAKE SO LONG THIS TIME. HIS TALKS NEVER LAST LESS THAN TWO HOURS!

WE'LL JUST HAVE TO PUT UP WITH IT.

...IN MY LATEST BOOK **JOURNEY TO MARS**, I CONSIDER THE TECHNOLOGICAL ADVANCES OF THE PAST 50 YEARS OF HISTORY IN ORDER TO ASSESS THE TECHNOLOGICAL DEVELOPMENT REQUIRED TO TAKE US TO MARS...

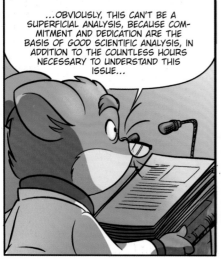

...OBVIOUSLY, THIS CAN'T BE A SUPERFICIAL ANALYSIS, BECAUSE COMMITMENT AND DEDICATION ARE THE BASIS OF GOOD SCIENTIFIC ANALYSIS, IN ADDITION TO THE COUNTLESS HOURS NECESSARY TO UNDERSTAND THIS ISSUE...

HE JUST SAID HE'D SPEAK FOR **HOURS...**

-SIGH!-

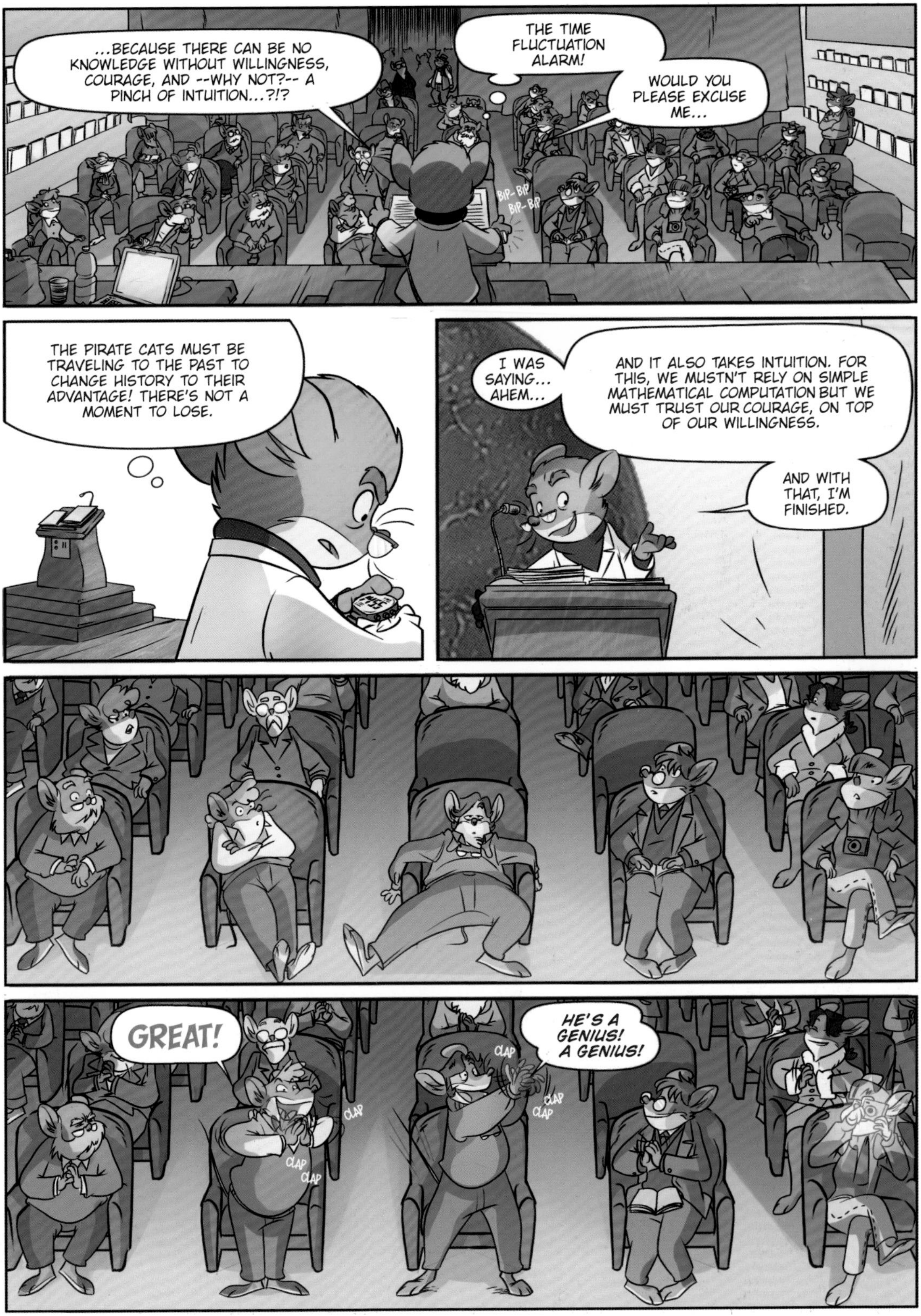

...BECAUSE THERE CAN BE NO KNOWLEDGE WITHOUT WILLINGNESS, COURAGE, AND --WHY NOT?-- A PINCH OF INTUITION...?!?
BIP-BIP BIP-BIP
THE TIME FLUCTUATION ALARM!
WOULD YOU PLEASE EXCUSE ME...
THE PIRATE CATS MUST BE TRAVELING TO THE PAST TO CHANGE HISTORY TO THEIR ADVANTAGE! THERE'S NOT A MOMENT TO LOSE.
I WAS SAYING... AHEM...
AND IT ALSO TAKES INTUITION. FOR THIS, WE MUSTN'T RELY ON SIMPLE MATHEMATICAL COMPUTATION BUT WE MUST TRUST OUR COURAGE, ON TOP OF OUR WILLINGNESS.
AND WITH THAT, I'M FINISHED.
GREAT!
CLAP
CLAP
CLAP
CLAP
HE'S A GENIUS! A GENIUS!
CLAP
CLAP

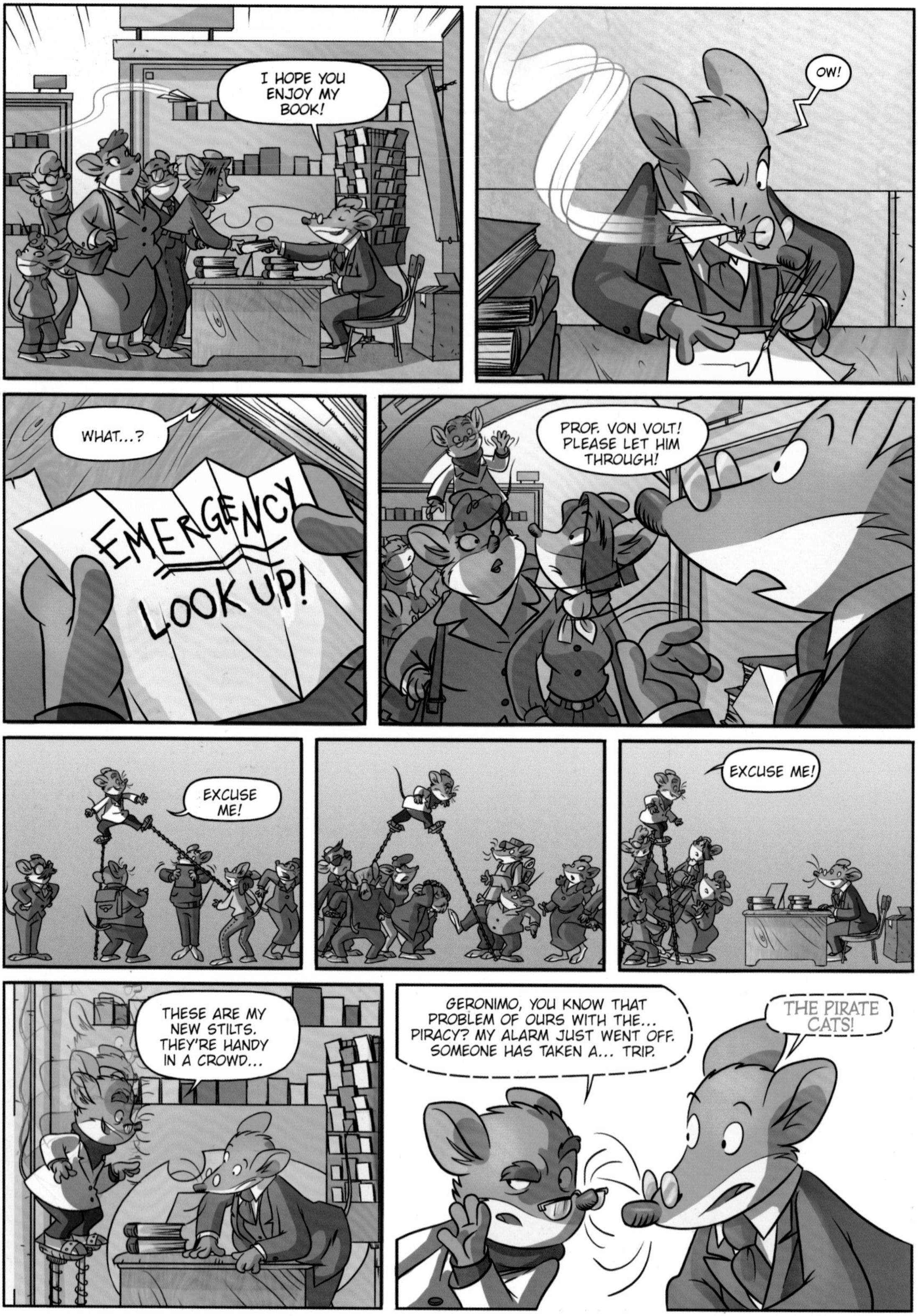
I HOPE YOU ENJOY MY BOOK!
OW!
WHAT...?
EMERGENCY
LOOK UP!
PROF. VON VOLT! PLEASE LET HIM THROUGH!
EXCUSE ME!
EXCUSE ME!
THESE ARE MY NEW STILTS. THEY'RE HANDY IN A CROWD...
GERONIMO, YOU KNOW THAT PROBLEM OF OURS WITH THE... PIRACY? MY ALARM JUST WENT OFF. SOMEONE HAS TAKEN A... TRIP.
THE PIRATE CATS!

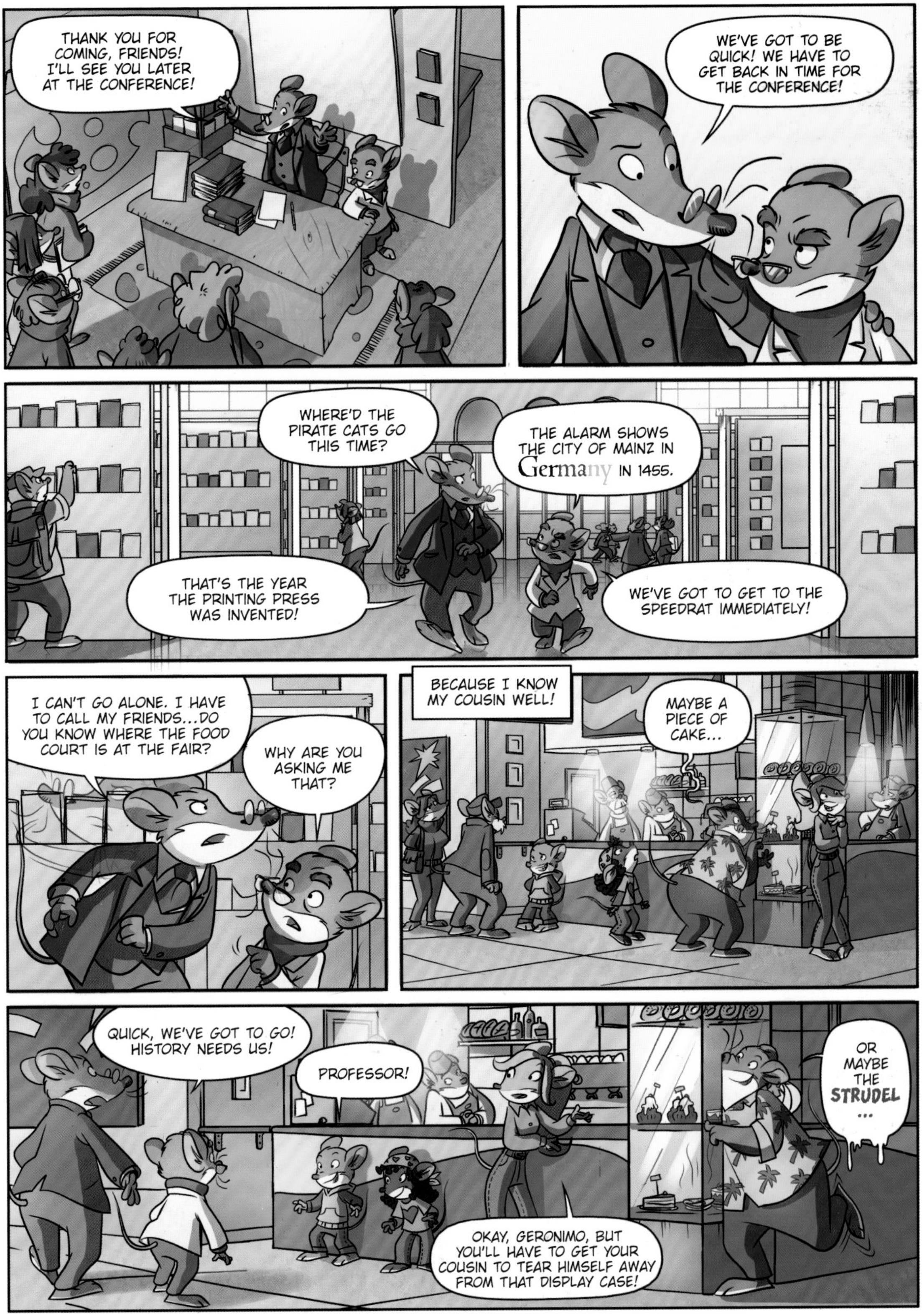
THANK YOU FOR COMING, FRIENDS! I'LL SEE YOU LATER AT THE CONFERENCE!
WE'VE GOT TO BE QUICK! WE HAVE TO GET BACK IN TIME FOR THE CONFERENCE!
WHERE'D THE PIRATE CATS GO THIS TIME?
THE ALARM SHOWS THE CITY OF MAINZ IN Germany IN 1455.
THAT'S THE YEAR THE PRINTING PRESS WAS INVENTED!
WE'VE GOT TO GET TO THE SPEEDRAT IMMEDIATELY!
I CAN'T GO ALONE. I HAVE TO CALL MY FRIENDS...DO YOU KNOW WHERE THE FOOD COURT IS AT THE FAIR?
WHY ARE YOU ASKING ME THAT?
BECAUSE I KNOW MY COUSIN WELL!
MAYBE A PIECE OF CAKE...
QUICK, WE'VE GOT TO GO! HISTORY NEEDS US!
PROFESSOR!
OR MAYBE THE STRUDEL...
OKAY, GERONIMO, BUT YOU'LL HAVE TO GET YOUR COUSIN TO TEAR HIMSELF AWAY FROM THAT DISPLAY CASE!

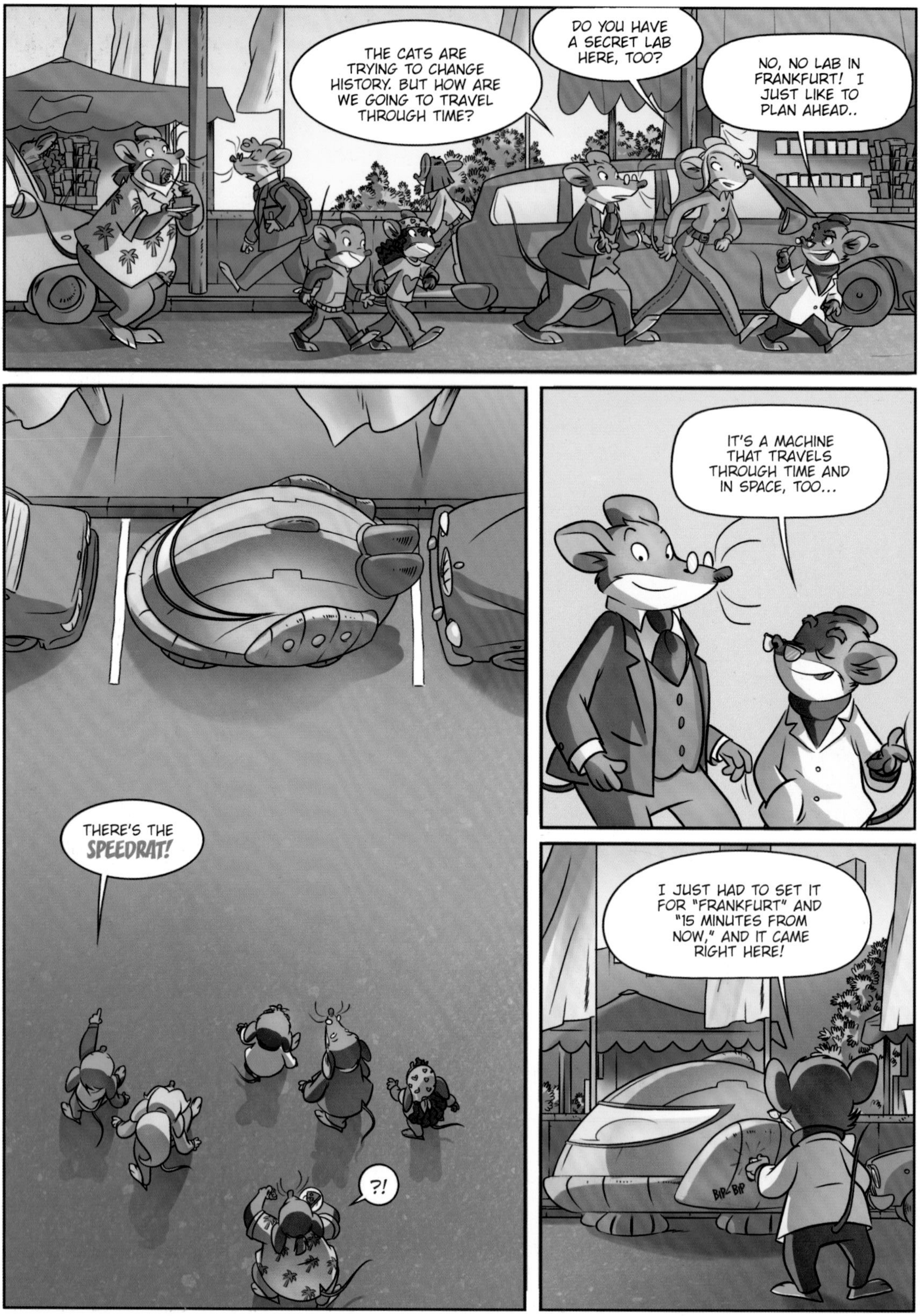
THE CATS ARE TRYING TO CHANGE HISTORY. BUT HOW ARE WE GOING TO TRAVEL THROUGH TIME?
DO YOU HAVE A SECRET LAB HERE, TOO?
NO, NO LAB IN FRANKFURT! I JUST LIKE TO PLAN AHEAD..
THERE'S THE SPEEDRAT!
?!
IT'S A MACHINE THAT TRAVELS THROUGH TIME AND IN SPACE, TOO...
I JUST HAD TO SET IT FOR "FRANKFURT" AND "15 MINUTES FROM NOW," AND IT CAME RIGHT HERE!
BIP-BIP

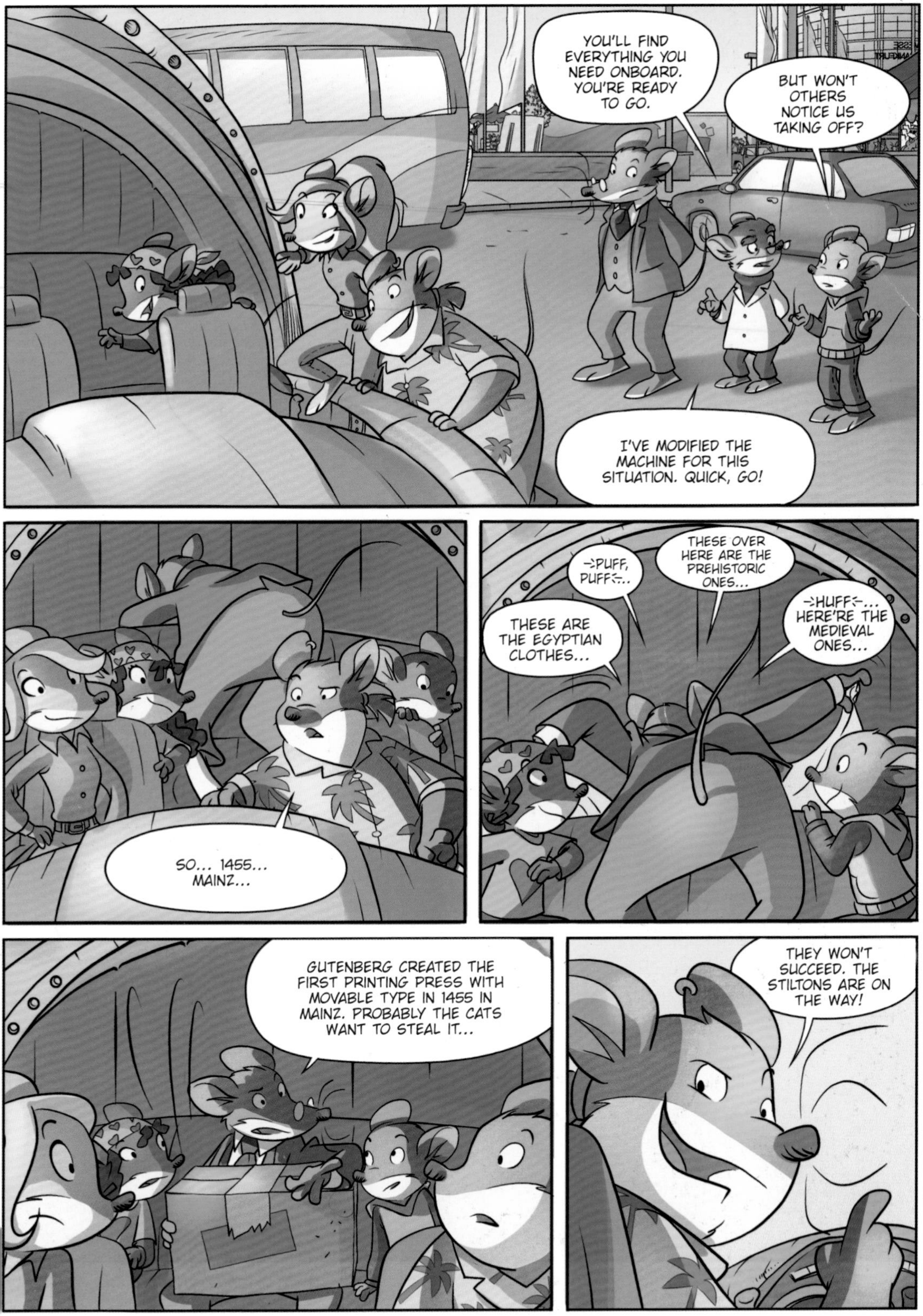
YOU'LL FIND EVERYTHING YOU NEED ONBOARD. YOU'RE READY TO GO.
BUT WON'T OTHERS NOTICE US TAKING OFF?
I'VE MODIFIED THE MACHINE FOR THIS SITUATION. QUICK, GO!
SO... 1455... MAINZ...
THESE ARE THE EGYPTIAN CLOTHES...
→PUFF, PUFF←...
THESE OVER HERE ARE THE PREHISTORIC ONES...
→HUFF←... HERE'RE THE MEDIEVAL ONES...
GUTENBERG CREATED THE FIRST PRINTING PRESS WITH MOVABLE TYPE IN 1455 IN MAINZ. PROBABLY THE CATS WANT TO STEAL IT...
THEY WON'T SUCCEED. THE STILTONS ARE ON THE WAY!

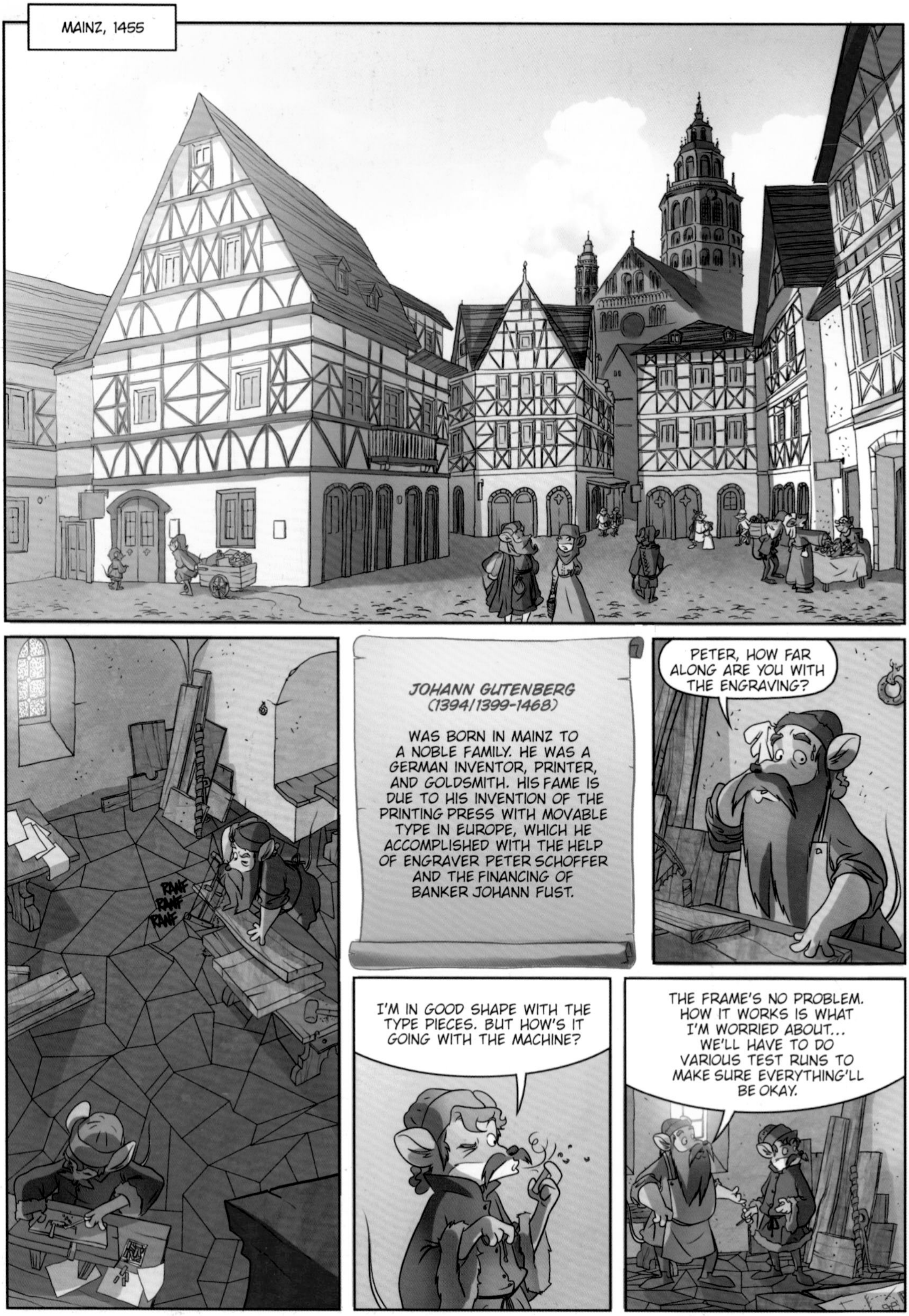
MAINZ, 1455
RANF RANF RANF
JOHANN GUTENBERG (1394/1399-1468)
WAS BORN IN MAINZ TO A NOBLE FAMILY. HE WAS A GERMAN INVENTOR, PRINTER, AND GOLDSMITH. HIS FAME IS DUE TO HIS INVENTION OF THE PRINTING PRESS WITH MOVABLE TYPE IN EUROPE, WHICH HE ACCOMPLISHED WITH THE HELP OF ENGRAVER PETER SCHOFFER AND THE FINANCING OF BANKER JOHANN FUST.
PETER, HOW FAR ALONG ARE YOU WITH THE ENGRAVING?
I'M IN GOOD SHAPE WITH THE TYPE PIECES. BUT HOW'S IT GOING WITH THE MACHINE?
THE FRAME'S NO PROBLEM. HOW IT WORKS IS WHAT I'M WORRIED ABOUT... WE'LL HAVE TO DO VARIOUS TEST RUNS TO MAKE SURE EVERYTHING'LL BE OKAY.

SO, ARE WE SURE THE BOOK WE'VE CHOSEN WILL CONVINCE FUST?

BUT OF COURSE! WHERE'D I PUT IT? IT WAS RIGHT HERE... THERE IT IS!

WE WON'T HAVE TROUBLE SELLING THE FIRST COPIES. IT WON'T TAKE LONG TO PAY OFF OUR BILLS.

THE MOST IMPORTANT BOOK IN EUROPE! THE BIBLE!

AFTER THREE YEARS OF WORK, I'LL BE ABLE TO SEE WHAT THIS BOOK WILL LOOK LIKE WITH MY ENGRAVINGS.

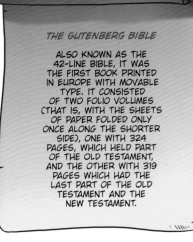

THE GUTENBERG BIBLE

ALSO KNOWN AS THE 42-LINE BIBLE, IT WAS THE FIRST BOOK PRINTED IN EUROPE WITH MOVABLE TYPE. IT CONSISTED OF TWO FOLIO VOLUMES (THAT IS, WITH THE SHEETS OF PAPER FOLDED ONLY ONCE ALONG THE SHORTER SIDE), ONE WITH 324 PAGES, WHICH HELD PART OF THE OLD TESTAMENT, AND THE OTHER WITH 319 PAGES WHICH HAD THE LAST PART OF THE OLD TESTAMENT AND THE NEW TESTAMENT.

BUT LET'S NOT GET DISTRACTED. IF WE DON'T FINISH THE MACHINE, WE WON'T BE ABLE TO PRINT ANYTHING.

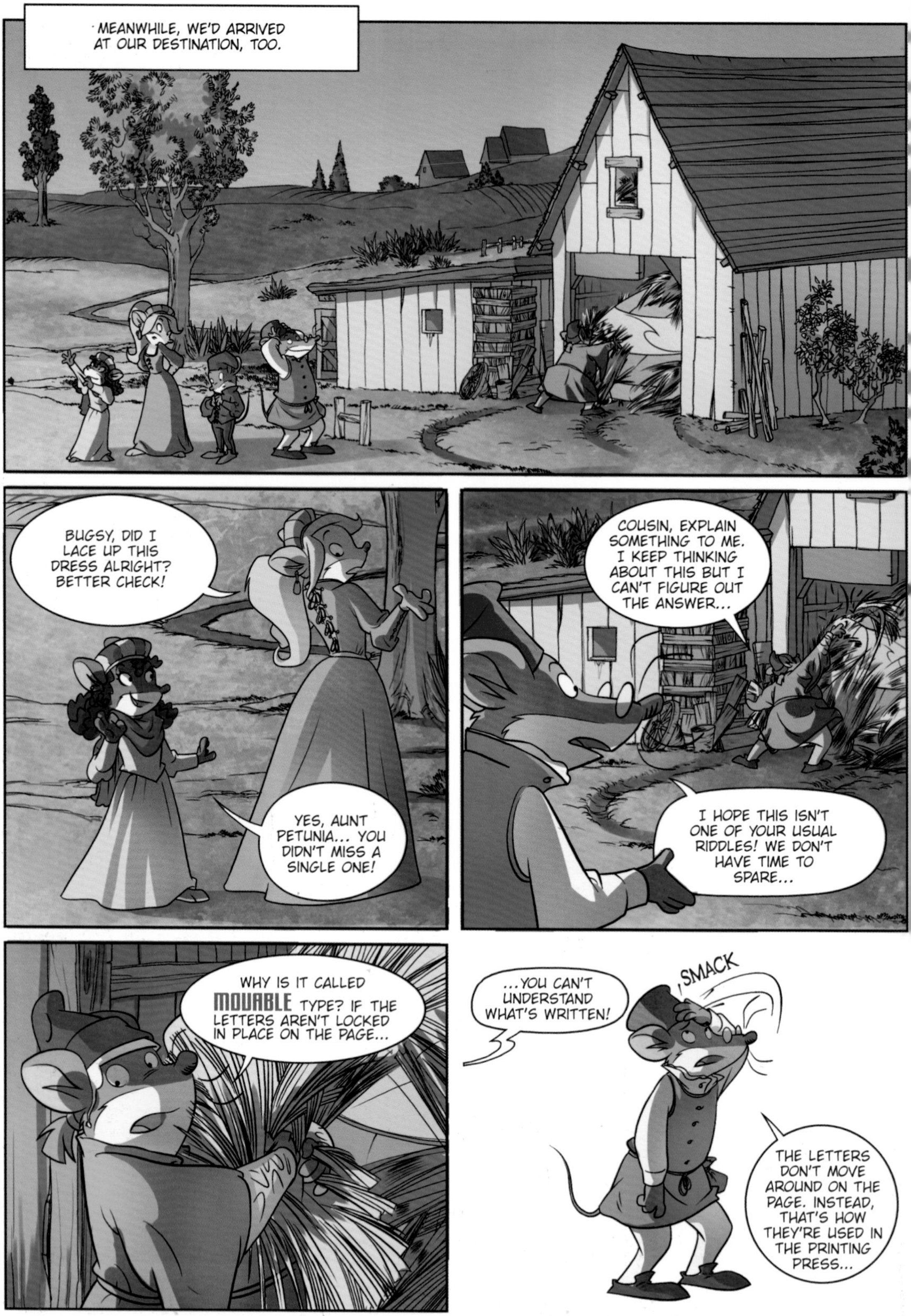
MEANWHILE, WE'D ARRIVED AT OUR DESTINATION, TOO.
BUGSY, DID I LACE UP THIS DRESS ALRIGHT? BETTER CHECK!
YES, AUNT PETUNIA... YOU DIDN'T MISS A SINGLE ONE!
COUSIN, EXPLAIN SOMETHING TO ME. I KEEP THINKING ABOUT THIS BUT I CAN'T FIGURE OUT THE ANSWER...
I HOPE THIS ISN'T ONE OF YOUR USUAL RIDDLES! WE DON'T HAVE TIME TO SPARE...
WHY IS IT CALLED MOVABLE TYPE? IF THE LETTERS AREN'T LOCKED IN PLACE ON THE PAGE...
...YOU CAN'T UNDERSTAND WHAT'S WRITTEN!
SMACK
THE LETTERS DON'T MOVE AROUND ON THE PAGE. INSTEAD, THAT'S HOW THEY'RE USED IN THE PRINTING PRESS...

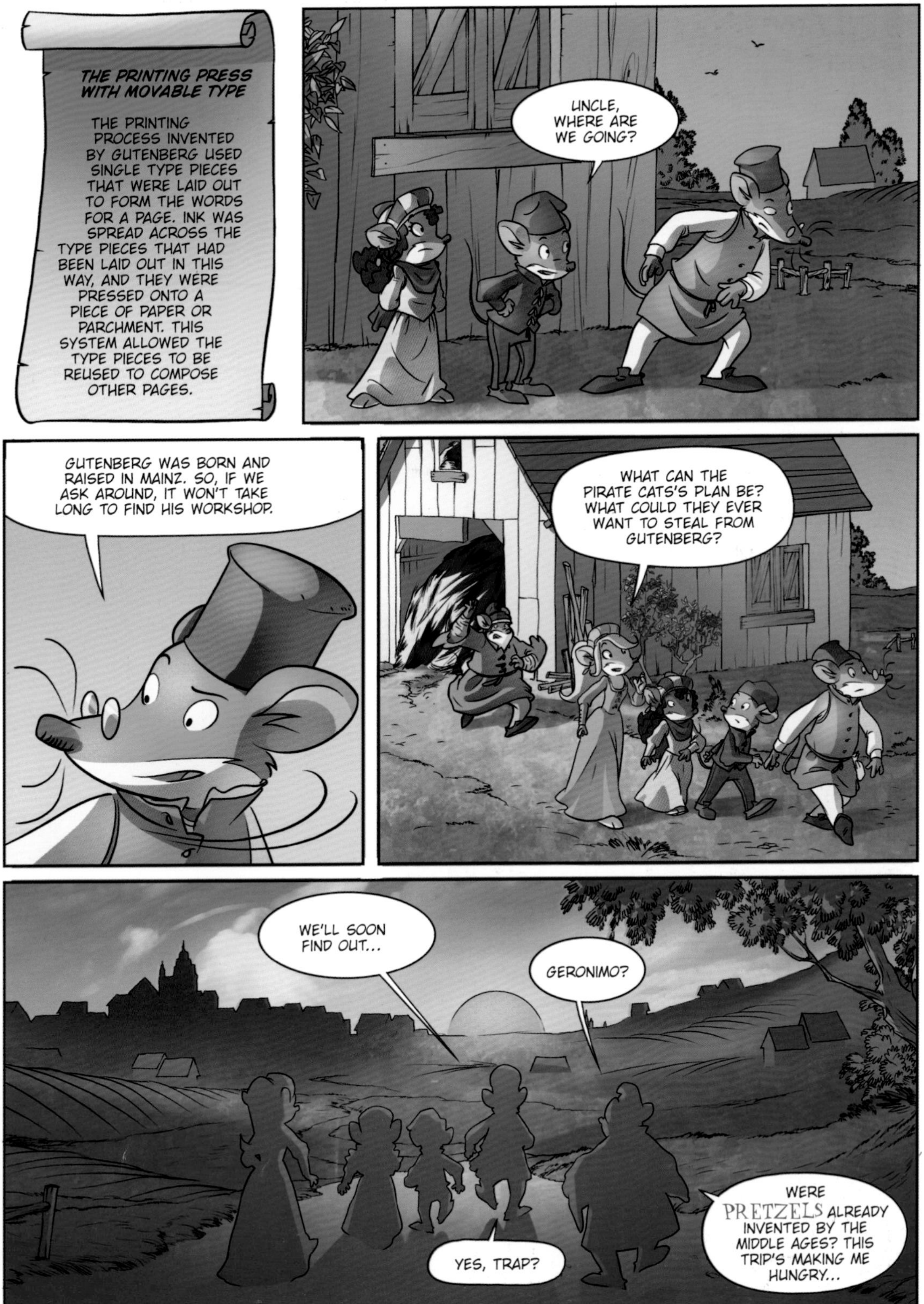
THE PRINTING PRESS WITH MOVABLE TYPE
THE PRINTING PROCESS INVENTED BY GUTENBERG USED SINGLE TYPE PIECES THAT WERE LAID OUT TO FORM THE WORDS FOR A PAGE. INK WAS SPREAD ACROSS THE TYPE PIECES THAT HAD BEEN LAID OUT IN THIS WAY, AND THEY WERE PRESSED ONTO A PIECE OF PAPER OR PARCHMENT. THIS SYSTEM ALLOWED THE TYPE PIECES TO BE REUSED TO COMPOSE OTHER PAGES.
UNCLE, WHERE ARE WE GOING?
GUTENBERG WAS BORN AND RAISED IN MAINZ. SO, IF WE ASK AROUND, IT WON'T TAKE LONG TO FIND HIS WORKSHOP.
WHAT CAN THE PIRATE CATS'S PLAN BE? WHAT COULD THEY EVER WANT TO STEAL FROM GUTENBERG?
WE'LL SOON FIND OUT...
GERONIMO?
YES, TRAP?
WERE PRETZELS ALREADY INVENTED BY THE MIDDLE AGES? THIS TRIP'S MAKING ME HUNGRY...

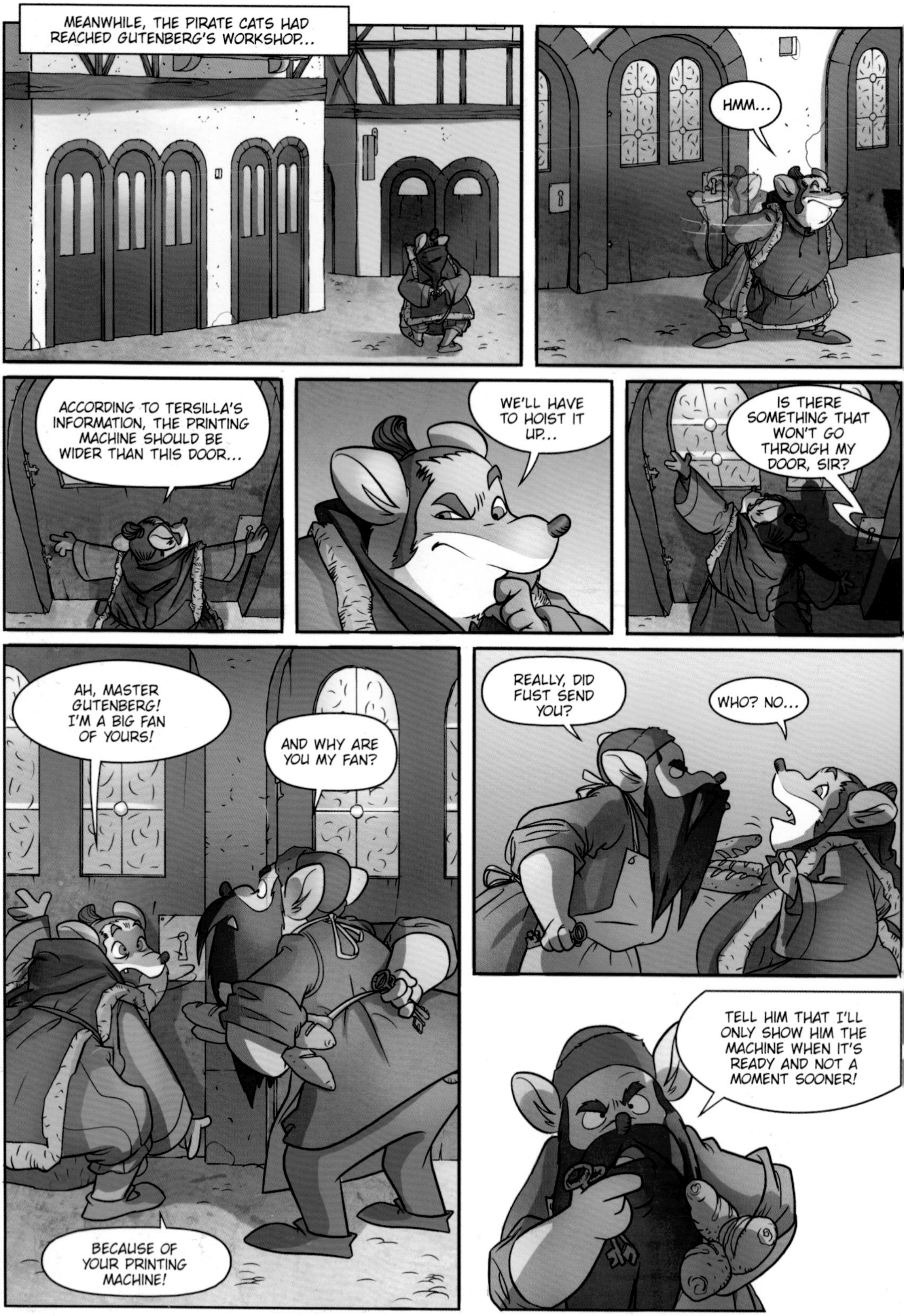
MEANWHILE, THE PIRATE CATS HAD REACHED GUTENBERG'S WORKSHOP...
HMM...
ACCORDING TO TERSILLA'S INFORMATION, THE PRINTING MACHINE SHOULD BE WIDER THAN THIS DOOR...
WE'LL HAVE TO HOIST IT UP...
IS THERE SOMETHING THAT WON'T GO THROUGH MY DOOR, SIR?
AH, MASTER GUTENBERG! I'M A BIG FAN OF YOURS!
AND WHY ARE YOU MY FAN?
BECAUSE OF YOUR PRINTING MACHINE!
REALLY, DID FUST SEND YOU?
WHO? NO...
TELL HIM THAT I'LL ONLY SHOW HIM THE MACHINE WHEN IT'S READY AND NOT A MOMENT SOONER!

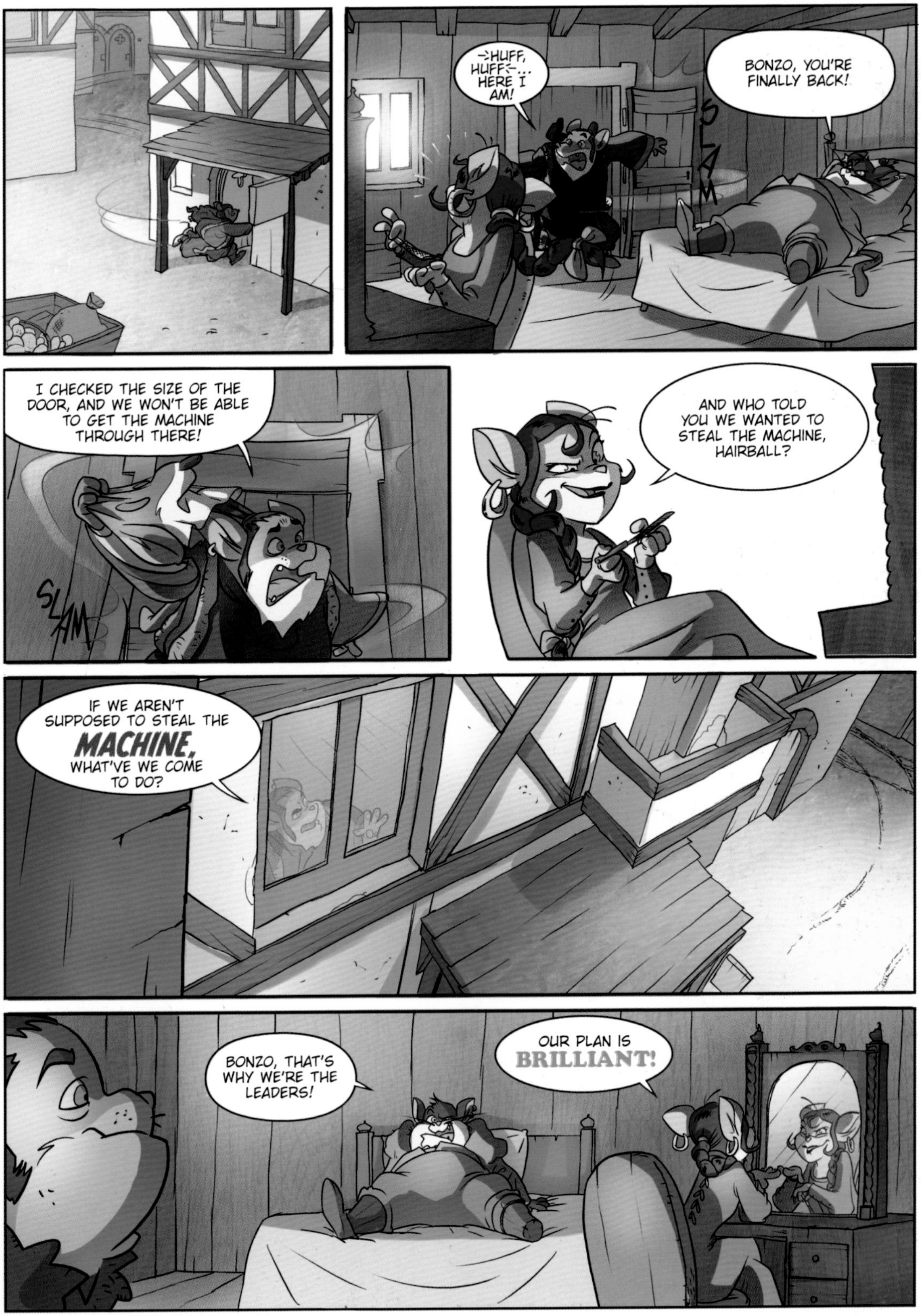
~HUFF, HUFF~... HERE I AM!
BONZO, YOU'RE FINALLY BACK!
SLAM
I CHECKED THE SIZE OF THE DOOR, AND WE WON'T BE ABLE TO GET THE MACHINE THROUGH THERE!
SLAM
AND WHO TOLD YOU WE WANTED TO STEAL THE MACHINE, HAIRBALL?
IF WE AREN'T SUPPOSED TO STEAL THE MACHINE, WHAT'VE WE COME TO DO?
BONZO, THAT'S WHY WE'RE THE LEADERS!
OUR PLAN IS BRILLIANT!

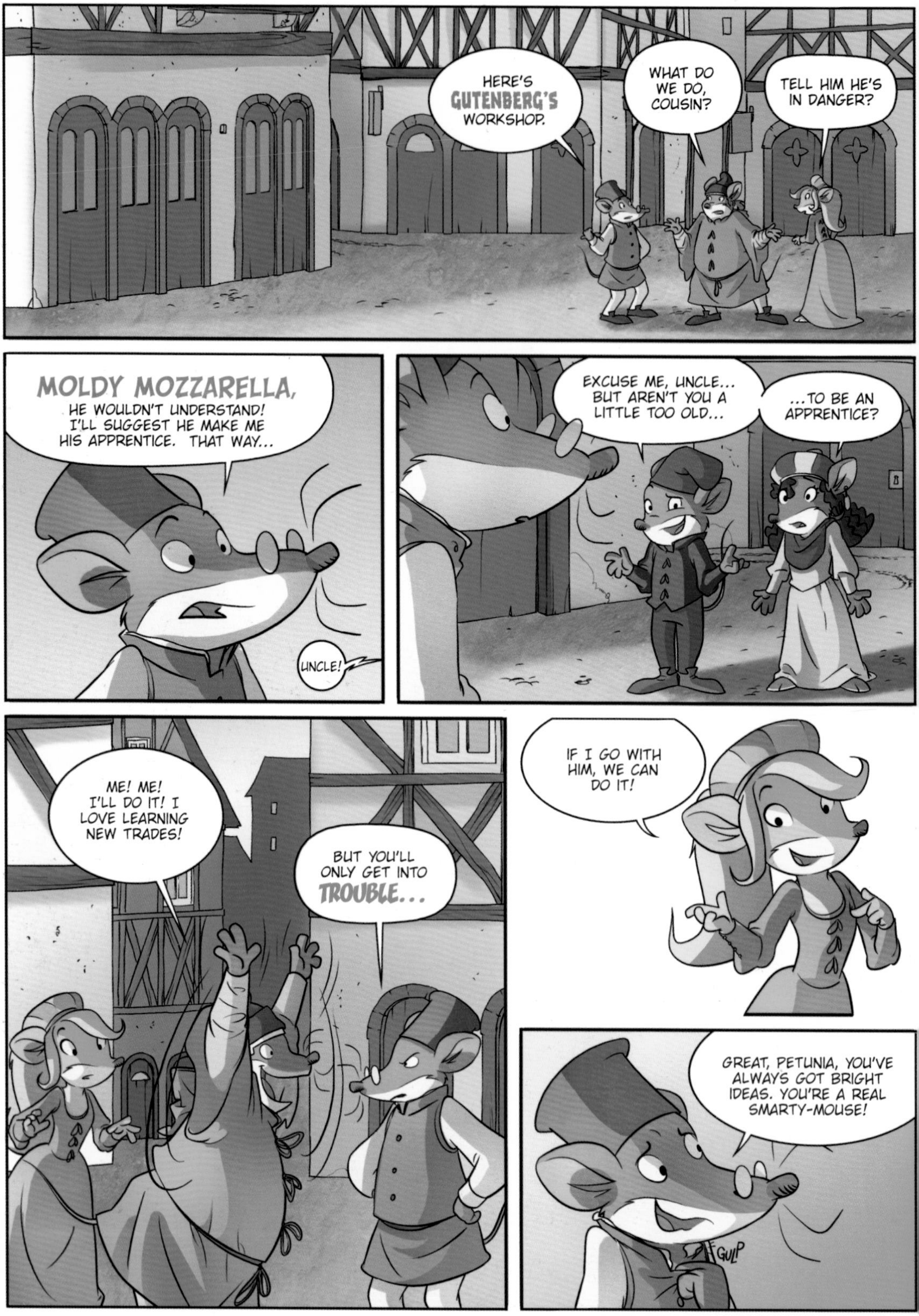
HERE'S GUTENBERG'S WORKSHOP.
WHAT DO WE DO, COUSIN?
TELL HIM HE'S IN DANGER?
MOLDY MOZZARELLA, HE WOULDN'T UNDERSTAND! I'LL SUGGEST HE MAKE ME HIS APPRENTICE. THAT WAY...
UNCLE!
EXCUSE ME, UNCLE... BUT AREN'T YOU A LITTLE TOO OLD...
...TO BE AN APPRENTICE?
ME! ME! I'LL DO IT! I LOVE LEARNING NEW TRADES!
BUT YOU'LL ONLY GET INTO TROUBLE...
IF I GO WITH HIM, WE CAN DO IT!
GREAT, PETUNIA, YOU'VE ALWAYS GOT BRIGHT IDEAS. YOU'RE A REAL SMARTY-MOUSE!
GULP

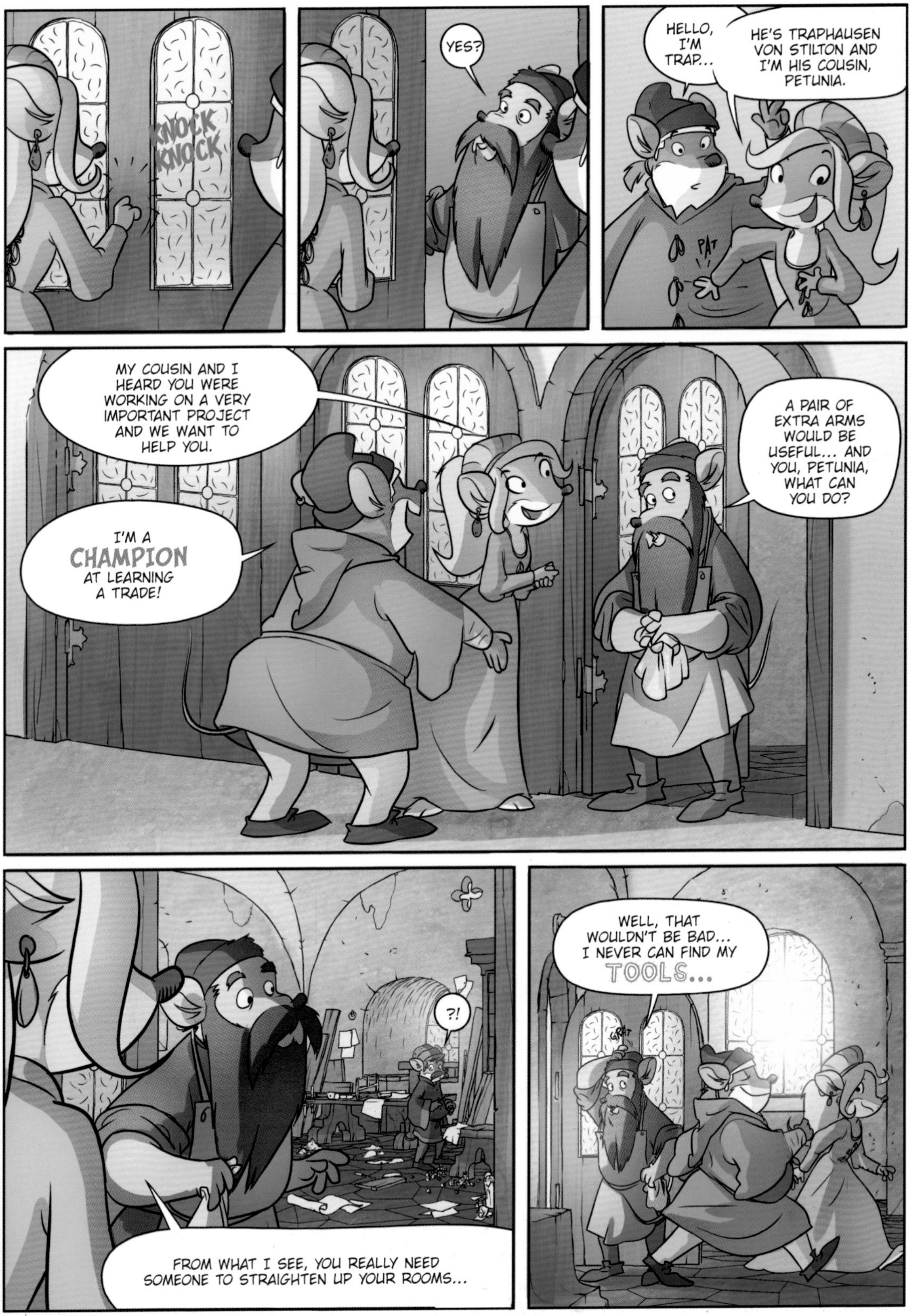
KNOCK KNOCK
YES?
HELLO, I'M TRAP...
HE'S TRAPHAUSEN VON STILTON AND I'M HIS COUSIN, PETUNIA.
PAT
MY COUSIN AND I HEARD YOU WERE WORKING ON A VERY IMPORTANT PROJECT AND WE WANT TO HELP YOU.
A PAIR OF EXTRA ARMS WOULD BE USEFUL... AND YOU, PETUNIA, WHAT CAN YOU DO?
I'M A CHAMPION AT LEARNING A TRADE!
?!
FROM WHAT I SEE, YOU REALLY NEED SOMEONE TO STRAIGHTEN UP YOUR ROOMS...
WELL, THAT WOULDN'T BE BAD... I NEVER CAN FIND MY TOOLS...
GRAT

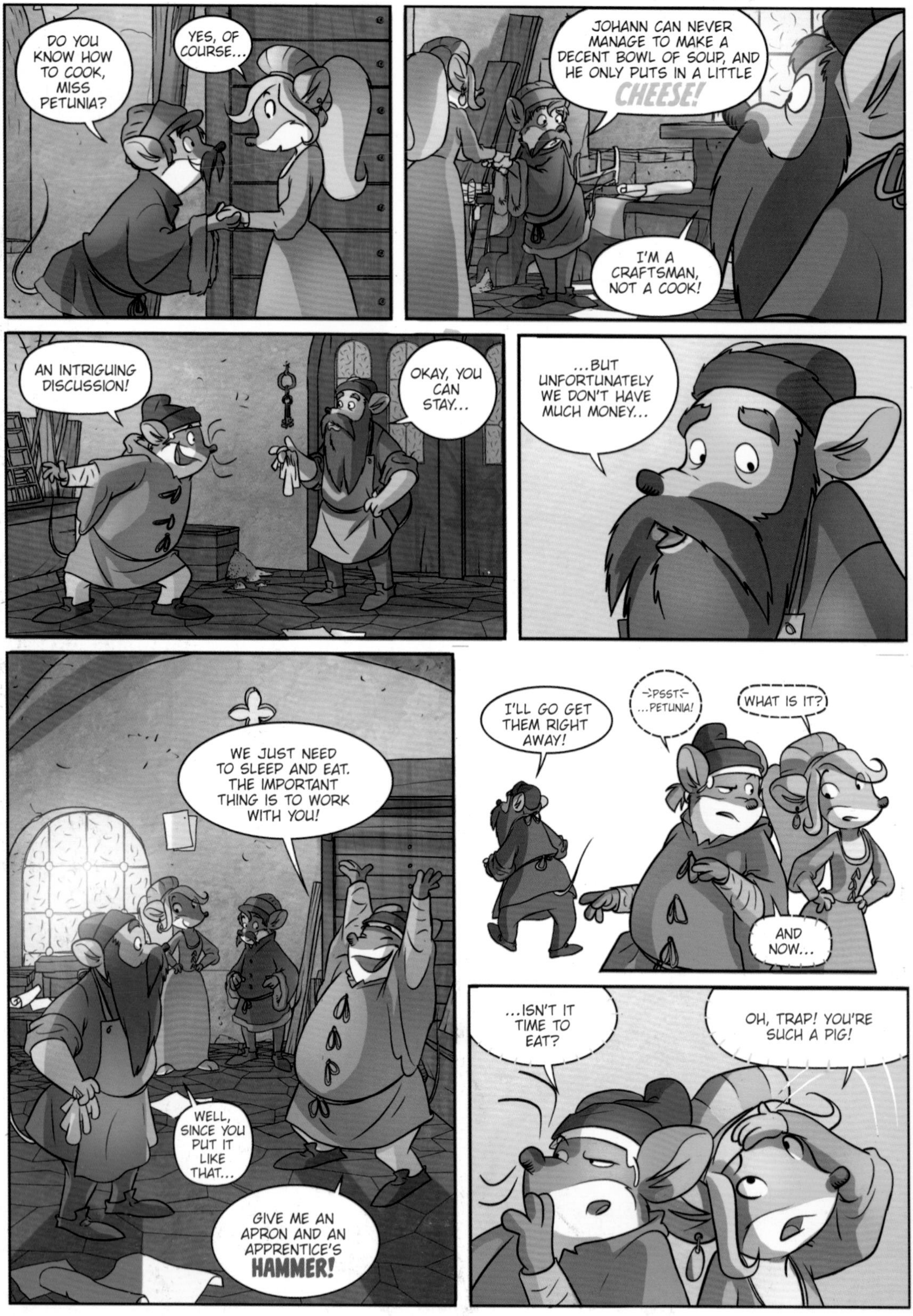
DO YOU KNOW HOW TO COOK, MISS PETUNIA?
YES, OF COURSE...
JOHANN CAN NEVER MANAGE TO MAKE A DECENT BOWL OF SOUP, AND HE ONLY PUTS IN A LITTLE CHEESE!
I'M A CRAFTSMAN, NOT A COOK!
AN INTRIGUING DISCUSSION!
OKAY, YOU CAN STAY...
...BUT UNFORTUNATELY WE DON'T HAVE MUCH MONEY...
WE JUST NEED TO SLEEP AND EAT. THE IMPORTANT THING IS TO WORK WITH YOU!
WELL, SINCE YOU PUT IT LIKE THAT...
GIVE ME AN APRON AND AN APPRENTICE'S HAMMER!
I'LL GO GET THEM RIGHT AWAY!
PSST ...PETUNIA!
WHAT IS IT?
AND NOW...
...ISN'T IT TIME TO EAT?
OH, TRAP! YOU'RE SUCH A PIG!

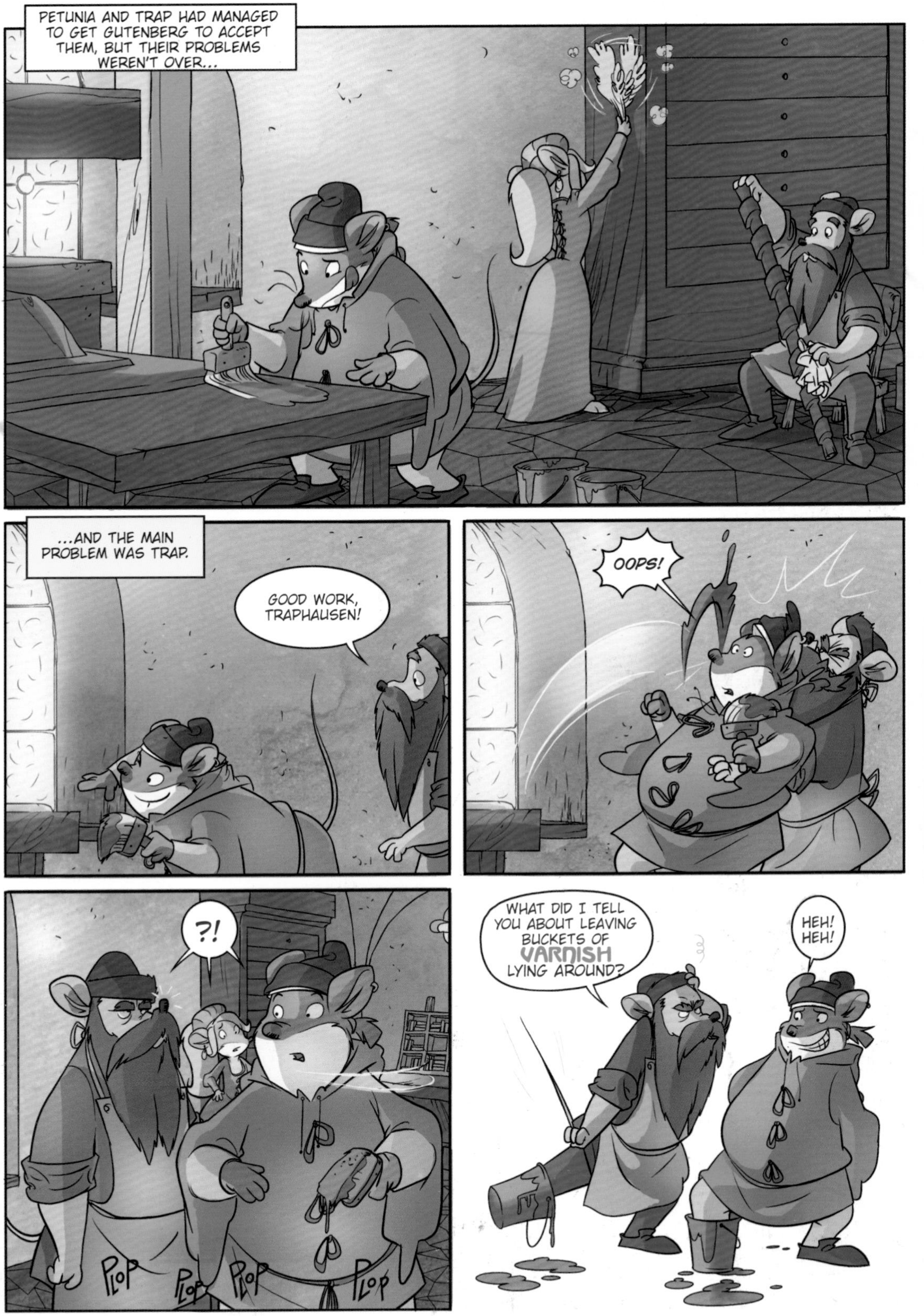
PETUNIA AND TRAP HAD MANAGED TO GET GUTENBERG TO ACCEPT THEM, BUT THEIR PROBLEMS WEREN'T OVER...
...AND THE MAIN PROBLEM WAS TRAP.
GOOD WORK, TRAPHAUSEN!
OOPS!
?!
PLOP
PLOP
PLOP
PLOP
WHAT DID I TELL YOU ABOUT LEAVING BUCKETS OF VARNISH LYING AROUND?
HEH! HEH!

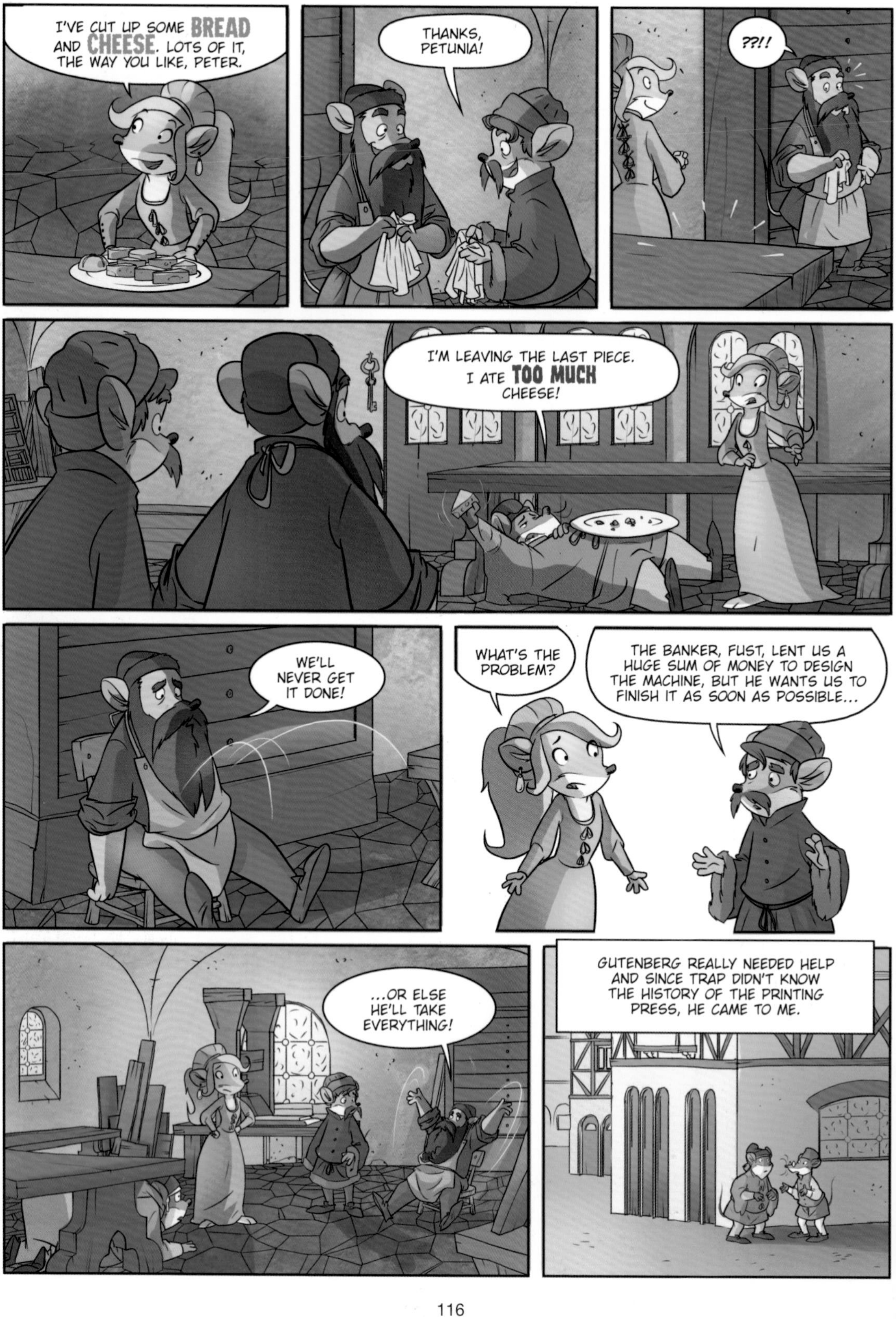
I'VE CUT UP SOME BREAD AND CHEESE. LOTS OF IT, THE WAY YOU LIKE, PETER.
THANKS, PETUNIA!
??!!
I'M LEAVING THE LAST PIECE. I ATE TOO MUCH CHEESE!
WE'LL NEVER GET IT DONE!
WHAT'S THE PROBLEM?
THE BANKER, FUST, LENT US A HUGE SUM OF MONEY TO DESIGN THE MACHINE, BUT HE WANTS US TO FINISH IT AS SOON AS POSSIBLE...
...OR ELSE HE'LL TAKE EVERYTHING!
GUTENBERG REALLY NEEDED HELP AND SINCE TRAP DIDN'T KNOW THE HISTORY OF THE PRINTING PRESS, HE CAME TO ME.

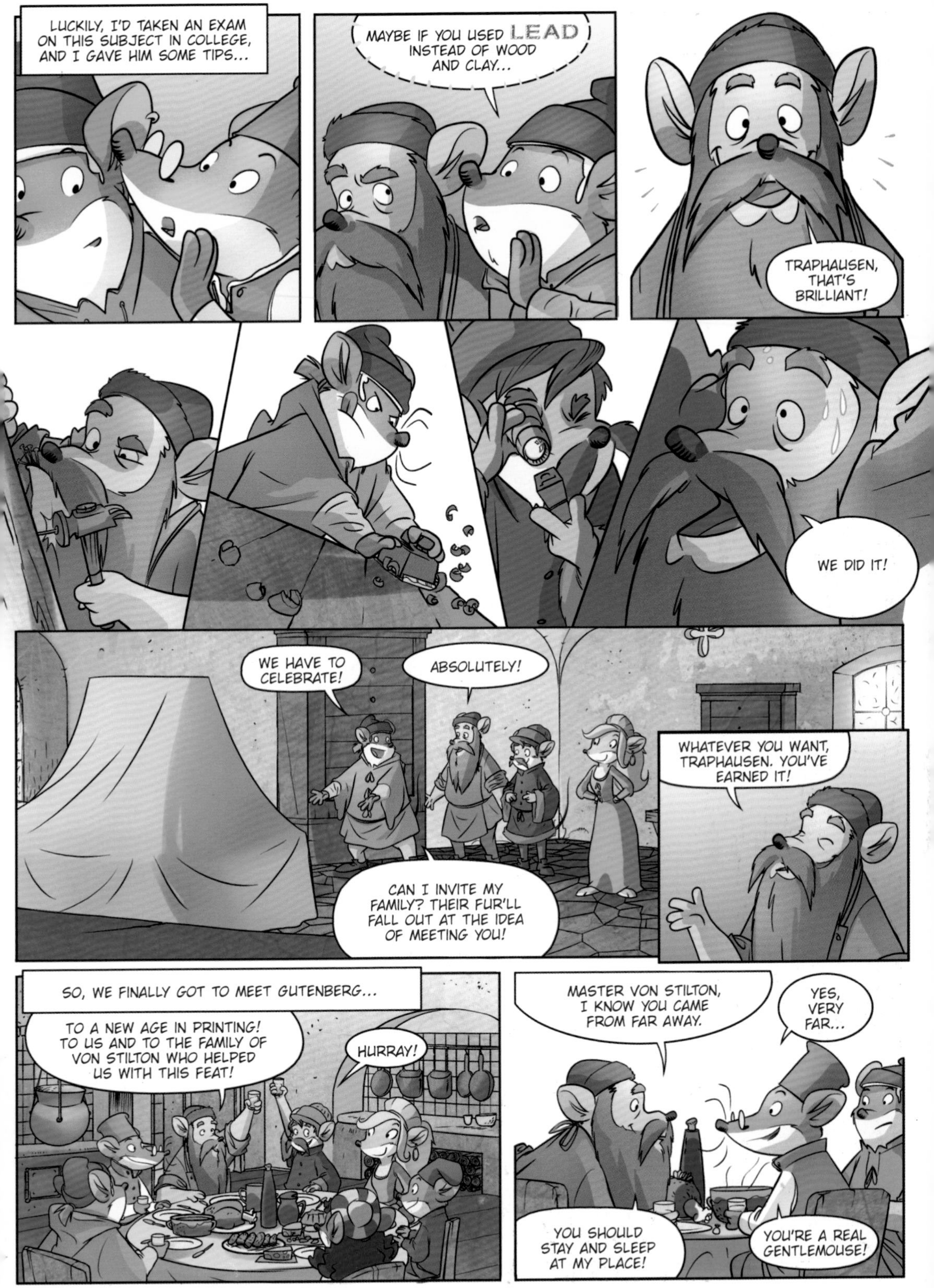
LUCKILY, I'D TAKEN AN EXAM ON THIS SUBJECT IN COLLEGE, AND I GAVE HIM SOME TIPS...
MAYBE IF YOU USED LEAD INSTEAD OF WOOD AND CLAY...
TRAPHAUSEN, THAT'S BRILLIANT!
WE DID IT!
WE HAVE TO CELEBRATE!
ABSOLUTELY!
CAN I INVITE MY FAMILY? THEIR FUR'LL FALL OUT AT THE IDEA OF MEETING YOU!
WHATEVER YOU WANT, TRAPHAUSEN. YOU'VE EARNED IT!
SO, WE FINALLY GOT TO MEET GUTENBERG...
TO A NEW AGE IN PRINTING! TO US AND TO THE FAMILY OF VON STILTON WHO HELPED US WITH THIS FEAT!
HURRAY!
MASTER VON STILTON, I KNOW YOU CAME FROM FAR AWAY.
YES, VERY FAR...
YOU SHOULD STAY AND SLEEP AT MY PLACE!
YOU'RE A REAL GENTLEMOUSE!

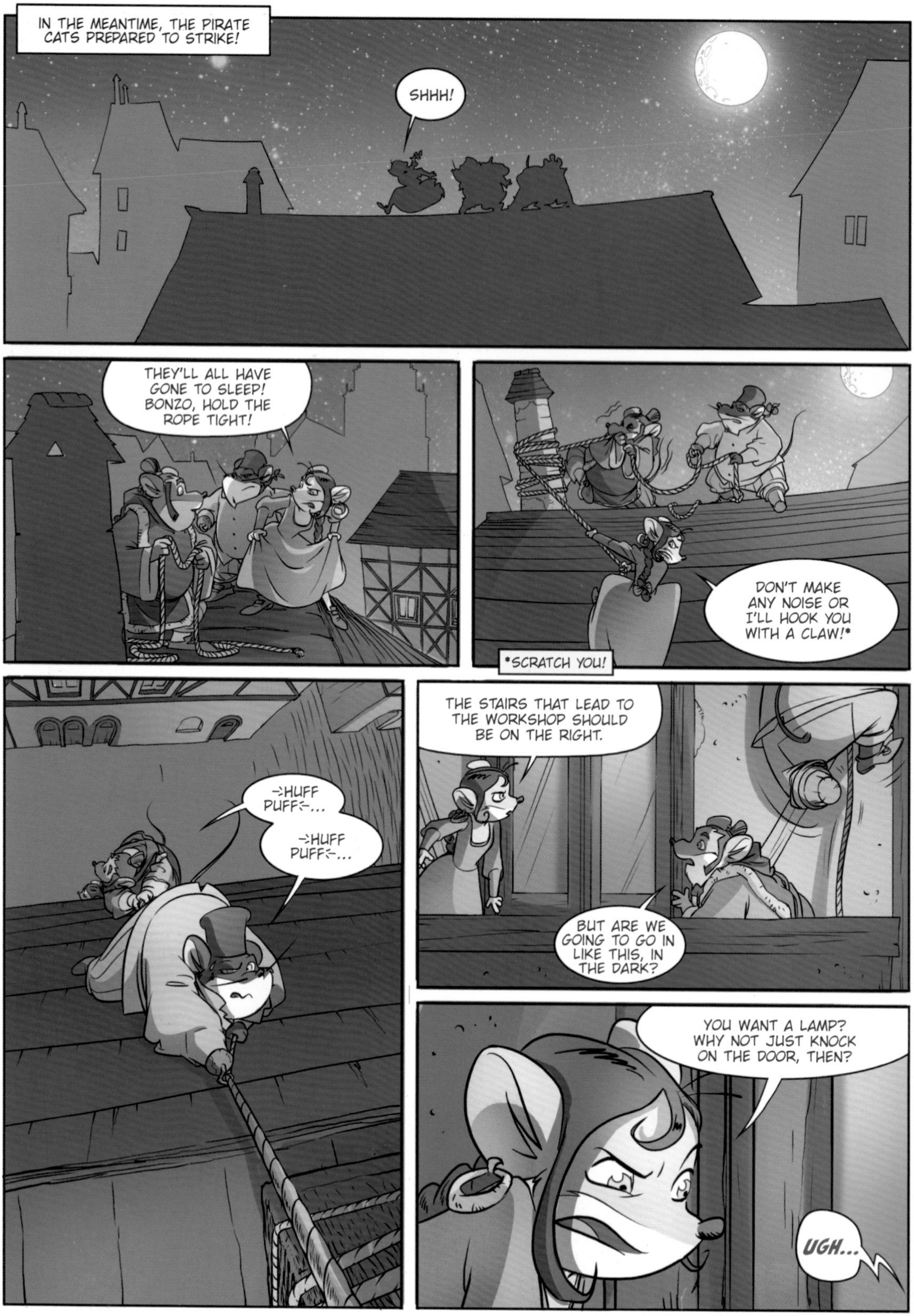
IN THE MEANTIME, THE PIRATE CATS PREPARED TO STRIKE!
SHHH!
THEY'LL ALL HAVE GONE TO SLEEP! BONZO, HOLD THE ROPE TIGHT!
DON'T MAKE ANY NOISE OR I'LL HOOK YOU WITH A CLAW!*
*SCRATCH YOU!
→HUFF PUFF←...
→HUFF PUFF←...
THE STAIRS THAT LEAD TO THE WORKSHOP SHOULD BE ON THE RIGHT.
BUT ARE WE GOING TO GO IN LIKE THIS, IN THE DARK?
YOU WANT A LAMP? WHY NOT JUST KNOCK ON THE DOOR, THEN?
UGH...

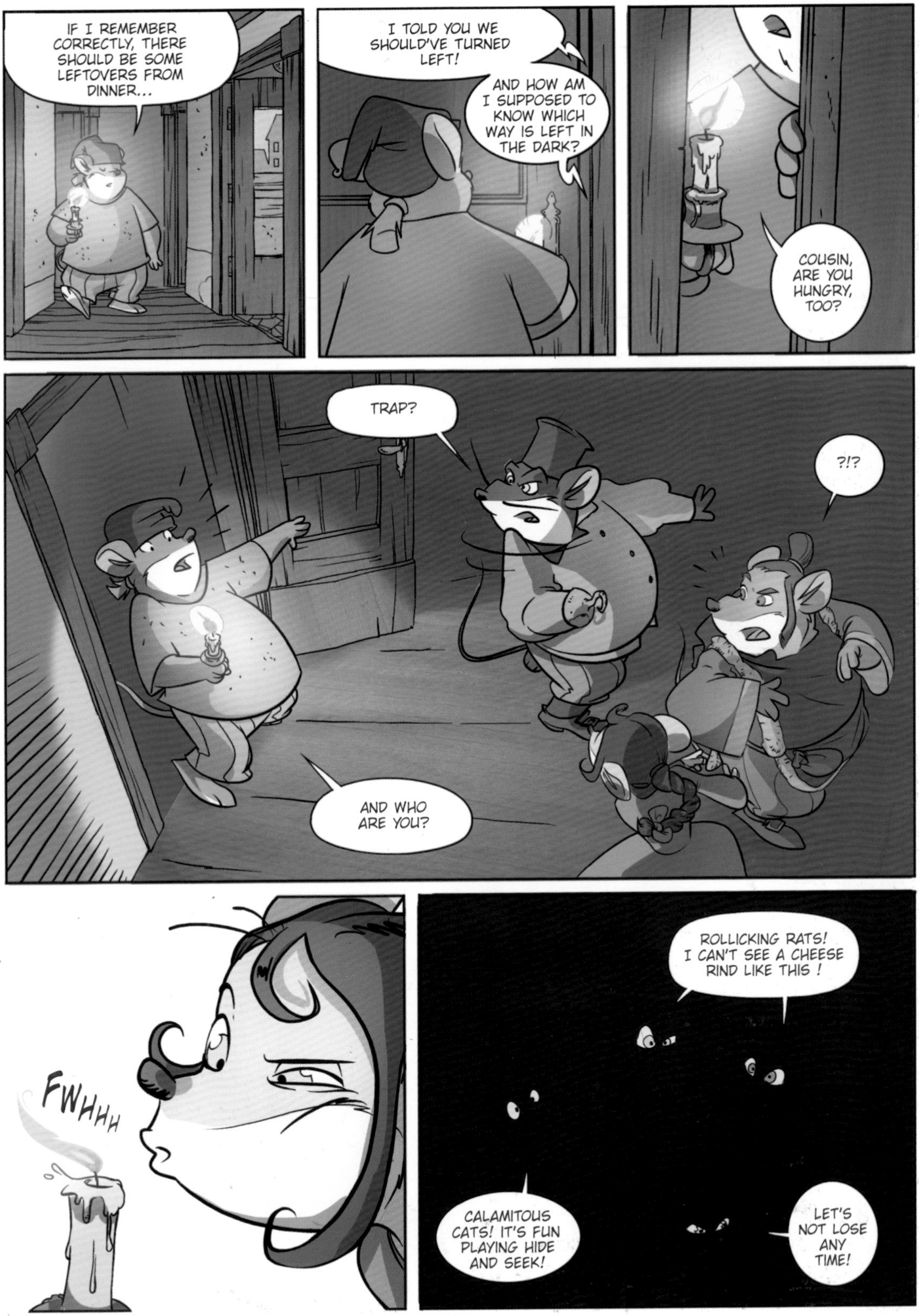
IF I REMEMBER CORRECTLY, THERE SHOULD BE SOME LEFTOVERS FROM DINNER...
I TOLD YOU WE SHOULD'VE TURNED LEFT!
AND HOW AM I SUPPOSED TO KNOW WHICH WAY IS LEFT IN THE DARK?
COUSIN, ARE YOU HUNGRY, TOO?
TRAP?
?!?
AND WHO ARE YOU?
FWHHH
ROLLICKING RATS! I CAN'T SEE A CHEESE RIND LIKE THIS !
CALAMITOUS CATS! IT'S FUN PLAYING HIDE AND SEEK!
LET'S NOT LOSE ANY TIME!

THOSE RATS WERE ACTING STRANGELY...

THEY COULD SEE WELL IN THE DARK AND THEY CRIED OUT, "CALAMITOUS CATS"...

RED ALERT! THE PIRATE CATS!

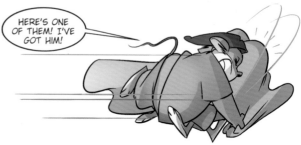

HERE'S ONE OF THEM! I'VE GOT HIM!

MOLDY MOZZARELLA! HELP!

I CAN'T, COUSIN! I'M HOLDING ONE OF THEM DOWN!

AT LEAST WE CAUGHT ONE OF THEM!

AHEM, TRAPHAU-SEN...

COUSIN, YOU'RE TOO HEAVY!

DO I LOOK LIKE A CAT TO YOU?

BUT IF THE CATS AREN'T HERE...

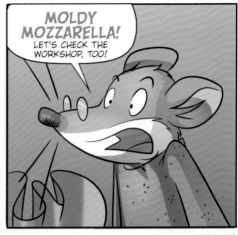

MOLDY MOZZARELLA! LET'S CHECK THE WORKSHOP, TOO!

THE DOOR'S OPEN. THEY GOT AWAY!

BUT WHAT DID THOSE CRUMMY CATS WANT?

MAYBE WE MANAGED TO WRECK THEIR PLAN...

OH, NO!

THEY STOLE THE TYPE PIECES!

WITHOUT THE TYPE PIECES, THE DEMONSTRATION WILL HAVE TO BE PUSHED BACK BY WEEKS!

THAT'S THEIR PLAN! WITHOUT THE TYPE PIECES, FUST WILL ASK FOR HIS MONEY BACK AND THE PIRATE CATS WILL PRINT GUTENBERG'S FIRST BOOK!

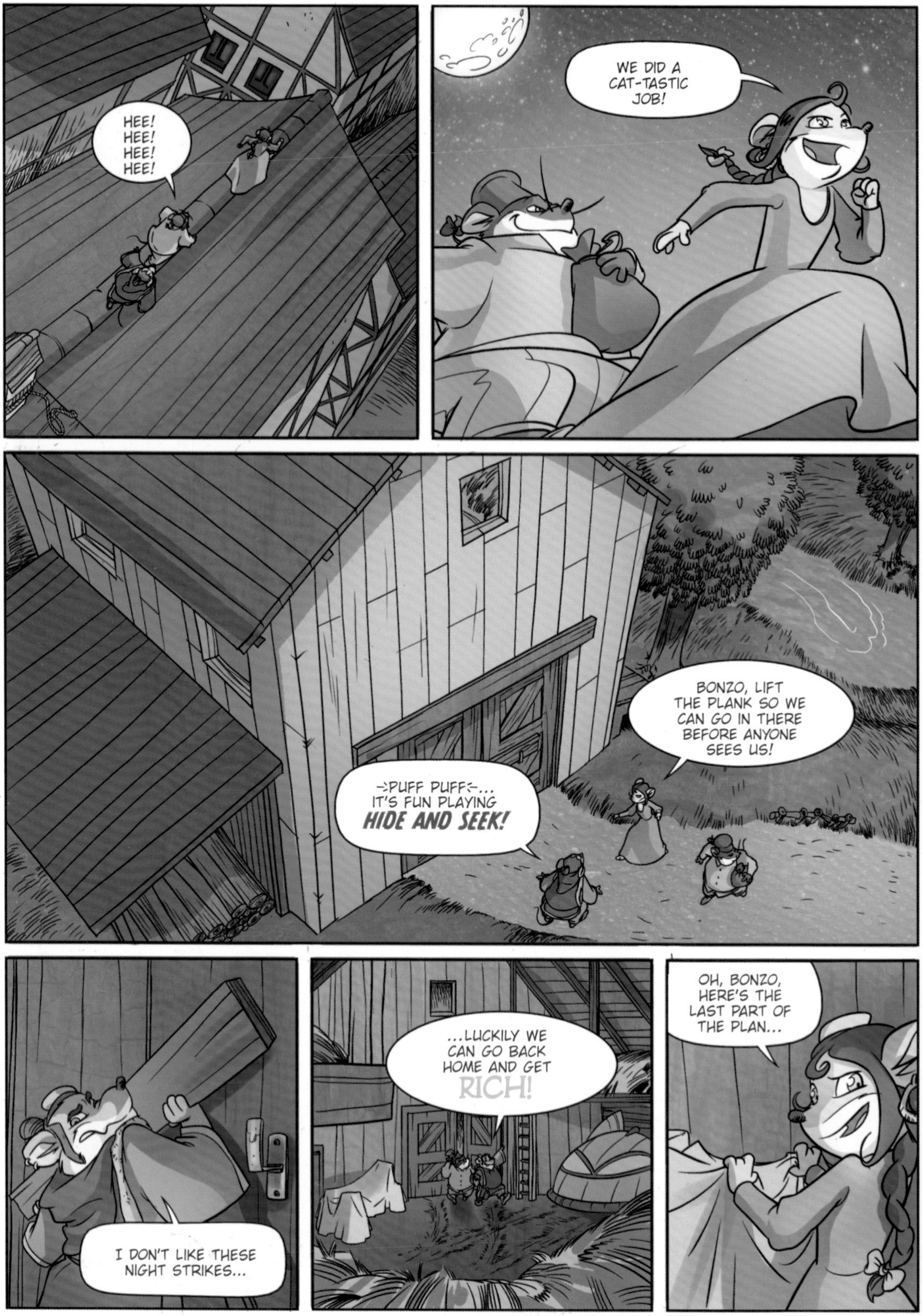
HEE! HEE! HEE! HEE!
WE DID A CAT-TASTIC JOB!
BONZO, LIFT THE PLANK SO WE CAN GO IN THERE BEFORE ANYONE SEES US!
⇒PUFF PUFF⇐... IT'S FUN PLAYING HIDE AND SEEK!
I DON'T LIKE THESE NIGHT STRIKES...
...LUCKILY WE CAN GO BACK HOME AND GET RICH!
OH, BONZO, HERE'S THE LAST PART OF THE PLAN...

WE STOLE GUTENBERG'S TYPE PIECES TO MESS UP HIS WORK...

HMM...

...WE'LL PRINT THE FIRST BOOKS! WE'LL FOUND A PUBLISHING DYNASTY THAT WILL LAST ALL THE WAY TO OUR TIME!

MAYBE IT WOULD'VE BEEN BETTER TO BRING A BICYCLE FROM THE PRESENT RATHER THAN BUILDING ONE...

THERE WASN'T ROOM. WE BARELY COULD FIT THE COMPUTER AND THE PRINTER...

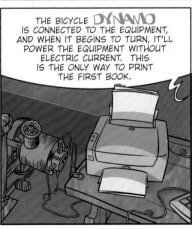

THE BICYCLE DYNAMO IS CONNECTED TO THE EQUIPMENT, AND WHEN IT BEGINS TO TURN, IT'LL POWER THE EQUIPMENT WITHOUT ELECTRIC CURRENT. THIS IS THE ONLY WAY TO PRINT THE FIRST BOOK.

THE BICYCLE DYNAMO

IS AN ALTERNATOR, A ROTARY ELECTRIC MACHINE BASED ON ELECTROMAGNETIC INDUCTION. IT TRANSFORMS MECHANICAL ENERGY (THE ROTATION, ITSELF OF THE DYNAMO) INTO THE ELECTRICAL ENERGY NECESSARY TO POWER ELECTRICAL DEVICES.

SOMEONE'S GOT TO **PEDAL** TO TURN ON THE COMPUTER? WHO'LL DO THAT?

I'D DO IT MYSELF, BUT I'M THE ONLY ONE WHO KNOWS HOW TO USE THE COMPUTER!

I HAVE TO PUT THE PAPER IN THE --PRINTER-- IT'S A DELICATE JOB THAT ONLY A ROYAL FELINE CAN DO!

I SHOULD'VE GUESSED...

BUT ARE WE SURE IT'LL HOLD MY WEIGHT?

DON'T MOUSE OFF! I'VE FOLLOWED THE CONSTRUCTION OF THE MOST MODERN BICYCLES IN THE FELINE EMPIRE. IT'S FOOLPROOF!

SQUEAK

SQUEAK

MAYBE...

UMPH...

SQUEAK

SQUEAK

COME ON, PEDAL! THE COMPUTER'S NOT EVEN TURNING ON!

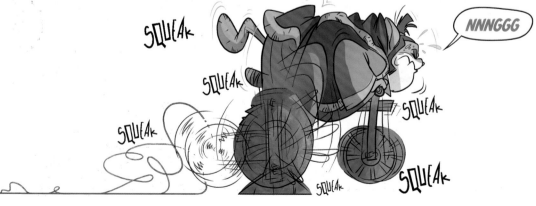

SQUEAK

SQUEAK

SQUEAK

SQUEAK

SQUEAK

SQUEAK

NNNGGG

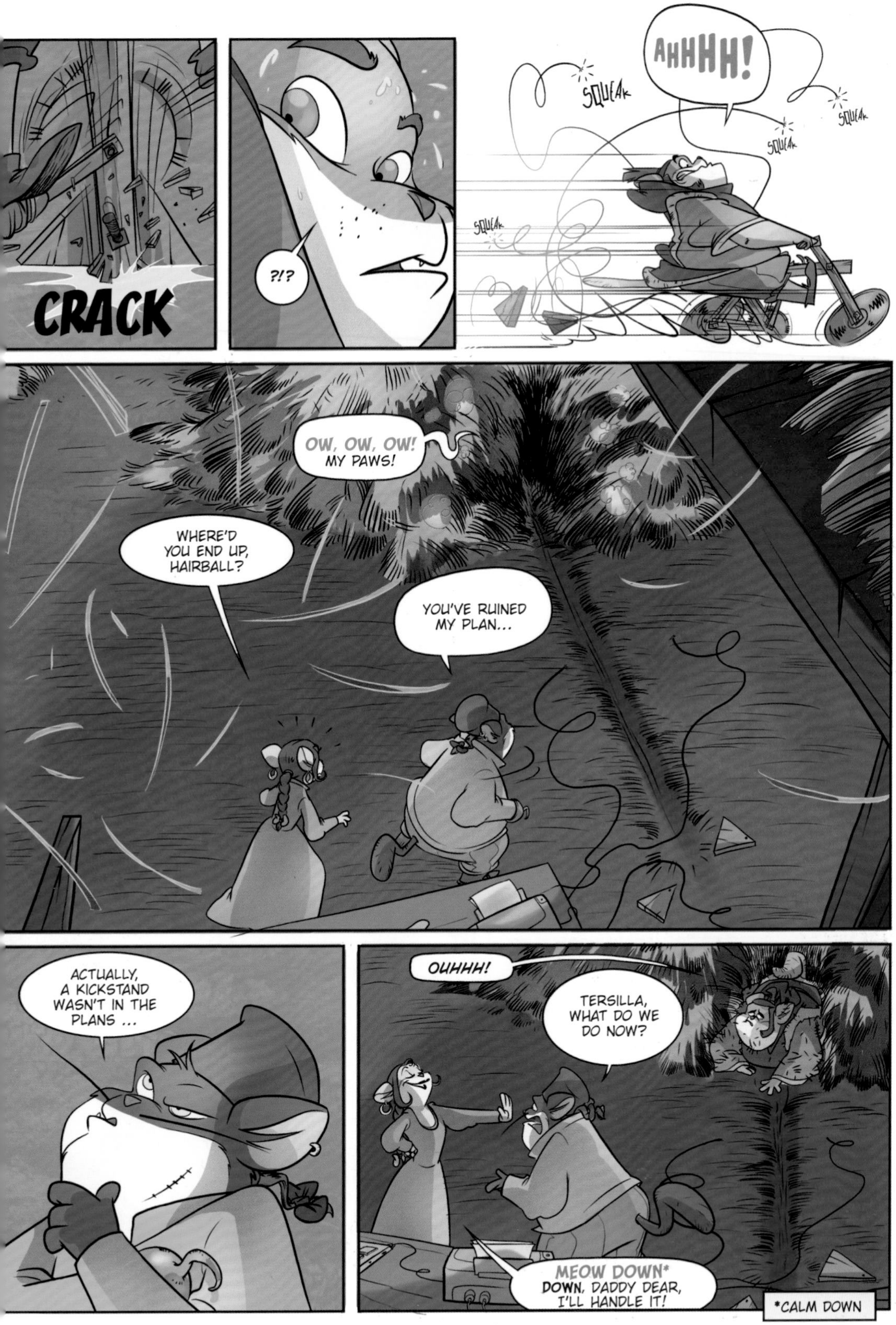
CRACK
?!?
AHHHH!
SQUEAK
SQUEAK
SQUEAK
SQUEAK
OW, OW, OW! MY PAWS!
WHERE'D YOU END UP, HAIRBALL?
YOU'VE RUINED MY PLAN...
ACTUALLY, A KICKSTAND WASN'T IN THE PLANS ...
OUHHH!
TERSILLA, WHAT DO WE DO NOW?
MEOW DOWN* DOWN, DADDY DEAR, I'LL HANDLE IT!
*CALM DOWN

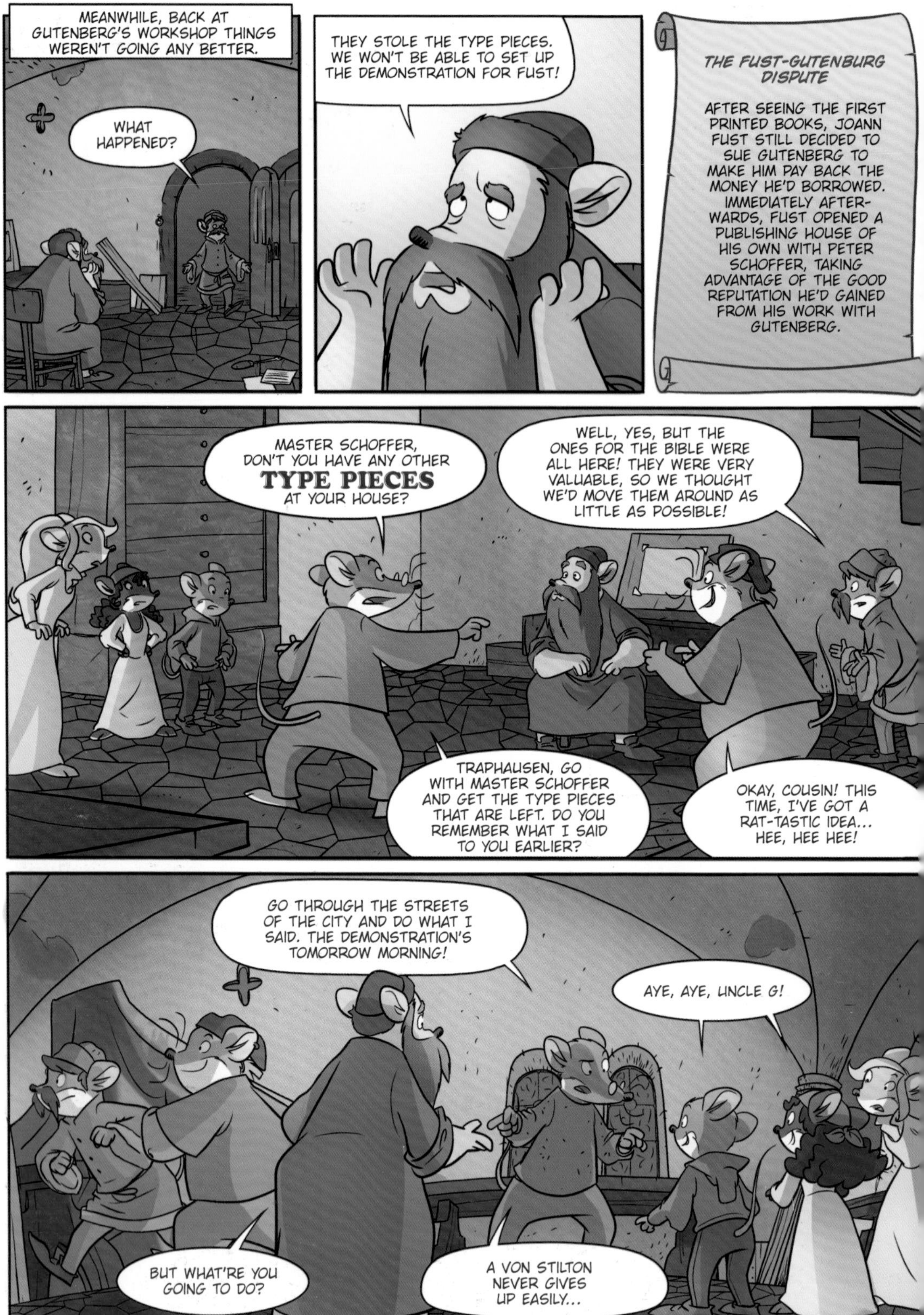
MEANWHILE, BACK AT GUTENBERG'S WORKSHOP THINGS WEREN'T GOING ANY BETTER.
WHAT HAPPENED?
THEY STOLE THE TYPE PIECES. WE WON'T BE ABLE TO SET UP THE DEMONSTRATION FOR FUST!
THE FUST-GUTENBURG DISPUTE
AFTER SEEING THE FIRST PRINTED BOOKS, JOANN FUST STILL DECIDED TO SUE GUTENBERG TO MAKE HIM PAY BACK THE MONEY HE'D BORROWED. IMMEDIATELY AFTER-WARDS, FUST OPENED A PUBLISHING HOUSE OF HIS OWN WITH PETER SCHOFFER, TAKING ADVANTAGE OF THE GOOD REPUTATION HE'D GAINED FROM HIS WORK WITH GUTENBERG.
MASTER SCHOFFER, DON'T YOU HAVE ANY OTHER TYPE PIECES AT YOUR HOUSE?
WELL, YES, BUT THE ONES FOR THE BIBLE WERE ALL HERE! THEY WERE VERY VALUABLE, SO WE THOUGHT WE'D MOVE THEM AROUND AS LITTLE AS POSSIBLE!
TRAPHAUSEN, GO WITH MASTER SCHOFFER AND GET THE TYPE PIECES THAT ARE LEFT. DO YOU REMEMBER WHAT I SAID TO YOU EARLIER?
OKAY, COUSIN! THIS TIME, I'VE GOT A RAT-TASTIC IDEA... HEE, HEE HEE!
GO THROUGH THE STREETS OF THE CITY AND DO WHAT I SAID. THE DEMONSTRATION'S TOMORROW MORNING!
AYE, AYE, UNCLE G!
BUT WHAT'RE YOU GOING TO DO?
A VON STILTON NEVER GIVES UP EASILY...

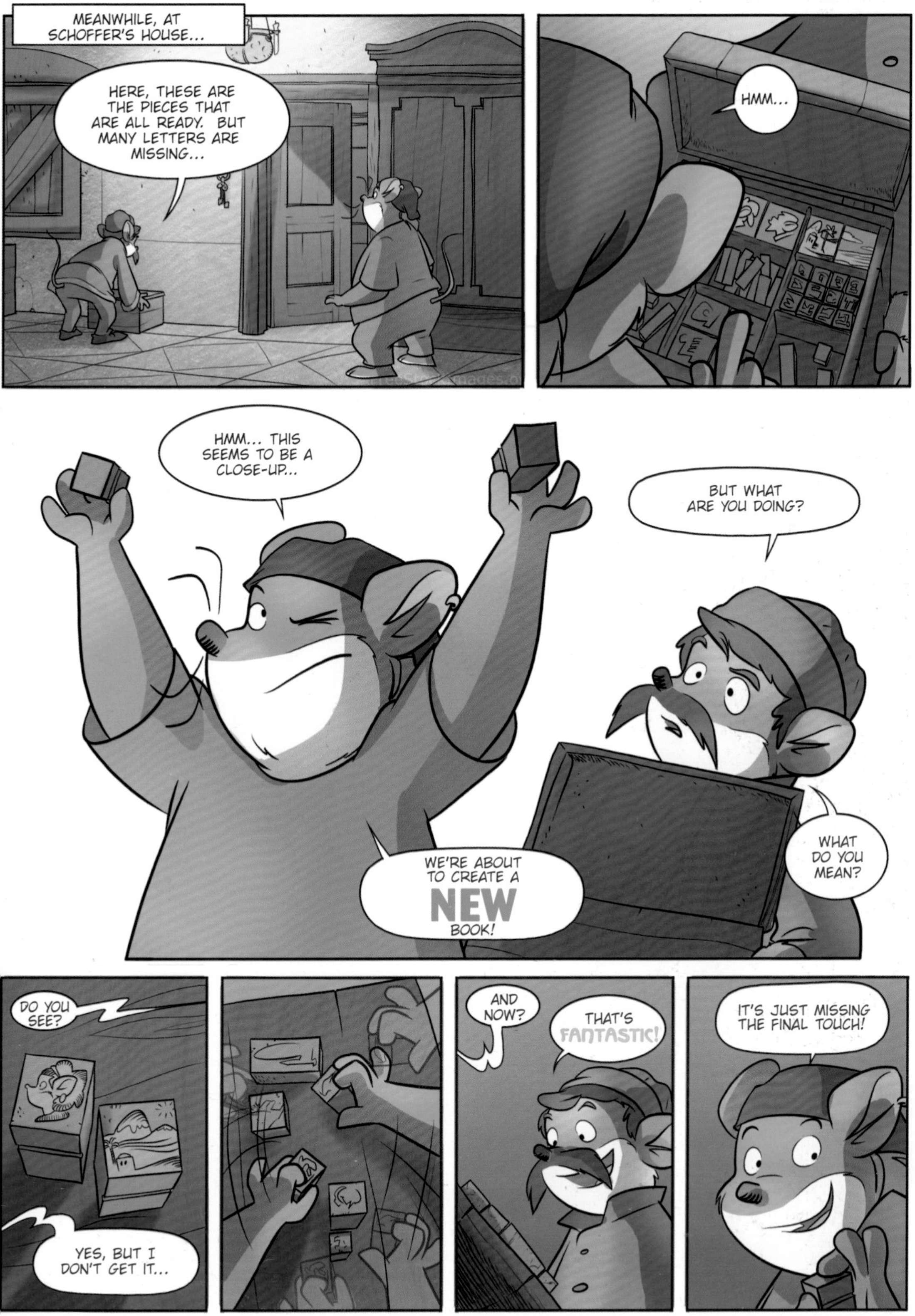
MEANWHILE, AT SCHOFFER'S HOUSE...
HERE, THESE ARE THE PIECES THAT ARE ALL READY. BUT MANY LETTERS ARE MISSING...
HMM...
HMM... THIS SEEMS TO BE A CLOSE-UP...
BUT WHAT ARE YOU DOING?
WE'RE ABOUT TO CREATE A NEW BOOK!
WHAT DO YOU MEAN?
DO YOU SEE?
YES, BUT I DON'T GET IT...
AND NOW?
THAT'S FANTASTIC!
IT'S JUST MISSING THE FINAL TOUCH!

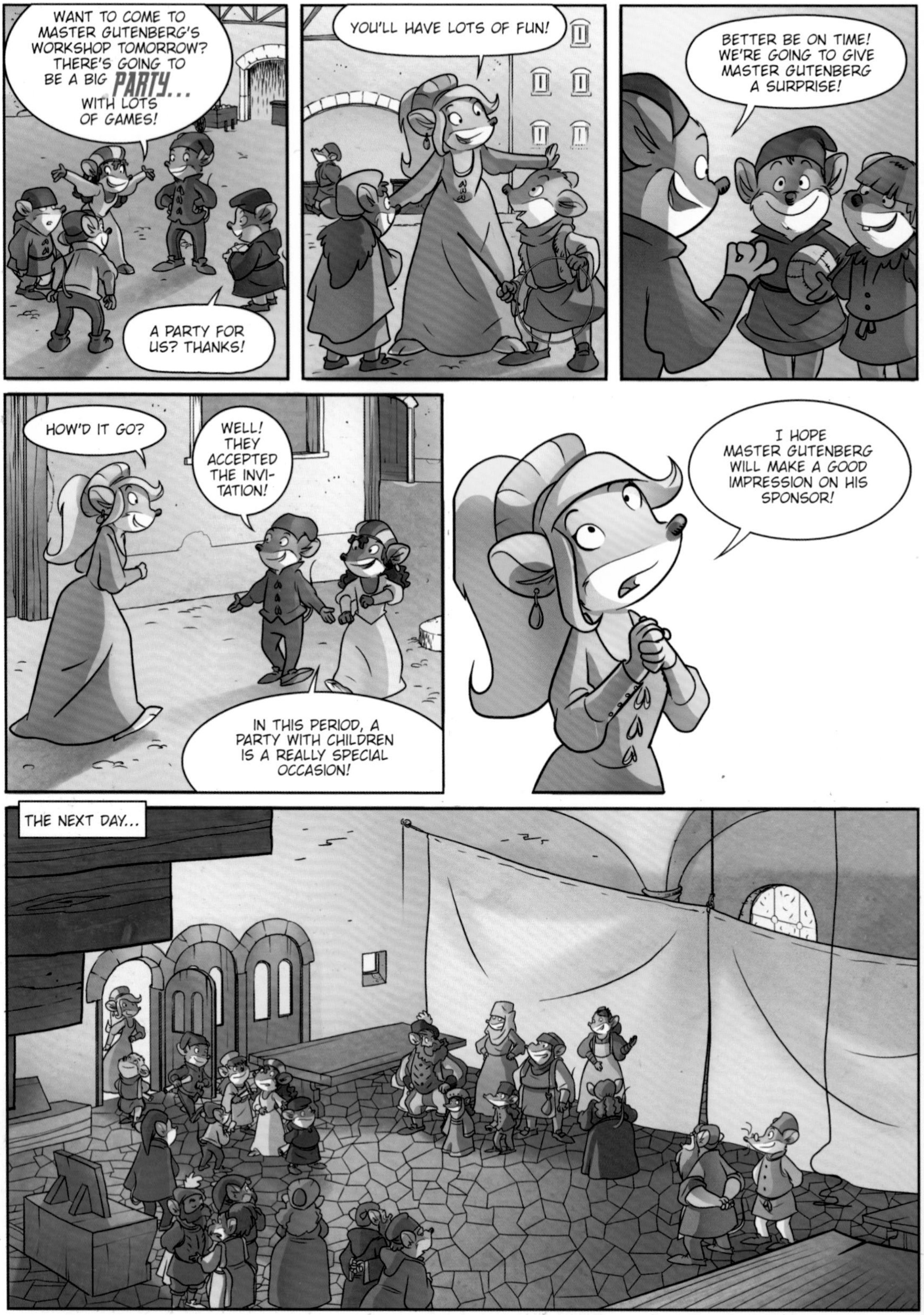
WANT TO COME TO MASTER GUTENBERG'S WORKSHOP TOMORROW? THERE'S GOING TO BE A BIG PARTY... WITH LOTS OF GAMES!
A PARTY FOR US? THANKS!
YOU'LL HAVE LOTS OF FUN!
BETTER BE ON TIME! WE'RE GOING TO GIVE MASTER GUTENBERG A SURPRISE!
HOW'D IT GO?
WELL! THEY ACCEPTED THE INVI-TATION!
IN THIS PERIOD, A PARTY WITH CHILDREN IS A REALLY SPECIAL OCCASION!
I HOPE MASTER GUTENBERG WILL MAKE A GOOD IMPRESSION ON HIS SPONSOR!
THE NEXT DAY...

TAKE ONE EACH AND THEN FOLLOW BUGSY WUGSY BEHIND THE CURTAIN.

ARE YOU SURE IT'LL WORK?

DON'T WORRY, THEY'RE ALL FANS!

THAT MAN NEXT TO THE MAYOR IS **JOHANN FUST!** WHEN I ASKED HIM TO SPONSOR ME, I EXPLAINED THAT I WANTED TO DO GOOD QUALITY WORK! BUT HE ONLY CARED ABOUT PROFITS, NOT WHETHER THE VOLUMES WERE PRINTED WELL...

HMPH...

SO, GUTENBERG, ARE WE GOING TO SEE HOW THIS MACHINE WORKS?

OF COURSE!

DEAR FRIENDS, I'M HAPPY TO PRESENT TO YOU...

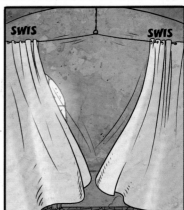

SWIS

SWIS

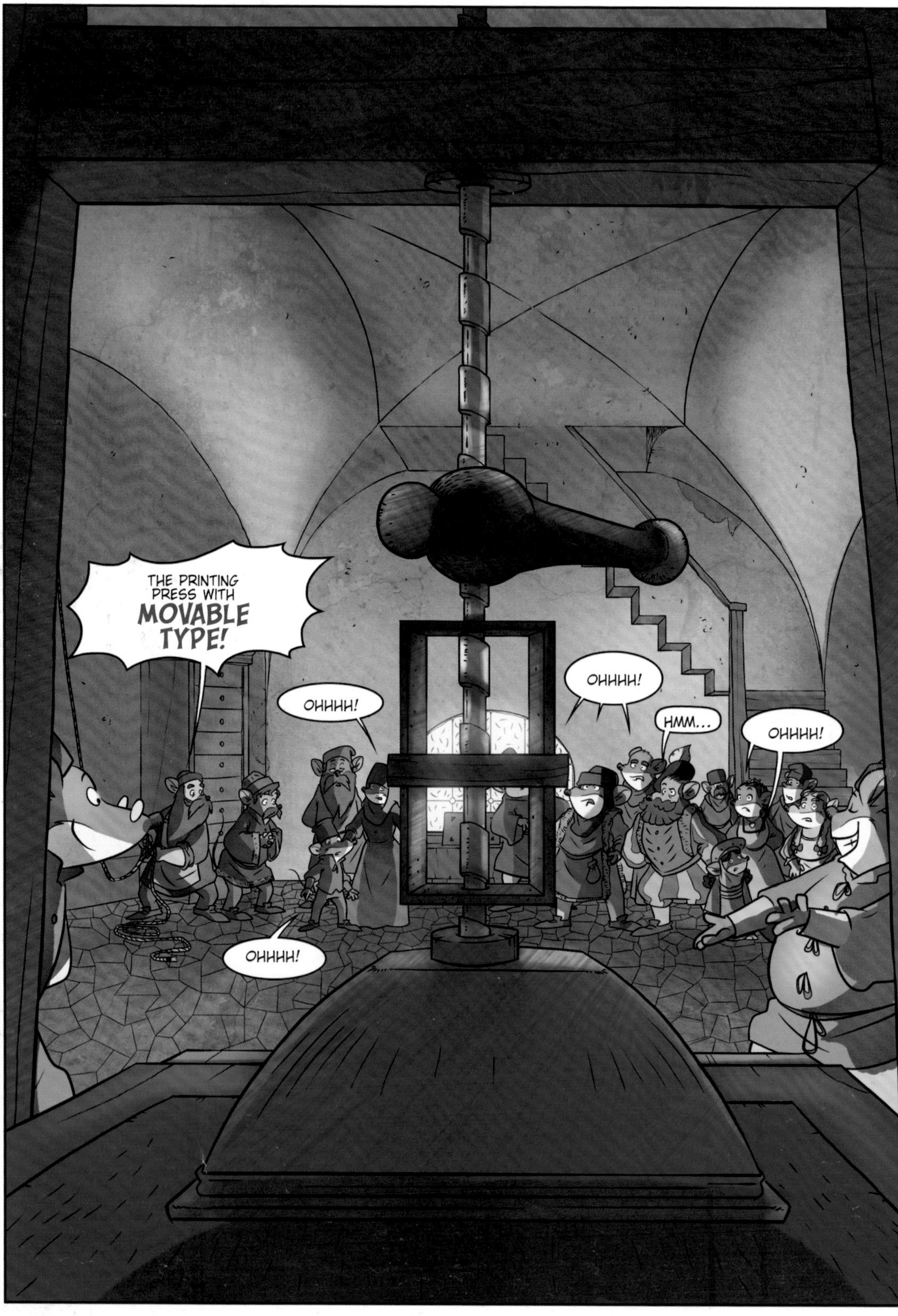
THE PRINTING PRESS WITH **MOVABLE TYPE!**
OHHHH!
OHHHH!
HMM...
OHHHH!
OHHHH!

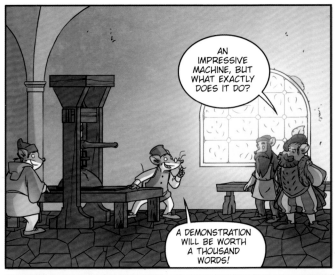

AN IMPRESSIVE MACHINE, BUT WHAT EXACTLY DOES IT DO?

A DEMONSTRATION WILL BE WORTH A THOUSAND WORDS!

START, TRAPHAUSEN!

RIGHT AWAY, COUSIN!

KCHOK KCHOK KCHOK KCHOK

MASTER GUTENBERG'S PROCESS CONSISTS OF LINING UP SINGLE TYPE PIECES...

...SET UP BY THE ENGRAVER FOR THIS OCCASION, TO FORM A PAGE...

...INK GETS SPREAD ACROSS IT...

KCHOK KCHOK KCHOK

...AND THEN IT'S PRESSED ONTO A SHEET OF PAPER OR PARCHMENT.

HERE'S A PAGE THAT'S ALL READY!

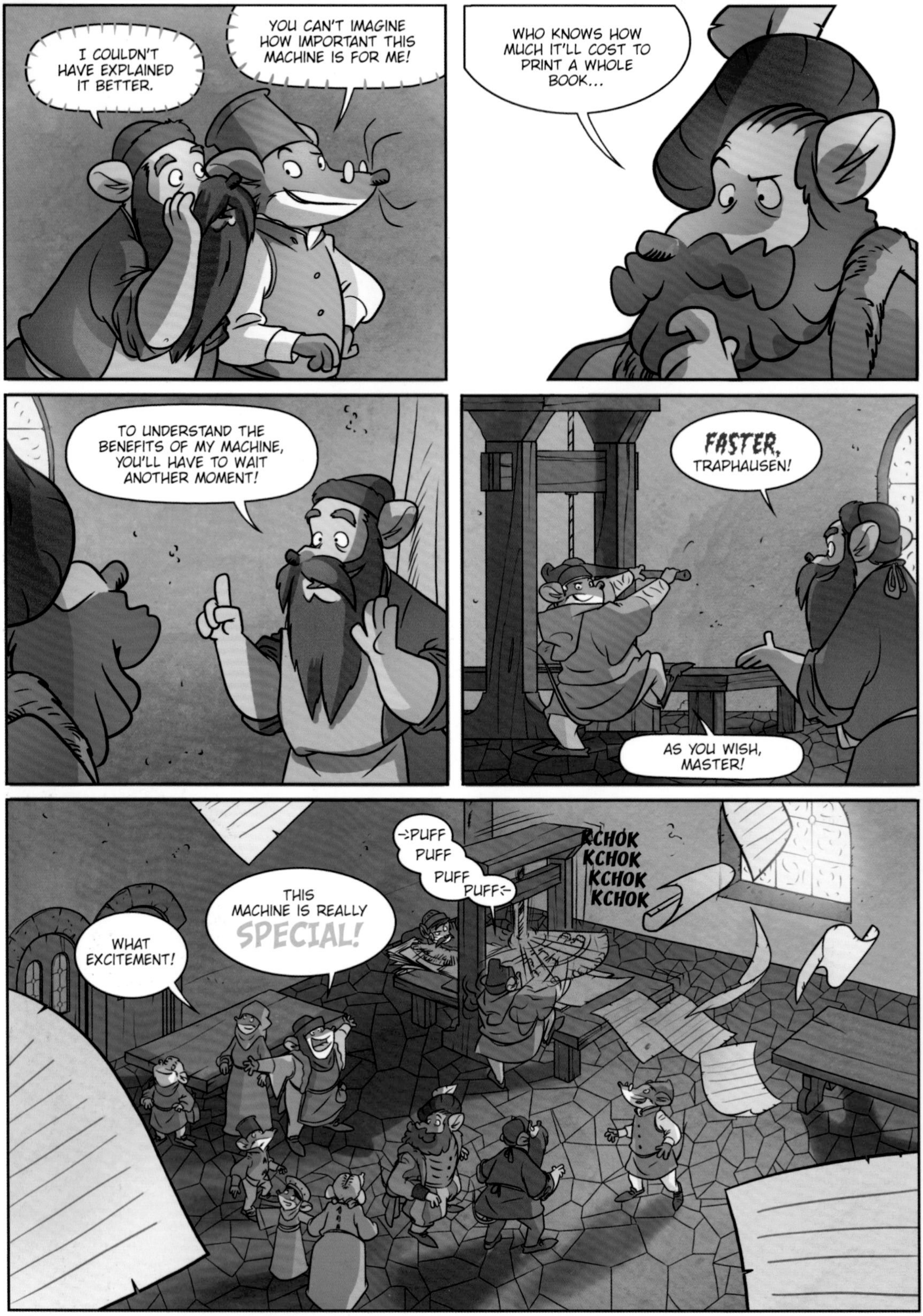

I COULDN'T HAVE EXPLAINED IT BETTER.
YOU CAN'T IMAGINE HOW IMPORTANT THIS MACHINE IS FOR ME!
WHO KNOWS HOW MUCH IT'LL COST TO PRINT A WHOLE BOOK...
TO UNDERSTAND THE BENEFITS OF MY MACHINE, YOU'LL HAVE TO WAIT ANOTHER MOMENT!
FASTER, TRAPHAUSEN!
AS YOU WISH, MASTER!
PUFF PUFF PUFF PUFF
KCHOK KCHOK KCHOK KCHOK
THIS MACHINE IS REALLY SPECIAL!
WHAT EXCITEMENT!

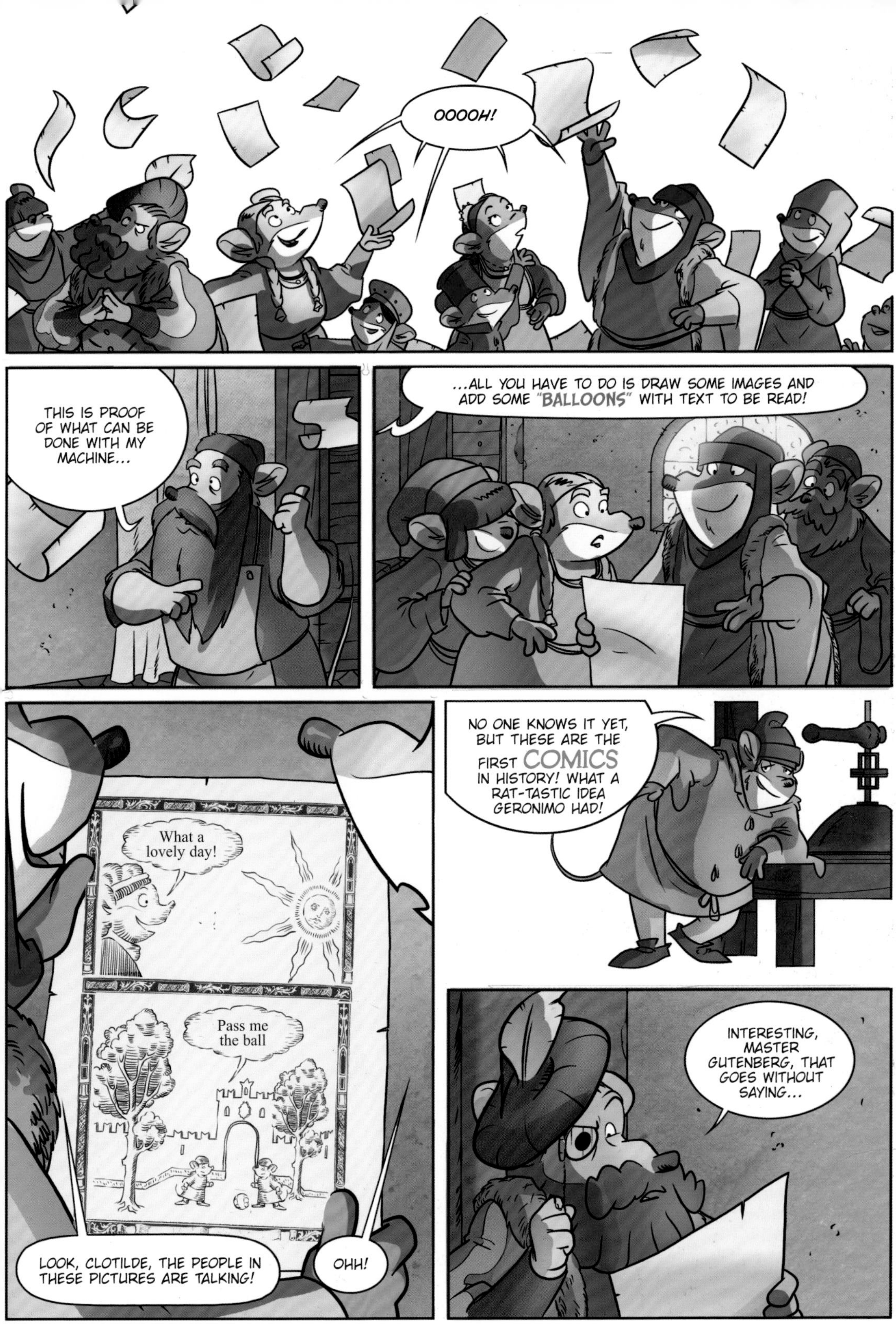
OOOOH!
THIS IS PROOF OF WHAT CAN BE DONE WITH MY MACHINE...
...ALL YOU HAVE TO DO IS DRAW SOME IMAGES AND ADD SOME "BALLOONS" WITH TEXT TO BE READ!
What a lovely day!
Pass me the ball
LOOK, CLOTILDE, THE PEOPLE IN THESE PICTURES ARE TALKING!
OHH!
NO ONE KNOWS IT YET, BUT THESE ARE THE FIRST COMICS IN HISTORY! WHAT A RAT-TASTIC IDEA GERONIMO HAD!
INTERESTING, MASTER GUTENBERG, THAT GOES WITHOUT SAYING...

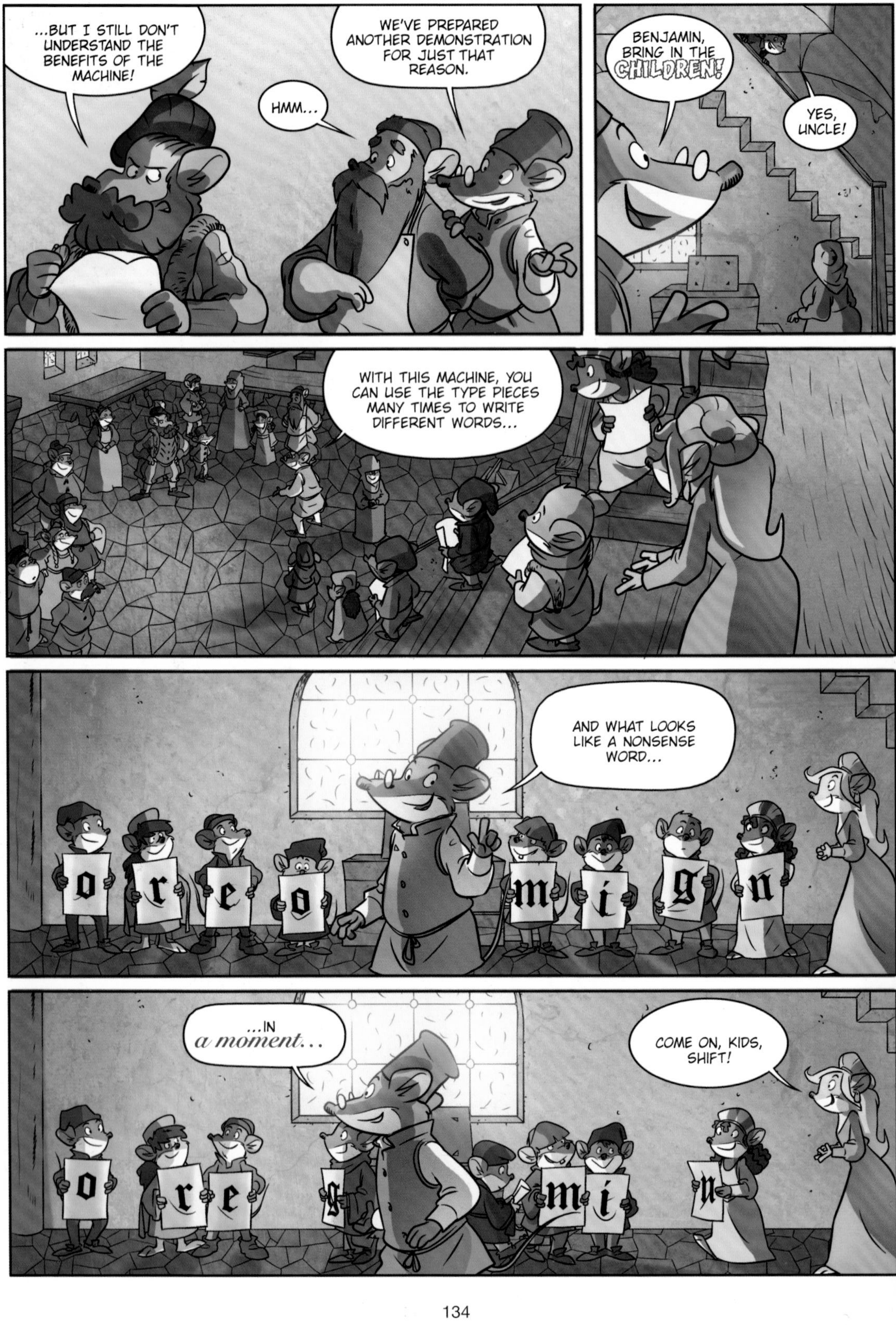
...BUT I STILL DON'T UNDERSTAND THE BENEFITS OF THE MACHINE!
HMM...
WE'VE PREPARED ANOTHER DEMONSTRATION FOR JUST THAT REASON.
BENJAMIN, BRING IN THE CHILDREN!
YES, UNCLE!
WITH THIS MACHINE, YOU CAN USE THE TYPE PIECES MANY TIMES TO WRITE DIFFERENT WORDS...
AND WHAT LOOKS LIKE A NONSENSE WORD...
o r e o m i g n
...IN a moment...
COME ON, KIDS, SHIFT!
o r e g mi n

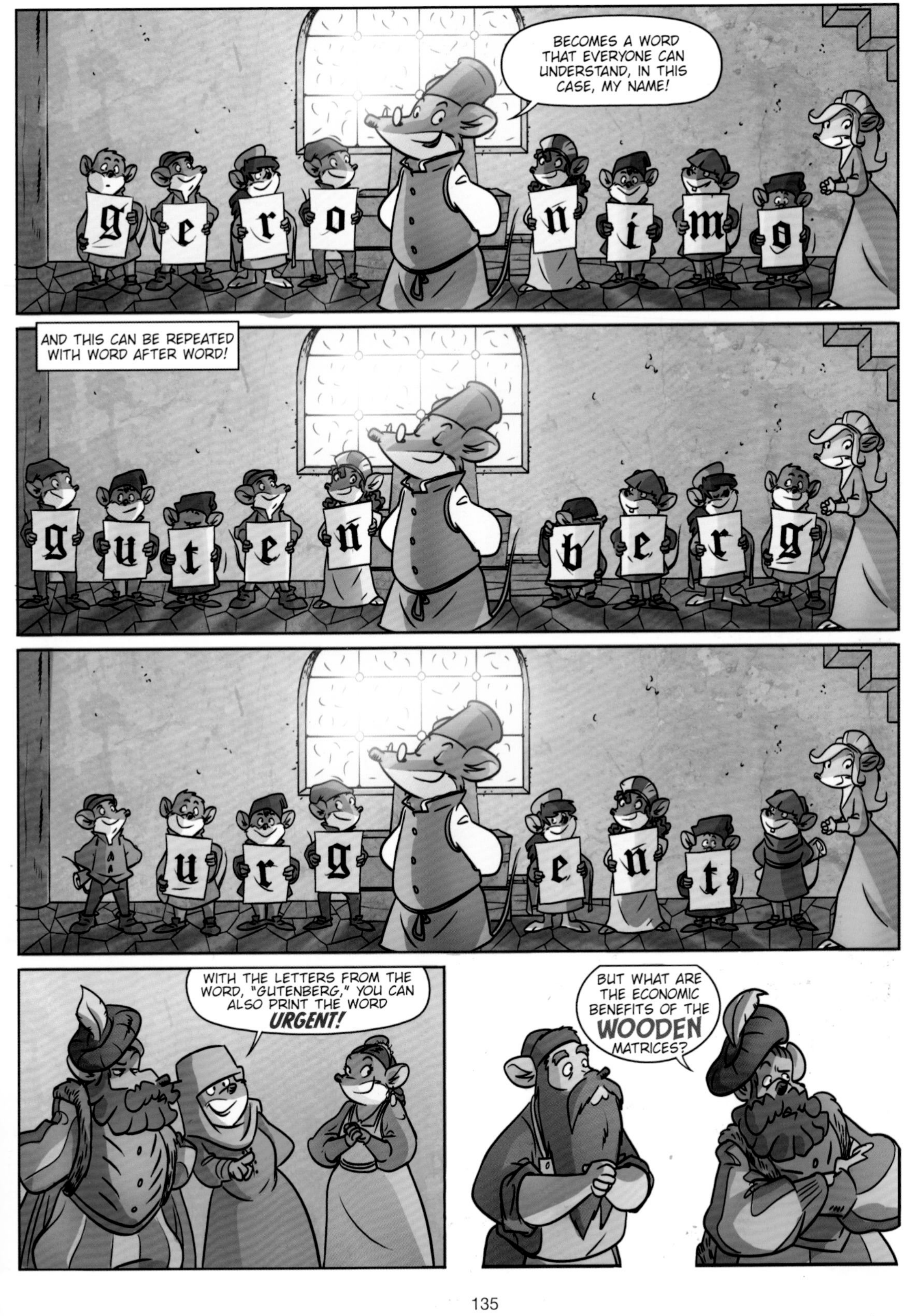
BECOMES A WORD THAT EVERYONE CAN UNDERSTAND, IN THIS CASE, MY NAME!
g e r o n i m o
AND THIS CAN BE REPEATED WITH WORD AFTER WORD!
g u t e n b e r g
u r g e n t
WITH THE LETTERS FROM THE WORD, "GUTENBERG," YOU CAN ALSO PRINT THE WORD URGENT!
BUT WHAT ARE THE ECONOMIC BENEFITS OF THE WOODEN MATRICES?

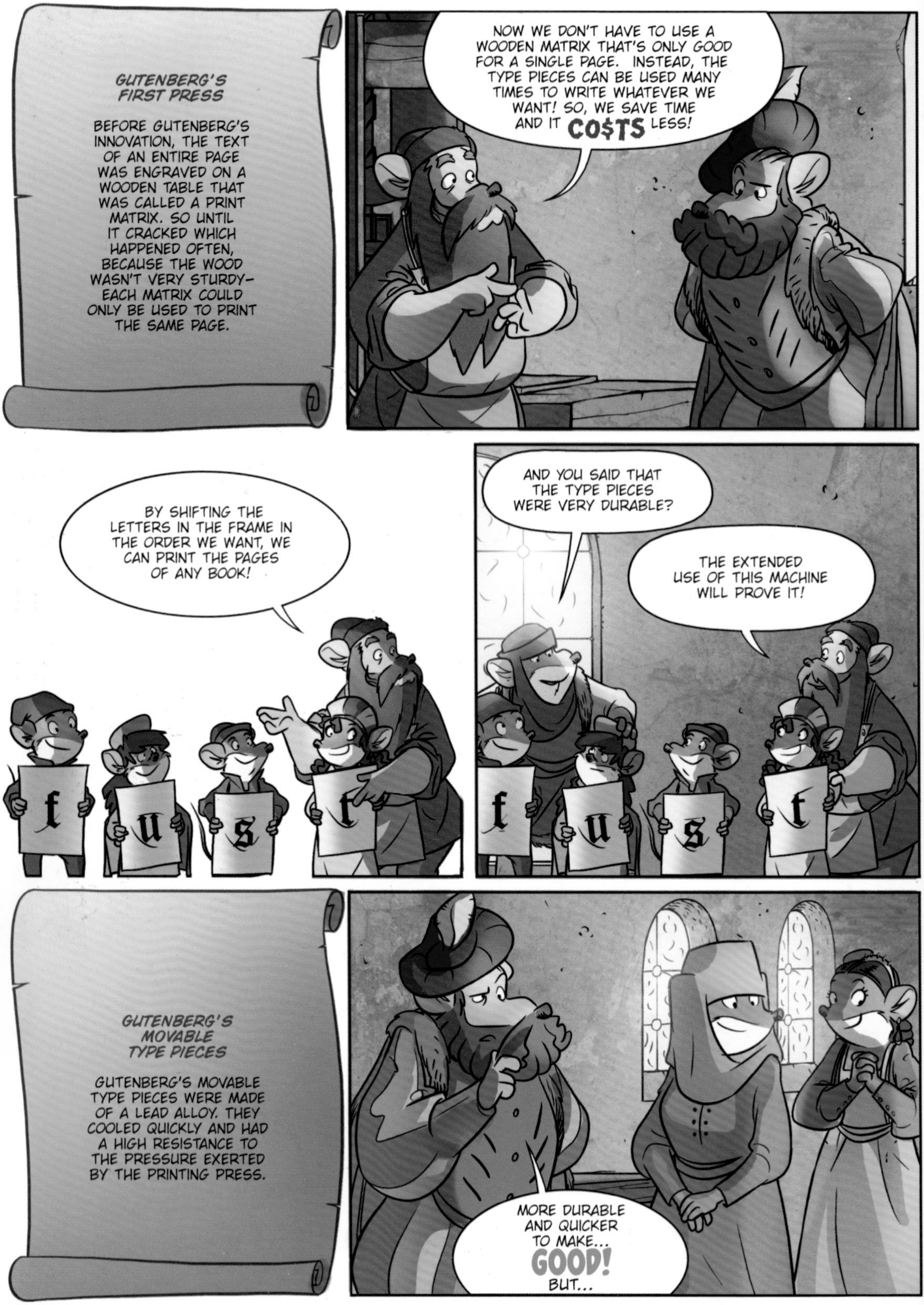
GUTENBERG'S FIRST PRESS
BEFORE GUTENBERG'S INNOVATION, THE TEXT OF AN ENTIRE PAGE WAS ENGRAVED ON A WOODEN TABLE THAT WAS CALLED A PRINT MATRIX. SO UNTIL IT CRACKED WHICH HAPPENED OFTEN, BECAUSE THE WOOD WASN'T VERY STURDY—EACH MATRIX COULD ONLY BE USED TO PRINT THE SAME PAGE.
NOW WE DON'T HAVE TO USE A WOODEN MATRIX THAT'S ONLY GOOD FOR A SINGLE PAGE. INSTEAD, THE TYPE PIECES CAN BE USED MANY TIMES TO WRITE WHATEVER WE WANT! SO, WE SAVE TIME AND IT CO$TS LESS!
BY SHIFTING THE LETTERS IN THE FRAME IN THE ORDER WE WANT, WE CAN PRINT THE PAGES OF ANY BOOK!
f u s t
AND YOU SAID THAT THE TYPE PIECES WERE VERY DURABLE?
THE EXTENDED USE OF THIS MACHINE WILL PROVE IT!
f u s t
GUTENBERG'S MOVABLE TYPE PIECES
GUTENBERG'S MOVABLE TYPE PIECES WERE MADE OF A LEAD ALLOY. THEY COOLED QUICKLY AND HAD A HIGH RESISTANCE TO THE PRESSURE EXERTED BY THE PRINTING PRESS.
MORE DURABLE AND QUICKER TO MAKE... GOOD! BUT...

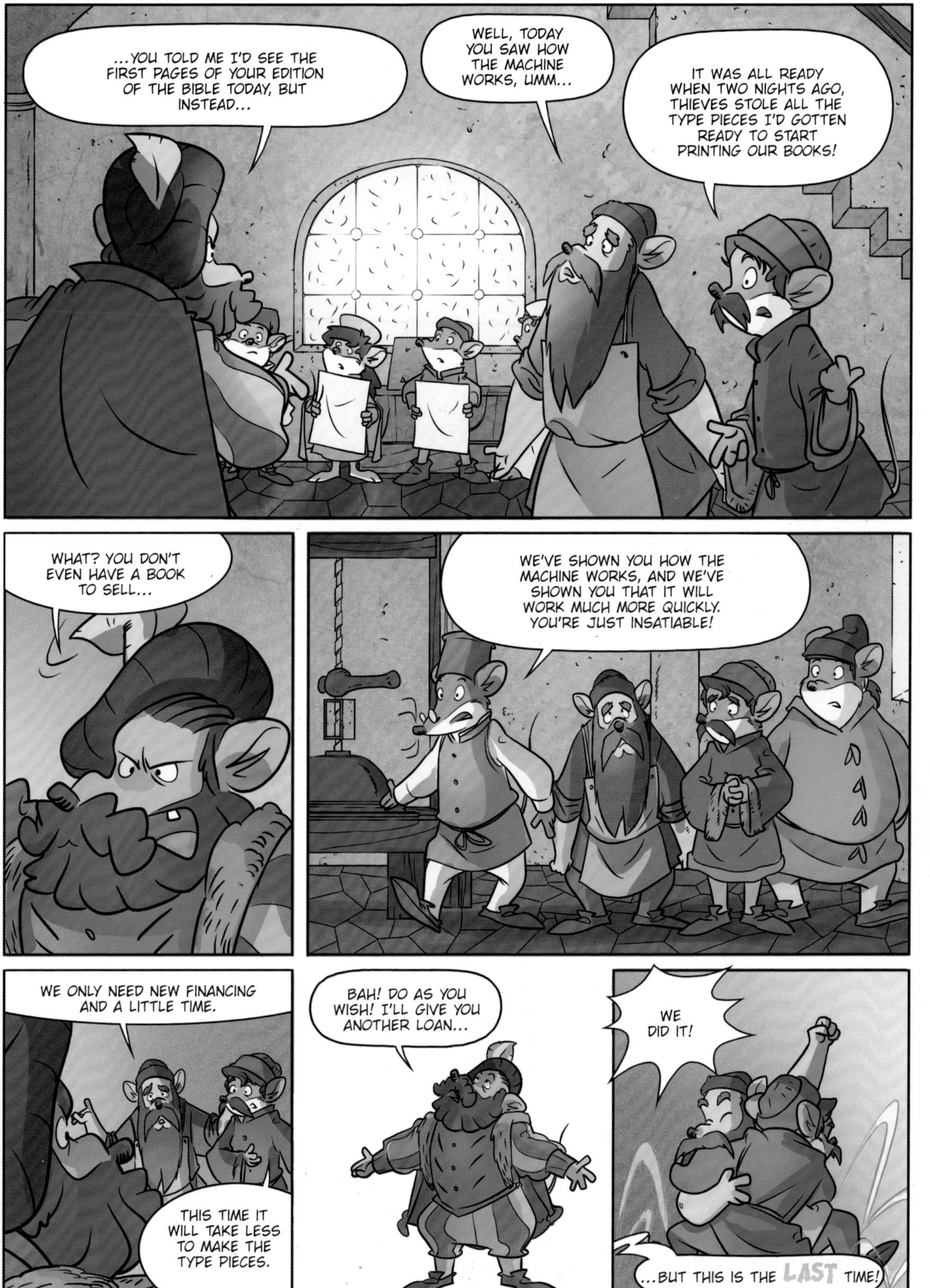
...YOU TOLD ME I'D SEE THE FIRST PAGES OF YOUR EDITION OF THE BIBLE TODAY, BUT INSTEAD...
WELL, TODAY YOU SAW HOW THE MACHINE WORKS, UMM...
IT WAS ALL READY WHEN TWO NIGHTS AGO, THIEVES STOLE ALL THE TYPE PIECES I'D GOTTEN READY TO START PRINTING OUR BOOKS!
WHAT? YOU DON'T EVEN HAVE A BOOK TO SELL...
WE'VE SHOWN YOU HOW THE MACHINE WORKS, AND WE'VE SHOWN YOU THAT IT WILL WORK MUCH MORE QUICKLY. YOU'RE JUST INSATIABLE!
WE ONLY NEED NEW FINANCING AND A LITTLE TIME.
THIS TIME IT WILL TAKE LESS TO MAKE THE TYPE PIECES.
BAH! DO AS YOU WISH! I'LL GIVE YOU ANOTHER LOAN...
WE DID IT!
...BUT THIS IS THE LAST TIME!

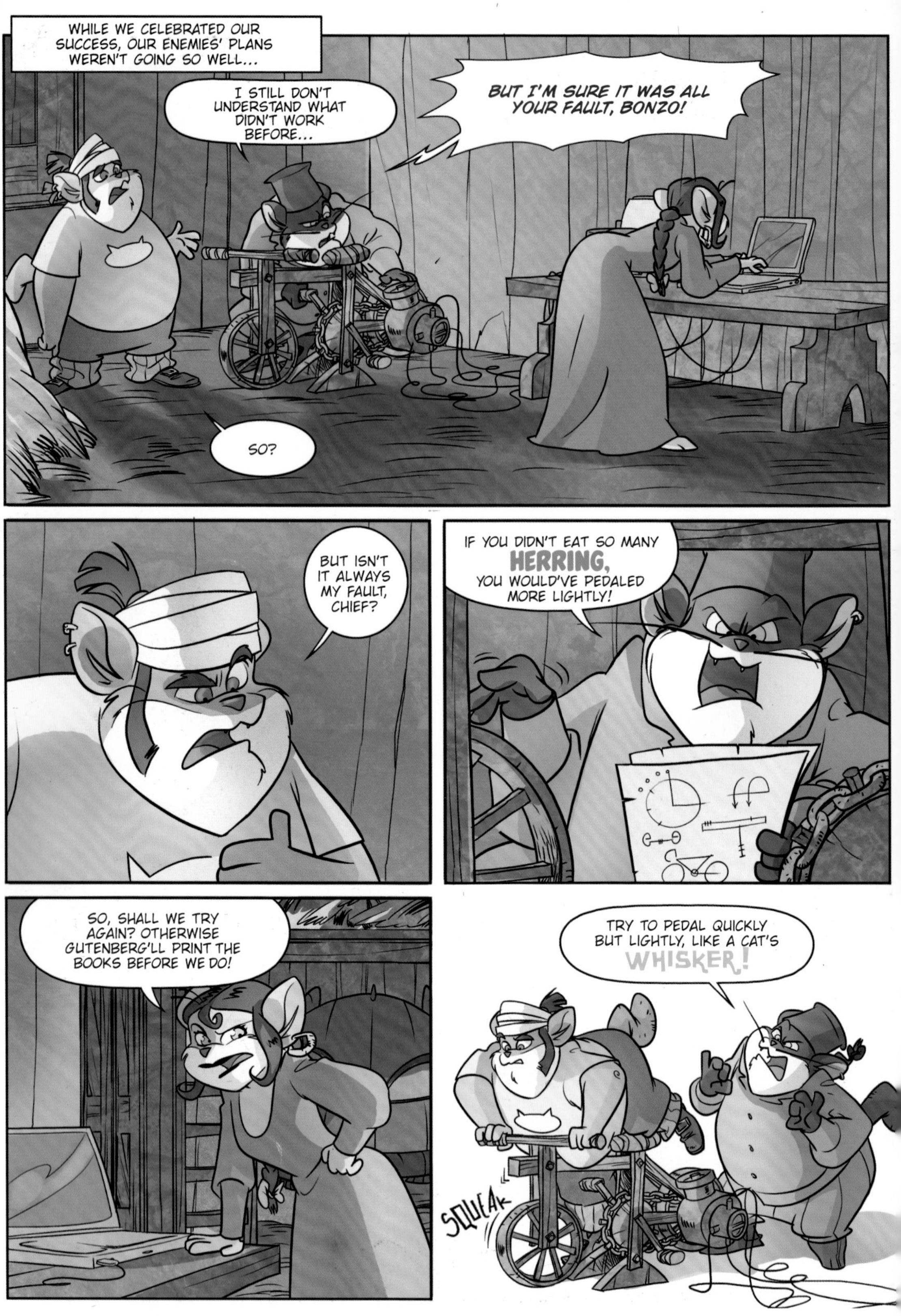
WHILE WE CELEBRATED OUR SUCCESS, OUR ENEMIES' PLANS WEREN'T GOING SO WELL...
I STILL DON'T UNDERSTAND WHAT DIDN'T WORK BEFORE...
BUT I'M SURE IT WAS ALL YOUR FAULT, BONZO!
SO?
BUT ISN'T IT ALWAYS MY FAULT, CHIEF?
IF YOU DIDN'T EAT SO MANY HERRING, YOU WOULD'VE PEDALED MORE LIGHTLY!
SO, SHALL WE TRY AGAIN? OTHERWISE GUTENBERG'LL PRINT THE BOOKS BEFORE WE DO!
TRY TO PEDAL QUICKLY BUT LIGHTLY, LIKE A CAT'S WHISKER!
SQUEAK

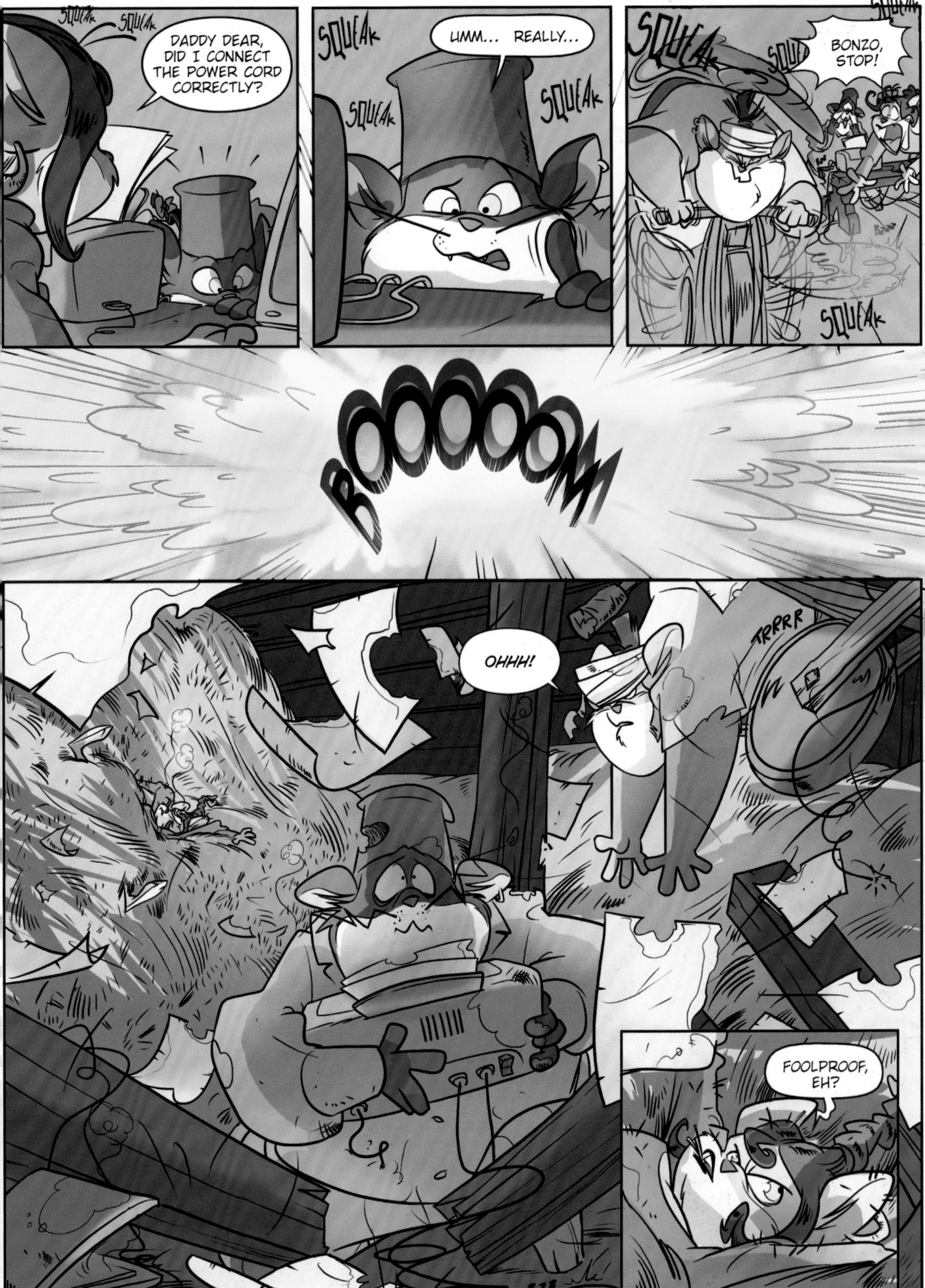
SQUEAK
SQUEAK
DADDY DEAR, DID I CONNECT THE POWER CORD CORRECTLY?
SQUEAK
UMM... REALLY...
SQUEAK
SQUEAK
SQUEAK
BONZO, STOP!
SQUEAK
SQUEAK
BOOOOOOM
TRRRR
OHHH!
FOOLPROOF, EH?

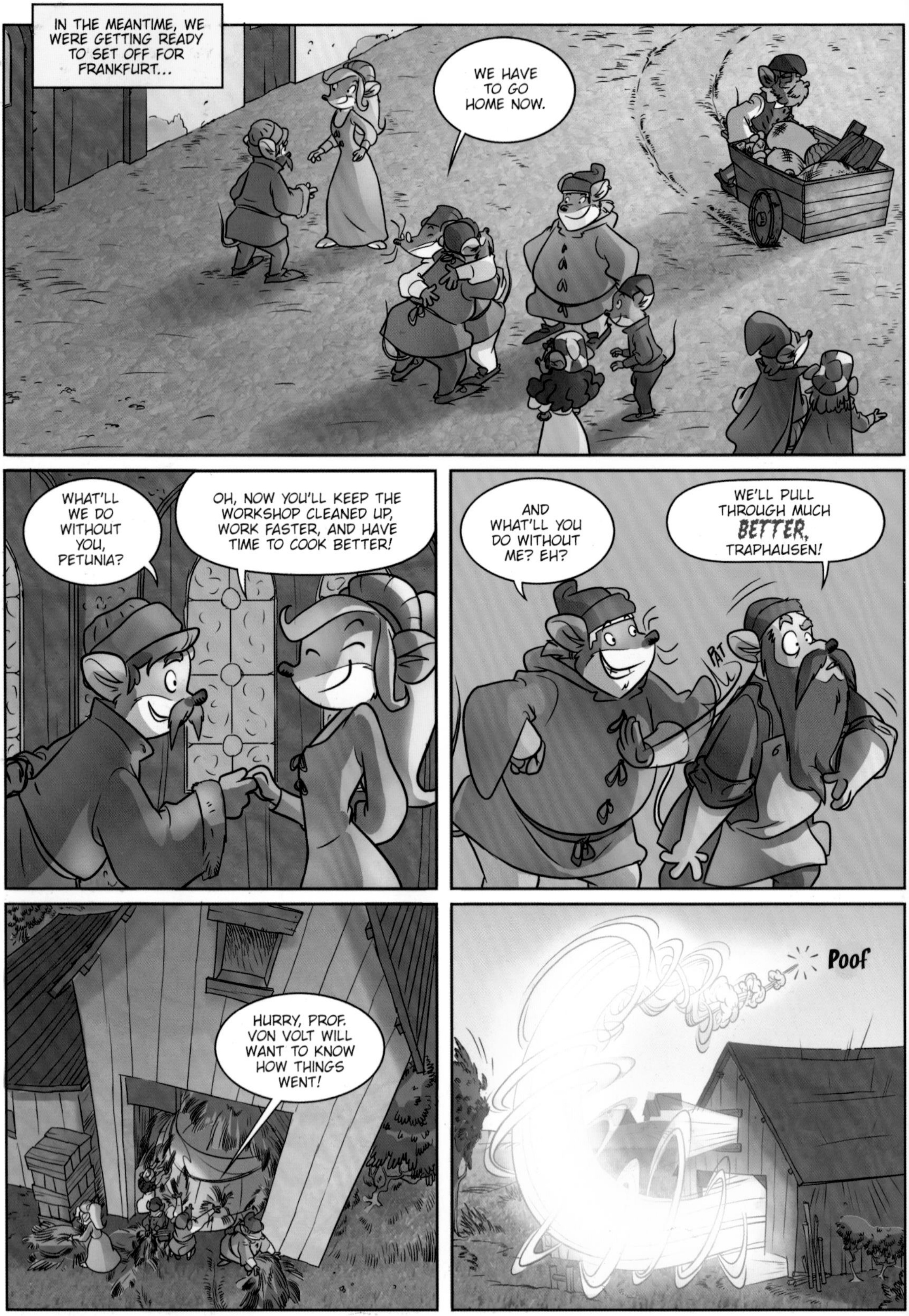
IN THE MEANTIME, WE WERE GETTING READY TO SET OFF FOR FRANKFURT...
WE HAVE TO GO HOME NOW.
WHAT'LL WE DO WITHOUT YOU, PETUNIA?
OH, NOW YOU'LL KEEP THE WORKSHOP CLEANED UP, WORK FASTER, AND HAVE TIME TO COOK BETTER!
AND WHAT'LL YOU DO WITHOUT ME? EH?
WE'LL PULL THROUGH MUCH BETTER, TRAPHAUSEN!
PAT
HURRY, PROF. VON VOLT WILL WANT TO KNOW HOW THINGS WENT!
Poof

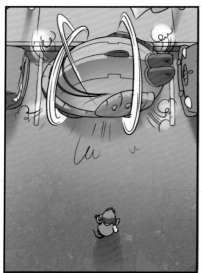

FRIENDS! SO, HOW'D IT GO?

...AND GERONIMO WAS ABLE TO HELP GUTENBERG DO A DEMONSTRATION OF THE PRINTING PRESS FOR HIS BANKER, FUST!

THEY STOLE GUTENBERG'S TYPE PIECES BUT THEN **VANISHED** WITHOUT MESSING UP ANYTHING ELSE...

UMM, THANKS, PETUNIA, BUT IT WAS ALL OF US... EVEN TRAP WAS VERY HELPFUL...

SPEAKING OF WHICH, WHERE'D TRAP WIND UP?

I NEEDED A **SNACK.** AFTER ALL, TODAY WE INVENTED COMICS!

I'D SUGGEST THAT STAY A SECRET, TRAP: WE CAN'T CHANGE HISTORY! AND NOW, LET'S GET BACK TO THE FAIR. EVERYONE'S WAITING FOR GERONIMO AT THE CONFERENCE...

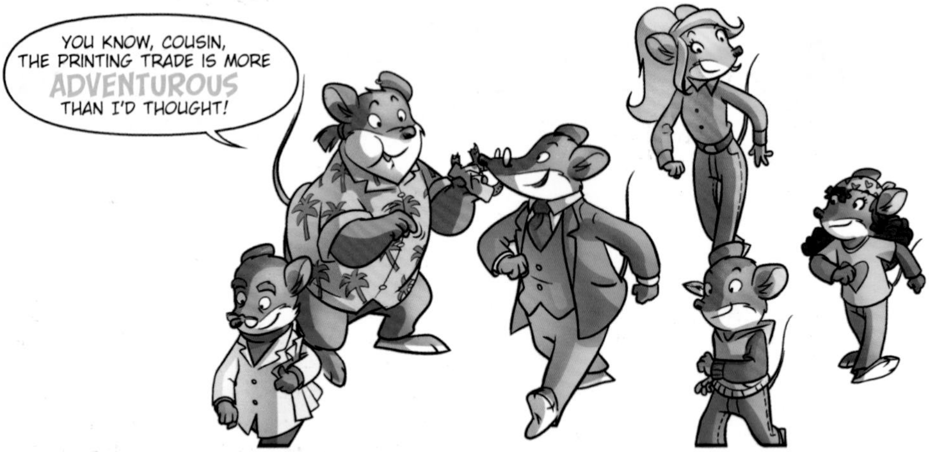
YOU KNOW, COUSIN, THE PRINTING TRADE IS MORE ADVENTUROUS THAN I'D THOUGHT!

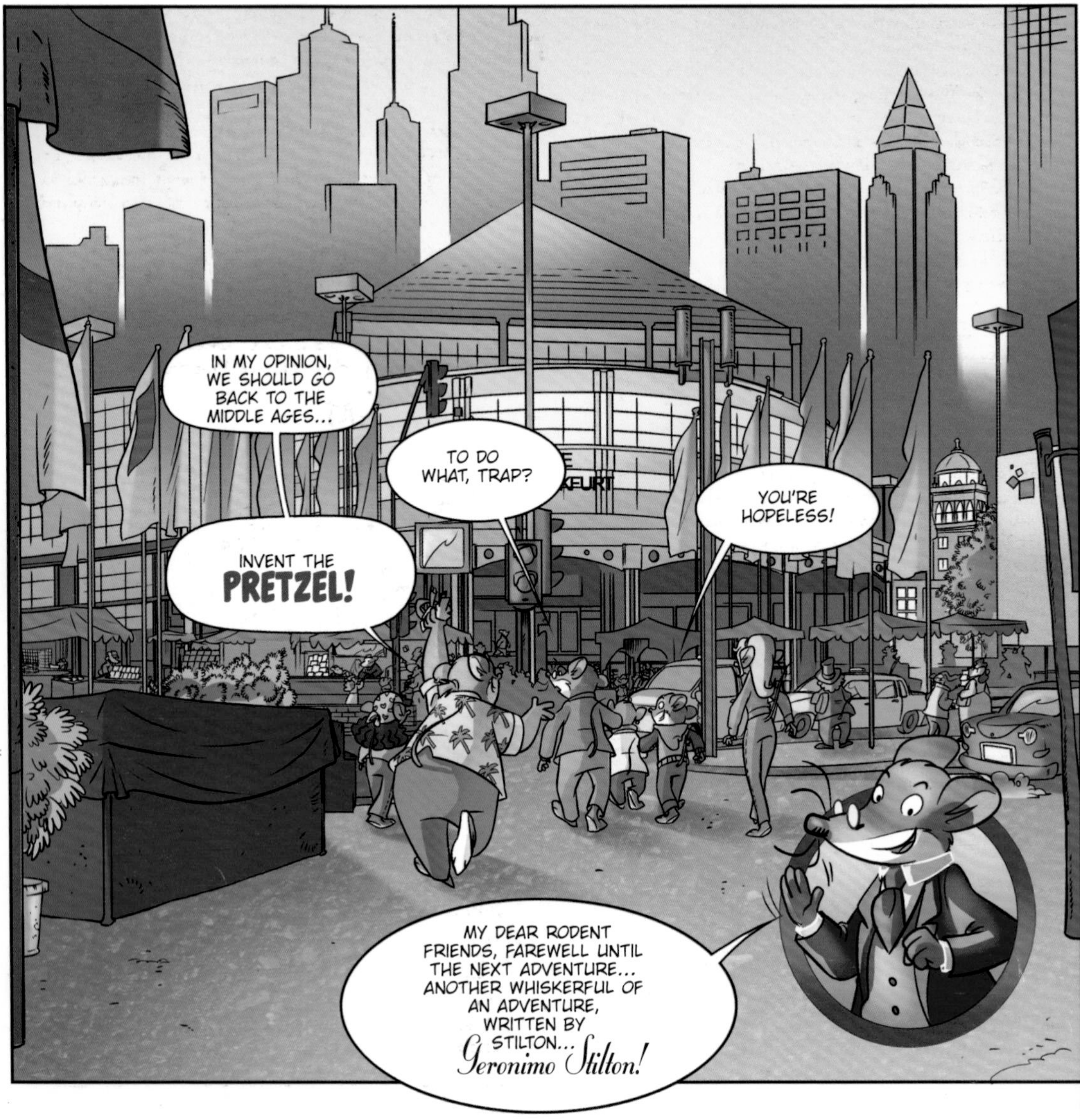
IN MY OPINION, WE SHOULD GO BACK TO THE MIDDLE AGES...
TO DO WHAT, TRAP?
INVENT THE PRETZEL!
YOU'RE HOPELESS!
MY DEAR RODENT FRIENDS, FAREWELL UNTIL THE NEXT ADVENTURE... ANOTHER WHISKERFUL OF AN ADVENTURE, WRITTEN BY STILTON... Geronimo Stilton!

Watch Out For PAPERCUTZ

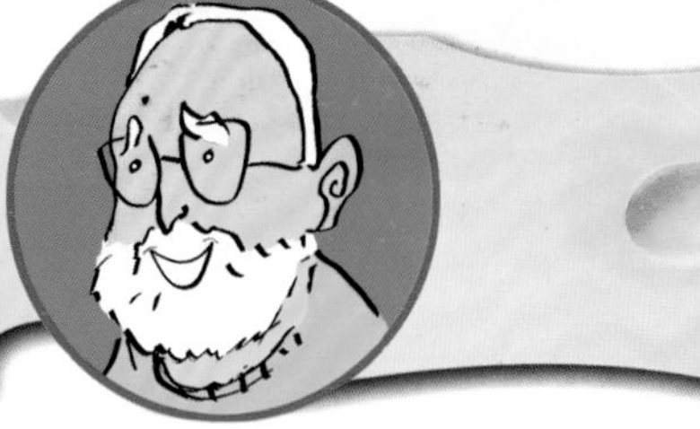

Welcome to the third time-travelling GERONIMO STILTON 3 IN 1 graphic novel, collecting three great GERONIMO STILTON graphic novels: "Dinosaurs in Action," "Play It Again, Mozart!" and "The Weird Book Machine," from Papercutz—those ink-stained wretches dedicated to publishing great graphic novels for all ages. Oh, and I'm Salicrup, *Jim Salicrup*, the Editor-in-Chief and Believer-in-Melowies*, here to chat with you a little bit and to even share a little philosophy with you...

For those of you who especially enjoyed "Dinosaurs in Action," there's a Papercutz graphic novel series we bet you'll also enjoy: DINOSAUR EXPLORERS! It's the adventures of a group of kids—Rain, Emily, Sean, and Stone—under the guidance of Dr. Da Vinci (Not to be confused with Leonardo da Vinci, who we last met in GERONIMO STILTON 3 IN 1 #2, in "Who Stole the Mona Lisa?," or any teenage, mutant, ninja turtles.), his assistant, Diana, and Starz, their helpful tiny robot, as they travel through time encountering not only dinosaurs, but even the prehistoric creatures that existed before the dinosaurs. Like the GERONIMO STILTON graphic novels, it's an exciting mix of science fiction (time travel) and historic facts (dinosaurs). Look for DINOSAUR EXPLORERS at booksellers and libraries everywhere.

And if you'd like to take a trip through time into the future instead of the past, may we suggest checking out THE ONLY LIVING GIRL series? It picks up right where the award-winning THE ONLY LIVING BOY Papercutz graphic novel series left off—on a strange patchwork planet filled the alien races and scary monsters at some point in the future. Created by writer David Gallaher and artist Steve Ellis, it tells the tale of two humans and their friends trying to survive life on a scientifically combined world.

But what about the future of Geronimo Stilton? What's he up to after repeatedly protecting the past from the dastardly Pirate Cats? Glad you asked! He's starring in an animated series, seen on Netflix and Amazon Prime, and a new graphic novel series from Papercutz titled GERONIMO STILTON REPORTER. He must have a time machine or something to be the star reporter on the Rodent's Gazette and the editor-in-chief—Oh, wait! He does. (Note to self: Get a Speedrat!)

And if you've been following the *Watch Out for Papercutz* pages in GERONIMO STILTON 3 IN 1 and GERONIMO STILTON REPORTER, then you know we've been sharing and talking about the *Philosophy of Geronimo Stilton,* as featured on geronimostilton.com. This philosophy is the guidelines used by everyone involved in creating Geronimo Stilton stories for every medium—chapter books, comics, and TV. In other words, these are the values embraced by Geronimo Stilton and expressed in all Geronimo Stilton stories. So, here's another dose of that philosophy...

> GERONIMO STILTON AND FAMILY
> For Geronimo Stilton, family and loved ones are fundamental: they are the backbone of his whole life.
> Family can brighten even the darkest of days.
> Disagreements between relatives and friends that can't be resolved don't exist, nor do problems that can't be sorted out.

We hope that you're as lucky as Geronimo and that you too have a loving family.

> GERONIMO STILTON AND FRIENDSHIP
> For Geronimo friendship is a fundamental value and he is ready to put all his fears aside and to face up to any difficulties in order to preserve it. Geronimo often takes the role of the "chance hero," who confronts danger in the name of friendship.

For everyone, even those not blessed with a loving family, friends are just as important as family. It doesn't hurt to ask ourselves, as often as possible, if we're doing everything we can to help our family and friends? Just spending time with someone who is suffering from loneliness can make a big difference to that person. And if you ever feel lonely, don't forget that you can always hang with Geronimo and his family and friends just by picking up the chapter books, graphic novels, or by watching the animated show on Netflix or Amazon Prime.

Oh, and it's also worth noting how Geronimo treats his friends and family with love and respect, just as they do him. None of them are perfect, and it's accepting that fact, and appreciating each person's good qualities that's important to maintaining good relationships with your family and friends.

Speaking of which, as we've said many times before, we greatly appreciate you. We're thankful that you enjoy GERONIMO STILTON graphic novels because we love publishing them. In fact, we hope you enjoyed GERONIMO STILTON 3 IN 1 #3, and that you'll be back for #4 which features the next three graphic novels: "Geronimo Stilton Saves the Olympics," "We'll Always Have Paris," and "The First Samurai."

See you in the future, JIM

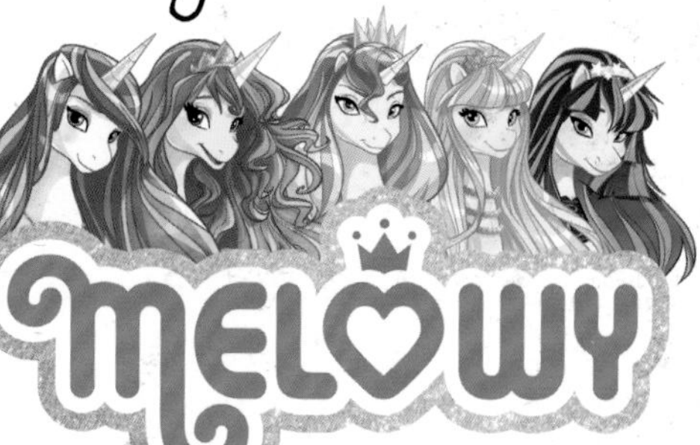
MELOWY

*You do know what Melowies are, right? If not, look for a Papercutz MELOWY graphic novel at your favorite bookseller or library. You'll thank us for it.

STAY IN TOUCH!

EMAIL:	salicrup@papercutz.com
WEB:	papercutz.com
TWITTER:	@papercutzgn
INSTAGRAM:	@papercutzgn
FACEBOOK:	PAPERCUTZGRAPHICNOVELS
FAN MAIL:	Papercutz, 160 Broadway, Suite 700, East Wing, New York, NY 10038

Thea Stilton

GRAPHIC NOVELS AVAILABLE FROM PAPERCUTZ

...ALSO AVAILABLE WHEREVER E-BOOKS ARE SOLD!

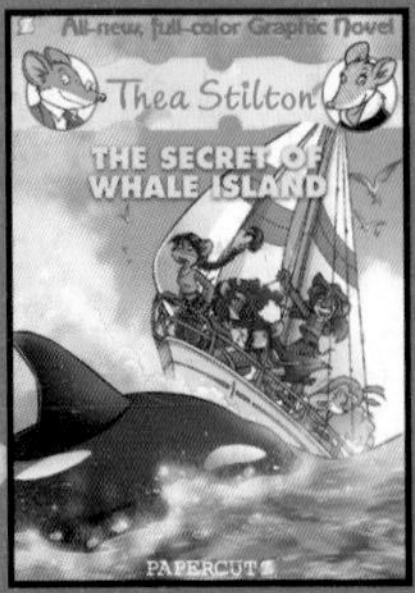
All-new, full-color Graphic Novel
Thea Stilton
THE SECRET OF WHALE ISLAND
PAPERCUTZ

#1
"The Secret of Whale Island"

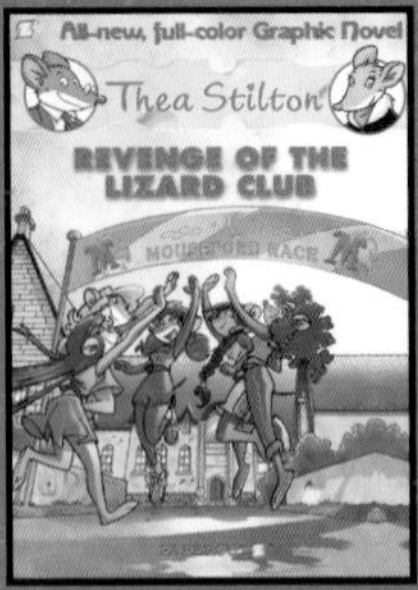
All-new, full-color Graphic Novel
Thea Stilton
REVENGE OF THE LIZARD CLUB

#2
"Revenge of the Lizard Club"

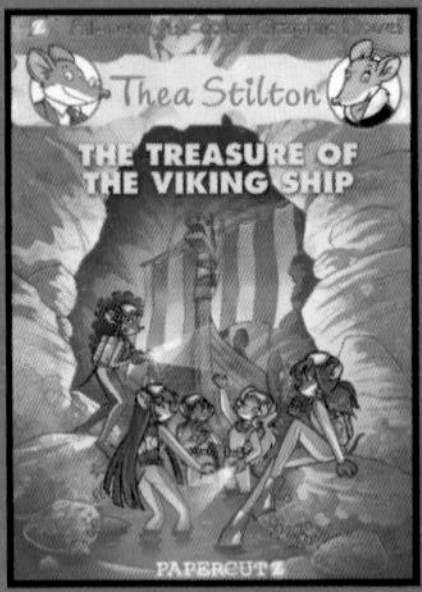
Thea Stilton
THE TREASURE OF THE VIKING SHIP
PAPERCUTZ

#3
"The Treasure of the Viking Ship"

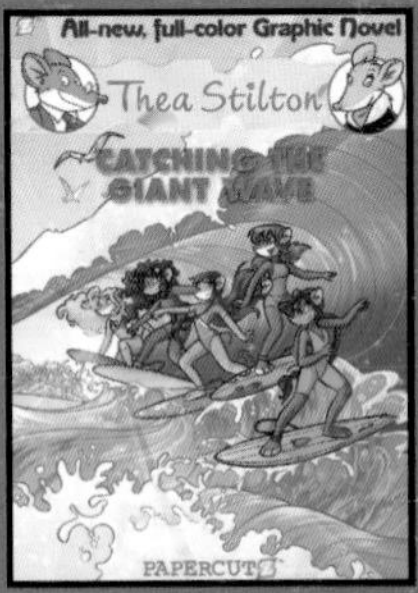
All-new, full-color Graphic Novel
Thea Stilton
CATCHING THE GIANT WAVE
PAPERCUTZ

#4
"Catching the Giant Wave"

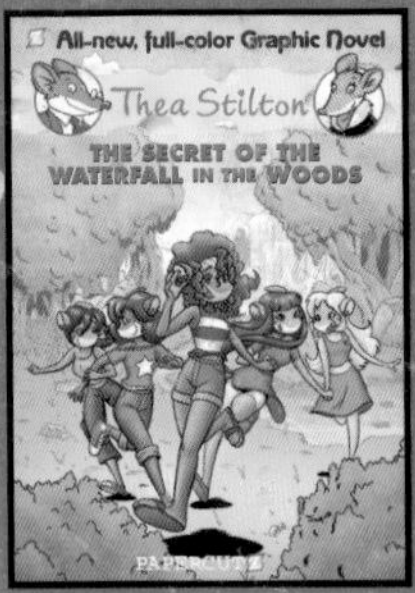
All-new, full-color Graphic Novel
Thea Stilton
THE SECRET OF THE WATERFALL IN THE WOODS
PAPERCUTZ

#5
"The Secret of the Waterfall in the Woods"

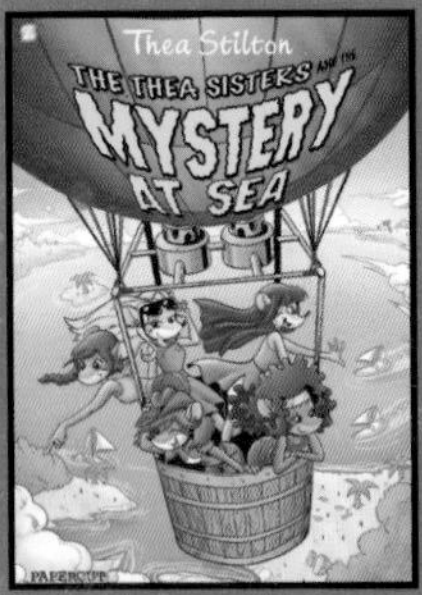
Thea Stilton
THE THEA SISTERS AND THE MYSTERY AT SEA

#6
"The Thea Sisters and the Mystery at Sea"

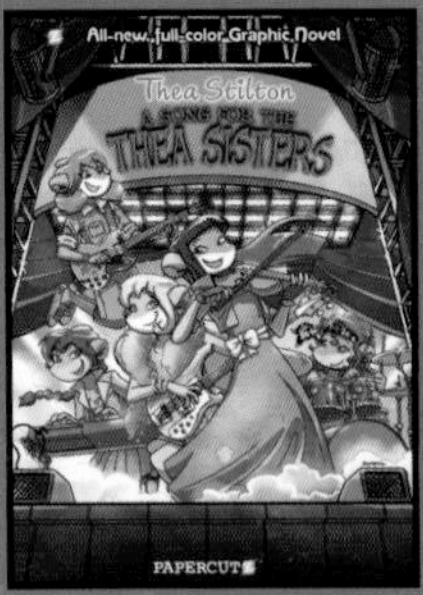
All-new, full-color Graphic Novel
Thea Stilton
A SONG FOR THE THEA SISTERS
PAPERCUTZ

#7
"A Song for the Thea Sisters"

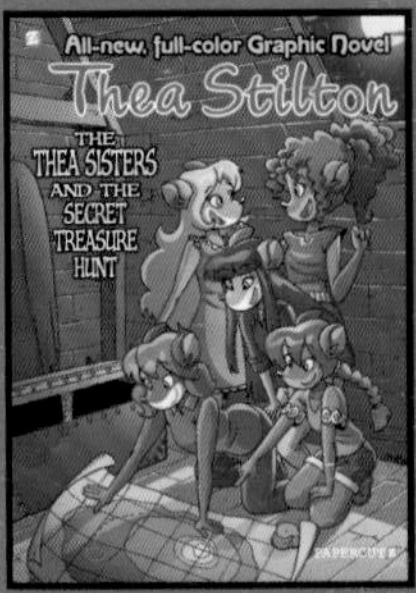
All-new, full-color Graphic Novel
Thea Stilton
THE THEA SISTERS AND THE SECRET TREASURE HUNT

#8
"The Thea Sisters and the Secret Treasure Hunt"

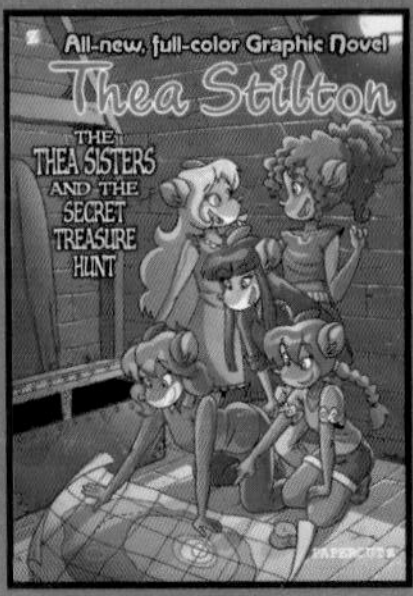
All-new, full-color Graphic Novel
Thea Stilton
THE THEA SISTERS AND THE SECRET TREASURE HUNT

#8
"The Thea Sisters and the Secret Treasure Hunt"

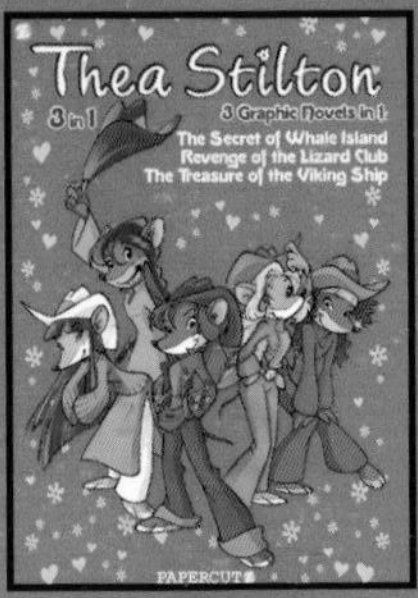
Thea Stilton
3 in 1
3 Graphic Novels in 1
The Secret of Whale Island
Revenge of the Lizard Club
The Treasure of the Viking Ship
PAPERCUTZ

#1
Thea Stilton 3 IN 1

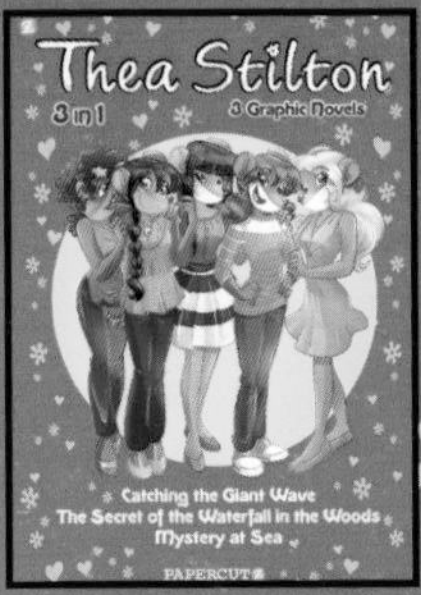
Thea Stilton
3 in 1
3 Graphic Novels
Catching the Giant Wave
The Secret of the Waterfall in the Woods
Mystery at Sea
PAPERCUTZ

#2
Thea Stilton 3 IN 1

See more at papercutz.com